Lucy Treloar was born in Malaysia and educated in England, Sweden and Melbourne. Her debut novel *Salt Creek* won the Indie Award for Best Debut, the ABIA Matt Richell Award and the Dobbie Award, was shortlisted for the Miles Franklin Literary Award and the Walter Scott Prize, and was published in Europe, the UK and North America. A winner of the Commonwealth Short Story Prize (Pacific), Lucy's short fiction and non-fiction have been widely published. Lucy is an Artist in Residence at the Meat Market in Melbourne. She lives in inner Melbourne with her family. *Wolfe Island* is her second novel.

Also by Lucy Treloar

Salt Creek

LUCY TRELOAR
WOLFE ISLAND

PICADOR
Pan Macmillan Australia

This project has been assisted by the Australian Government through
the Australia Council, its arts funding and advisory body.

STUDIO PROGRAM

First published 2019 in Picador by Pan Macmillan Australia Pty Ltd
1 Market Street, Sydney, New South Wales, Australia, 2000

A catalogue record for this
book is available from the
National Library of Australia

Typeset in 11.9/16pt Garamond by Post Pre-press Group, Brisbane
Printed by IVE

The characters in this book are fictitious and any resemblance
to real persons, living or dead, is purely coincidental.

MIX
Paper from
responsible sources
FSC® C018183

The paper in this book is FSC® certified.
FSC® promotes environmentally responsible,
socially beneficial and economically viable
management of the world's forests.

For David

The island is sinking. The isles fled away and the mountains were not found.

Revelation 16:20

The strangest thing after living alone for so long: some young people have come to stay and everything has changed.

Kitty Hawke, *Notebook of Wolfe Island*

Part I
The Island

Chapter 1

MY FATHER ALWAYS said with a name like Kitty Hawke I'd surely fly away. He said my mother should have thought of that before she named me. It was the way on the island, time out of mind. Mothers had the naming of the daughters and the girls took their mother's name, and fathers had the naming of the sons and the boys took their father's name. I had some trouble with Hart on this score, since he came from elsewhere, but history and tradition had their way.

My mother was Anna Maria Hawke and my father, an outsider, was Harald Schonfeld. They had no son, just the two girls, Bette and me, both Hawkes, the oldest name on the island, so his name died with him. I don't know how he felt about that, but I felt some lonesomeness on his account when I saw his name on the gravestone on the main after it was rescued and relocated to be with the others from Wolfe Island, after his bones began to wash loose on the shore and my mother's soon to follow, how he was the only one of his name there. He came from an island further up which went when he was a child, so it may be that there are other gravestones in other cemeteries of relatives of his I never knew. I hope so for his sake. Or it may be that their bones are now

3

rolling about on the sea floor like piano keys never to make a tune again. Schonfeld's a good name in its way. It would mean beautiful field, I suppose. The father of my children is named Hartford Darkness – an old mainlander name – and our son's name is Tobermory Darkness and our daughter's name Claudia Hawke. She, Claudie, kept up the tradition in the face of her husband's will, hers being stronger in that small regard at that time. Her daughter, my granddaughter, is Catalina Hawke.

The islands were worlds and you didn't move lightly from one to the other, and people's way of speaking wasn't quite the same from one island to the next. If we ran into each other on the main – a no-man's-land to us – we saw our resemblance to each other, and heard our own foreignness in each other's voices and prickled up and felt the eyes of people on us, assessing us for threat in the same way that we did them, resenting them for it and feeling their resentment towards us. We called ships 'shups', like we were gulping a sudden mouthful of air; further up they called them 'shee-ups' – something like that. And so on. It might not seem like that big of a deal, but these things mattered to us; we thought the way other people spoke ridiculous, but were too polite to comment. We felt the unease of all outsiders then.

My mother was not a worldly woman and my father had to explain to her why a Kitty Hawke might be more likely to fly away than any other Hawke, and despite my reluctance to leave the island even to go shopping, and the unease I felt when Hart persuaded me to go journeying on the main and the relief I felt when I returned, and it seeming that my mother had been right for so long, it turned out as it so often did that my father was right after all, which he greatly loved to be.

He would have teased my mother and she would have laughed, not really minding, because him being happy made her happy too. They were good people, and would have been shocked at what I did and what I became. Neither family was known for its murderers. Times are different now. I think that's what I'd tell them if they were here to ask me.

Slice a life any way you like and it'll tell a different story. Each cut shows something new; each might surprise or confound. Some parts you must expose with a delicate blade to keep them whole. It's not an easy task; it takes patience. Not everyone likes to know this. You decide for yourself the things you want to know about yourself, even if not in your entirely conscious self; you choose not to peer down into the mess of it all. That's what I do, I'll admit it. I turn away.

Two things come to mind, one real and one a dream and each as true as the other.

The first

I say, 'Girl, Girl,' and she comes to me like a myth, her coat sleeked smooth, her tail back out. She is a line, a ripple through the long grass, and butterflies and hoppers rise in her wake, lifting like spume and catching the light. She passes me by with a rush of wind and her sweet wolf scent, leading the way to anything. Bosum's dock is Daddy's old piano with its keys unmooring and the black notes are the dark water beneath and Girl is a dance on its broken rhythms. She looks back at me: Come on. We run down the steps to the boat and she drops in and takes her place in the bow facing the main. I loose the old rope and step in, my feet feeling about through my thin soles for the wood and the heaving water beneath. There it is, a rise and fall, a grave pull that goes through me. Then we are together: Girl, water, boat, me.

For a minute we are moving through the salted ossuary of ancient docks: here a ribcage, there a raised arm, and at the ends of each dock the old oyster shanties, which somewhat resemble skulls with their sunken rust-weeping eyes and raddled paint. Lines of silvered posts strike out to sea, and if I were very tall and steady of foot and impossibly agile I would leap from one to the next across the water and at the last one turn and see this lost world anew: a low stretch of grasses standing and falling like the pelt of a living thing on the ocean's surface, and on it, rising from it, my house, high and vast, appearing to thrust what's left of the island beneath the waves.

I pull away from the island. Soon even the grasses have disappeared and the house is nothing more than a cut-out picture, like a theatre set smacked up against the sky and the sea.

The second

In the distance, in the milky light of morning, he dandles the baby over the smooth cold water and its hovering mist, taunting the baby's mother. Their high pure screams, mother's and baby's, ripple in the still, a queer ancient sound. The mother's arms are outstretched and her mouth is open and her head tipped back to release her anguish. She is as old as time in that moment, and so am I.

I run. When I get close I roar, 'Put the baby down. Now I say. *Do* it.'

'You going to make me?' he says.

'I am.'

He crouches swiftly in the boat, which dips and slithers against its moorings and beneath his land legs. 'Oops.' He gives a foolish grin – insolent, you know? – which I imagine he perfected at school, though he is not a child any longer.

The baby is scarlet, screaming, and writhing as strongly as a ten-week baby can.

The man holds her around her chest, a hand beneath each arm, tightly, and lowers her, dipping her feet in the icy water. Her knees jerk up and her screaming cuts off. 'Oh, you like that,' he says in a mocking way. He looks up at the baby's mother and at me, and the sunlight shines into his blue eyes and makes them blaze. 'What you going to do?'

I feel in my coat pocket for the cold thing nestled in the fur and grip it hard. Everything has led up to this moment and everything will lead away.

Chapter 2

Winter

IT WAS LATE winter when they arrived, too early for butterflies, a different kind of day. At first light I headed to the main for fuel and supplies, enough to keep me going until the weather warmed and I could get the garden going again, not so much that it sank the boat. Rough weather was coming – it was there in the yellow air and the oily sea – and the wind was gusting by the time I got back. It would have been sensible to stay close to the house, to read or attend to my makings or dig the walled garden or thin the seedlings in the greenhouse, but town made me edgy (all those people in their bright clothes looking at me, their faces saying, My God, who does she think she is?) and storms made me restless. I watched birds wheeling the sky and plummeting to shelter when weather hit, and thought I understood them.

I could have gone inside and made soup and got Girl her dinner, and watched the storm through the windows, but I needed to smooth my feathers, so to speak. I pulled my mother's rattling old bike from the barn and headed up the road, riding into the weird light as if diving through shipwreck, past ruins scattering roadside and shore. The water champed on the seafront, dragging back morsels. Girl roamed around,

8

hoping to stir up small creatures to snack on. A tiny bird swooped and lifted around me like a dolphin about a boat and I began to belong again. My hair flailed, and there was not a soul to say, Come on now, Kitty, tie it back, it'll tangle, and I was glad of it. Girl, I should say, is my wolfdog.

I passed the Fisherman's Confederation Hut where the watermen had drunk at day's end, crab pots stacked high in the green-gold light, two tatterdemalion shanties on the water, and the meandering marsh walkway, then the silent power station and the old excavator with its head rearing from the western sea. Soon I was swallowed by the sky and marshes and I disappeared even to myself. There was just the briny smell, the *whump* of air at my ears, like there was some hypnosis in the air. The path dipped and the grit turned to half-frozen slush and dragged on the wheels. The wind whined in the power lines and my coat was a sail and there was still time if I'd known to turn back and live oblivious. But why would I? The island narrowed to its marsh-edged hourglass centre and flared again and then I was in Stillwater (three houses remaining). Beyond Pine Point storm clouds piled like forests of seaweed reaching for the light. That's when I saw it, a skiff lit by sun, a fair way out still, skittering the waves and heading my way.

The reckless ignorance of being out in this weather told me they weren't from here. Recalling previous troubles, I pressed my hand to my pocket, feeling for my gun. There, I could look after myself, no need to worry. I could deal with whatever came.

They drew closer, the wind dashing them towards the shore. I pulled my hair back to see. I couldn't help being curious.

It was a girl at the tiller, with a pale face and long loose dark hair flying. Two boys – young men, I suppose – one dark and one fair, sat on the seat, and crouched at their feet was another dark head, a child. I knew this was strange the same way an animal does, and was wary.

I watched as if they were a thousand miles away. The sea rose and shattered around the boat. More than once I thought they were gone, fighting the grain of the water that way, but the girl held her line, slowing and looking along the shore. Then she caught sight of me and lifted her hand, and there was no pretending any longer that we weren't in the same world. My arm felt heavy as I raised it and pointed towards the north-east end. They would have foundered otherwise, I'm sure of that. Two lines of government-built jetties were submerged out there, jagged rock banks waiting to tear out the bottom of any passing boat. The boat seemed to pause and I saw the girl's hesitation, the wish to obey the water's rush for shore. But she eased off, keeping a respectful distance from the coast, riding the waves, disappearing into troughs and rearing out of them again. With the wind behind me now I rode in the same direction. Girl streaked ahead.

I was at the docks before them. After some minutes they came from behind the low point over the harbour, circling wide and coming in straight, threading down the timbers towards a dock with more meat on it than most. The blond boy sat up straight and turned to the girl. She shrugged, but didn't reply or look at him and didn't move her face. She was a fair boatwoman or knew how to hold her nerve; either way it meant something bad had driven them this way. The dark-haired boy steadied the child – a little girl, I saw now – and held her hair while she was sick over the side. The fair boy gripped the side. He stared at my towering Watermen, beings of protection that I had made a few years back. The dark boy's face was guarded. His glance touched on me and went past, sweeping the island's marshes. If it was flight he was after, Wolfe Island might appear as much a blind alley as a sanctuary. He looked at the older girl and seemed to gather himself. The little one might be his sister, from his tenderness and their black hair, which was glossy as a starling's wing.

The boat slumped deeper, and the water fell away in folds as thick as cream, holding and falling and renewing behind them so they seemed to be travelling down a hollowed-out path of water that had been waiting for them. She sidled the boat close, slung a line over a pile and stepped cleanly onto the landing stage, gripping the boat while the others clambered out. The little girl gave a cry as the skiff slid beneath her. The big girl grabbed her hand and heaved her clear. The flying wind pushed them towards me; behind, the yellow water slapped, the sky was low and grey and the light was the same queer yellow as the water. They were a walking dream in it as they passed the Watermen, looking at them and quickly away, understanding the warning that was in them, as everyone did.

I knew the older girl immediately – but none of the others. She had long legs and a long slouching step and a narrow face. Her hair blew across it. She swept it aside and in a swift movement twisted and thrust it beneath the collar of her short black puffer, and kept coming, like she was coming for me. I remembered the exact movement from years before. She had been taking pictures and her hair had blown across the camera lens and she'd scooped it away. It was one of the school field trips that used to visit – maybe four years ago.

The big blond boy, in khakis and a football jacket, a half step behind, scanned the docks and beyond like he was inspecting a piece of property, which made my neck prickle and Girl's hackles rise a little. I put a finger on her shoulder. Last came the little girl clutching her brother's hand, doing a little jog step once in a few to catch up. She wore a pink satchel and held a blanket-wrapped doll in one arm. Her brother was broad-shouldered and heavy-browed and had a kind of deep seriousness about him, as if spirits too high or too low would expend energy he couldn't afford. He had a black and swollen eye, a cut cheek, and hunched one shoulder, favouring some hurt to his ribs or chest. It seemed he was getting through each moment: now and now and now. I knew that feeling, like blood.

'How may I help you?' I called. I only meant to slow them, because I knew from the sickness in my stomach and the dream-like way they seemed to be moving that everything was about to change. The little girl peeked from behind the boy, her skin looking half-drowned from seasickness and misery.

'You,' I said to the big girl.

'Yes,' she said. 'Kitty Hawke, right?'

'Yes.'

'Then you're my grandmother.'

She came closer and I knew she was telling the truth. She had flecks of green in the brown of her eyes, which were wide like her mother's. Last I saw her that I knew of – much more than four years ago – she'd been a tiny thing, spitting and hissing like a kitten, refusing to be dolled up in pink, and Claudie was in a state because she had no idea what to do with her fury. That child swayed from memory, across a chasm. This girl didn't know me, or I her, and I felt a fool now for not recognising her when we last met. I don't know where the years went. They'd moved before she started school – a nine-hour round trip at least – too much for one day and no welcome at the other end. I could never find a time that suited Claudie.

'Claudie's girl,' I said. 'Catalina.'

'Cat.'

'Cat. You might have told me that other time.'

She ignored that. 'Josh, Luis, Alejandra,' she said, pointing to the others in turn.

I nodded at them. 'What on God's earth brought you out here in this weather?'

'We're looking for somewhere to stay,' Cat said.

'Is Claudie okay?'

Cat, puzzled, said, 'Of course.'

'You were caught in the storm? Is that why?'

'Not with you exactly. I was thinking of one of the other houses, just for a few nights.' She looked about. 'I thought there were more. I remember more.'

'You remember right. We've lost some since then.'

'But there are still some?'

'Some,' I said. 'Would you mind my asking what you're leaving behind?'

'Who said we were?' Josh asked.

'You're out in this weather, you want shelter for more than a night, and there's a child here without her parents. You tell me what you're doing.'

'We can leave. We've got other places,' Cat said.

'I didn't ask you to do that. If there are other places, they'd be easier to get to than this, which makes me think the other places are . . .'

Cat glared.

Balls of rain began to hit. I listened to their scattered sound.

'We need to leave behind some things that are happening,' Luis said.

'I don't pay too much attention to the world – some, but not a lot.'

Cat said, 'We can't all pretend.' Still a spitfire then. The boys shifted their feet like bull calves in a field wondering about bolting, the way they do when they're spooked.

'And I'm not going to start pretending to you. I didn't say I wouldn't help. You're here. Only a fool would go back out on that sea. You were lucky on the way here.'

'I know what I'm doing,' Cat said.

'You know a little. I could have been more welcoming.' I touched her upper arm lightly by way of apology, and she put her hesitant hand on mine, which startled me, unused as I was to touch. It was real, then, this strange day. 'There's no going further now. You'll be staying with me tonight.'

'Grandma,' Cat said.

'Too late for that. You can call me Kitty, same as everyone. Rain's coming.' I turned and didn't wait to see if they followed. What else were they going to do?

'Luis, Luis,' panted Alejandra, running along, the crunching of her footfall light and fast.

'What?' he said.

'What are those things?'

'Sculptures, I guess, like art. Someone made them.'

'Me,' I said.

'They have funny faces,' Alejandra said. 'What are their faces?'

'Sh,' Luis said.

I looked over my shoulder. 'Skulls. Cattle skulls.'

'What's that mean?'

'The bones inside cows' heads,' Cat said. 'That's pretty gross.'

'Meant to give pause,' I said.

'Is that a wolf, Luis?' Alejandra's piping voice.

'Wolfdog,' Cat said. 'Like the island, Wolfe Island. There's always been wolfdogs here.'

Without turning, I said, 'Name's Girl.'

'Did you hear, Luis? A wolfdog. What's a wolfdog? Why do you keep looking?' Alejandra said. 'Luis, why?'

I turned. Luis's head was skywards, checking behind. 'Looking for trackers?' I asked, and at his wary look added, 'I'm not completely ignorant. Set your mind at rest. Girl'd hear them, even if I didn't, which is not likely. Eagles don't like them either. We hardly see them out here.' I slowed until they caught up. 'You're runners, you and your sister here. That it?' His face stilled and he put his arm around her shoulder and pulled her in close.

'Is that a problem?' Cat said.

'I meant it as fact, not accusation. Doesn't matter to me. Why would I be against them? They've done me no wrong, but that's not the end of any story, you know that.' My life was quiet but I'd read enough to know the word and what it meant. If they were runners and people were looking for them, what did that make Cat and the other boy, Josh? 'And you,' I said to him, 'what have you got to say for yourself?'

'Nothing much, ma'am.' He grinned. He was one of those boys like a side of beef, hanging there waiting for the admiration to hit him like an appreciative slap, the sort of boy who might have given Tobe a hard time for nothing more than amusement. I know I shouldn't have judged him straight off like that.

'You should,' I said, and saw his certainty waver. 'Don't let other people speak for you.'

Cat frowned, like she planned on saying something, but changed her mind, pulling her jacket closer and tucking her chin into its high collar. The wind blew the hair across her face and she let it.

I said, 'There's a storm coming. Won't that be nice for us all.' I turned again, and the crunching of their feet on the path resumed.

'Why does the lady speak so funny?' Alejandra.

'She doesn't speak funny,' Luis said, low.

'She does so.'

'Island talk,' Cat said. 'That's just the way they talk here. Always have.'

'How do you know?' Alejandra said.

'Everybody knows. My mother can even talk like that if she wants to, the exact same way. I always liked it.'

'Some things you can't forget,' I said over my shoulder. 'Can't take the island out of the girl.'

'My dad tells her to quit it.'

'He would.'

'Ha.' Cat laughed – a good sound, and there was the pleasure of making someone laugh.

Alejandra darted to the path's edge, to the old picket fence and the shells lining its base. 'Look, Luis. Can I have one?'

'I guess.' He called louder to me. 'Is that okay, ma'am?'

'Sure. They don't belong to anyone in particular.'

'What kind are they?' Alejandra asked.

'Oyster.'

'*Arster?*'

I tried again, bending my mouth. 'Oyster. A shellfish. Good to eat.'

'I want to try one.'

'If you can find one, good luck to you.'

The rain hit my cheek in earnest and I could not help myself and began running. There was nothing for me to escape, but I was fleeing something even if I didn't know what, and was frightened – not of these people, but of what they might mean.

Above my panting breaths and the whack of my boots and the wind buffeting my hood the little girl called, 'Why is she running, the lady? Why, Luis?'

'I don't know,' he said.

They were all running to keep up, as if they thought they might lose me, which might have been what I wanted, even if it was not possible. They weren't to know that.

I think of that day and what I could have done different. Could I have let them founder on the rocks and drown, shown my gun at the docks, or shot in the air or bellowed at them to get on, to leave on by for the next island (Shakers was not so far away, though as I have said it was not the day for travel in such a boat), or made Girl growl and show her teeth? Did I want company? If I did, it was not in my conscious self. I understood in that moment that if you know someone or have met them, and have no reason to hate or mistrust except because they are human, then it is hard to turn them away.

Chapter 3

THEY WATCHED AT the kitchen table as I pulled a meal together: biscuits and cheese, tomato soup. Cat shook herself into politeness (a glimpse of Claudie reminding her of her manners). 'Thank you. We won't be here for long, we hope. A couple of days, or weeks maybe, we're not sure.'

They were all weary, Alejandra most of all. She rested her head on the table as if it was the softest pillow. Her hands fell in her lap, and her eyes looked about. Cat stroked her cheek with the back of a finger. Alejandra blinked. Luis's gaze rested on them without moving. Josh pushed his chair back from the table and stretched out his legs, which he crossed and rocked on one heel. I pushed down a forgotten dread of obligation, of people to be tended to and failed. It didn't matter if I didn't know them. There would be no stopping it. The windows were filled with thrashing rain and small things – leaves, branches, perhaps a small creature or two – hurtling through the air. They paid no attention to the tumult. The island was just a place to them, shelter, not a living thing under siege.

'We'll go looking tomorrow. You want to stay together?'

Luis sat up a little. 'We don't want to put you to any trouble, Mrs . . .'

'Kitty. You've got enough of your own by the looks.'

He put a hand to his cheek up near the eye. 'A fight.'

'A bad one,' I said.

He shrugged. The side of his upper lip twitched, pulling at his face. He pressed a hand to it, hard, and when he took it away he had mastered himself. He didn't look at Cat or Josh then for any sign of understanding or care. Not a one of them looked at any other, and their expressions became fixed.

But Alejandra sat up, as if a shadow was passing overhead, and pushed her face against Luis's arm and then hid beneath it. He rolled his eyes at the awkwardness. The smallest word, the breath of a memory, could set her burrowing for refuge. I learned that, but this was the first time I saw it, and already I didn't want to add to her sadness. In a second she was on his lap with his arms around her. He was worn out – no more than seventeen by my estimation – but he didn't give himself a choice, just shrugged a little, rested his chin on her trembling head and exchanged subdued smiles with Cat. It seemed as if Alejandra's fears were a regular storm he must deal with.

'What happened?' I asked.

Josh might have spoken, but Cat pressed his knee.

'Sorry to pry.' I measured flour and butter, sugar and salt, and cut them and rubbed them together, not too fine, then added the cream, lightly, and mixed them in a bowl to make a dough. 'As long as Claudie knows you're safe.'

'I left her a letter,' Cat said.

'That you're here?'

'That we're okay, not to worry.'

It would have to do for now. Luis preferred not to speak of private matters – 'for the safety of some people,' he said. I considered the load his spirit seemed to carry. He was a serious person and he cared for his sister and when I asked about his family, he met my gaze directly: all things in his favour. 'We'll try to let them know. I wonder – might I enquire as to whether I could use your computer, ma'am, if you have one?' It seemed an effort for him to make this request. 'We were advised to shut everything down . . .'

'Sounds awfully heavy,' I said.

'Being careful,' Cat said.

'Most people have a reason for being that careful.' They didn't say anything to that, only looked away vaguely, maybe waiting for my attention to slide by, the way Claudie and Tobe used to if something had happened at school – Tobe in trouble usually, skipping classes to go wandering down to the docks, out on the boats, anywhere to escape a room with a closed door and windows. But it was worse than that now, as if we were paused above something dark.

I patted the dough together and tipped it onto the floured board, dabbed it out with my fingers, cut it and put the biscuits in the oven. 'You can help next time, if you'd like,' I said to Alejandra. She stared.

Josh went to the window and put his face to the glass. 'Looks like there's a couple of houses to choose from.'

'They're standing; doesn't mean you'd want to live in them, but there might be one that would suit.'

Luis took Alejandra over and they looked through cupped hands against the window, wiping away the moisture from their breaths now and then.

'What happened? I mean that one.' Josh pointed. 'No one there?'

'No one anywhere. No one but me.' I didn't have to look to know the house he meant. 'Beauforts' summerhouse – nothing but a shell. The mansard roof was always trouble. Fanciest house on the island but it leaked like the dickens.' I wiped down the benches. 'My mother didn't care for the portico but I always liked it. We had some good times up there – threw a rope over and shinnied up when the summer folk left.' My mouth was running. 'As to what happened, it was the same as everywhere round here. The island started falling into the sea. No one likes the ground moving, or water coming through the floorboards.'

I stirred the soup, and got out plates and bowls. 'If you could set the table?' I said, but they were all at the window by then.

They would be seeing a ghost town, cold and ruined, when I remembered lit windows, people moving through light, laughing and talking, children running, crowds in summer, parties and festivals, days of men out on the water – winter for oysters and summer for crabs – and women picking crabs and talking: some new way with a mayonnaise dressing, who made the best layer cake, whether Maya and Jesse would make a go of it, take over his daddy's business now he wasn't so well, and the new teacher soon to arrive. Wolfe had been a world that things orbited – boats, fish, birds, people, business, life, and all the seasons of those things. If anyone talked of the future with worry, there was always one person to say, 'We'll be right. Always have been.' It seemed like a fairytale now, but there had been a dark side to it all along.

Houses fell into the sea, insurance and health premiums went sky high, government relocation packages enticed the skittish folk, the school closed, and even the church by degrees. They weren't helping; they were shutting us down. It seems fast written like that, but it took all my years of growing and a few more.

These days, rusted cars and ruins were just things I moved around, no different from trees, though like people variable in the ways they fell apart. Morning glory and orange trumpet vines rampaged in summer, trying to drag things back into the ground, and in winter turned sodden brown. Choked gables thrust out still, tattered curtains licking the air. I'd tried for a while to keep things looking respectable, but it was too much for one. It was hard to see things happening so slow, and I had become accustomed to the dereliction. I would not go so far as to say that I found it poetic, as Hart once claimed, but there was something in it that suited my way of feeling. I was protective of it and would not forsake it, for Tobe's sake most of all, as if I might still be able to call him home.

I lit the lamps. (It saved power for the freezer.) Outside, darkness began to fold around everything, growing and hiding things by degrees, the smudge of it coming closer, flickering like an inconstant memory, obscuring the island's shadowy promontories which reached finger by finger into the iron sea. I fed Girl and set the table myself, and by then the biscuits were ready. We ate our meal and didn't say much, since I had nothing but questions and they had so few answers, though Josh did mention a friend driving them from Calverton and someone in town who'd lent them a boat. Cat gave him a hard glare and he fell quiet.

Later, I made up beds in Tobe's and Claudie's rooms. The thought of other people sleeping on the island and the sounds of their whispering voices as they settled kept me awake in the dark, as if my ears were pricked and swivelling like Girl's. She looked at me – surely I'd do something – and when I didn't she rested her head on her paws and made a whistling sound in her throat. It seemed like Wolfe was rippling with their presence, as if the island was a pond and they were thrown stones.

At breakfast Alejandra snuck Girl pieces of waffle under the table, while I pretended not to notice. I went upstairs and fetched the box with the keys people had left with me, at first for safekeeping over winter and later after they left for good, so I could show their houses to anyone who 'might be interested'.

I looked from the landing window towards the island's north end, where two houses stood at the edge of shallow washes of water, as queer as tombstones against the drizzling sky. From the opposite window Stillwater might have been a watercolour on Wolfe's south coast.

I went downstairs. 'Yep, the south end is shot.'

They looked up, startled.

'A raggedy place no good for boat or person. No, that end I do *not* recommend. No way to leave the island and the marsh road's only open once a day. Tides cover it. It might seem quiet now, but we used to have fun . . . Hundreds of people in summer,' I said.

If I looked out of the window my sister Bette would be strutting the balustrade of Beauforts' portico, and the rest of us would be drinking sneaked beers below or making out in sandy dips near the marshes, wherever we could find. We mocked the summer folks' ways, some of that from envy. Bette would be cranky when they were gone and my mother had no patience with that. 'You should be proud of what you are, and all you want to do is run.'

Girl, as impatient to be out as I was, stood at the door with her nose snuffling the crack to let me know. It was our exploring time of day. I went to the window and watched the rain slow and finally stop. 'Ready to go looking?' I called. The wind was still moaning and apart from Alejandra they looked at each other in a raised-eyebrow way from their warm place by the stove, but gathered themselves, putting on jackets and woollen hats and scarves. It would have been hard to face the next unknown thing, I suppose, having arrived at shelter, but it was what they were here for. I opened the door and we went into the blustery wind.

'Girl, Girl, come on, come with me,' Alejandra called. Girl let her rest a hand on her head, which she didn't really care for. She understood before I did that Alejandra needed gentleness above anything. They walked together down the broken road.

Beauforts, as expected, was hardly more than its outside walls, like a well filled with shattered building material. The tombstone houses at the north end were mottled and had a scum of frothing water on their front paths, and the air around them was salt-sour. Cordgrass filled their yards. We pulled our coats in tighter. I would have gone on, but the others wanted to peek in. There wasn't much between the two houses: their roofs gone and the sky falling through their mangled guts. The stairs had broken loose from the landing in one, ending midair, and the ceilings drooped heavily or had fallen into middens of slats and plaster. Desks and sofas lay on their sides like beasts tied for branding. We began to cough.

That left the two houses on the small spit of land hugging the other side of the docks, the last ones in the street that had once ended with the Barlows' place – the first house at the north end to be eaten by the sea.

I was the one who found it one stormwrack morning the year I turned seven. The Barlows were away to the main for

some celebration and I was out checking for first-light glean-
ings, as we used to call the things washed up after a storm. The
house appeared to have stumbled: knees in the sand and body
aslant. I was paralysed at first, watching the waves repeat. Water
billowed and slammed and swilled about its ruin. I could feel
it in my feet. I ran next door and told them. Word spread
like a contagion and a crowd gathered, the adults sombre, the
children excitable. It was a kind of death and a portent of more,
but declarations of doom or plans were private, for later – the
hopeful warmth of a kitchen, or if financial ruin beckoned
the dim lit end of a hall. I overheard a few such murmured
conversations, as children often do, and learned that day that
things could change and we could not stop them. I slept poorly
for a long time after, imagining the same happening to our
house, until my father told me our house would outlast them
all. I believed him.

I had some hopes of the remaining two houses since their
shingles were intact and windows unbroken, though I seldom
visited this way. It made me think of Tobe and his nearby
shanty and his last days here. The fallen realtor's sign out
front said: *Absolute ocean front view.* 'That view got any closer
you'd be swimming in it,' I said, an old island joke, and they
smiled politely.

The front yards of the houses facing the dock weren't so
bad, being merely scattered with salt-damaged shrubs, but
looking down the side of the first house, all I could see of the
'oriental-style' gazebo and neat dock of memory was a stretch
of water, a ruined boathouse and a line of stranded timbers
on which five black gannets hunched against the wind. The
second house ran along the shoreline's fingernail rise with its
windows keeping lookout in all directions. Stiff grasses bent

and straightened with the wind in endless repetition at water's edge. It had got worse since the last time I came this way, whenever that was, which I didn't want to think. Water was stealthily approaching the back of that house too, and I hadn't noticed a thing.

Alejandra skipped the mossy oyster shell path from road to porch of the second house – white like every other place on the island. 'Will this be our house, Luis?'

When he didn't answer I told her maybe, and that seemed to satisfy.

I poked at the weedy path. 'A few barrows of rock and shell. A nice couple used to live here. They kept it up. Shipleys.' Up on the porch, I rummaged for the key. 'Here you go.' A turn of the key and a shoulder to the door and we were in. There was more disarray – furniture and boxes abandoned in the entrance hall. People seemed to leave in such a rush at the end, as if fearing they'd be marooned. We proceeded gingerly, feeling our way and sniffing, throwing shutters and windows open to let in the cold air. The stairs were spongy beneath their red-flowered runner, but – I bounced on the bottom stair and shook its rails – were still connected to landing and ground floor. And it smelled dry. It was cold and bleak – that was the truth – but it wasn't hopeless and that made it seem almost hopeful.

'Seems like the one,' I said. 'There'll be three rooms up there, maybe four. Screens are shot, but that doesn't matter at this time of year. Summer now . . . never mind. You won't be here. I'll leave you with this, just in case.' I handed Cat the key box. 'There might be things you want in other houses. Linens and such, maybe up at Stillwater. There were a few good housekeepers up there. Careful where you put your feet. Get the fire going first is my advice, and sort out your wood.'

26

The kitchen, overlooking the water, wasn't too bad. Its long bench had a phone and several flyers, saucepans left behind, and an old takeout menu, as if the Shipleys had been on the point of ordering and departed the island instead.

I began to read it. 'How about that? A Patty's menu. That was a diner. Corn custard. I haven't had corn custard in years. I'll make you one.' I folded it in two and tucked it in my pocket.

Alejandra picked her way across things like a little cat, peering into any cupboards she could open. Luis cleared rough pathways to each window, which he peered through, and opened every door on the ground floor until he found one leading to the storage area and the back door. Only then did his manner calm.

'You can see even more from upstairs,' I said. He gave me a swift look, as if he'd revealed himself in some way that he regretted. 'If you're wondering.' I spoke lightly to set him at ease, but he didn't say anything or go upstairs, just set to clearing more floor space, stacking things neatly against the wall. Josh disappeared upstairs. His heavy footfall moved about as he opened doors. He returned to the landing and called down: 'All good up here.' And then came a whipping 'Woo!' which Luis ignored. Cat went outside and returned with some wood. There was a box of matches on the living room mantel and she began a fire, and soon its living heat and sound and flickering light brought the room to life.

A walk around the house discovered the solar system panel at the back door. I turned it on and a green light lit up. With any luck it would still work. Orderly folk like the Shipleys would have emergency lighting somewhere. Alejandra made a game of the hunt and finally called out, 'Kitty, Kitty, come see.'

She had found three lamps and a can of fuel in the utility room off the back porch.

'Well done you,' I said. I filled them and adjusted the wicks and lit them.

'Oh, pretty,' Alejandra said. I agreed. Their light softened everything and held things together.

There were a few candles and plenty of matches but no torches.

'I'll leave you to it. You're welcome to come up for lunch,' I said.

From the porch I looked over the water to my place, stark and forlorn in the pale winter light, but tidy enough. New growth and a few pots of flowers would make it more cheerful come spring. Towards the mouth of the gut was the Shipleys' old oyster shanty (later Tobe's), stranded since its long walkway went years back.

Cat came out, holding the edge of the screen door and swinging it lightly, watching it, glancing at me, as if the door was more interesting than anything either of us might say. 'We won't bother you, don't worry about that.'

'You're no bother.'

'That's not true.'

'Well.' Maybe she meant it and maybe she didn't. She spoke lightly, but her words weren't light. I would have to wait to find out. 'You haven't asked for much.' Not the right thing to say. No one likes having to feel grateful. 'You go ahead and bother me. I don't mind.'

'I'm sure you've got your work to do.' There was an edge there. Something had changed in her.

'You're my girl's girl. I'm glad to have you here.'

*

They'd been around twelve years old, those girls, some of them quiet, others as bounding and high-spirited as half-grown pups, excited to be away on camp. Their teacher was a young woman, small and pretty, with a long braid of fair hair and a high colour in her cheeks. She wore old jeans and a worn brown jacket, everything washed out and not suiting her at all, yet the girls looked to her as if she was the sun and they were flowers and could not help turning towards her. She lit them up. 'Fly on your angel wings and make me some art to remember,' she told them. And they didn't laugh. It was something to watch.

She'd shown them a film made not long before about my work and my solitary life on the island. They visited my makings room and I probably said a few things. Then they roamed outside taking photographs.

It was Cat I remember. I was on the porch drawing, Girl at my feet, when she sidled up.

'Have you always lived here?' she said.

'I have.'

'Do you like it?'

'I don't think about it like that. I belong here. I *can* live here. And I keep living here. That might tell you something.'

'You don't miss people?'

'*Some* people. But I have Girl here.' I stroked her idly with one foot and she blinked at me.

'She's a wolfdog, right?'

'She is.'

'My mother says they're good dogs.'

'They can be for the right person.'

'We have a Maltese.'

'Oh yeah?'

'It's my dad's.'

'Nice dog?'

'He's a little shit.'

I laughed and she laughed too. Her eyes were bright as a house sparrow's.

'He's not really a family dog. My dad says it's irresponsible to have a wolfdog.'

'Probably is for some people. They're not for everyone.'

'I wish I had a dog like that.'

'Maybe when you're older.'

'Yeah.' The thought seemed to please her.

Written down it might seem like a fast conversation, but it stretched out. She would ask something and I would think before replying and she would think some more, poke around among the dahlias growing below the porch, or sit on the steps, and come back and ask something new. She had something I liked.

'Anyway . . . I better get going.' She seemed reluctant and looked through the open doorway of the house. I like looking through doorways myself. You can tell a lot from them. It was pleasant with my grandmother's rag rug, the old hall table, a bowl of pomegranates, and the small making I kept there. The light fell in a particular way, as if it was visiting from the past. 'We're supposed to take some pictures.' She paused and corrected herself in a sort of mocking tone. '*Capture* some *images*.'

'You do that. Cake later.'

'Cool. See you, Girl.' Then, 'See you,' she said to me.

Even though she didn't look like Claudie, she reminded me. (That could be the backward-looking eye; maybe all I mean is that finding out who she was these years later wasn't altogether a surprise.) I should have known. She was the one who was curious; she was the one who bothered to talk.

Now, standing on the porch, *her* porch, I said, 'That time.'

'Yeah?'

'You were checking me out.'

'In a way. I was checking my mother out too.'

'I thought it was a nice day.'

'Did you?' She moved her head very slightly as if it was up to me to decide whether she was agreeing, she didn't mind.

'You're different.'

She shrugged. 'Just older. My mother used to talk about living out here on the island. I should have told you who I was.'

'I imagine you had reasons.'

'Not very good ones. I wanted to see for myself what you were like. I wanted to piss my mother off. Not as much as I did.'

'She didn't like it here. My sister Bette was the same. Claudie and Tobe were the last babies born here. Did she tell you that?'

'About a hundred times.'

'That was his shanty out on the gut.' I nodded across the water, which washed about the shanty's pilings, all grey and weathered.

'Uncle Tobe's?'

'When he came back from the war.'

'She never told me. What's a gut?'

'Just a creek. They're mostly called guts around here. Anyway, I'm glad I didn't scare you away.'

'You might have now.' She permitted a half-smile. 'No, I don't think you would. Alejandra likes you.' That seemed to weigh with her, but she didn't say more and I was about to leave when she said, 'Wait, Kitty,' and took hold of my arm. 'I have to say this. It's important. You must remember.' The next part she recited like a list or a poem she'd memorised.

I can't recall it exactly, but it went something like this:

Don't talk about us to anyone, in any way.
    Even if someone else mentions us, or hints they have heard of us, or has heard from us, or has seen us passing by, do not say anything, do not betray.
    You don't know until you know.
    Silence is safety. Don't be the one to break it.
    Don't betray any secret.
    Remember this: it's lives we are saving.

'That's awfully heavy for a sixteen-year-old,' I said. 'Say it again?'

She did this without a pause.

'What is going on? What is it about Luis and Alejandra?'

'He's a guy we know from school, from this kind of group we're in. He's a good friend. Things are bad for them, that's all.'

'Don't runners run?'

'There's more to it with them.'

'And what about Josh and his parents? And school?'

'He's eighteen.'

'You're not eighteen.'

'I'm not your responsibility. I'm just here. Please remember what I said, or we'll have to leave.'

'Why would I not tell your mother?'

'Because we will leave, and Luis and Alejandra will be in . . .'

'Trouble?'

'Something like that.' Then she seemed to reconsider. 'It's

dangerous for them. You have to get that. I can't say more. It's not my business to.'

This is how I remember the conversation, trying to keep up. She was setting the rules. She did not seem sixteen. I believed her, but I didn't understand. I was rattled by her intensity. What kind of world had she come from?

I took my leave and walked around the edge of the docks, heading home along the marsh's edge, past the sign for Peachblossom Road stranded in its middle, a boat tethered to it (someone's idea of a joke), and over the bridge. It was not my usual route. Before I could stop myself, I was looking down the gut. Tobe's shanty looked worse side on. The ridgepole had bowed and the next stage, its broken back, would be the end. Keeping it up had been a point of pride for Tobe (the waterman in him), even though he grew to hate the dream, the way it wouldn't let him go. He'd coil and recoil his ropes and clean and stack the crab pots. When I asked him why, he said, 'I like to be busy.' He'd head out almost radiant with hope at the beginning of each season, sometimes anchoring on the water overnight to get an early start. He was going to show people there was a future in it. He did that for a couple of years after he finished school, then, his spirit broken by the empty water, he joined up, and later, his spirit broken in a new way, returned to his shanty.

I would try not to think about all that, just do what needed doing now, try to keep it up for his sake. A small gut along the roadside had broken its banks and water was running across. I'd shore up the spot with stones and shells and rubble: cold work, but it might help save that spit of land for a while longer, and therefore the dock and maybe my house too further down the line. The whole island was like dominoes lined up. I was always eyeing which part might be the next to fall.

Chapter 4

THERE WAS A cold snap a few days later, or what counted as a cold snap these days – nothing like the year my grandmother died. It was colourless outside but for the hollowed-out skins of two pomegranates still hanging on the tree and the waxy orange hips of my mother's roses. The cold struck through walls and waterfalled from windows and came through any cracks it found.

Girl and I went walking. The sky was that faint blue and the sun was as pale and distant as if ice covered it too. The water in the inlet had frozen overnight and was as motionless as a photograph for a while. I took twenty-seven seconds of footage, and nothing moved during that time but an eagle scything across the frame. I watched the still hard water for a long time, stamping my feet intermittently to keep the blood moving. Girl roamed around sniffing at things. The water seemed to have gathered itself mid-breath and stopped – held its movement and energy within, its peaks and troughs, slight as they were, intact – until with an imperceptible loosening around mid-morning it slumped, the icy rime at land's edge fell back, the water levelled and the current, a sliver of darkness from around the bend of a hummock, began to merge into the still bay. One or two gulls glided by to inspect, and by late morning a small flock was paddling the melt line. Does a bird like novelty as much as a person? On the way home, grass slipped and crunched under my feet, and I gave a puddle a whack for the pleasure of seeing it shatter. Girl was extra prancy; the weather suited her too.

Back home, I stoked the fire and Girl and I curled up on the sofa near the old woodstove with its iron doors opened wide. I'd slept there before if the cold didn't let up. Things were so quiet it was as if the others weren't even there.

Later in the morning, Cat and Alejandra came up the road, their hands plunged into their pockets and their chins tucked inside their collars. Girl went to greet them, waving her plumy tail.

They stood hunched before the fire when they came in. Alejandra's puffer had a milky stain down the front. It was cold there in the mornings then. She'd been wearing it when she ate her breakfast.

'Warm enough down there?' I said.

Cat held her hands over the stove. 'We ran out of wood last night. They're getting some more now. Just the nights are a little chilly. Isn't that so, Alejandra?'

Alejandra gave a small proud nod. Her hair slithered on her shoulders and she scraped it back from her eyes, like she knew what Cat meant, that they were okay on their own, they didn't really need me.

'You need some good big pieces of wood to keep burning overnight. There'll be some around,' I said. 'Think about what matters most: hot food, light, warmth, being clean. That's what you have to work out with your power. You've got lamps and you've got wood for fires. It's a waste using power for them.'

'Got it,' Cat said in her quick, almost terse way.

We went up the narrow attic stairs to get some extra bedding, and stopped to look out of the dormer window. It was as if the whole world had become glass-topped, that old glass with a hidden life in it: faint waves, pinpricks of air. It was dish calm, or *deesh cahm* as we used to say. Any object on it, boat or hummock or buoy, appeared to hover above its surface like a hallucination. Cat and Alejandra tried out some furniture, which I said they could take if the boys could manage carrying it. Cat found some bags of quilts and woollen blankets and we stood at the top of the stairs and threw them down and down through the house. Alejandra laughed – the first time I'd heard her do that. She put her hand over her mouth, but her eyes were still bright. Cat noticed it too. 'Fun, hey?' she said, and Alejandra nodded.

I couldn't help noticing and trying to make sense of them and the things they did. It seemed like they were settling in, yet I didn't ask about the time stretching out. It wasn't because they made me feel good. I never felt as lonely as when I saw them all together and knew myself apart. I mention these things so you can see how quickly I began to change, how they became an intrusion into my mind. When I sat with my sketchbook, my ideas came to nothing. In the makings room my things were silent. Trying to wrench my life back, to get back on my own path, I went walking with Girl and turned my attention to the south end of the island, looking from the windows facing that way, walking that way, collecting that way. I had work to do: that's what I reminded myself. And still I said nothing to them about their plans.

I visited Tobe's shanty, which had been on my mind since talking to Cat. It hadn't changed. I looked along the shelves, its ropes, chains and pulleys, boxes of floats, lath crab baskets, pliers and wires, hammers, mallets, hoop-handled shears, leather straps, awls, a brush for the shanty chimney, iron dustpans, sailcloth remnants for repairs, wooden carrying trenchers and things I recognised but did not understand. It was too tidy. It was like a makings room with nothing to make and no future. I hadn't noticed when I was visiting Tobe. There was a draughts board and a half-finished game of Scrabble that made me weep. I stayed for a while on his bucket stool inside the doorway until the moment passed. On the way out I picked up an unused notebook from Tobe's bookshelf. I hoped he wouldn't mind.

When they, the Shipley household, had come to use the computer the first time, only a day or two after they arrived, I'd been in my makings room, which if my house was the telescope that it somewhat resembled would be at its narrowest end. They knocked. It was a courtesy they kept up, not only from politeness, but I think to stay separate: our paths were different and the sharing of our lives temporary. Cat called, 'Kitty?' (She had a clear voice, deeper in anger.)

'Keep coming,' I called back.

Their footsteps sounded on the old wooden floors as they approached, and they came in, pushing the door wide. Cat exclaimed: 'Oh, it's the same.'

Alejandra prowled around, looking at the things that filled the shelves: bottles, oars, driftwood, cans, stones, signs, tin cans, bottles, wire, metal, bones, stones, arrowheads, insect husks, tiny skulls of birds and other creatures, and large bones too. Luis and Josh stared, as people always did at first sight. It was unusual, I suppose.

'What's it called again, what you do?' Cat asked.

'Different things – bricoleur, assembler, sculptor. I make sculptures – makings, I call them – from stuff I find.'

'There's a documentary about Kitty,' Cat said, with a little pride. 'There's a bit I always remember about that lady who found you.'

'My agent? Mary Dove.'

'I liked how she said it was as if the Watermen – that's their name, right? – were calling her across the water.'

'I nearly shot her by mistake. They left that bit out. Mary's always been very good about that.'

'Shit, Kitty,' Cat said.

'Why would you do that?' Josh asked.

'I *didn't*. I only *nearly* did. I told you that. She crept up one day when I was working. A few things had made me jumpy – a story for another time.'

They came up often after that to use the computer, as Cat did perhaps a week after the cold snap, when I was at my work table one morning. She said little but hello before she settled in, her dark head bent in concentration over the computer. It gave me a bad feeling.

'Did I do something to you?' I said.

She raised her head. 'No,' she said lightly.

'That can't be true.'

'I know you've got work to do. Me too.'

'I see.'

'Family's not your thing. I get it.'

'That's not true. I like having you here.'

'But you left your children?'

I can tell you, those words left me breathless. 'Claudie . . .'

'It doesn't matter. I didn't know you to miss. But you left my mother, and Uncle Tobe. I asked her about it.'

'After you visited?'

She nodded. 'She never said until then. I thought you'd had some argument. I used to think you were kind of cool after that film came out, like an outlaw or something. You've got to admit, it is weird what you did.'

'It's not like I abandoned them on a roadside. They had their father. We visited back and forward. They came out here, and I went to the main. Claudie wasn't even there when I went to town. If she was, she wouldn't talk to me.'

Cat glared.

'You know how old Claudie was when I moved back here?'

'Like eleven or twelve.'

'Your age.'

That stopped her.

'She's not the one who left, though, is she?' Cat said.

'That's true. She's always wanted to fit in – nothing wrong with that. I didn't know how. I did try.' I thought some more, fiddling with some pliers. 'I embarrassed her, I think. She was angry. It seemed like it was easier when I wasn't there.' I could have been trying to persuade myself on that point.

'What about Uncle Tobe?'

'Yeah,' I said. 'Tobe.'

When I didn't say more, she returned to whatever she was doing. I did too. My work was a mess. Nothing hung together. It didn't mean anything. When Cat stood to go, I dropped my tools. 'What are you doing there?' I don't know what made me finally ask – irritation at her maybe, wanting to make her as uncomfortable as she'd made me.

But she didn't mind a bit. 'Waiting for news.'

I would know them from the sound of the keyboard if they didn't call out coming in. Cat wrote short things in a rush, sometimes impatient, sometimes angry, or there might be a growl of frustration before she left. Mostly, she was bored, I think. Josh fumbled around typing and deleting – searching for things, I supposed. He wiped his history, so I wouldn't know. Long streams of rattling keys meant Luis.

Boldly, I asked him one day what he was doing. He paused and considered me. 'Looking for my mother,' he said. 'She was picked up by agents. There's an immigration lawyer and a couple of church people I check with. They're making enquiries – good people. I don't want to worry Alejandra.'

'No,' I said.

'It happens.'

'But this is your mother.'

'Yes.'

'Let me know if I can do anything.'

His expression brightened somewhat. 'Do you know anyone?'

'Out here, you mean? No one. I don't know why I said it.'

'Thank you anyway, ma'am. For your help.'

'It's really nothing.'

'It is something.'

I knew it wasn't. What was I thinking? Anyway, at least I know a little then.

Claudie sent me an email, asking how I'd been and whether I'd been busy, had anything been happening. Since she hardly contacted me from one Christmas to the next, I surmised she was looking for Cat but couldn't admit she was missing. I said I was well, and busy preparing for my next show. Winter was my best time: the garden lay fallow for a few months and it was just me and my thoughts feeling their way along. I felt some guilt about concealing Cat's whereabouts, but I had Cat's rules in mind. I sent Claudie my love.

The truth is that my work was going badly. My thoughts kept turning towards keeping everyone fed, and their plans, such as they were. It was a couple of weeks after they arrived that I began writing in the notebook from Tobe's shanty. First I sketched a boat filled with people on a stormy sea, then wrote: *The strangest thing after living alone for so long, some young people have come to stay a while and I'm not sure how I feel.* After that I began writing about things that had happened and things I was wondering. (I still haven't caught up.)

The past is here all the time, running alongside the present, their currents flowing, connecting here and there, warm above and cold below, or fast and slow alongside each other, that sort of thing. Sometimes I'm touching both at the exact same time. I might be looking towards Stillwater and it's like Tobe is about to come home from a morning's explorations up a gut, while looking in the other direction his niece, twenty years later, is gathering kindling. My mother might be in the pantry; I can almost hear her. I wonder whether to Tobe and my parents (and to all the people who've lived on Wolfe for thousands of years) I might seem like a ghost from the future, if they caught sight of me.

As to what started me writing, it was as if something rescued me. My mother would say an ancestor was holding me close. Bette would call that superstition. My father would smile and say, 'If it makes you feel better, sweetheart.' I was slow at first, trying to distract myself from my worries and from thinking about Hart, who I was missing after all this time. It might have been seeing the closeness at Shipleys. A strange thing: I was going to say the closeness between Cat and Luis. They laugh and talk. They are friends, I suppose. Josh doesn't seem to mind.

I'm not sure who I'm writing for – perhaps for Hart and Claudie, in case something happens to us, or for the long arc, so people will know I tried to do my best, whatever the outcome might be. I might even be talking to myself. I do a little writing, catch up with my thoughts and things that have been happening, and set free somehow, I can start work.

Observations of the Shipley household from the first month
- *Alejandra lying on the dock edge dangling a line into the water, the milkiness that seemed to hover on the water and around her. It's like watching memories, first of me and Bette and Doree, second of Tobe and Claudie. I imagine Claudie telling Cat stories and Cat passing them on to Alejandra. I would like to have heard them.*
- *Cat and Luis keeping Alejandra company; them laughing, and Luis forgetting what weighed so heavy, and Cat noticing. He looks stricken sometimes. I wish he would talk, but he is careful in the things he says. He might talk his troubles over with Cat, but I think not with Josh. At least, if he did, I never saw it.*
- *Josh puzzling at the mechanisms of a hundred-year-old crab trap, as if he'd ever need it in winter – or summer these days, for that matter. Very occasionally I saw a crab rising towards something, or slinking aside, and stayed very still and hoped it would survive. But that was in summer, and it was winter now.*

They moved furniture balanced on a wheelbarrow, once a floral sofa from one of the tombstone houses, which kept tipping the wheelbarrow over. They laughed and shouted – I assume from the sounds and the ways their bodies moved. They righted it where it fell not far from the Peachblossom Road sign and sat there for a rest, and I think they might have left it there if Luis hadn't got them going again.

They tried fishing, then tonging for oysters, which is cruel work. Cat fell in once while wielding the giant pincers. Josh pulled her up one-handed and they laughed together and he gave her a kiss. He can be sweet with her. Luis looked away. Josh and Luis hauled up bottles and whitegoods before giving up. You have to know what you're doing with oysters, and these days you have to be lucky. They were raised for a different world.

They scavenged through the old houses and sheds across the island and wheeled back their treasure – old tins of food and so forth. This, they could do.

- *Luis looking out to sea, scanning it, scanning the sky, doing this often.*

Later on the day that Cat fell into the water while tonging for oysters, after everyone had finished laughing and teasing and she'd gone inside and changed, she came out again and joined the others, putting her hands to Josh and Luis's backs in a friendly way, rubbing a little. Then she shoved them both in. When they bobbed up, Luis laughed; Josh did too, after a pause. I like a man who can laugh at himself freely. I always feel it's a good sign. Hart was good in that regard – in fact he was laughing the first time I met him – but then I liked everything about him.

*

The first time I saw Hart my throat stopped as if I was drowning. Doree told me later that she'd overheard a couple of women say he was the hottest man on Wolfe in two generations.

My mother sat two rows ahead of me for revival meeting that year. It was summertime in the 'tent' (a tall open-sided wooden pavilion) in one of its final years, and her dark hair took the evening sun. Her cheeks were high and apple-ish, and her narrow eyes kept watch. I don't know that my mother believed in what went on at revival. Her father had turned against God and the church after his wife's death one harsh winter. My mother spoke sometimes of a vision she might have had at the time and her belief that her mother could have returned to life if she'd been truly faithful. Since she loved her father she respected his scepticism and even shared it to some degree, but she'd felt what she'd felt, so she sat through revival each summer, watching the goings-on, fanning herself languidly with a folded song sheet against the heat. I liked the songs. Marilynne Jims from the Craft Guild Confederation shop led each line in her ringing voice and we'd follow along more or less, the sound billowing like the murmurations of birds we sometimes saw and which our fathers shot. Starlings were a pest, they said.

That summer I was fifteen I broke free. There was a scuffle up in the rafters, among the doves perhaps. Their feathers drifted and fell as soft as autumn leaves – everyone watched them, even the minister – and I started laughing and couldn't stop. Pastor Kevin was preaching a wistful reminiscence of his vodka days. He slumped to the Wurlitzer when the sadness of sobriety overcame him, and broke into song and let the Lord take him, staring up at the dark-planked roof as if it was God rather than pigeons up there. Pastor Kevin's kids played on their handheld games, the greenish light shimmering on their indoor faces; his wife Lorraine looked like she was weighing up whether to make a chocolate fudge or a strawberry cream layer cake the minute she got home. Hearing my laughter, Hart, who I had not met, turned and stared at me in a particular way and shook his head, pretending he was shocked, and that started me up again.

Doree dug me in the ribs and grinned. 'Shut up,' I mouthed to her and she shook her head and tick-tocked her finger and mouthed, 'You are going to hell.' (We were practised in the art of lip reading.)

I marched right up to him after the meeting was over. A desperate resolve had overtaken me. He would be gone so soon and my life would not be worth living if we didn't converse. 'What are you doing here?' I asked.

'I came for the meeting,' he said.

'Are you religious then?' What a disappointment that would be; I had decided I was not.

'Curiosity. Anthropology. Meetings like this are a dying artefact, don't you know? We're living in the end times.'

'You should have been paying attention then,' I said.

'You're probably right.' Then he paused. 'Trouble was, I couldn't look away.'

No one had said such a thing to me before. People on the island weren't bold in their words, at least not to the people they felt boldly towards. He was teasing and telling the truth together.

'What's your name?' I asked.

'Tell me yours first.'

I waited, which was a different kind of boldness.

'Hart,' he finally said.

'That's it?'

'You want the whole thing?'

I nodded.

'Don't laugh.'

I crossed my heart.

'Hartford Darkness.'

'Well,' I said. He waited. It mattered what I thought and I knew that. 'That is a heavy burden to carry.'

'You don't know.'

'I'm Kitty Hawke,' I told him, and held out my hand to shake his.

'Ha!' he said and took my hand and threw back his head and laughed.

I went home and lay in a darkened room to keep my feelings pure. My mother came in and when I shouted at her, she laughed and said, 'You do have it bad,' and let me alone.

Two afternoons later she sat heavily at my side on the porch swing. 'That idiot Tolstoy, what did he know? And Shakespeare. He's another one, telling us.' It was her way of saying sorry, which I didn't understand until years later when I read some Tolstoy and Shakespeare – those long island winters. In those days I thought lightweight, light-hearted things *were* unimportant. Some years later I thought they held the world together. Things like comfort, pleasantness and sufficiency were reliable and constant, whereas love (and hate and retribution) complicated everything. I was wrong about that too. It is merely that all these things exist as the world does, as people do, each as implacable and destructive as any violent storm.

The first time Hart came back to the island he travelled in darkness, which is never wise. I was sitting on the stoop below our dock shanty when a boat took shape. I should have been cautious, pulled into the soft shadows, or called out, 'Hey,' and listened for a familiar voice in reply. But I didn't. I watched the shape walk along the line of wooden slats, its feet hardly sounding above the water. There were plenty of stars out but only a sliver of moon and there wasn't much to see. It was as if my mind was catching up with what my body knew and had been waiting for. It was Hart's walk, which I knew by the shape of the darkness around him. Even though I'd hardly touched him except for that handshake, I threw myself at him when he emerged into light and stood there so straight and bright and young, and he held me as if I was the answer to every question he ever had.

There were some setbacks on account of his parents, who wanted him to finish college and had plans for him that a girl like me could only ruin. But he visited, and we weren't as careful as we might have been, and got married when Claudie was on the way, although I was still so young. Hart travelled back and forth to the island until he had finished his degree; his parents insisted on that, and had some leverage as trustees of his grandmother's estate. (It took a year or two for him to finish his studies, and another year before the old doctor retired and he could take over.) They never approved. I could have moved to the main then, but I wanted to stay on the island and live the old life.

Chapter 5

THERE WAS A low mist one morning, what my mother would have called a 'simmerin' mist'. Its surface seethed and spread, while a 'smotherin' mist' lay waiting to stop your breath. Watching it from the landing window was like floating above the clouds. The second storey of Shipleys rose like a fairytale, shadowy figures moving about or gliding past windows. One of the windows flew up. Luis thrust out his head and looked around, and shut it. At another window Cat and Josh appeared and disappeared from the square of light. They'd be downstairs, like birds in a cloth-covered cage. Smoke began rising from its twin chimneys. The low cloud above began to glow grey and then white and pale gold and fell away, and finally the sun broke through and hit the mist, striking through it in places and lighting up bushes and boats and the Watermen above the docks, and finally melting it away.

Luis came up, quite friendly, relieved that the mist had gone. 'Freaky, wasn't it?' he said.

'I love the sound. Did you hear it?'

'I didn't hear anything.'

'That's why. It soaks it up. Kind of eerie.'

He scanned the horizon. He seemed to breathe easier

when he could see what was coming. He went in to use the computer and I went to my kitchen window seat to work on my notebook. He came out in a while and told me someone thought they had a trace on his mother, or someone like her. I could see how he didn't want to get his hopes up. 'We'll see,' he said.

'That's a good sign,' I said.

'I guess it is. It is, isn't it?' Times like this I could see how he was still a boy.

It was the beginning of winter's end. Over the week that followed the air softened a little more each day, and buds blushed and the days suddenly seemed longer. In the kitchen one afternoon, I set the kettle to boil and leaned against the counter, considering the pale room. Maybe another chair or a sofa and a few cushions by the fire would make it more welcoming, just in case. I didn't think the Shipley household was going anywhere soon. They were waiting for more news. I went and looked at the vegetable garden, which was sheltered against a rickety shed, and bordered on the other side by a stand of pomegranates (hopeless gaunt things in winter) and surrounded by trodden paths. If Wolfe was a book, I was the only one who could read it. The wisps of corn that clung to verges, the remnant mulberries and pomegranates from when they were going to make us all rich, the overgrown ossuaries of animal bones, and the white shell paths that threaded the island were all that was left of its seas of corn, its orchards, its meadows of livestock, its teeming seas.

Rising salt was the new crop. It had arrived in my garden a few years back after a decade creeping in from the shore.

Things began to grow stunted: the corn no more than waist high, the tomatoes and peppers spindly and wan-leafed. I sweetened the soil with grass clippings and vegetable peelings, fallen leaves, and goat manure too, when I still had them. One beautiful year I believed I had it beat and bought an orange tree, the winters being milder by then. I loved that tree, the waxy sweetness of its blossom and its bright leaves. The flesh from the one small orange I got from it was as dry as shed snakeskin and tasted of nothing and I wished I'd left it on the tree. The fruit stopped setting after that, bees having disappeared, perhaps blown out to sea, and after that there was nothing for it but to hand pollinate – a tiresome task that went on all summer. Each year I built the beds higher, and mounded hills within walls, anything to keep ahead of the rising salt.

There was nothing new in worrying about crops and vegetable gardens, but people had always paid more attention to the island being whittled away. Seawater coming up your hallway is disconcerting, I suppose. Every once in a while, right up until a few years before the last islanders left, there would be campaigns for a new jetty when the old one failed, and people ran fundraisers and sold cakes. Islanders watched the tattered shores and kicked at them and said, 'She'll turn around again, just you wait. It's always been changeable.'

TV people used to do reports on 'the situation'. They'd put some folk in a room – watermen mostly, ten-year-old Tobe once as 'a representative of the future' – and some pretty young girl would say, 'How do you feel about your world disappearing?', and Tobe would shrug in that way of his. 'Like, how do you think, sweetheart?' I wanted to say. They'd act like something might come of it but nothing ever did.

We were 'the island that time forgot', then they'd go right ahead and forget us again. A politician claiming some importance rang the mayor once and told him not to worry; everything would be fine. 'Believe me,' he said, and most islanders did. Thank *you*, mister. He turned out to be the biggest liar of all. The world wouldn't stop for us. Some believed in the power of prayer. Others were waiting for the rapture. 'There's no reasoning with such people,' my mother used to say.

So a few years ago when a documentary filmmaker emailed to ask if I would care to be part of a project I thought it was the same old thing. His name was Chas Dartmouth. You might have heard of him. Perhaps he thought me a relic of an old way of life. People couldn't get enough of the way we spoke, like it was a birdcall or scat that must be analysed. But it turned out Chas Dartmouth was interested in my art, which he had seen at a recent show in Escher, and the ideas of decay and renewal in my work and my environment – his words, not mine. He thought it symbolic or metaphorical or resonant – something like that. That was the second time in my life someone took me seriously, and it was a strange feeling. So we made that film and it was shown around and things went well for my work. I quit making jams and preserves, except for my own pantry. People came to Wolfe to talk to me about my makings. If they were artists or sculptors or assemblers I would offer them cake and coffee; if they were not, I told them not to touch anything, went inside, and kept an eye on them until they left. That died down after a bit. Word spread that I was not easy company. A few people said I was a recluse. It was not true, but it suited me for people to think so. I worked on another project with Chas a couple of years later and he became a friend.

*

'So you're like the last of the Mohicans?' Josh said to me one day, poking around for a way to get into my good graces. The way he presumed he was charming irritated me so, and I think he felt that, even if he didn't understand its cause.

'Not really,' I told him. 'I have visitors, and I go visiting. There are islanders around, just not so many *on* the islands as there used to be.'

Something in his question must have stung. I went around for days thinking of better answers, and made a list of last year's activities, so I was prepared should he ever ask again.

Visitors to Wolfe
- *School groups x 3 (art, biology, history)*
- *Two scientists of my acquaintance, Jean and Lloyd, who I first met when they were measuring Wolfe's erosion for a government project. The funding dried up, but they came out anyway for coffee and cake and a day of peace, and told me stories of the main that were so queer I could hardly credit their words.*
- *Several birders, who I kept an eye on, since some of them bother the birds.*
- *Two out-of-season hunters who I sent on their way by introducing myself as the island's caretaker and wildlife officer.*
- *Mary Dove, my agent, who visits once a year.*

Visits to the main
- *Shopping visits to Blackwater x 2*
- *Visits to prisoner x 3*

It was true that I preferred not to visit the mainland. In fact, it was not until I was almost seventeen that I spent a night away from Wolfe. Hart wanted me to see the world. He might have been hoping I'd fall in love with it. Some people don't mind mountains and trees in the way; I was used to the edges of my world falling away like water from a plate. In the mountains, the trees were dark and tall by the roadside, turning the sky into another kind of road that was distant and travelled by solitary birds that hung above us, and it seemed as if time had stopped and I was looking back at someone else's memory. We walked a trail. There were butterflies, the light was green and sweet, the wind hissed in the trees. We lay in a clearing on leaf litter that was the fallen worlds of thousands of years. I smoothed his fringe. He smiled and I loved him and told him so. I wonder if he remembers.

The second trip was to a beach, while I was still travelling between Wolfe and Blackwater, trying to keep things together – biding my time, though I didn't know that then. It was a beachfront hotel with a plastic-looking portico. The hotel staff had faces like carnival heads. The sun was brassy on the horizon line and the sand seemed to sicken on the beach. We went walking early and came upon staff clearing up dead fish that had washed onto the shore. Hart acted like it was everything he'd ever dreamed of (apart from the fish), mostly to annoy. On the drive west towards home, my spirits flung upwards like a kite and I hummed old songs as if the sky had sent the words down to me. The signs along the roadside, the grassy ditches and pines lining the route and the crops between turned familiar. Hart was in a mood to quarrel and for the first time in a week I was not. I put my hand on his leg and said, 'Sweetheart, let's get drunk tonight.'

Not long after, we passed a farm prison where illegals and children, perhaps their own, all dressed in orange, were in trees picking fruit. It was the first I had seen of that sort of thing. When someone at the children's school told me they guessed Wolfe Island was a kind of prison and I must be glad to have broken free, I'd learned enough to tell them they were wrong. They didn't believe me. That's the trouble with people. They have to see things for theirselves. Well, I didn't understand exactly why Luis was still so watchful. I sometimes thought it excessive, but I had no idea what he was fearful of or what he might have seen. His manner should have been enough to tell me that he had good reasons.

I took a cake or two down to Shipleys. Cat was tired and not eating right and losing weight, but I wouldn't know if she ate any. She said, 'Thanks, Kitty,' in a cool sort of way and not much more.

I didn't know the world they were raised in, what had made them and how they felt about those things, so they might just as well have washed up like wreckage from a foreign country with strange lettering printed all over. The idea of our isolation never occurred to me when I was growing up. Islanders didn't care too much about what was happening elsewhere. The mainland was another world and we couldn't see the difference it made. I knew some of it, but not much. I began to look at the news, trying to understand what they had left behind.

I read about militias and vigilantes running wild more or less in some counties, and authorities making use of them to do their work while they looked away, laws turning wispy and insubstantial in the face of life, zealots working for the rapture to arrive. They ploughed fields of solars and felled wind turbines to hasten the Lord's coming. It seemed like there was a lot of pretending: people saying one thing and doing another. (I'd seen plenty of that on Wolfe. Practically everyone I knew said they'd never leave, but they did anyway.) I had not known a tenth of what was going on. It's easy to miss small changes in a place you live, and it's easy to misunderstand the things you're seeing. A trip to the main was like getting a glimpse through a tiny window into a crumbling old house.

On one visit to the main I saw police talking to a small dark-haired woman. She looked into their faces with worry and distress, and away as if someone else might say something to save her, and then, holding onto her dignity, the only thing she had in that moment, she got in their car. Maybe she was helping them, or maybe she was in deep trouble. I say that now, but I didn't think about it then. I didn't bother. I was thinking on my own problems. I'd heard talk of 'the situation' and 'the way things are right now', and saw more people carrying guns and heard announcements in shops. But it didn't seem so strange. I carried a gun myself. I felt better for it.

Now I looked at Luis and Alejandra and Cat and Josh – runners and runaways – and wondered about more than what kept them together. Cat and Josh were bored rather than frightened, but Luis looked out to sea as if staring from a cage. Sometimes he ran and ran up the marsh road, up every road and every track of the island he could, beating against its edges – but he wasn't imprisoned in a way that I was familiar with, except by circumstance. A true prisoner can't see beyond their walls. Perhaps he was one then.

I'd begun visiting the prisoner I mentioned earlier when Chas Dartmouth 'reached out', as he called it, while working on his next project, about the lives of prisoners who lived in solitary confinement on death row.

He came out to Wolfe for a meeting and we sat on the porch drinking iced tea and looking over the water, which had turned brittle in the late sun.

'You're against the death penalty? Because I couldn't care. Really, I could not care,' I said. 'Why choose me? You imagine I'm some sort of prisoner and I'm going to change my thinking?'

Chas shook his head and blinked rapidly behind his round black glasses, unsettled by my agitation, but still gentle. He was a good man. He wanted to understand people, and I respected him for that. He waited for me to settle. 'No, Kitty. I do not. I don't know what's in you – what you think and feel. I don't want to change you. It's not that at all. I don't even know why I'm interested. I mean, do you always understand why you try things out? All I know is this is what I'm thinking about and what I have to do.'

It was a reproof in a way, a plea too, and I listened. He told me about the prisoner, whose name I will not mention here. Chas had known of my connection to him from when we first met. It might have been on his mind, and when the man was sentenced to death he'd got thinking. It was a hard thing to take in, but I was curious to meet the fellow he was talking of, I will not deny that, and I agreed.

It was autumn, two months later, when I met Chas in the prison car park. We were silent on the walk to the great gates where we paused to be checked in. There were red maples, their leaves falling, and the red leaves drifted and rustled onto the asphalt in the breeze.

'You okay?' Chas asked.

'I think so.'

'There'll be a pat down, nothing to worry about. And a metal detector.'

'I'd best leave this in the car then.' I took the gun from my pocket – that gave him pause – and went back to the car and put it in the glove box.

'Nothing to worry about,' he said again.

'I'm not worried,' I said.

'I am.' He gave a short laugh and pushed his glasses up. He was sweating, though it was not warm.

The prison was a deathly place: close, sour, antiseptic, and humming with dread. We walked through the narrow guts of the building. We might as well have been inside a carcass for the view there was of the outside. Everything was grey and the doors were grey iron, numbered, with narrow flaps. The guard was soft-looking, with close-cropped hair, his belt pulled in snug beneath his belly, and his gun holster rubbing against his thigh like a loose dick. He touched it once or twice as he walked in front of us. The keys and cuffs he carried sounded against each other in a calm and repeated way and he cared so little about it that I was quickly terrified, as if I was being walked in to begin a sentence myself. Sweat prickled at my hairline.

'Here,' the guard said. He opened the door. 'You can set up. I'll get him.' He left.

We sat on one side of a table in a room so narrow that the table divided it almost exactly in two. There was a door on the other side of the room and the door that we had entered by, and this room connected two worlds. The walls were grey, the ceiling was grey and low, lit with two fluorescent strip lights, and the floor was grey linoleum spattered with red as if in anticipation of stains to come.

57

Chas fussed with his camera and tripod, trying to get the right angle. The door opened and the meeting proceeded. I remember little of the visit, except for one bit that I try not to dwell on, which was when the two guards came for him. They opened the door and came in and each put a hand on his shoulders. 'It's time,' one said.

'Okay,' the prisoner said, and then, to Chas and to me, 'I thank you for the opportunity.' He stood immediately and without hesitation. He had to lean forward to shift his weight, his wrists being shackled to his metal belt. His ankles were shackled too, so he moved like his body was broken. The part I could not bear was when he said, 'Okay,' for a second time. Sometimes I can't help thinking of this.

They turned him around as if he was a thing – a shopping trolley, say – and he shuffled out without a backward glance, like a child who has learned the futility of making a scene, and has reason to expect punishment if he does. He was as broken as a person can be, had been broken long ago. How would he ever become whole again? Who would care if he did not? Life had whittled him to nothing. He was a sorry thing, but a hard kernel in me would not loosen. I am not sure what it was – not hatred, not exactly. Maybe it was the sadness of him sitting alongside the sadness he had wrought around him and in me. It had become part of me, and it's not easy to let such things go. Who would I be without it?

I had borrowed Doree's Dodge to get there. There was a long, high bridge I had to cross, and on the drive back I thought of the bridge ahead – its flimsy sides, the cars hard up against its edges, the speed of the traffic, the space beneath – and the journey to come through ruined country, where ducks swam in blackened ditches, lone buzzards patiently circled, and big-headed dogs roamed free. For some distance the bridge climbed a low hill rising from a fishing village outgrown itself, and from shopping malls and gas stations, until suddenly unshackled it soared. The ground fell away and disappeared. There was only water and air and movement, and at my elbow the edge of the highway. A seagull sauntered through the draughts alongside, looking in curiously at my moist eyes. Surely I would fly too if I drove through the low wall at my side. The car touched the edge and the metal screamed. Leisurely, I drew away. The steering wheel pulled under my hand like a strong dog. I held it tight then and it was like the quivering of the wheel felt its way into me until I was shaking too, as hard as I ever had. A car drew alongside, the driver's mouth wide and black in its depth, his eyes going from front to side, to look at me and howl out his rage. I could have killed him, just run into his side. I didn't think the world would miss a person like that much. I didn't think it would miss me.

Chapter 6

Spring

I WENT TO the marsh walkway, a structure that ambled above the eastern saltmarsh like a caterpillar in search of a leaf. It had a way of clearing my mind, which was muddied then by many worries: about the future, and about Claudie and what she knew, and whether I should tell Claudie about Cat, and what I suspected about her.

The walkway had been intended to bridge a widening gut, but failed before they quit building, the water having moved too fast, and after some distance the structure stopped suddenly as if its purpose had not after all been to cross the encroaching sea but to greet incoming storms. It had been good pasture all around for as long as anyone knew, 'speckled with Jersey cows the colour of caramel chews', my mother told me. That farmland turning to saltmarsh was the end of dairying on Wolfe – a terrible blow to the island.

But the walkway hadn't been wasted. People promenaded its length of an evening, and visitors had enjoyed looking at the *unparalleled vistas of this historic region*, as the sign below promised they would. Children thought it haunted, but no one could agree by what: a pair of poisoned eagles, a drowned dog or fisherman, a murdered wife.

I sang one of the old songs, a habit of mine when out there, not really thinking.

Will you come with me, come with me?
Stay with me, stay with me,
Be with me, be with me
My dear one, my heart
Will you be with me now
And forever, forever
Oh, let it be now and all will be well.

It has a strange melody in a minor key. My mother once said, 'Everything has its own tune, Kitty. But you must learn to hear it.' The island has its own tune, which I sometimes hear at the end of winter when I haven't seen a person in months. It is mute to me this year. Girl got restless and howled to the wind, a different kind of song, an old one. Maybe she thought my singing a lonely sort of howling, which wasn't a great compliment to my singing. I hummed some more and looked over the fallen farmhouse enmired in the marsh nearby, the wheeling sun, the circumscribing sea, and the old bridge linking north and south ends, a quaint thing of Willowware design.

Girl doesn't like Josh. He makes her uneasy. I try to be welcoming to him to put her at ease, but she shies away from him and is watchful. He approached her too fast one morning and tried to pet her. Girl growled. I put my hand to her shoulder. Menace was running through her.

'She safe?' Josh said.

'How do you mean?' I stroked her head.

'With strangers?'

'She keeps an eye out for me. She won't bother you if you don't bother her.'

It's the opposite with Alejandra. Girl always approaches her with her tail swaying, and touches her hand with her nose, and Alejandra touches Girl's shoulder.

Girl found Alejandra lurking on the marsh road on the last day of winter and brought her out on the walkway. The cold whipped her cheeks pink and made her eyes water. She was quiet for the most part, only whispering into the ear of her doll, Luna, but she liked it I think.

She began to come about with me late in the morning (she did schoolwork first thing with Luis, she said), pretending she'd happened upon me by accident. It seemed polite to pretend the same. I let my eye roam over the mucky ground at the fallen shore and around the marsh mudflats, looking (not intently, more like waiting for a fish to bite on a line) for things of a different colour or a peculiar shape, or feeling for things with a stick tool I had, but not too hard. There it would be, whatever it was, just there. I bent down and felt about and if I could I'd winkle the object out with a finger.

'What are you doing?' Alejandra asked from a nearby hillock.

'Looking for stuff.'

'What stuff?'

'Things from the past,' I said. 'They call it mudlarking in England – progging around here. I prefer mudlarking – though that used to mean oystering hereabouts. Words are shifty in their meanings. You'll find that out. I've got a friend there who does the same, except along a river. She goes out and finds things from thousands of years ago. She makes ugly things beautiful, but she only cares about telling the truth. That's what she says.'

'That's a funny thing to say.'

'Isn't it?'

She, Irina, has a Russian mother and a Kurdish father and grew up in a refugee camp in Italy and now lives in Essex on the Thames, not far from London. I wonder how she answers when people ask where she's from, since she's lived in so many places. What things make her recall her past and the countries that have been her home – a dish, a colour of sky, the first soft wind of spring on her face, the smell of a smoking fire? Nothing on Wolfe is truly strange to me. I have a memory for every part of it. Show me an old drink can and I'm dandling my legs over the side of a skiff, tossing it or any other litter overboard, as everyone did back then. ('Nature's trash can' we called the water. No wonder there's so much to be found.)

Thready roots connect me to the island everywhere I go. Wolfe Island folk had known each other's families for generations; the Willowware bridge was built by my great-great-grandfather; my mother had an old family word that she used for Pine Point on the island's southernmost tip. There had always been a tall tree there, she said; it was important to keep a new one coming along or it would be bad luck for the island. 'Superstition,' my father once said. My mother looked at him with a hint of something knowing, and tartly replied, 'And who is to say that doesn't matter, pray tell, Harald Schonfeld?' And he, hearing her tone, would say, 'Why, no one of any sense, my dear, I am sure.' I loved my father, but agreed with my mother in this regard. What we feel is as true as what we think.

My mudlarking stick has a flattened crook on the end that I drag across the muddy surface. I did this now and the crook caught the edge of something and lifted it. I teased it free. It was a pointed thing, triangular. An arrowhead? Alejandra scrambled across the tussocks towards me. I dipped it in a pool of water, sluiced it clean and looked again. Too big and the wrong shape for an arrow and cold in my hand.

'What is it?' she said.

'Shark tooth. Millions of years old by the size of it. Rare.' I held it out and she touched its serrated edge and looked at her finger to see if it had left a mark.

'Why do you do this?' she asked.

How could I explain why to a seven-year-old? So one day I can say I lived in a place where such things could be found? To remind me that sharks swam here once and might swim again? 'I like to find things,' I said. 'They're nice to hold in your hand. Imagine that great big mouth. I'm holding the past right here. It's like it's swimming past.'

I handed it to her and she turned it over carefully, smoothing it. 'You can have it,' I said on an impulse. Her face lit up. 'Look after it, mind. There're more people than shark teeth. Folk will pay for such a thing – good money. We might be able to find out about it when we get back. Keep it somewhere safe. Do you have a deep pocket?'

She pushed her hand into her jacket pocket and waggled her fingers.

'Don't lose it now.'

She shook her head and looked at it again before plunging it into her pocket and doing up the zipper. She ran off. It seemed like she'd had enough. A good shark's tooth, millions of years old.

But Girl swayed her tail and suddenly Alejandra was back, a stout stick in hand, and began poking the marsh's surface, watching for anything that might appear.

'That's right,' I said. 'Like that. Careful now, not too hard, you don't want to miss anything.'

'Okay.'

'I'll get you something else – make it easier for you.'

'One of them?' She nodded at my mudlarking crook.

'A bit smaller.'

'Okay.'

She seemed to like doing things with me.

Luis didn't mind. 'If she wants to,' he said. He asked if she talked.

'A little,' I told him, and he said, 'That's good, that's really good. She's been kind of quiet for a while.'

'Kids don't like change,' I said, and he said he guessed not.

I asked her once where they were staying before she came to the island and what she'd liked to do. She stared at me in confusion. 'Are you my friend and Luis's friend?' she asked finally.

'I think so,' I said.

'I – I don't know . . . Luis said . . . he said I . . .'

'Oh, it's okay, honey. He said not to say?'

She nodded furiously.

'It's okay, sweetheart. Don't worry. I was just chatting. Don't say anything you don't want to, okay? Do you want to go out in a skiff? That's a little boat.'

'On the sea?' She looked stricken in a new way now.

'No, just on these little creeks – the guts, we call them. We can just paddle around and see what we see, that's all. Just for fun. Girl likes being a ship's dog for a change. Better check with Luis first, though.'

'Okay.' She went running down the road and a short while later came panting back. That was the first time she came exploring the old waterways, where the water sometimes stayed clear to the bottom.

'What's that?' Alejandra said. 'That thing down there.'

'Coke bottle. We better get it. Wait.' I stilled the boat, passed her the net. 'There you go, lean over now, not too far or Cat will kill me and then we'll both be dead. Better stop laughing or Girl'll be dead too.'

'Not Girl!'

'No, not Girl,' I assured her. 'She's a good swimmer. Lean now.' She leaned.

In the makings room I have cleared a table for Alejandra which she calls her work desk. She arranges her discoveries on it, shells especially, and investigates them online and in a book on shells I found in someone's house. We found another notebook at Tobe's and she has begun keeping one too. Alejandra wanted to visit his shanty again, but I said it was kind of private, and she seemed to understand my meaning. We both had quiet places in our pasts. Girl sits at her feet, or at her side on the sofa beneath the study window, while Alejandra reads.

Luis began spending more time at my place too. 'If you don't mind,' he said. 'It's a help.'

'It's no bother,' I said.

'Cat and Josh.' He didn't elaborate, but sighed.

'Fighting, kissing, or too many rules?' I asked.

He laughed. 'I'm trying for some rules, but, yeah, you pretty much got it.'

He and Alejandra have a quietness that is easy to be around. Cat is like a firecracker, a slightly damp one these days, her spirits being subdued.

Luis tapped at the computer, as intent as if he was picking crabs, getting that last bit of meat from a claw. I went into my makings room and once in a while he knocked on the door, though it was open, and waited for an invitation to come in, and if Alejandra wasn't there (if she was washing shells or reading the internet herself, for instance) he sometimes began to talk, as if this room was a kind of confessional.

'I don't mind if she talks about our mother or little sister with you,' he said one day.

'You have a sister?'

'Just a baby. Selma. She might talk about her. She loved playing with her. She used to feed her breakfast. Anyway, I don't mind is what I'm saying. But there're some things it's better if you don't . . . It's better this way. It's better if she forgets.'

'It's fine. Really.'

So I did ask her about her mama. Alejandra said she was very nice, and that Selma was only good at smiling and waving. 'She can't even *crawl.*' She made a face at the thought, then stopped talking, the memories' effects on her face like leaf shadow. I thought she might cry, but she didn't.

After a big tide we fossicked the trash line, which my grand-father had called the wrack line and we didn't talk so much then.

Items recently collected from the trash line and elsewhere by Alejandra and me
- *5 branches, different sizes, with good silvering and move-ment (Pine Point, Beauforts ditch, and Deadness gut)*
- *Cattle skull, one broken horn, otherwise intact, washed clear near the marsh walkway*
- *Fisherman's white plastic bucket, east side*
- *Length of blue synthetic rope, frayed, knotted, with three floats attached, Deadness outlet*
- *53 plastic bottles*

- *Sea glass, different colours and sizes, one rare sapphire blue*
- *Shells, various*
- *A half wine barrel*
- *3 bottles: poison, whisky, ointment jar (chipped)*
- *A car tyre*
- *A leather satchel of a handy size, with the embossed initials HLG. Fairly fresh, so it might come good with care (washed onto a bank of Deadness gut)*

The satchel held sodden papers and a real find: a cunning knife, its handle inlaid with the initials EHG, and a blade like the edge of a gull's wing with an elegant rise at its tip – a loss to someone. I wiped the satchel clean and, sitting before the fire, rubbed in several coats of old boot dressing. It might make a collecting bag. Luis saw it there and seemed surprised that I'd found such a thing. He brushed his fingers across the lettering, admiring the workmanship, I think, so I showed him the knife. He seemed reluctant to take hold of it and was quiet. I touched my finger to the blade, showing its filigree inlay work and the initials. He hissed through his teeth. 'Careful,' he said. 'It's sharp – looks like it is. Where'd you say you found it?'

'Deadness gut,' I said. 'Near the walkway.'

'Strange things must wash up here.' He handed it back, handle first. I couldn't tell whether he was relieved or disappointed to let it go.

'You're telling me.' I returned the knife to its sheath.

I don't know if the notebook was teaching me to notice or teaching me to remember so I could write it in my notebook later. It might have been both. Sometimes things caught in my mind – I don't know why – and I did remember this.

*

Cat and Josh went to Blackwater one morning and returned loaded with supplies. They must have been running low on food or were tired of the old tins. It was the first week of spring. I was out of patience with them on account of Cat's manner, which continued aloof, and went down to tell them they better be careful, even though they didn't care what I thought. I just wanted to give the line that connected us a good old yank. Cat was on the porch sofa, her hands clasped loose on her belly, her eyes closed, and she had such a stricken look, tormented really. What was going on in her mind? She opened her eyes at my footfall and with some effort put on her mask of indifferent waiting.

'You're staying,' I said.

'Is that okay?'

'How long?'

'Does it matter?'

'Not to me.' I sat on the top stair.

'Why ask then?'

'I want to know you're safe. You've got money?'

'Enough. For now. And we used cash so they can't trace us. We're not idiots.'

Josh came and stood in the doorway, leaning against it, tapping his toe at the screen door to keep it open.

I said, 'Good to know. Something else: people are going to notice you if you're there too often.'

'No one knows us there,' Cat said. 'Who would care? Luis and Alejandra didn't come.'

'It's a small town.'

'Why would that matter?' Josh said.

I shifted against the stair post to see him more easily. 'You know how people are. They see something new, they start talking. They see you shopping like that again – two kids who look like they should be in school – they'll get chatty, they'll ask you things and they'll pass that on. Are you ready to answer? Say someone comes to town looking, then what's going to happen? Someone says, oh yeah, I saw them just last week, came in a boat. And they start looking at security cameras.'

'Got it,' Cat said sharply. 'But why would they come looking here?' She came to the porch railing in agitation, running her hand along it, up and down.

'I don't know. Are you *all* wanted? And how much do they want you? There's a reason you washed up here and if anyone's looking for places you might go, any relatives could come up, and they might check things out down here, even if it's just to cross Blackwater off a list.'

Cat glared down at me. 'Why do you care?' she said.

'Because I do.'

'So we're screwed with the shopping.'

'Not what I said. You've got to think in an island way. It's spring, time to plant, get things growing. Get some corn in, tomatoes, salad greens, beans, carrots. Potatoes. Think about preserves. I can do a little shopping for you, but people will ask questions if I do too much. We'll check everywhere for seeds, any drawer we come across.'

I was alert for visitors after the shopping trip (it was too early for birders and day-trippers) and Luis kept Alejandra close.

'Tell me, Kitty, where would you hide if you needed to?' he asked a couple of days later.

I knew him a little then. It wasn't an idle question. 'Not in a house or any building. Out in the marshes, I guess. You'd be cold and you might get wet feet, but not a person could find you without a dog helping. Girl'd take care of that. Yeah, the marshes for sure.'

'Thank you,' he said.

But things were quiet and the sense of danger receded. We began a search for seeds. Old breakfronts yielded best. We found folded packets of seeds: *Grandma's squash*, *Eggplant (striped)*, *Scarlet runner*, *Tiger beet*, *Glory's best*, *Royal carrot*, and other such things. Doree's mother had been a wonderful gardener. Her yard had hummed with bees and what seemed like the very sound of plants growing every summer.

Not a one of them – Cat or Luis or Josh – knew about planting or tending a garden. They were townies. Alejandra said their mother had one, and she used to pick the tomatoes and corn when they were ready, and she had little yellow flowers too. 'Marigolds maybe,' I said. 'Let's put some in.'

It's a beautiful time of year. Sitting here in my makings room, gazing south through the open doors right now, I have a strange feeling of contentment at all the new life. I write a little and look out. Girl is lying in the sun. Spring is flooding the island in waves of colour and light and warmth: the pink blush on the shrubs bursting into leaf, new grass thrusting from dead clumps, the sky colouring deeper, more birds arriving. With them have come a few birders – the first of them last week – as seasonal as the birds themselves. They're no trouble, just moving quietly on pathways near the marshes. Luis and Alejandra go inside and lock the doors at the sight of them, in case people are tempted to poke around inside, just from curiosity. It's happened to me more than once. A dog is useful.

They've been building a new vegetable garden, skimming off any sweet soil they can find from around the island and hauling it back in the barrow. I showed them how to plant and quite a few things have begun to peek up. Josh seems to find gardening demeaning, as if he imagines a crowd of jocks might pass by and jeer, but Cat and Luis don't mind. Alejandra loves watering best, not that it's needed just yet. She goes about with an old can of Tobe's. He used to love it too. 'Some for you, and some for you.' She tips a little on each plant. 'Some for you, Girl?' But Girl doesn't want any. She has a bowl of her own.

The prisoner told me once how much he'd liked watering. It gave me a strange feeling, knowing that, and thinking of Tobe. After the prison film was made, his lawyer asked if I'd visit him again to relieve the loneliness of his confinement, which was solitary, and I said I would. I'm still not sure why. His family didn't visit. They might have been too poor and too far away.

I visit him a few times a year, though it's a while since the documentary came out. Chas had wanted to show the faces of the inmates, what that closed-in life did to them, and to hear what they thought. It was hard to forget their faces. That might be one of the reasons why I go.

He was worn out and ready for everything to end the last time I saw him, as if he didn't care about the future, as if it had ceased to exist. The few times before that, his lawyer was appealing his sentence, and it seemed he still hoped, despite everything, that his life might turn out not so bad in the long run.

'What do you do out there on your island?' he asked.

'I garden a lot,' I said. 'I have to so I have fresh food.'

'I never had a garden. But my pop – grandpop that is – he had a garden up on his roof, up this little ladder. You could see some light coming in around the edges of the trapdoor up top. I'd wait for him to open it and go through. The light, it hurt your eyes, you know? It was so bright after the dark.' His eyes wandered around the grey room and the line of white light above. 'I'd go about with him up there. He was okay.'

Another time he said, 'I had a little, like, can of water I took around with him to, you know, water the plants. That was okay.' His eyes tracked around my face as if he was trying to judge if he'd made any impression on me. On this point I was not always sure myself, whether he had or not. I was not at my best at the time.

He told me about this and I remembered the way that Tobe had of coming about with me when he came back from a day out on a boat. He'd tell me about drudgin' and jimmies and sooks and a big one he'd heard of that had oysters growing on it. He spoke in the old way that he refused to forget, which Hart discouraged, telling Tobe to aim for better grades and think of a worthwhile career, one with opportunities. Tobe looked at him in his sweet way and went on doing what he did. Hart couldn't change him and maybe Hart was right and I should have tried. I should have tried. I didn't like thinking about Tobe and the prisoner together, but I couldn't stop it happening.

Things kept pulling the prisoner into my mind, like that watering can, like Luis running. The settled feeling that we'd had for a while – the Shipley household and me – didn't last. How could it really? I had a letter from the prisoner asking if I'd stop by soon. A date had been set for his execution and he had a favour to ask me. And in mid-spring Cat and Josh left the island early one morning. None of us knew where they'd gone.

Chapter 7

THERE'S NOT A one of us knows what we might do if things
go wrong, if the people we love are in danger, or if we're taken
from our home and all the things that make us. I tried to think
the best of Josh. Getting Shipleys in shape, scavenging through
houses for things to please Cat – a ladder-back chair, a flow-
ered plate, a wicker settee – those things he was part of. He
used his muscles; he hefted wood. He threw his arms around
Cat and kissed her. They had escaped something all right, but
they were together, and wasn't that something? So when they
left the island, and returned later without any shopping, it
seemed at first like they'd just decided to go out, almost as if
they'd gone on a date.

Luis and Alejandra came up to see me in the afternoon like
lost people wanting someone to say, No, you're not lost. We're
here together, so we can't be.

'You know anything about it?' I asked.

Luis shook his head.

They returned at dusk. We saw them from the porch, and
when we wandered down, casually, they didn't say anything
about their outing.

'Where were you, Cat?' Alejandra asked.

'We had some things to do. Helping out.' They wouldn't say more.

When they went again the following week I asked Cat about it – was it anything to do with Luis's mother? She said, 'No. Kitty, you know the rules. It's safer for everyone this way.'

'But are you safe?'

'I'm a good driver,' was all she'd say.

The messages she'd been waiting for seemed to be arriving. I worried about it, I did, but still didn't ring Claudie. What would happen to Luis and Alejandra if I did? If Cat had been filled with high spirits and adventure, I might have spoken up. But she was neither anxious before a trip nor excited after. The thought of sending her home to be looked after was ridiculous. She would just run again. Being away from the island and doing something that had a purpose seemed to settle Josh too. He stood taller somehow, with some pride.

They were away more often as the weather warmed, some-times overnight. I worried each time that they'd drowned. Luis did too. More than once I saw him staring out to sea towards evening while I was doing the same. When we saw their boat, we went inside.

It got so their being away for a night didn't seem so bad. (One good thing: they were able to shop on the way back. They avoided going to the same place twice, Cat said, and never shopped close to the island. But as to how they paid, I don't know. Surely they would have run out of cash by then.) Then it was two nights, and I told Cat that was my limit. On the second night I had pictured them drifting on dark sea and sliding beneath waves, so vividly it seemed more vision than imagination, and I thought of Claudie. When they finally returned late morning, I went down to Shipleys, where Cat was poking around the kitchen making coffee and Luis was sitting in the nook writing. I told her she would have to tell me what they were involved in or I'd ring the coastguard or her mother. It was her choice and I made that clear. Cat was a fierce person. Coercion was bitter to her. She turned from the sink and balled her fist and punched her leg, and the look on her face made me step back. Still, I was ready to insist, but in the end it was Luis who broke through.

I might have expected his emotions to rise, but he was quiet, almost distant, not pleading for his own sake. He rested his chin on one hand, idly stroking his cheek. He laid down his pen and said: 'Alejandra has nightmares when you're away. She didn't sleep last night. She's lost three people in her family already. She is frightened of losing one more. You are her family now. If there is something I could say to reassure her, it would help.'

'Oh God,' Cat said. 'I didn't think.'

They called themselves railroad drivers, she said. 'We drive people places – runners. We have a section. We pick people up and drop them off. That's all – a transportation service. No one looks twice at us. The two-night trip was because another driver fell through. Something happened, I don't know what.'

'You should have told me,' Luis said, still quiet, but there was an edge in his voice now, and he glared. 'What you're doing is dangerous. You need protection.'

Cat returned his look. 'I've got Josh, and you've got enough to worry about. You think I was going to add to that?' She wouldn't say she was sorry.

'You should have anyway,' he said.

'But you're safe?' I asked, as I had before.

She shrugged. 'I'm a good driver, I told you. I don't draw attention to myself. Drivers never meet each other. We don't know the names of the runners or where they're from; we don't talk to them about anything personal, we stick to the rules. I make sure of that, you know me. And we're minors, so . . .'

'Whatever would happen to minors if you got caught.'

'Yes.' It seemed like there was something else on her mind, but I knew there was no point in asking.

'I wish you'd tell your mother.'

'About what?'

'Where you are, what you're doing, your *life*, Cat.'

'I've sent a couple of messages. She knows I'm okay.' I made some sound of irritation. 'You don't know what she's like,' she said.

'I know how a mother feels.'

'Do you?' she asked. I thought she was being sarcastic, but she tilted her head quizzically, looking at me all the while, as if she really was considering whether I might have motherly feelings.

'I most certainly do,' I said, and left.

After an afternoon's gardening they often stay to dinner. They sat before the fire one cool night in the middle of spring, Josh leaning forward, elbows on knees, and glancing at me earnestly, as if thinking to recruit me to his cause. He has a golden quality that draws people in. I guessed he'd always been protected; he took slights so hard. Tell him he'd pulled a lettuce by mistake and he looked ready to hit someone or something. I mention these things so you can understand the kind of attention that he must have got at school, and how that might turn a person.

I know I made allowances for him on account of it. I wasn't surprised at the way Cat looked at Josh, but I did wonder how long it might last.

It was raining outside and they began talking, and it might have been that to them the house, dry and warm and shadowy in the lamplight, was a safe-seeming cocoon. I listened to their tangled talk and for once they didn't mind if I asked them questions. He, Josh, had become involved in the railroad through Cat, and an art teacher at school and a friend of hers, he said. It was an accident of life that had set him on this course; he only had free time because a knee injury had sidelined him from the football team.

I asked why he'd run. 'My parents didn't like the company I was keeping,' he said mockingly – mocking his family and the company both, I thought.

'Meaning me,' Cat said. 'My parents thought the same about him, of course.'

'You don't have to protect me,' Luis said. 'We know who they meant.'

'Yeah. It wasn't you,' Josh said, serious for once. 'They don't even know you. They just didn't want me getting political. It's like they don't see me. I'm just another one of them. But what if I don't want that? I've always done what they said and I never thought about why.'

'You want to know who *you* are?' I asked.

'I don't know. I guess.' Josh scratched the scarce stubble on his chin, thinking it over. 'Something like that.'

Luis didn't say as much as the others, but Cat turned to me sharply once, as if there was something I had to know now. She said, 'They probably got Luis's father last year. Assholes. His family hasn't heard from him.'

Alejandra abruptly began attending to Luna, straightening her wrappings and murmuring all the while.

'Where would Luis and Alejandra go? Nowhere *to* go,' Josh said. 'We had to do something.'

'Josh,' Cat said.

'What?'

She glanced at Alejandra.

Luis asked his sister to fetch some wood and she left the room.

'You weren't born here?' I asked.

'Only Alejandra and the baby,' Luis said. She'd be on her own or in foster care if he was deported, which meant the danger of that system on her own or entering a different world of danger with him. Sometimes children disappeared, or were sold or lost, or used and then tossed away. There weren't enough people to keep them safe or to keep track of their whereabouts. I wanted to say then, immediately, that I would care for her. I would. But they didn't have their papers and without them, trouble would always be following them. Luis knew that. He had worn a path with his thinking.

'It's not that we don't have family,' he said, 'but they are not here. Our father disappeared a while ago. Then they came to our house for my mother. She was out, so I rang to tell her don't come back. We moved to the church and we lived in the basement there. We kept going to school. Then it got more difficult. If my mother got in touch during the day because she'd been taken, we had to get our bags and go. One day they pulled my mother over at a red light because of the way she looks.' He repeated this quietly – 'The way she looks' – and touched the side of his face. 'I got Alejandra from school and we left. "Do not hesitate," our mother said. It's what we agreed.'

'Sins of the father,' I said.

'Excuse me?'

'Never mind. I'm not saying it's right, only that it happens, that innocent children suffer.'

'He did not sin,' Luis said quietly. 'Sometimes people have no choice.'

'I think they do.'

'People who don't know think that,' he said.

'It's the consequences of actions I'm talking of, how our children suffer because of us, how we wish it were not so. But why are you doing this?' I asked Cat, wondering what Claudie might have done to her.

'Because I'm alive and I'm not wasting it.'

The way Josh spoke about the turn their lives had taken made it seem like an adventure, driven by high spirits as much as a cause. His voice rose and his eyes shone. Luis watched until he was done, then said, quietly, 'We were worrying about our parents going to prison.' (I thought of the boy on death row.)

Cat leaned and pressed her forehead against Luis's upper arm. He sat very still.

'What about your things?' I asked Luis.

He shook his head. 'They took everything. My mother made us swear that we would find a way to go north so there is a chance we can be together again. This was her hope and our promise to her. We're grateful for this safe place, Kitty.' It was the first time he'd called me Kitty. It was an effort for him, a gift to me, and I was almost overcome.

Alejandra came back with a shell from the makings room she wanted to show everyone. She'd forgotten about the wood.

'I wouldn't give you away for anything,' I said. 'Anything at all.'

He nodded once as if it were a contract, the most courteous contract. I thought he would be a person who ran straight and true in all that he did. He was smaller than Josh, and less showy, but he was the kind of person people might remember years later and wonder about. I knew I would. It might have been his determination with his life and his gentleness with his sister. The word dangerous also came to mind, unsettling me. I had no reason to use it, but it stayed just the same. Once or twice on other occasions he spoke to me about their troubles. It was rare, though – a way he had of talking to himself.

I had felt like a prisoner in Blackwater even if I went to live there willingly. School didn't suit Tobe's quiet ways. It was the opposite with Claudie. We moved the year she started high school but it made no difference – she had already pulled away. Everything was unsettled. At night I imagined flying over Wolfe Island, looking down. It was how I lulled myself to sleep. A tree in Blackwater was felled that year to make way for a new slipway. It was a sycamore. Children had run beneath, leaping at its spinning seed pods, and creatures had lived in its shelter. After the tree was gone birds wheeled its ghost canopy for days, as if branches might yet reappear. Where did they belong now? The tree had run through them like a path or a memory. It *made* them. Without it, they might as well have been pictures in a book. Take stories from their source and they were vases of dried flowers. Who was I now, on the main?

After Claudie and Tobe left for school and Hart had gone to work I fled to Wolfe and pretended for a while, rocking on the porch swing in the sun, walking, collecting a few things, watching the soft heaving sea.

The dragonflies were about. Oh, I loved them – their flighty movements and uncanny stillness. They were fierce. A dragonfly's wings beat fifty times a second; they can fly at forty miles an hour; they can see in front and behind at the exact same time. I liked knowing those things. I loved their names too, which I considered poetic, and have noted some here so you can see what I mean. (Some are known by name only these days, which I consider a loss.)

Dragonflies
- *Ruby Meadowhawk*
- *Little Blue Dragonlet*
- *Comet Darner*
- *Swamp Darner*
- *Harlequin Darner*
- *Unicorn Clubtail*
- *Spine-crowned Clubtail*
- *Black-shouldered Spinyleg*
- *Blue Corporal*
- *Common Whitetail*
- *Eastern Pondhawk*
- *Tiger Spiketail*

Time was nothing on those Wolfe days until I saw where the sun hung in the sky, and I'd race to get back before I was discovered. Hart was someone different on the main, as I was. I believe I became pitiful in his eyes. It's possible he was trying to protect the children and me. He mentioned the hairdresser and bought me a lipstick. I should not hang clothes to dry outside in the good clean air. I left the laundry to him since he cared so much. The suffering patience of him.

I lost myself and couldn't find my way back. I stopped making things, let passing thoughts pass, misplaced my notebook and didn't care. I watched women in the street with their long curled hair and new clothes and high shoes walking together beneath the tall trees, slowly, talking without cease, as if time and place and people would never change. I knew they might, so to me they seemed like dreaming creatures. There was some innocence about them that nothing could shake. Stubborn, you know? There is no certainty, only the dream of it lived so perfectly that a person can believe it as long as it endures.

I practised another voice, as if I was a ventriloquist and its doll together. People didn't comment on my new accent, but I wouldn't speak like that to family. What if they preferred a woman with neat hair and a bright mouth and a mainland voice? She had nothing to do with my past or me. I stopped her dead. At first it was an effort to speak again in the island way. I took some pleasure in people's stares – at an exotic, a remnant, seeing their childhood memories flying at them: boats slicking and bright water, the fat claw of a rising crab gripping the thing that would lead to its death. It shook something loose in me and I began working on small makings, feeling my way. I didn't have room for anything else. The bigger things I kept for visits to Wolfe.

Family visits were never enough. The first time I stayed on the island alone was for three nights. It was the end of a hot, still day. Through narrowed eyes Hart and I watched the sun falling like a red-hot penny into a slot machine. A rich swampy muddy smell drifted from the salt meadow on a quiet breeze. Birds called out in their different ways. Time and sound and light were slow.

'Why don't you go on back without me,' I said to Hart. The words came out unthought, as if a secret person had delivered them for utterance. I didn't look at him. And what I'd said seemed so obvious that I went on. 'It'll be easier to clean the house without you tracking mess through.'

'What mess?'

'Everything. I'll make it nice for next time.'

'It's already nice.'

'I'll be back on Friday.' It was Tuesday that day.

'School starts Monday.'

'And I'll be back before then. Plenty of time.'

I suppose people judged me for leaving my children behind.

It is not entirely true, what I said earlier. Claudie wasn't always the way she became. One time she said, 'Mama, come back with us.' She must have been sixteen by then. Hart had brought them to the island when I didn't come back after a couple of nights – who knows why? To check on me, to persuade me, which there was no need for in my mind. I would be back; I was merely delayed by a making. 'I'll be there tomorrow,' I said.

'Home – you mean home,' Hart said.

'Sure,' I said.

Tobe wanted to stay. I should have backed him up. But I was in the middle of something and the timing wasn't good.

'A couple more days and I'll be finished. You'll be okay,' I said to Claudie.

I am sorry about that. I didn't go back; I stopped pretending.

While I'm talking of untruths, I should correct another. I said that I wasn't lonely on my own on Wolfe. The truth was I didn't think I could stand being there on my own at first, despite my years of dreaming. Tobe stared back at me when they got in the boat; I waved from the dock and called out, 'See you soon, have fun now,' stupid things to hide the truth. Tobe's eyes were hidden beneath his thick dark fringe, so like Hart. Hart did not look back, which I thought hard at the time. He saw before I did how things would unfold. They were close to grown by then. Claudie had nearly done with school. Tobe might have been thinking it wasn't fair that I was out there and he wasn't when he wanted to be too, for his own reasons. I couldn't see the difference I made to them. Claudie hardly said a word to me. My accent embarrassed her, I think. She didn't say that, but I felt it. I was working seriously again and didn't care what people thought. My mind wasn't really on them. I was probably thinking of how to join a spoon to a bicycle chain.

When light fell the first night I went down the street, my old dog Sweetie came gliding beside me in the curtains of dark. The light from our house was as blizzard-like as a slow photograph. Higher up, moonlight carved the air in clean bright chunks: there was the space between church steeple and a birch (a diagonal on one side, filigree on the other). The solar poles (blown away now) framed the emptiness of the streets. Sweetie leaped on a rat and it screamed. She squeezed her teeth into it and tossed it once or twice. It dragged itself away on its tiny hands, and she bit again, feeling its body with intelligence, feeling for the fluttering of its living heart. She picked it up and padded along with me. A listening quiet settled over Wolfe. Anything could be in the shadows. My voice speaking softly to Sweetie seemed foreign, almost indecent, the sound of a vagabond interloper.

We walked the long way home by the docks and the gutter bridge, Sweetie, her rat, and me. It was the first chill of autumn and my breath plumed white. I might have been breathing fire, I might have been a dragon, I might blast everything in my way. At home the wind hummed in the lines of the boat, and the metal cleats chimed in the night, a high and mournful sound. The wind struck the roof and I waited for it to fly away. Aeroplanes floated across the flat luminous grey. Later, red or white lights blinked low on the water, moving past – boats, dragging their sounds behind. There was some quiet triumph in my feeling. Nothing could stop me and nothing would get in my way.

Chapter 8

I WALKED FROM the Blackwater dock to Main Street and everything was strange. The ground was hard, when it yielded responsively at every step on the island. The two places might have been different planets, their orbits connected by nothing more than my boat, as if a slingshot had flung me across time and space, not only sea. The houses here were painted as pretty as playhouses and left me stranded between many feelings: at this moment the mystery of civic pride persisting when the world seemed to be falling apart. The truth is mostly irreconcilable with everyday life.

'Kitty, honey,' Doree cried from the other side of the road, as if I was the very thing she'd been waiting for. When I'd crossed she gave me one of her hugs, which are thorough but make me feel my boniness.

I was in town for food and gardening supplies and to drop off a bottle collection for Doree's shop. Girl had dissolved into shadow in her effortless floating gait – some business of her own to attend to, perhaps with the rare, shadowy coydogs and coywolves that had been sighted in the forested areas around Blackwater.

Inside the shop a radio was playing a lonesome country

song. We moved down the aisles to the counter past starfish, boat wheels, decoys, candleholders and soaps, weathervanes that would never feel a breath of wind. The song stopped and a voice – high and chipper – broke in, as if offering a rare treat. 'Remember the three Ps everyone! Federal agents *are* authorised to search premises, persons *and* possessions at any time, *and* to examine and destroy *any* unaccompanied baggage or to take *any* suspicious persons into custody *for* further questioning.'

'That's a new one,' I said.

'I had some agents through last week. I've seen people stopped.'

'I had no idea.' (That wasn't true. There had been that woman getting in the police car.)

'People just pretend. It's like: "A bomb's gone off. What shall we have for dinner?"' She rolled her eyes. 'Anyway,' she said, 'you got something for me?'

'I do.'

She checked things over and took all but one, and looked up her books and paid for the last batch.

'Now, you're staying for lunch, I hope. I won't take a no.' There was good reason to stick to routine so I let her persuade me the same as usual.

It used to be that she'd tell me how well her boy Wilt was doing. For a while he was studying hummingbirds to see what could be done to save them. A year or two later she told me he'd given the hummingbirds away. They couldn't make a camera small enough for them to carry about without them dying she said, try as they might. I didn't know what to say. If you ask me, dominion, which Pastor Kevin had preached so often, is an evil thing. I was glad my children had never done such work. I didn't say anything to Doree on that subject, though. Tobe was back from war by then, holed up in his shanty over the water, and a delicate quiet had settled between us on the subject of sons. Wilt was a big strong boy. I don't know how he escaped the war and I never asked. Mothers will do a lot to protect their children. I didn't know how to with Tobe.

I used to row to Tobe's shanty, a pot of stew or a pie at my feet. He'd look at me sidelong, as if he'd been comfortably drifting away and my visits dragged him back to shore and he resented it. But he had beautiful manners. People used to remark on them. 'Thank you,' he said each time. 'That smells so good.'

He covered his eyes with the palm of his hand. Finally, his hand slid down and he stroked the tiny blue teardrop tattooed below his right eye. He'd got it to match one a friend of his had done when he was doing time – 'So he's not alone when he gets out, you know?' he said when I saw it. What would I say? 'You're asking for trouble, sweetheart,' was what first came to mind. I wish I hadn't said it. We watched the swifts lifting and darting over the water. Tobe belonged in this world because he rose from it. It had made him.

After one long silence he said, 'I have to find work, I know that.'

I waited before I spoke in case it was one of the pauses that marked his speech. Finally I said, 'If you want to. Take your time. You've been through something.'

'I've done that. It's not coming back. None of it is. I was writing a book about . . . everything. I'll show you.' He went inside, and came back with an old notebook, a school one, carefully kept. He must have scavenged it before the school fell. (I can't remember how many years ago that was.) 'Here.' He held the spine nestled in one hand, and riffled the pages with his other. 'It's nothing.'

'I'm sure it's not.' I couldn't take my eyes from that book. He held it so loose over the water. I could see him spinning it free, the water dragging it down, and the pages staring up like a person's face falling away.

But he didn't. 'I'm done with all that, all of it. It's not worth a thing.' He took the notebook inside and placed it carefully on the shelf. I found it there later. I plan to read it one day when I'm ready.

'You could live with your father in town. He'd love to have you.'

'It's hard living there,' he said.

'I remember,' I said.

Sometimes he talked about the old watermen, and the times he went out on their boats, with Owen Jims especially. Owen had lasted longer than most. I came upon him once standing on the road at Stillwater outside his fancy-lettered oyster shed and mountain of crab cages, tugging at the stump of a finger. His wife had gone shopping and he didn't know what to do. He was ghostly, his clothes as faded and worn as his skin.

'The tanks in there were full of crabs, if you can believe it, we were into the main every week, hard times too though,' he said without a greeting. His words flowed like water, the way they might have in his mind.

'They could be.'

'It was a beautiful life.'

I agreed.

'She'll be back soon, tell me what to do.'

'I'm sure she will.'

There were plenty like him towards the end, chewing things over at the Fisherman's Confederation Hut. 'Chub biting in Coffin Bay,' one old man would say. 'Yup, yup,' a weathered feller would reply, feeling the white bristles of his cheeks with his hands grown soft and his nails grown long and filthy at the quick, recounting the names of the old oyster reefs: Eight Mile, Jimmy's Best, Sutters Line and so on, as if they were incantations.

'I know what I'll have to do and I know I'll hate it,' Tobe said.

'What's that?'

'Work in the prison.'

'Tobe.' It was true there wasn't much around. 'You could go back to college.'

He shook his head. 'I don't know.'

'That tear might have to go.'

He put a finger to it, quickly, as if it needed protection.

The thought of him in a prison was cruel. Tobe used to putter the island in his boat. He had the whole island mapped in his head. You could ask him anything and he'd know – about muskrats, birds, currents, everything. Only island people could see the beauty and skill in that, and the sadness, since the island was going. It's not easy for a person to live with. It's a particular kind of burden. People turned from it. He reminded them. I was no help to him. Now, I think education, conservation, water management, ecosystems, biodiversity. I was stupid.

He went to work at the prison and came back when his shifts allowed. The tattoo went but he seemed to feel it still brimming on his cheek. He touched the place often.

*

Now, sitting over our lunch, Doree said, 'Something on your mind?'

'New seeds. They don't keep like they used to somehow. This weather.'

'Something else if I know you, but you go ahead and keep it quiet. You always did.'

I thought she had something on her own mind, but didn't ask what it might be. Her eyes flickered out of the window to her boathouse. She was on edge.

I went shopping before lunch, checking my gun as advised by the sign at the supermarket entrance: *STOP! Please ensure your safety catch is activated on entry. Have a nice day.*

Folks said the same as always: how glad I must be of a change of scene, civilisation, fries, what was I doing in town, and so on. A woman tried to pet Girl. Had our daughters gone to school together? 'Here, girl,' she said, and when Girl shied away she asked, 'What's her name?'

'Girl,' I said.

I went back to Doree's. 'The questions they ask.'

'They don't mean any harm,' Doree said.

'I was just trying to do some shopping.'

'Oh, Kitty, you make me laugh sometimes.' And she did laugh a little.

'Honestly.'

Afterwards I took our plates to the sink and looked down the long garden, where I saw a curtain moving and a light swaying. 'Someone in the boathouse?'

'A friend of a friend passing through,' Doree said. 'And that's a big shop you've done. Not asking why, mind.'

'Oh, didn't I tell you? Claudie's coming for a holiday.'

'Is she? You've heard from Claudie?'

'I had an email last week. It'll be nice to catch up.'

It was not clear to me where we were up to in this conversation, what we were saying to each other and what we each believed of what the other said. Why didn't I ask Doree outright about her boathouse? Why didn't she say, 'Kitty, I believe you're lying'? We would have once. Secrets had entered the world we lived in – I'd learned that from Cat – and now they were in our lives and between us, old friends that we were. People didn't know who to trust. We pulled back from this delicate point and had lunch and a glass of wine or two, but even then we kept our secrets.

Sometimes, way back, I'd call Sweetie in the afternoon and we'd take the boat to town. Not wanting to upset Claudie or Tobe, old though they were, we'd wait at the docks and when darkness fell and house lights began to go out, like fireflies dying at summer's end, and doors stopped banging and people stopped calling to their pets, we walked beneath the tall trees to Hart's house. The key was there beneath a limestone paver under the hydrangea where the air was cool and damp. There was a rustling – some other life running alongside mine. I crept inside, upstairs, listened to Hart's slow breathing, saw his arm reaching, and peeled the cover back and pressed myself along his side.

'Kitty, girl.' He pulled me close.

I stayed a little later after they'd grown and left home. In the morning I dressed and braided my hair and Hart watched. One day he said, 'You can't live in a dream your whole life.'

'That's where you're wrong. The whole world does, or tries to. Why shouldn't I?'

At the door I turned to look at him lying there with his hands over his eyes.

'Stay,' he said.

I went back and kissed him. I didn't know what else to do.

'It gets lonely, Kit,' he said.

That was the night that Tobe met trouble. I will never stop wondering if things might have been different if I'd lived in town all those years. I thought things would stay the same. I didn't think of Hart changing. The last time I visited, a few years ago now, the key was gone. I turned every stone to make sure, and in the end threw one or two, high and hard. Dogs began barking and two faces – one of them Hart's, the other a woman with fair hair – came to an upstairs window, what was left of it. She stared as if I was a creature from myth. Hart disappeared. I gave a high whistle to tell Sweetie 'come quick', and loped off down the road.

'Kit,' Hart called, following after.

'Nothing to say. You go on back.'

He caught me up and took a hold of my arm. 'You expect me to be here.'

I pulled free.

'I'm supposed to hang around wondering whether tonight, if I'm lucky, the wind might be blowing in the right direction.'

'I never asked.' I kept on. Sweetie came out of the darkness, like shadow turning solid, suddenly at my side, touching my hand with her nose.

'What do you think that's like?'

'Wind's changed. It won't happen again.'

We reached the boat, both out of breath. The darkness was filled with the thrum of a thousand air conditioners.

'You can't go at night.'

I got in the boat. 'I know my way. I won't trouble you again.'

That was the last time I saw him or spoke to him. I thought of him, though.

All the way back after my shopping trip I was thinking about husbands and fathers and sons, secrets too. I felt the pull of Hart still. I missed the soft talk, the quiet moving around each other in the house, or sitting before the fire, getting the dishes done, drawing the curtains so we were warm and safe within.

We docked. Girl leaped out and prowled the shore of Wolfe, uttering staccato yips I couldn't interpret. She lifted her muzzle and howled, a sound that made me shiver.

Luis came out to see. 'Something up with her?' He watched her for a moment.

'She just does that, I don't know why.'

He had a strange look on his face, almost excited, even hopeful. I'd never seen him look that way. 'What's happened?' I asked.

'My father got in touch.'

Chapter 9

Cat came down to help before Luis could tell me more. He began taking the bags inside.

'Thank you,' Cat said with distant courtesy, standing by the boat. 'That was nice of you. No need though.'

I felt more myself than I had for a while, perhaps from being away from them, and succumbed to a spurt of anger. 'Listen to me, Catalina, sweetheart. I'll take this from Claudie; she's got her reasons, or thinks she has. You don't. This, the way you're talking right now, is nothing to do with me. So quit it. Two parents and a world of security, and look at yourself next to Luis. Do better.'

That made her step back.

'And another thing.' I let my eyes sweep across her belly. 'I thought you might be the one to break the run.'

'What run's that?'

'Having a baby so young. You'll be seventeen, same as me; Claudie was an old lady: nineteen. When were you thinking of telling everyone? It's not going to disappear if you keep pretending.' And I went on by pulling my trolley, Girl at my side.

*

I heard more from Luis about his father later that day. Things were still difficult, he said. He was in hiding, but closer to home, and wanted to see his children.

'Wonderful,' I said. It seemed the right thing even though his face was twisted with worry. 'How long's it been?'

'Early last year.'

'But . . . something's troubling you?'

'He mentioned going home – not home here. Home with him, south.' He stopped. 'I don't understand why he'd say that. It's not safe. That's why we left. It's always been north, never south.'

'What about your mother?'

'That's what I asked. I'll write again. I'll find out.'

We had a celebration at my place that night anyway. I got out the *Camp Meeting Cookbook* and cooked up a storm: crab boulettes, angel chicken and a peach cream pie. We had a fire in the yard for the fun of it, and when the flames had died to coals we roasted marshmallows. I told them about a long-ago midsummer night when it had been pale on the horizon and the fire on the beach had burned frail, and we'd done the same. Doree and Bette and I had got up, a restlessness upon us, and gone running down the beach in the moonlight, and our strides felt ten feet long, and we felt ten feet tall, and our shadows were twice that, and we were immortal. (The very next day Bette left the island, she left us all.) Alejandra wanted to try it, the moon being full and bright.

'The beach is gone, sweetie,' I said, but seeing her disappointment we ran along the road with her to make shadows, rushing into their darkness ahead.

Afterwards we had hot chocolate at my place, and while looking up recipes Cat found an old flyer in the back of the cookbook. 'You'll love this one, Kitty. *If the threat of nuclear obliteration is playing on your mind, why not allay your fears by making sure you're prepared? First find a large stable building.'* (It was like she was reaching out to me and saying sorry both.)

You can imagine how we laughed about that. 'Might have been from that Korean scare,' I said. 'North Korea was going to bomb Guam, but people wouldn't even leave the beach. They'd had scares before that came to nothing.' In my observation people mostly incline towards the thought that things will work out until something happens to them. It's how we sleep at night. I include myself. The water wasn't at my doorstep yet. I'd see what difference that made.

'Allow one gallon of water per person and a three-day supply of non-perishable food,' Cat continued. 'Wouldn't want to be carrying that.'

'Especially on foot.' I stuck the pamphlet on the notice-board and read it occasionally.

Cat found me in my makings room the next day. 'Are you going to tell my mother?'

'Claudie doesn't know?'

'Of course not. I know what she'd say.' She put on a velvety sort of voice. '"That's not the person we raised you to be. You're better than that." All that shit. Imagine the family meeting. No kid of mine's ever going to a family meeting. You didn't have them, did you?'

'One or two. There was a fashion for them.'

'They're so . . . embarrassing. "How do you feel about it?" "How about *you*?" "Don't you think you should be doing your chores, young lady?" "Don't you think you should quit nagging?"'

I couldn't help laughing. She was a good mimic. 'There's the health insurance. You might want that. Claudie doesn't mean anything wrong.'

'Don't tell me what my mother means.'

'She's respectable, I mean. She's like her father.'

'I know that.' Cat sat so still then and her face was also still. 'I was thinking about a termination, but a friend of mine nearly died.' She covered her eyes, then took her hands away. 'I just want them behind me.'

'Any plans for the birth?' I asked.

She took a shuddering breath, and shrugged helplessly. She had no idea about having a baby – I mean in the logistical sense. It was strange to see when she was so certain about everything else.

'What about Josh?'

'I've got some time.' She started the computer; it was as if she'd closed a door.

Girl opened an eye. I stroked her side with my foot and went into the garden, where Luis was trenching the edges of a vegetable bed.

'Great job,' I said.

He kept on, breathless from going so fast. He said, 'I do it for my mother, because I promised her. And I do it for Alejandra because she has no one else.' He stopped and straightened and a look of disgust crossed his face, like some dark thing was nearby. He jabbed his spade hard into the ground and it made that sound I hate, the crunch and hiss of a grave being dug. 'Yeah, that's a lie. I do it for myself too.' He glanced at Cat through the doorway, just a flicker. So that's the way the wind was blowing. What a mess.

Two days later, Luis wrote to his father, asking about the

change in plan, but his father didn't mention the south again. He wanted to know about Luis's life, where he was staying, how his darling daughter was.

'Did you tell him?' Cat asked when she heard this.

'I didn't tell him where; I just said near the sea.'

'Good,' she said.

I don't know when the others found out about Cat and her baby. Luis might have known that afternoon we were talking. It might have been part of his anger that day. He was on edge waiting to hear again from his father. There was something going on with Josh, too.

In the days that followed my trip to the main, pretending seemed to fall away. For instance, I had believed they lived in harmony in the other house. They might have wanted me to. Now they started talking things over with me – little things – and they got careless with what seemed like truly private talk. I began to overhear the hissing ends of conversations or their broken middles.

Once, Josh said to Cat, 'They've got nothing. They can't pin it on us.'

'They can't pin it on me because I wasn't there. But you – if someone saw you . . . It was a stupid thing to do.'

'I didn't mean that. I meant—'

'The other? Be quiet about that,' Cat said.

Another time he said, half pleading his cause, 'You've got to make a statement. Smoke and fire, some noise. Something that'll make the news.'

Cat cut him off. 'If you hurt people, you lose people.' That was the end of the conversation.

Most of all, I saw how her attention was sliding away from him to what was happening inside. She grew impatient with him. She'd ask him to do something, and add slyly, 'If it's not too much trouble for a jock like you,' and smile to show she meant it for a joke. That's the sort of thing I mean. He flared up. I heard him shouting once.

I took them a batch of cookies. Josh came to the door and took the container from me and ate one: 'Dee-licious,' he pronounced, and grinned, presuming he was charming me.

'They're for everyone,' I said.

Luis came outside with a basket of washing. Josh pulled him in close by the shoulder. 'We're doing all right aren't we, man, looking after you and the kid?' and knuckled the back of Luis's head and laughed. He glanced at me then at Luis again. 'Got your backs. Got to look after people.'

Luis smiled. 'Sure.' He rubbed his head and left.

Josh was like a sail fallen slack. I didn't think a lot about the way he might have been feeling. He liked my granddaughter and that was something. It was not my place to share my thoughts on Josh with Cat. Better for her to find out for herself. I had spoken my mind with Claudie and it did not end well.

It was exhausting being around people and noticing them, thinking about them. I felt roughened and coarse now, as if I was rubbing against the grain of Wolfe Island. It used to be that I could forget myself and *be*, spend hours in the marshes watching the tides and the grasses, birds walking over my feet I'd been still so long, listening to the unintelligible wind. I was part of it then, and insignificant. I missed that. The writing helped a little, but only a little.

*

Later that week, from the living room, I spied Luis and Alejandra on the porch, silently rocking, pressed close together. They must have had news. A haze was hanging along the shore, as if a fire was smouldering somewhere down that way. The water was dark grey and the sky a lighter grey, and the vaporous light looked like a shroud around the island.

I didn't know what to say so I left them alone, thinking they might like some privacy. A little later they still hadn't moved, except on the trapped arc of their swing. They weren't talking. Girl and I went out. Luis lifted his eyes. Girl sat before them, shuffling close to get their attention. She rested her head on Alejandra's knee.

'What is it?' I said, and when they didn't answer I drew up a seat before them – 'What's happened?' – and touched each of them softly on the knee. It woke them from the dark place they were lost in. And now I knew how much I cared for them. Once that's happened, it's too late. I was part of it before they said a word.

Alejandra's eyes shifted towards me, and she put a hand on Girl's neck. 'Girl,' she said. There was a catch in her voice. It frightened me.

'What? Luis, what?'

'Maybe we should go south with our father. We can start again.' He pulled Alejandra closer. 'He will be there.'

'But Mama . . .' Alejandra said.

'She did nothing wrong – *nothing* except try to keep us together.'

I touched his shoulder.

'I heard from the lawyers. Mama said there would be word – she did not know how. "A letter at the post office, a sign in the wind, a feeling in your heart if it is so that I am safe," she said. Her words. I know what she meant now. I felt things were going bad for her. I hoped I was wrong. But we have word, and I know it is true. Mama and the baby are in jail.'

They had truly lost everything. I knew I couldn't do anything, but I asked anyway.

He said, 'The legal team are trying to get them released. They don't know if this will be possible. I hope it will. I don't know who my father's in touch with. I'll tell him.'

I knew so little about Luis. I didn't know his family name, or the names of anyone in his life: lawyer, teacher, friend. He could seem aloof, though I believe that was from preoccupation not pride. He was never above any task. He was doing what he could to gather his broken family together. The island was just a way station in his life. What other choice did he have? He had a kid sister filled with fears that only her doll knew. I would do anything I could for them.

I kept working all week, though the news of Luis and Alejandra's mother hung over us all. 'Are we mudlarking today, Kitty?' Alejandra said each time she arrived. It settled her if she knew what was coming next. She would make plans about where to explore, and whether by boat or on foot, and tell me. When we got back she washed her finds and cleaned them with a toothbrush in a bowl of soapy water. She never tired of it.

'Cat and Josh are shouting again, Kitty,' Alejandra announced as she and Luis arrived one afternoon. Luis shook his head at her. 'They are, Luis! You heard them.'

'You don't say it.' He went to the computer.

'Why not?'

But Luis had disappeared from this world.

He found me outside later where I was hammering some cans flat for a new making. I stopped when I saw the elation he was squashing down. I knew before he said: his father had sent another message. He wanted to arrange a place to meet up. Luis's manner made me wonder if his father had always been some sort of treat, not to be expected or counted on, as if he was an idea as much as an actual person. It made me sad for Tobe. Hart had been anxious for him, which made him incline towards criticism: work harder, get involved, have some ambition. It had made Tobe wary. Why would he be otherwise when he could never please?

Luis would have arranged something for that afternoon if Cat and Josh hadn't talked him down. He might have been looking for hope; how much he must want to lay down his burdens. After some time he could see the sense in Cat's suggestion, which was to arrange a meeting place. 'Not here or in town – somewhere an hour away at least,' she said.

'An hour away,' he repeated.

'Harder for someone to trace us. I'm sure they won't. I'm sure we'll be fine.'

Josh offered to drive, but Cat and Luis had things worked out by then. He didn't like not being the first pick, but held his temper. 'You should wait and watch to see who arrives. Hang back. You don't have to be the first ones there,' he said, and I think we were all surprised by this sound advice.

They left early next morning, so Alejandra arrived at my place early. She thought Luis had gone to see a lawyer about their mother; I didn't disagree. We walked up to Stillwater, which I hadn't properly visited since the day they came, a time that seemed distant and wilder. I pointed out Nate Strudwick's house and told her about his oyster farm.

'He had a whole boat filled with them. He pulled them up when I came visiting, the whole boat, it came out of the water like a shark.'

'What did you do then?'

'We ate a couple, straight from the water. Alive.'

'No! Kitty!'

We looked across the broken docks. 'It'll be out there. And all the oysters, I hope.'

'I'm not eating one.'

'Me neither. Dock's not safe.'

He'd been one of the last to leave. He was trying to get some books written first, a trilogy as I recall: *Dystopia*, *Revolution*, *Utopia*, something like that. It was going to make millions, he said. He dressed like someone out of *Apocalypse Now*, and had nothing but his oysters, the 'minners' he raised for fish bait and a typewriter for company. It was quite a few years ago. Perhaps he'd published them by now.

We crossed the marsh just before the tide spilled across the road.

After lunch Josh came and shored up the corner on one of the stone edging walls. He liked being around people, even people such as us at a pinch. I was making something new, a cartwheel attached to a stand, which resembled a twirling umbrella or a maypole. Things hanging from it flew around: people of sticks with feathered wings, dogs of driftwood, birds of wire, three infant pomegranates that had shrivelled dry.

'I like this one,' Alejandra said. 'Only it's not very nice hanging them by their heads, Kitty.'

'It's not, is it? That's the way it is, though. The problem is what to call it. *Time* or *Midsummer* or *The Circle*? I'm not sure.'

'No, no, no.' She shook her head. Later, she looked up from her work and said, '*Carnival Ride.*'

'Oh, perfect, macabre. Clever girl.'

She was pleased. She climbed on a stool to spin the wheel and all the small creatures threw out their limbs, obedient to the force. 'Are you going to move the strings?'

'I don't think so.'

Skulls and skeletons, the brokenness of life, people and creatures strung up: what was I thinking? Sometimes it was as if the world had been postponed. I didn't think of the future. Even then, as much as I cared for her, I didn't think of her first.

Luis and Cat looked like they'd been in an accident when they returned; they could have been sitting on a roadside, dazed and waiting for help. Alejandra had thrown herself at Luis. It was late afternoon, almost evening by then, so they must have driven some way.

They didn't mention the town they'd been to, and I don't know if they'd stopped at Shipleys first when they got back, or come straight up to collect Alejandra. Cat probably wouldn't have come for that alone. She might have come to talk. I brought them a drink and they sat on the porch, mute. Surmising the news was not good, I gave them some time and came out after a bit to ask how many might be staying for dinner. Cat's face was still in the late sun. Luis's leg bridged the gap between his seat and hers and he rocked her gently, watching her. The sight seemed to soothe him. Alejandra left Luis's lap and clambered up with Cat. Cat opened her eyes and put an arm around her when she snuggled in close.

They swung some more until Alejandra fell asleep. Girl sat at their feet looking out, her eyes narrowed against the glare. It's hard for some people to let themselves be peaceful. Cat was a person like that, and it was strange to see her like this, especially after such a day. Luis glanced at me and knew I'd seen how he felt, and seemed to be pleading with me to say nothing, acknowledge nothing, pretend I'd seen nothing even to him, because there was nothing that could be said or done that would make things right. But this, the way he felt, was some solace for him.

Josh came to the gate. 'Hey, you could have stopped by,' he called. I put a finger to my lips to shush him. 'So?' Josh said when he'd climbed the stairs.

It wasn't a long story they had to tell.

They'd arranged to meet Luis's father in a park pavilion in a town about ninety miles north. It was close to the road, Cat said. She'd passed it before on other journeys. They were there early and parked at a nearby corner, where they had a good view of the pavilion, planning to emerge only when Luis's father arrived. It was quiet. There was a young couple sitting on a bench. A person wearing a cap and dark glasses walked by and stood further up near a traffic light – waiting for someone, they thought.

Then a young man who might have come from a long way south, judging by his appearance, entered the park. When he passed the couple on the bench they stood and dragged him from the path. The man punched him hard – he knew what he was doing – and he folded to the ground. They pulled a wad of papers from his pocket. The woman looked up the path and called out (they heard the sound, but not the words) and the man who had been waiting by the lights ran down to join them, removed his glasses and stood over the man they'd hit. He might have said something. He might have kicked the man, or he might have stopped himself before he made contact.

'I don't get it,' said Josh when they were done. 'That's it? It wasn't Luis's dad?'

'The one they attacked? No, he was just a young guy. He got up and left,' Luis said. 'His papers were good, I guess.'

'And you came home?'

'Yeah, we did,' Luis said.

'Why not wait longer?'

Luis looked at Cat. He said, 'My dad was never going to be there. But Cat and I knew him, the guy with the glasses. I saw him at the church after school a couple of times. I didn't know his name, though.'

'Who was he?' Josh asked.

'Your dad. It was your dad, Josh,' Cat said.

Luis looked at him with sadness – that's the closest I can come to describing it – as if he'd let him down, or maybe as if he understood what it might feel like to have a father let you down. Josh looked like he'd been hit. 'My father? What? No fucking way would he— How do you know? Why would you even say that?'

Cat said, 'I know your dad, Josh. I know him. And he's in Homeland Security. It was weird.'

Josh said quietly, 'I know he can be an asshole, but this isn't even his level. He's not a street guy.'

'I told you it was weird,' Cat said.

'It was a trap,' Luis said. 'I don't know why he'd want me, unless it was to get to my dad.'

'You think you've been emailing with my father all this time?'

'I guess it was him.'

'Did he say anything about me?'

'Why would he if he was pretending to be *my* dad?'

'How'd he get your address?'

'I don't know.'

'My father.' Josh got up and leapt down the stairs and headed towards the marshes.

I watched his dwindling figure, and said, 'I don't understand. Could they have caught your father, Luis?'

'I don't know why they would want me and Alejandra if they had,' Luis said. 'I don't think he's around. I don't think he ever was. He never used Alejandra's name. Maybe he didn't know it. I should have realised when he mentioned going south. The plan was always to go north. I was stupid. We got lucky today.'

'What did you do?' I asked Cat.

'Reversed up the side street.'

'Slowly,' Luis added.

Josh came back and was quiet through dinner. He was shrunken. We couldn't talk about it since Alejandra was there. It was the way Luis wanted it, but Alejandra knew something was going on. Her eyes moved between people's faces, assessing, trying to fit things together. Later, when she'd gone to get something from her desk, I asked about the church, whether they might have passed on Luis's contact details by mistake to someone claiming to be his dad.

'Why would you think the church would be the good guys?' Josh said.

Cat and Luis turned sharply at that, all apprehension.

Seeing my interest, Luis said, 'A church guy gave us some trouble once.'

'The fight,' I said, thinking of the bruises and cuts Luis had when they first arrived.

'You remembered that? Yeah. He doesn't work for them now.'

While they waited to hear from the lawyers, Luis thought they were as safe on Wolfe as anywhere – safer, since they wouldn't be stopped or searched. How would anyone find them on Wolfe, much less capture them? It was hard for Josh, realising what his father might do, and that we knew too.

I went to visit the prisoner later that week, as we'd arranged a few weeks before. I don't recall ever before being relieved to leave Wolfe behind, but I was then. I passed graveyards for cars and boats and people, boats marooned in stubbled fields, the rusted hulks of vehicles nosing around forest edges. Factories lined the highways outside of towns. I passed a lot the size of an airfield filled with shipping containers, with a sign out front: *For All Your Home and Storage Needs!* No surprise – I'd seen it all before and wondered. People lived there on tidy streets of containers that were dark grey or rusted to the colour of dried blood, or in the nicer streets prettied up with a hope-filled lick of paint. One had a garland of flowers painted each side of its metal door. Each had a narrow path leading to the door, small windows punched in, and an outdoor chair or two or a rocker, and even a pot that might have flowers in summer – geraniums or sunflowers, perhaps. Chimneys poked from the roof of a couple, and smoke oozed out, falling and drifting along the ground, the air was so heavy. In the middle of the metal village was a dirty white farmhouse office, the only thing left of its country past.

The land can't ever have been much – not enough of it to show a profit, or maybe the soil went sour, or maybe those who owned it got sick and lost their money. There are so many ways to be trapped and not many ways to break free. Behind it all were dead woods and silvered pines, stark and stiff, their branches beginning to snap off in the winds. Salt ruin. But it was better than a prison.

I felt almost free driving down the highway on my own. Even my thoughts had become noisy on Wolfe. I rarely felt at peace.

The prisoner and I talked about my garden, and what I should plant in it – he liked green beans, he said, and carrots, and these little white flowers his pop had grown up on that high roof – and about Girl, who he wished I could bring inside with me for a visit. 'I always liked dogs,' he said. I told him about my family – I used that word – who had been staying with me for a few months. I might have been more animated than usual, seeming further away. He made himself listen; he was being brave, though his eyes fell to his manacled hands, his fingers moving together. I didn't realise that until the drive home. I wished I hadn't mentioned them.

There was a sweetness in him that reminded me of Tobe. I hated that. I wanted to smash him in those moments. But I noticed threads, not between them, but within each of them. It seemed like the rooftop garden was where the prisoner felt safe and the place he wanted to see again, and that was like Tobe and Wolfe Island, like Luis too, just then. Sometimes it seemed as if Tobe's own dark side had killed him, as it would the prisoner in the end. I asked the prisoner if he dreamed about it. A sick look came upon him then, a bad look, like his dreams could not be spoken.

'Not about, you know – I mean your pop's garden.'

He looked as if I'd released the noose about his neck. 'I think about it,' he said. 'I remember little things, you know? My pop had a cookie in his pocket once. He gave it to me up there. It was nice of him. I think he might have liked me.'

'Were those little white flowers Queen Anne's lace?' I asked.

'Kind of tall and fluffy, it looked like one flower but it was lots of tiny flowers, kind of flat,' he said.

'Sounds like it was. The prettiest weed in the world. Or it might have been hemlock. Looks about the same – hemlock's poisonous, though. It can kill you. I hope he told you to be careful in the wild.'

He dropped his eyes, embarrassed that he'd killed my son, embarrassed that the subject had come up – that in the end everything between us led to that – when we'd been getting along so well. He wished he'd thought of another flower. He might have wanted to spare me or he could have been thinking of his own mother's sorrows. I thought about that. 'I've never even been in the wild, ma'am,' he said. 'I wouldn't know how to get there.'

'There's a patch of wild country not far from here,' I said. 'Not too big, but it gives you a feeling for it.'

But he'd come in a prison transport without a window to see from. He hadn't seen the outside for years.

I left the prison then. Girl was waiting for me in the car, windows down. She could have jumped out if she wanted to. (I mention this in case anyone thinks I'm ignorant about dogs and cars and the dangers of overheating. I know it.) It helped to think about her waiting when I was speaking with this broken creature, who I actually hated as well as pitied.

*

112

'They're taking babies away,' Luis said, and it was like ice water thrown over us all. 'I heard this afternoon.' In this way, when I returned from the prison visit that afternoon, I was plunged back into the complications of their lives.

Cat said, 'What?'

Luis put a finger to his lips. Alejandra was on the other side of the garden and he didn't want her to hear. He spoke softly then. 'From their parents. To make them agree to things or to tell things, to scare people.'

'From people who are running?'

'And illegals. I don't know if it's everyone.'

She looked horrified, a subdued horror that had struck somewhere deep. 'I didn't think. Why didn't I think of that? I shouldn't be doing this. I won't be able to do this.'

'What?' I asked.

'If I got caught, what might happen with the baby . . .'

I said, 'Cat.'

'Love makes you weak,' she said, looking at neither of us.

'Don't say that,' Luis said. The thought seemed to pain him terribly. 'It makes things clear. You learn who you are. You know what matters.'

'I loved before this and I could do what I should,' Cat said.

'Were any of those people threatened?'

After a pause she shook her head slowly. 'Not before this.' She hugged her belly.

'That's when you learn,' he said.

'What use am I now?'

'This is not all you are. You can stay in touch, do the checking and arranging, and Josh can do the driving,' Luis said.

'That's a shitty thing to ask him.' Cat walked around a bit, rubbing her belly with her flattened fingers, pushing lightly against a small movement from within. 'I will ask him.'

They hung around until I asked if they cared to stay for dinner – Josh too, if he was hungry.

'He can find us if he wants to,' Cat said carelessly.

To see Cat's swelling belly in profile at the window – she was such a slender thing – was to know that we were drifting. I asked her for help in the kitchen so we could talk about the baby: where she'd have it and who would help. I was thinking of Doree, I told Cat, even if I wasn't sure how to explain the situation to her. I thought telling Doree as much of the truth as possible would be the best approach, leaving out Josh and Alejandra and Luis.

'Your friend Doree in town? I didn't know she was a nurse.'

'Why would you know? But yes – she still does a couple of shifts. I think she'd help out. You're sure you don't want to go home?'

She gave me a wild look at that, like I was about to take her baby and deliver it to hell.

'I'm asking you, not telling them,' I said.

But the truth was that the choices were Doree, returning to Claudie, or driving for miles to the nearest hospital when the time came and throwing herself on their mercy. Whether they would admit her I didn't know. Everyone knew stories of people who'd died because they couldn't pay.

It was a good evening. Alejandra told Luis about the old clothes in the attic, and when he said he didn't believe it she dragged him and Cat up to see. Their laughter and conversation rang through the floors, and for the next while the girls were up and down in crinolines and frilled nightgowns and corsets, straw hats and panamas, bell-bottom jeans and parasols, waistcoats, caftans and dainty muslin jackets.

'I told you, Luis. You look very nice,' Alejandra said, admiring his pinstripe suit.

I found some music – some kind of waltz – and we began to dance. It was unfortunate that Josh arrived at that moment and saw us all. Girl ran at him and barked, and he hung at the door until Cat said, 'Oh, come on, Josh, you just surprised her. Here, Girl,' and Girl let him be.

It was too late for him to pick up the thread of the evening. He stayed when I thought he wouldn't, backed into a corner of the sofa, arms crossed, unsmiling. His eyes tracked Cat as if he might otherwise lose sight of her – as if he suspected that was her intention. The attention he conferred on her had always seemed like a form of self-regard: how fortunate she was to have captured his eye; how special she must be to deserve it. And now her patience and maybe her feelings were wearing thin. What was wrong with her? his manner seemed to say. Cat became louder, gayer. It seemed half taunt to me, or as if she was caught and could not quite break free. Alejandra – tired, I supposed – subsided to a chair in a distant corner of the room. Finally, Cat took pity on Josh and led him away. Alejandra asked if she could stay the night, which Luis didn't mind, so I made up Claudie's old bed and Alejandra sat up in it like a lady in an old white nightgown, all pintucks and frills, a lovely thing. Girl jumped up, soft and heavy, and sat on her feet. Alejandra's eyes shone. When I went downstairs to bank the fire and put things to rights, Luis had fallen asleep on the sofa, a boy again. I found a warm quilt and laid it over him and left him there.

In the morning over coffee Luis told me that the authorities had taken Selma away from their mother. No one knew where she was. He didn't want Cat or Alejandra to know. He pressed his fingers against his eyes. His shoulders were convulsing and a terrible sound came from his throat.

Later, I watched as Josh, Cat alongside, brought the boat into harbour, slow and careful, three or four times, until he was ready to do it solo. He sped out on the water so it flew away on either side, suddenly free, and harnessing his high spirits he turned in a wide loop and came back slowly, finally berthing the boat. On the dock he sort of shook himself into place, letting the tension of it go, and flung his arms around Cat and spun her so her legs flew out behind. That was the last time I saw that sort of thing between them. He thought she was coming back to him. He couldn't see that she had cut him loose.

Chapter 10

Summer

SUMMERTIME. WHEN I wake early I can pretend things haven't changed. I wait for this moment: first light arriving on the plain of Wolfe Island like a can of paint-wash water of clearest watermelon pink flung in an enormous delicate rush. I go out to the garden, adjust the shades to suit the forecast, do some pollinating, throw some water around, wonder about the failures to thrive, and think possibilities and adjustments. I make coffee and watch the world and listen too, before people obliterate the sounds.

A day or two ago, Girl and I rambled the nearby shore, she sniffing and me poking around for what might have washed up – a sick bird or an old packing case or plastic from a long way off with lettering on it I couldn't understand. Then I went to my makings room and its long benches, touching things, holding them, not thinking anything in particular, moving things about, seeing how they might create together. I went out and picked a few flowers, took one from the bunch and laid it down alongside a spoon, and then inside the spoon, as if I'd been fishing for flowers with it, and look at this one that came up – chicory, almost blue and almost purple. What would I make a flower out of? I had a piece of hammered blue tin that might work. Oh, believe me it would be exciting stuff to watch. Slow air came through the window, and the sound of a bird.

The air turned ponderous and hot. I sprayed garlic about my yard to keep the mosquitoes down, and mowed the verges of the road between my house and Shipleys. The lawnmower fumes made a blue haze in the air. Pomegranates hung in the trees. Butterflies flickered. The marshes were as beautiful as I ever saw them, speckled with pink mallows and banks of snowy marsh hibiscus, their buds unfurling and shrivelling within a day, and the orange trumpet flower vines and honeysuckle scrambled and hung from every building, scenting the heavy air until every bit of it was sweet.

Despite that old beauty I began seeing things – signs or occurrences – that gave me pause. It was as if a deep breath had been drawn, as if it might be needed for a race or a deep dive, and we were waiting. I began a list.

Recent observations
- *Alejandra would have eaten handfuls of pokeberries one hot afternoon if I hadn't banged on the study window and shouted. The poor girl jumped and the berries tumbled about her. Everything about the livid colours and fleshy stems of pokeberry bushes screamed poison to me but Alejandra was as helpless as a baby where nature was concerned. What else might she do?*
- *The stump of Wolfe's Pine washed free in a storm, roots and all, and there was nothing to take its place. My mother said there must always be a pine on Pine Point, and a young pine coming through. But the young pine had died of salt already and the point has already begun falling apart.*

- *It's bad luck to kill a summer goose. Who doesn't know that? I couldn't believe it when I saw Josh stalking them in the north marshes with a hunting rifle one morning. Girl and I went out. I hollered and called to Girl just to kick up a noise and even sang snatches of a song. Girl barked in a cooperative spirit. The geese exploded into the air, almost vertical in their haste.*

- *Alejandra found a dead bird in the berry patch. She pressed a strawberry to its beak, but it did not wake, so she stroked its head. An adult passes a dead bird and they kick it aside; a child makes a coffin-nest filled with soft things and berries, a crust of bread, and puts soft old cloth (a silk scarf, say) as a lid on top to stop the dirt falling on its sightless eyes, so it continues its deep and pleasant sleep. They are kind to creatures in death, even if cruel to them sometimes in life.*

- *I began looking at the sky and the clouds, the shape of the waves and the direction of birds' flight, how they had all changed, and wondered what they meant. I knew how they felt; my direction had changed too.*

- *The prisoner told me of a belief he had from his family or had heard elsewhere: 'You need someone with you as you – you know – cross over.'*

  'Cross over,' I said stupidly, thinking he meant the bridge I'd travelled once already that day.

  'To the other side.' He waited for me to catch up.

  'Oh, right. I'm sorry.' I realised then what he was asking of me. 'You mean me.'

If I were as superstitious as my mother, I might have paid more attention to things that were happening, but it wasn't until I considered my list that I understood its meaning. Bad things were coming.

I taught Alejandra Chinese jump rope to keep her busy, hammering in four poles, notching them, and attaching elastic so she could play on her own. I thought of my sister Bette, the queen of games. There had been quiet when people watched her. Up she'd jumped, up, legs twisting, then down to her casual triumphant landings, the dust puffing at her feet. Our bodies in lilac evening intersected with those of dragonflies and hoverflies and midges, darting, lit up and graceful. Mothers paused in windows and looked out. One year a sporting scout came to see her and she left and things changed after that.

Bette came visiting once and watched our games with a half-mocking smile. How island we were. Her eyebrows were plucked into fingernail moons and her hair was yanked back so tight it hurt to look at. We ignored her. Late in the afternoon she stepped forward. Everyone stepped back; she was the queen, after all. She went the whole way through, and even threw in a couple of flips. When she had finished we didn't clap and she walked away and never once looked back. Everyone went home.

Next day we went out in my skiff, the champion gymnast and the island girl puttering around hooking bottles for pocket money.

'Boring here for you,' I said.

'Yeah, my life is really great.' She tugged a reed free and whipped the surface of the water until drops flew.

'Don't let us keep you.'

'I'll be gone tonight, don't worry, I won't take up your space.'

I rowed along.

'You're so stupid,' she said.

She gave gymnastics away not long after. 'Coach was a jerk,' she said.

We read about him later so we knew what she meant. That was hard for my parents, who'd encouraged her in that foolishness, as they now saw it. Somehow everyone felt ashamed.

She plumped up, working at Patty's diner until it closed. Visitors sometimes told her she reminded them of a gymnastics champion from a couple of years before. She met a guy on a tour one day who said he liked a handful. They've got a little house fifty miles south on the main. I haven't seen her for a long time. My sister.

I told Alejandra about Bette. Alejandra told me about her baby sister, Selma, who was too small for Chinese jump rope and too little to leave her mama. 'Do you think she's walking yet?'

'Maybe.'

'I miss my mama,' she said.

'I bet she misses you too.'

And then she chanted this rhyme, which I wrote on a piece of paper I make sure I always have in my pocket.

'*Silly Selma, silly Selma, one two three*
Called for Mama, called for Mama, from the trees.
Policemen came, picked them up, but they forgot about me
Luis, Cat, Kitty, Girl, set me free.'

She stopped jumping.

'I would come for you if you were in any trouble, and Girl. And Luis and Cat are with you already and are not going any place without you. And your mama would be here if she could.'

Alejandra's face got that old blank look I hadn't seen in a while. 'I've had enough now, Kitty. Bye, Girl.' She stooped to pat Girl, who lifted her head. 'Bye, Kitty. Thank you.' She gave her low wave, her hand at her waist, and turned and walked home.

That time I found Josh hunting I asked where the rifle was from, and he told me, 'Just some house,' he forgot which one. I didn't like the thought of it, but what could I do? He was bored, I think, since there hadn't been any runs for a while and he found the gardening so dull. Darts of meanness came out of him from nowhere.

Alejandra had her own job in the garden fertilising the tomatoes and the zucchini. Each morning she took a little paintbrush I'd found for her. 'Some for you,' she'd dab a flower, 'and some for you.'

She did a good job and I told her so. Josh said, 'Pretty easy when you're only a kid. Everyone else does the work, right?' He said it in a half-joking way, but she knew he meant something else and was wary.

'I'd be lost without her,' I said.

'I'm talking about work.'

'So am I. Have you seen her? She's one of the seven wonders of the world. Any tomatoes we eat will be down to her work.'

Alejandra gave a little proud shake of her head, like she was settling her feathers back into place.

'Come up later and I'll show you something about the geese, around sundown.' I smiled at Josh, trying to be pleasant for Cat's sake, not mentioning him hunting for them. It's always been better to get along out here. Don't threaten, don't involve the law: two island rules I don't recall ever being broken.

Alejandra and I cooked bean stew, corn, tomato salad with basil, baked potatoes with Alejandra's snipped chives and strawberry shortcake for dessert. There was a change in the weather and we opened the doors and windows and the salt breeze moved about.

Everyone except Josh came. Luis said Josh was busy fixing something. Cat made a disparaging noise. 'That's not it. A message came through today and I told him I wasn't going on any more runs.'

'And?' I asked.

'He's pissed,' she said. 'He said he'd do it if I wanted him to, and I said he should do it because it was the right thing.'

'Oh dear.' I removed his place setting.

We talked softly as we ate. Girl took a cob of corn into the yard and chewed the kernels off it.

The sun dropped and turned orange and sank through clouds that were low on the horizon, and in the air, faint at first in the distance, came the honking of a lone goose. It came closer and circled down, drifting like a scorched leaf against the burning sky before it dropped to the water at the shore's edge. The sound of its splash reached us a half-beat later.

'It's come home,' Alejandra said.

'Only one?' Cat said.

'Wait. Listen.'

The goose honked again in that hollow reverberant way.

'Is it lost?' Alejandra asked. 'Maybe it's lost its family.' She held my hand hard.

'You'll see,' I said.

The goose called out three, four more times before there was an answering sound, so high and faint at first that I believe we all thought it was in our imaginations. It seemed

123

a perilous venture. The sounds became clearer, pulsing backwards and forwards, call and answer. Then they were there, circling in low, blurred shadows, more absence than presence in the failing light, their calls turning to a gabble of relief and reassurance even before they met on the water.

We sighed a kind of release, knowing the tension with the loss of it.

'There's always one that calls them,' I said. 'Hard times coming.'

'How do you know?'

'They circled three times. It's just a superstition, but I've known it come true.'

'Are there more?' Cat asked.

'Superstitions?'

She nodded.

'Well . . . If you scatter rose petals about your house, your true love will find you there. A lone goose foretells a lone stranger. If you see one you must look for the other or trouble will come. A creature lurks beneath Bosum's dock. Never linger on a bottom step. Raspberry sun, good things to come. It's hard to remember them when there's no one else who knows. We'd remind each other as we went along.'

Josh decided to do the runs anyway, anger or not. He came looking for Cat after his first solo run two days later. He might have thought she would warm to him again if he did. She had become the centre around which we slowly circled. We all have a story we tell ourselves. He might have been thinking the loss of her attention was temporary – it was the baby, his baby, who had it for now, that was natural, but surely it would return. She was at my house to escape the mosquitoes and a sulphurous smell that had settled in the marshes approaching their house, and to sit under my fan.

'Hey,' she said vaguely, lifting her head from a book when he walked in, as if he'd just appeared from the garden. 'Any trouble?' And that was all.

He stared in disbelief. He was burned by sun and wind. He'd been gone since sun-up, and it was evening, long after dinner, by the time he got back. Even I felt sorry for him.

'All good. Hope you had a good day too,' he said. 'See you later.' And he went back down the road.

She called out but he didn't turn. She pressed her hand to her side, distracted. 'Not yet, baby.'

I should have paid attention to Josh. I didn't think. No one did. It seemed like it would always be summer, Cat would always be pregnant, Josh would always just be holding together, Luis's mother would surely be saved and Selma found if not tomorrow then the day after, and Alejandra would grow up fine and straight and undamaged and I would have helped that to be so.

The weather turned the following week. It was almost summer's end, not long until Cat's baby was due – another few weeks we thought. A thin waterspout writhed past the island. The algae began its torpid blooming further out, like a bloodstain, and a few choked fish washed up. One black night a spout churned the red sea into blue spangles – the prettiest thing. There were two waterspouts the next day, closer, and it seemed safer for Cat and everyone to move from the shore to my place, and to stay indoors. The heat was a clamped-down lid and but for shifting the shades over the vegetables and doing the watering we didn't venture out.

Alejandra found the old family Bible in the shelves. She turned its tissue pages carefully. 'No pictures?' I shook my head. She kept on politely, skipping somewhat, not wanting to concede defeat, and came to the last pages where she stopped in consternation. 'Someone wrote in it.'

'Everyone from this side of the family – my mother's, that is. My father came from somewhere else. It's about them, when they were born and died.'

'Are they all died?'

'No, no. Some have moved off, but I know where they are. Pretty sure I do.' I wasn't sure at all. What a speck of nothing I was, the last person – one of the last, I mean – to live on Wolfe.

'Where are you?' she asked.

'Here.' It was almost the last one, in my father's intricate beetle-foot hand. Tobe's entry was not finished. I should do that – sometime I would.

'And Cat?'

'Here. The last one.'

'I am?' Cat said. 'Show me.' So I did. 'I didn't know.' She liked it, I think. She got what my mother used to call a secret look.

'Would you like your name in there?' I asked Alejandra.

'Am I family?'

'You are to me.'

'Okay.'

I wrote her name – 'just Alejandra,' she said – her birth date, and the date of their arrival in brackets.

She went to show Cat, who was in the window seat. 'Nice,' she said. 'That makes us like sisters or cousins or something.'

Alejandra looked like she'd burst with happiness, and its shadow that was always there for her: loss. 'And Luis? And when we find Mama and Selma?'

'Sure, if they'd like. We'll ask.'

'Luis would like it. I know he would.'

But I forgot to ask. Maybe Alejandra did and he told her no. He remembered his parents, he remembered them being all together. But Alejandra had truly become family. I don't know how, only that seeing her on the old sofa wiggling her toes in Girl's fur, thinking of her name in the Bible made it so.

I would do all I could to keep her safe. Having her name written there within those old pages might help. How would I know? How would anyone? We all believe things, many of them strange, generation after generation: the first snow must be fashioned into a snowman or a lantern, no matter how small; a candle must burn through the longest night of the year; people must walk through streets behind idols or saints on the longest day and sacrifices must be made on the shortest; warriors must drink from the skulls of their vanquished enemies; and a child should not be named until they are two so the devil can't find and kill them. We don't like to tempt fate. We do anything we can to keep the ones we love safe. We will thwart fate and live and prosper, dear God (if there is such a being) in heaven (if there is such a place), we hope.

Chapter 11

I TOLD DOREE only that Cat had run away from home and was staying with me for a while. Doree was surprised – 'Lord Jesus and his mother Mary,' she said in a very island way – but willing to help. She had the number of a doctor friend who could assist in an emergency. I was thankful for that. I loved Cat for her own sake, but there was Claudie too. I could not be responsible for her girl's loss and I could not betray her daughter and I didn't see how everything could be right.

The week after, a hurricane ran the edge of the island like a zipper, and the land frayed and spilled afresh. I say that like it's nothing, but you can't know until you've lived through it. We couldn't see for rain. Girl howled and paced. Afterwards, Wolfe was more water than land and quaked and gave to footfall, as if we were walking on a dead creature – one of the caramel-chew cows of my mother's memories. Water pooled in our footsteps and remained. The sea turned unpredictable. Winds blew up and the grain of the water changed, running counter to itself, and waves lifted from nothing in minutes.

I began to fear for Cat and what might happen if we were caught or forced to battle through uncertain seas. I was thinking of my grandmother and the winter of her death. We carry our families with us in our actions. My mother made sure not to conceive a baby that would be born in winter. Summer storms and hurricanes were a new danger. No sense in giving her more to worry over. There was no chance of Claudie forgiving me if anything happened – not much chance of her forgiving me anyway.

Not without some misgiving, in a calm spell, Cat and Girl and I left Alejandra, Luis and Josh to fend for theirselves while we went to the main to wait for the baby to come. I wondered if Josh might like to come, but Cat became vague. 'Oh, I don't think so,' and she put her hand to her belly and stroked it with her thumb. 'He's not really that interested.' They weren't together anymore, she said. 'No fight. Actually, we haven't talked about it. I'll tell him. I will.' She looked across the bay towards their house. 'I honestly don't know *what* I saw in him. I don't even like him.'

'He's very good-looking.'

'But so what? I think I went with him just to give Dad a fit. That worked. Everyone wanted him.'

'You looked like you liked him.'

'I must have for a while.'

'Well,' I said, 'it'll sort itself out in its own time. One way or another.'

'It won't,' she said.

I went walking around town for a change of scene, ignoring people's sidelong glances. I happened to pass Hart's place. Blackwater isn't a large town – it wasn't even before it started to whittle away. A walk around the harbour took me that way, I would like to be clear on that point. I had time to kill and a restlessness to be spent. Cat had gone inside herself and her waiting and had shut out the world.

'You could walk around to your grandfather's,' I'd said. 'See if it gets things moving.'

'Why don't you go see him? You're the one who's interested.'

'I'm certainly not.'

She'd given me a sort of look, so I left, Girl at my side.

Now I stood in the shadow of a red maple I used to admire from our bedroom window. The house was neglected. The grass was too long – someone putting it off – and everything needed a lick of paint. It had been spruced up and painted butter yellow with white trim the last time I'd seen it, six or seven years before, under the influence of Hart's new woman I presumed.

Cat was napping on the living room sofa when I returned. Doree was out. Girl went into the yard. Beyond her were the harbour and the clutter of dogwoods and picket fences and brick paths and houses close together – much the same as always, even with the changes: the water higher, the fishing boats fewer, that sort of thing. Girl pricked her ears at the sound of strange dogs or coydogs or coywolves or even wolfdogs, and melted into the shadows, heading towards the forests out of town, maybe searching for a mate. (I had a feeling she was coming into season. It was too late to stop her now.) There was a bird in the tree above, and another in the reeds. It was like a dream. People prefer to live like this, ignoring the things that might wake them, as if ignorance might force the world into returning to its proper course. I did once have the glancing thought that living on Wolfe was not so different.

Next morning, while I was putting the coffee on, wraiths of mist were lifting from the dewy grass, and Girl, back from her night of roaming, wandered curiously towards an old brown car behind a dogwood on the dirt road at the back of Doree's. A woman was hunting through things in the trunk – plastic shopping bags and the small colourful bags that children like – which she dumped on the ground when she'd searched them. Softly, I whistled Girl back. A child poked its head from a window and the woman saw Girl. She took her phone from her pocket, and faced the house. It seemed as if she was looking at me, and I was on the point of waving. I heard Doree's voice upstairs. Quite suddenly, the woman shoved the phone into her jeans, threw the bags into the car, shut the trunk softly, jumping to add her weight, and got in. The car pulled away quiet and easy.

Doree came down the stairs – there was one step on the turn that squeaked – and when she came in I was getting creamer from the fridge. She glanced from the window. 'Oh, coffee. We're going to need that. Cat's pains are starting.'

I went in to see her late in the morning. She was moving restlessly from bed to window, pausing there to lean against the ledge, bowing her forehead to her arms and rocking and groaning, poor girl.

'I want Claudie,' Cat said. 'I want her.'

'I'll see if I can . . . I can ring her. I think I've got her number, if it hasn't changed.' I put a hand to Cat's back and felt the great humming energy at work in her.

'I want it to stop,' she said.

'I know you do. I'll get Claudie, okay?' I went onto the landing, looking through the tree branches while the phone rang.

'Mother?' Claudie said in that wary way of hers.

'It's Cat,' I said.

'You've got her?'

'I promised I wouldn't say. And I haven't *got* her. I didn't *have* her before. I just know where she is.'

'She's on Wolfe?'

'Not right now.'

'How do you know where she is then?'

'I'm not getting into that. Cat said she let you know she was safe. I told her she had to.'

'*Did* you? And you trusted her? That girl—'

'Did she leave you a letter?'

'Yes.'

'Well, then. Not my business to betray a confidence. Did you wonder why I might be ringing?'

That got her going. How dare I keep her daughter from her, and so on. After a while she wound down and I took the phone to Cat and left them to it. When Cat began to groan again I went back. The phone was on the bed and Claudie's voice was still pouring out of it. I picked it up.

'It's me.'

'I want to come.'

'Oh, good. Cat wanted you to.'

'What's happening?'

'She must have said something. Can't you hear her?'

'She doesn't want Rob there, she says.'

'I believe not.'

'Don't,' Claudie said. 'Not one word.'

'I said I believed you were right.'

'She should be in a hospital.'

'Too late for that. Can you come?'

'He'd know.'

'Claudie, you're her mother. She's the one you think of. He can look after himself.'

'Don't say it like that,' she said. 'Don't say it. Don't say it. Where could I be going?'

'I don't know. What do you do with yourself? Could you be helping someone move?'

She didn't say anything but I could hear her breathing.

'What if I need your help?' I said.

'Why would you?'

'People do. Broke my leg. Laid up with pneumonia, cholera, typhoid, chemo, nervous breakdown. I don't know. You'll think of something. Take a bus.'

'I'll drive. Where are you?'

'Blackwater. I'll meet you at the docks. If I see Rob with you, I'm turning around. Cat doesn't trust him.'

'He's her father. He's got a right.'

'No he doesn't.'

'Mother.'

'Claudie.'

She made her sort of angry growling sound then. She was just my daughter and nothing to be frightened of, but she frightened me anyway with her sad fury. 'All right then,' she said. 'I'll be there in the morning.'

I felt tired already.

Poor Cat kept on through the afternoon, and by dinner had a fevered look. She was grateful for ice chips and cold face washers and the drugs that Doree had got from 'someone'. (That was Doree all over; she knew everyone it might be useful to know, and every such person owed her for some kindness.) It was late when I heard the baby's cry.

Doree came out from Cat's room. 'All fine. Just going to

clean up and make them nice. She's perfect. Both of them are. A wee girl.'

I brought warm water and soft towels and clean sheets and took away the bloodied ones that Doree passed out, and quite late – stars were out over the harbour when I passed the round lookout window – I went in to see Cat and the baby. She was holding her and kissing her cheek ever so softly, again and again. 'Treasure. You are.' She could hardly drag her eyes away.

'Well, look at you two.'

'That's what I'm calling her.'

'Treasure . . . That's a good name.' I sat on the edge of the bed. 'What will Claudie think?'

'She can just stick it up her patootie, or whatever she says.'

'Patootie – oh, patootie. God, I haven't heard that for a while.' I laughed. They'd survived. I felt like running down the street. 'Claudie always did like that word. How about Josh?'

'Didn't want me to have her, no interest, so he doesn't get a say, does he, Treasure?' She kissed the baby again. 'Asshole. Not you sweetheart, that daddy of yours.' She kissed the baby's head and rubbed it with her cheek. Treasure's eyelids and mouth fluttered but she slept on. 'But let's not mention that asshole again.' Treasure was as dark as her mother, with a good bit of hair and eyelashes like sparse fans trembling on her cheeks.

'Why that name?'

'Because she is my treasure and I will always keep her safe. Nothing, *no one*, is going to stop me.'

'I believe it.' I sat on the edge of the bed, on Doree's old childhood candlewick bedspread from Wolfe. 'She's a sweetheart all right. Remember that feeling. Hold it tight. Somehow it can wear away . . . They have other ideas.' Cat looked fierce. 'Sorry,' I said. 'You'll do it. I know you will.'

Cat pulled Treasure close, then slowly she passed her to me, as if all the time she was considering and reconsidering the wisdom of it. But she kept on and I felt the weight of the baby passing from Cat to me. Feeling Treasure in my own arms and looking at Cat's face I remembered. She looked not light or loving or soft, but ferocious, like she knew things she hadn't known before, and had been through something she didn't know she could. No one can prepare you for it. You've been somewhere. Your body's surprised you. Whatever you've felt before meant nothing. *Nothing.* This is the thing that matters. Nothing is more important; nothing explains more. You're holding the world.

Claudie was in a mood. She never could stay still if she was upset. I dreaded what was to come even before I reached her. She was pacing the brick path and leaning against her slippery-looking car and pacing again as if she'd been there for hours instead of a few minutes. Her hair, which was the colour of dark honey, was long and waved about the golden skin of her face. Every bit of her was tended to. There was the push of her sleeve just so, a little way up, to reveal her wrist and her gold bangle. The silky fringes of her patterned scarf moved in the breeze. The laces of her boots weren't tied, but I presumed that was a kind of casualness that let anyone who wondered know that fine clothes and the appearance of wealth were the least of her concerns. What, this old thing? every part of her seemed to say. (In case you are curious about my attire, I was in jeans with well-worn knees, a plaid shirt of Tobe's with the arms cut out and a leather jacket I found in some island ruin when I was scouting around for new books.) It's what she wanted. That's the trouble: things you don't expect arrive without invitation. She might learn one day, as I did. She ran at the world so straight and undaunted that she convinced me she knew what she was doing – like Cat had been doing all year. Well, she had a way to run yet.

'Claudie,' I said, when I got closer.

She allowed herself to be hugged. 'Mother.'

When had I become Mother? 'Come on, Claudie,' I said. 'Come meet your granddaughter.'

She rolled her eyes. 'I'm not even forty. I've got friends my age with babies of their own. It's embarrassing.'

'It is a shock.'

'You're a great-grandmother.'

'Please.'

'You started it.'

The misery and worry on her face. I put my hands to her cheeks, and she let me. I stroked a blowing strand of hair back. 'Let's go see them. We won't worry about the rest for now.'

Claudie's boots made a tapping sound on the path, and even though she was a half head taller than me in her bare feet, a tall girl, she was slower – those preposterous heels. 'They're beautiful together. She's something, that Cat. You should be proud of her.'

'Don't tell me what I should be.'

'I'm sorry. I'm never sure what for, but I am anyway.'

We fell into silence, and kept walking, crossing Pork Street and Chewton, and then Claudie said, 'It is pretty here,' which was her way of apologising. It reminded me of my mother.

'It is that.'

'Quiet, though.'

'Season's finished. You don't come here to see Hart?'

'He comes for Christmas every other year, him and his new wife. Old wife.'

'What?'

'You didn't know? I thought he would have said. They broke up.'

'Poor Hart.'

'Liar,' Claudie said calmly.

I laughed, feeling suddenly lighter.

'Mother,' she said sternly, but she bumped against me and stayed there for a moment, almost friendly.

'What happened?' I said.

She gave me a sidelong look. 'You'd have to ask Dad.' We crossed another street. 'If you ask me, he missed you and she knew it. She was just so pleasant. She was too much.'

'Perhaps she was restful,' I said. 'Here.' Doree's house was all lace and flags and green shutters, and had myrtles and hydrangeas and sunflowers blaring outside. The whole street was done up in the same style, though different colours. (Everything on Wolfe is white, which I consider peaceful.)

'Isn't this – isn't it Doree's?'

'It is.'

'I should have known.'

I was glad for Doree's sake that she wasn't home. Claudie curled her lip at the gingham.

I went upstairs and poked my head in Cat's door. 'Claudie's here.'

'Better send her in.'

Claudie stayed for two nights. Mostly I remember the arguments. I would have returned to Wolfe to give her and

Cat some time alone – and mostly to spare myself – but Cat wouldn't hear of it. 'She'll kidnap us.'

'Don't be ridiculous. She's your mother.'

'Exactly. She'll call Dad. She won't be able to help herself. You stay here, Kitty. No going out.' She leaned forward – 'I mean it,' she hissed fiercely. 'I'm trusting you.'

I didn't hold out much hope for reconciliation between them, but I took the occasional laughter that gusted from Cat's room as a good sign. Doree and I had a quiet dinner; Claudie took a tray up to Cat's room and kept her company through the evening. Several times in the night I heard Treasure's piercing wails and Cat's murmuring replies.

By next morning, Claudie's hair had collapsed and she'd pulled it back into a loose knot. We sat in the kitchen drinking coffee. 'I like your hair like that,' I said.

'You would.'

She ate a piece of dry toast and went up to see Cat, her head, body and finally her feet being swallowed by the floor above as she climbed the stairs. There was the sound of her knocking, then quiet and then voices getting louder. Perhaps twenty minutes later she reappeared, her suede slides scuffing.

She came to the kitchen archway. 'You must think this is all pretty funny. You must be just about killing yourself laughing inside.'

'Why would I be doing that?'

'I suppose you'd call it karma.'

'I certainly would not. I don't believe in such twaddle. Choice and free will is what I believe in.'

'*Twaddle*, Mother.' She couldn't help a snorting laugh. She pulled a tissue from her pocket and blew her nose. 'Hay fever.' She moved about the kitchen as if she was in a pinball machine. 'She's refusing to come with me. We could report her, you know that? As a delinquent minor. Would you like to know what she did?'

'I know what they told me.'

'*They?*' she said. She wheeled around from the sink and came towards me. 'You mean Josh? He's on Wolfe too? I should have known. Vandalising golf courses. Burning the clubhouses, poisoning the greens, cutting the fences. His father is very important, you know.'

I don't know how I stopped myself saying something about Josh's father then, but I did. I remembered Cat's list. I hung onto it hard.

Claudie folded her arms in that fancy way where the palm of one hand cradles the elbow of the other. I let her stew, and looked at the news and checked my emails, and began a reply to one. Claudie straightened the table runner. 'I hate gingham,' she said. 'It's just so . . . so phony.'

I didn't reply.

'I made sure she fitted in,' Claudie said.

'You can't make them want what you want. I suppose we all try.'

'You did what you did and you decided it was okay.'

'So did you, and now it's Cat's turn.'

'I hate it. She won't come home, she won't go back to school.'

'Different issue.' I poured some coffee and added hazelnut creamer, a mainland treat. 'She's like you. Both of you doing what you have to. I am sorry I got in your way.'

Claudie breathed rather loudly and wildly like there was plenty more to say. Finally, she wailed, 'She's a single mother.'

'Oh, Claudie, who honestly cares? You've got a smart daughter and a healthy granddaughter. They just need some support.'

'Well thank God I've got you here for the parenting advice.'
That was the first morning.

By next day Claudie's gloss was entirely gone. She was thin
and tired-looking – like a tall gaunt horse. She ate an egg
white omelette for breakfast. She gathered crumbs on the table
surface, and straightened a spoon and centred the vase of late
summer flowers and began to rearrange them, stabbing the
stalks into place. The tea towel hanging from the stove rail
shifted as she passed. 'My hair,' she wailed, trying to smooth it.
'This place.' She yanked the lace curtain back and peered out.

'It's not so bad.'

'Then why was it so bad moving here? I suppose now's the
time you remind me about Tobe and his *incredible connection* to
the land.' She did that finger thing around the words. 'Which
consisted of killing everything he could. "Go play with your
brother." Meaning checking his death traps: crab pots, fishing
lines, muskrat cages.'

'It was just the island way.'

'Can't really complain there's nothing left, can you? I know
he was your kid. But did you ever think that might not be
my thing?'

It was coming back, the cold fog of it approaching, which
was not only because of the way she was, but the way things
were between us when we left Wolfe. 'I have to go out now,'
I said.

'Of course you do.'

Girl and I walked fast down the street beneath the plane
trees. It was warmer today and another time it might have
been pleasant moving down the long green tunnel they made,

the morning light sending shadows across gardens and houses, falling everywhere, fallen like leaves. Oh, that feeling, that dread softness in my chest. I kept on.

It was mid-morning when I got back and Claudie was getting a sandwich for Cat.

'That looks nice,' I said.

She rolled her eyes.

'I see you're still sixteen.'

'Sarcasm. Nice parenting there.'

'You think I favoured Tobe.'

She poured juice into a glass and put it on the tray, then leaned against the bench and folded her arms.

'I didn't,' I said.

'Doesn't matter now. It wasn't his fault. I worked that out in the end. I'm glad we were talking.'

'I worried about him. You made friends the first day at school. Remember that?'

'Yeah, what a *great* day that was.' Every word was on the same note, and if 'great' was a piano key it was like she gave it a good whack. 'You shouldn't have left.'

'Well I did. You didn't want *me* there – but your father was. And I wasn't there for Tobe, and you were all right and he wasn't. That's what I live with.'

'Why do you suppose I have one child?'

'How would I know?'

'So I couldn't have a favourite. Pretty funny, don't you think?'

'Claudie, I'm sorry. I am. I don't know what else to say.'

'Nothing. Now you can send my daughter home.'

'As if I could make her.'

Chapter 12

Autumn

THE HOLLOW-EYED WATERMEN beckoned from a distance, and there were the few houses, the dock, and the figure of Alejandra running down its length. Families are as alive as a dog or an island or a country; each has its own drive and way of being. It's not easy to change its direction. I hugged Claudie more than once in parting, but I knew that wasn't the end. We hadn't learned in an instant how to be mother and daughter any more than she and Cat had. But I told her I loved her and I had no reason to lie about such a thing and she had no reason to disbelieve me. There is hope built into that. It was another kind of family on the island.

We slid into harbour, feeling the change in the water, the way it accepted the boat. Cat looked about – for Josh, I suppose – but there were just Alejandra and, a little way behind, Luis to meet us.

'Where's the baby? Show me the baby. Where is she?' Alejandra clamoured, jumping about. 'Girl!' she squealed.

Girl leaped out of the boat and I followed. Alejandra threw her arms around me and I kissed the top of her head. 'Hello, miss. Tell me everything.' She quieted at that. 'Did you forget the garden? Doesn't matter. It's enough to see you.'

Luis helped Cat and Treasure onto the dock and we all had to admire the baby again. Treasure had made Cat a different person. What was Luis now? I gave him a half-hug, which he took quite well. He smiled, anyway.

'She okay?' he asked in a quiet aside.

'She's wonderful. And Treasure – exactly like Cat.'

'It's hard to tell when she's all wrapped up.' His face was very still right then, and mine was too, and I thought that we'd explained to each other quite well with our faces that we were each relieved that she hadn't taken after Josh.

'Things okay around here?' I asked.

'Yeah,' Luis said.

'No they're not,' Alejandra said. 'Josh got really mad yesterday, Kitty. He even punched a wall.'

'Did he? Why would he do that?'

'I think he might have got an email,' Luis said, trying to tell me something with his eyes.

'I'll go find him.'

But I couldn't find him. I went back to my place, where I felt like a visitor, as if everything was pretending its familiarity. There was one more conversation I had with Claudie that wouldn't leave my mind. But I'm aiming to be truthful for Claudie, or whoever might read this, and writing it down might help.

We were walking down to the harbour when Claudie burst out, 'You've got to leave Wolfe, Mother. It used to be eccentric, but it's just weird now.'

'I can't.'

'You really can. Winter's coming. What if something happens with Catalina or Treasure? I just can't believe you.

I can't believe myself. I should have the police here. I should have got Rob.'

'We've got phones, computers, and there are rescue planes.' But I was thinking in an island way and she wasn't, and she worried and worried at me until finally I burst out, 'I'm not letting Tobe down again.' It didn't come out right. I meant that the island was the place he loved, and giving up on it would be like turning my back on him again and walking away.

'Oh my God. Of course it would be about Tobe. He is dead, Mother, *dead*, and even he knew he couldn't stay there forever.'

'That's enough, Claudia.'

'*Claudia*,' she mocked. 'You can't send me to my room now.'

'Don't be ridiculous.'

'Mother,' she said, with slow patience, 'Tobe left Wolfe.'

'Because we made him.'

'Only the first time. Feel whatever you want to about that. It's on Dad too. If you ask me, you should have left years earlier, you should have seen what was coming. The second time, Tobe left on his own. He hadn't given up. He wasn't a victim of the *changing world* or whatever you want to think. He was fighting for himself. He was thinking about his future.'

'He was miserable.'

'Who isn't sometimes? He was seeing a doctor, he was working on it.'

'He would have been safe on the island.'

'He was twenty-four, not four. He came to see us.'

'What?'

'A couple of times. He was looking for other work, getting involved. We talked about you . . . how we thought it was time you left. And that's a while ago now.'

My face, my chest were boiling. I put my hands to my cheeks

to try to cool them. Anything to stop the feeling. 'I work out there. I'm not just sitting around. I've been working the whole time. That's my job. It's connected to that place.'

'I've seen the films – my mother, Kitty Hawke, artist, outlier. Did you have to go buddy up with a murderer?'

'Claudie. You have to stop.'

'And now you've got my daughter out there.'

'She ran away.'

'Lucky me. I've had a mother *and* a daughter run away from me now. How special am I?' Her eyes glittered and furious tears began spilling. 'I was going to be better than you.'

'Claudie, Claudie, sweetheart.'

'*My* turn to say enough.'

That's how it went. It was exhausting.

Late in the afternoon I spied Josh on the marsh walkway, and went that way, calling out so I didn't startle him.

'Kitty,' he said, when I drew closer.

'I came to say congratulations.'

'Oh yeah? Cat didn't tell you then, that she's breaking up with me? Or broken up apparently, nice of her to let me know, said we were too young, some shit. My parents would have liked it. They always wanted a daughter.' He spoke in a bitter sort of way, and scratched his unshaven cheek.

'Maybe later.' But later what? I'd seen how he made her hate the thought of being tricked by the way other people saw him. She'd thought better of herself. How could he not see that?

He made some disbelieving sound, and rubbed a thumb over the knuckles of his other hand. They were red and grazed, puffy-looking. Seeing my attention, he thrust his fist into his pocket. 'I'll fix it.'

'It doesn't matter. The house won't be there for much longer. Something to keep in mind – for all of you.'

'I don't even know why we're still here.'

'Luis is waiting for word. Cat was waiting for the baby. You were waiting for her. Isn't that it?'

'They're not going to free his mother, Luis knows that. He's scared of what comes next.' And then he said, 'She didn't give me a chance.'

'Might be time to move on?'

'That's what I told her.'

'For you, I mean,' I said. 'Make your own way.'

'As long as she's here, I'm not leaving.'

'Even if she's turned from you.'

He seemed wild and stricken somehow then, looking at his injured fist again and pressing it to his front, as if that could stop all his terrible feelings, and I took pity.

'Come on,' I said. 'We'll fix up your hand. Things will seem better soon.'

He came along, seeming comforted by my quiet lie.

It was like the air itself was crackling after that. Girl raised her head and looked about for its source. (Another complication: I was pretty sure Girl was expecting. It might have been that night out in the forests, or while Claudie was at Doree's and I was distracted. She was eating more, and was touchier.) It was as if we'd dragged the mainland back with us and couldn't shake it free.

Three weeks after we got back from the main Josh left on a

run – a one-night job, and he was gone for two. As afternoon deepened on the second day Cat watched from the upstairs window. I thought she might be missing him. 'If he's been caught, if he talks,' she said as I came up the stairs. 'Where could we hide Luis and Alejandra? Stillwater? If he's done something stupid.'

'There's plenty of places,' I said.

Josh returned at dinnertime the next day, coming through the door after a short knock that made us all leap. We were on edge by then. Cat ran at him and his face lit up; he thought she was glad to see him. 'Where were you? You couldn't find somewhere to send a message? We didn't know whether you'd been caught.' She stopped herself from shoving him, though her hands came close to his chest. 'My God, you stink.'

He reared back. 'Real nice welcome.' He stepped around her to the table and sat. A strong smell of fuel wafted about him, his cheeks were smudged, and his hands were marked by burns and a wound that he'd wrapped roughly in some torn cloth. Mostly I noticed his feverish brightness, the way his legs jittered, and he rubbed his arms, and grinned as if he didn't know any of us anymore.

'Something happen?' Luis asked.

'All good, man,' Josh said. He rubbed his mouth with the back of his hand and returned it to his knee and pressed it. He shivered, and shook his hand as if trying to flick something away.

'Josh?' Cat said.

'What?' It came back hard as a punch. 'I'll tell you once.' He shook his head in a rhythmic way. 'First night, picked up the runner. All good. Just another guy heading north. Then, about an hour in, we were pulled over coming into a town.

147

Unmarked car, plainclothes officer, and they saw him. It was like your mother, Luis. They just took him. No papers. They asked if I knew him, I said no. He'd nearly made it, that guy. Not much older than us.' He was shaking. 'They wanted my licence.'

'No,' Cat said.

'Don't worry – I'm sure you won't. I had my fake. I said he was a hitchhiker. They got my details, and the car plates. I told them the car was borrowed. That was okay. It's the truth. It'll need new plates and papers for whoever they get to do the next run – don't want them making any connections.' Here, he glanced at Cat. She nodded. 'But I'm finished. They took photos of me and the licence. They let me off with a warning – can you believe it? I thought it was a trick, they'd put a tail on me, see where I went. So I went driving all over until it got darker. I drove into a forest and stayed there until it was night and ended up at an old friend's from school. We did a few things that we maybe shouldn't have last year.' Cat was on the point of speaking. 'Nothing to do with you,' Josh said to her. 'We got talking. That's all you need to know.' He looked at his hands and held the fingers out, and shivered again.

'I have some anaesthetic cream,' I said.

'You do? They hurt. I forgot how much.'

I got the first-aid kit, some antiseptic, and a few clean soft cloths. They watched as I carefully cleaned the dirt and charred skin and the greasy residue of some rich smoke away. He swore, but under his breath, and it didn't seem directed at me. It was like he was an injured animal we'd picked up from the roadside. No one talked. I dabbed some ointment on the burns and wrapped the soft gauze on the larger ones, loosely. I mention

148

this because I think we hadn't given up on him yet. In our minds he was still one of us and something bad had happened.

'I'm really sorry,' Luis said.

'I thought of your mother. I didn't know that guy from shit. But your mother . . . I could see how it would have been. *My* mother, my father . . .' Josh was looking inside, not seeming to find anything he cared for.

Luis clasped his shoulder briefly.

Alejandra had gone to sleep and Luis didn't have the heart to move her. He sat quietly on the porch steps watching the dark shapes of Cat walking Josh back to Shipleys.

'Strange night,' I said. He nodded. 'Something the matter?'

He lifted a shoulder and let it fall.

'You can tell me.'

'Lone goose. Saw it come in tonight.'

'Superstition.'

'Don't say that.'

There was a heavy frost next morning, the first of the season. Everything was white, the dainty spiderwebs too, all glittering and hard. Girl went running, looking back to make me gambol with her, so I did my best, and it seemed like she was laughing at me. She loves the cold.

That was the first thing. Of course the frost had killed the vegetable garden. The tomatoes, beans and peas were black and drooped by mid-morning, and the pumpkins were showing off and the last tomatoes blinked from the ruined plants like the brightest eyes. Alejandra had joined us by then. She got a bowl and began picking the tomatoes and anything else that hadn't been spoiled. Cat and Luis came out with steaming cups of coffee and sat on the garden wall with Treasure, admiring Alejandra's collection. We were laughing about something, I don't know what, because it was sad too. They'd made the garden and now it was done. The laughter might have been to hide the sadness.

Girl looked up then. She stood with her ears pricked. She stared at me and yipped and I looked up too, but everyone else was still laughing.

'Quiet,' I hissed, as if someone invisible was among us and they might overhear. They were quiet. I heard the buzz then. 'Quickly now, get inside fast. That's a drone.'

Cat ran with Treasure into the makings room. Luis scooped Alejandra around her middle and ran after her. Alejandra was still holding her watering can and the water slopped a trail behind. I went down the path, looking up all the while. There it was, a dark thing so like a dragonfly that it seemed close at first, though it was still quite high. I hate them anyway, and I hated this one for what it might mean. It dropped lower. I leaped the porch stairs, went inside – 'Stay down,' I shouted through the house – and pulled my rifle from the top of the kitchen cupboards and was outside again, taking aim.

The shining thing was nosing along the street a few lots down by then, like it was looking for the right address. I shot it and broke a wing and with the next shot hit its carapace and it lay down. It was as intricate as a brooch, buzzing still, and even though I knew it wasn't a living thing I wanted it perfectly dead. There was a rock at Beauforts' front gatepost. I heaved it free and dashed it onto the metal.

They poured from the house and came to look.

Josh came up the road shouting. At the sight of him Alejandra took hold of my hand and pressed into my side.

'A drone,' I said when Josh reached us.

Cat said, 'You idiot. You used your phone to pay, I know you did, and they've found us.' She was almost panting with rage. Alejandra and I stared down at the crushed metal.

Josh said, 'I had to. I'm not going to steal. But seventy miles away. God, what is wrong with you? Why wouldn't it be you? Who saw you in town – both of you?' (Here, Josh looked at me.) 'And don't tell me no one heard the baby. Why wouldn't it be you?'

That shut us up.

He crouched by the drone, lifted the rock aside and peered close.

'Do you know anything about them?' I said.

'My dad brought a few home to try out,' Josh said. 'His line of work. I've seen similar.'

'Who was controlling it?' I said. We looked to the sea, but there was no boat to operate it from out there, and no one had arrived at the docks. I hoped everyone had got inside before they'd been filmed.

Cat said, 'Bury it.'

I said, 'Drown it. Deadness gut – that's the deepest, always been the best place for secrets. Get some salt water into it.'

I picked the drone up by one of its stubby limbs and left Josh and Cat on the road talking, I don't know what about, though I did see Josh take hold of Treasure's hand and her pull it back, and his look of hurt.

I strode up the marsh road and took the path to the gut's edge and slung the drone into its depths. It sank fast.

'Hey!' a voice came from behind. I swung around. Girl was already planted four square and growling before me. It was some khaki-clad birder coming up the path, binoculars and cameras slung across his chest, a baseball cap and heavy sunglasses against the glare.

'Where'd you come from?' I said.

My tone would have pulled him up even without Girl between us.

He pointed down the path to Deadness beach, or in the direction it used to be. 'Back that way.'

'Dangerous waters.'

'Good charts,' he said. 'You seen a drone around?'

'That was yours?' He held up the control. 'What was it for?'

'Birds,' he said. 'Survey for the Audubon Society. The picture went dead when it was going up a road.'

'It would have. I shot it. Should have run your survey past me. If I'd known . . .'

'Who are you?'

'Wildlife officer. I always shoot a drone if the eagles don't get it. I don't allow them. They frighten the birds. You should know that.'

'Not if you're careful.'

'Better take more care next time then.' I turned away. I looked back once and he was standing by the gut looking in. It was his problem now, and if that was the stranger foretold by Luis's lone goose, we'd seen him off.

The closeness of the night after Josh's last run and our relief over the drone were short-lived. Alejandra told me Josh had moved out: 'to that little shanty up the gut'. Tobe's shanty. No good would come of him brooding over there, separated by water.

'Why'd he do that?' I asked.

'I don't know. He's been staying in another room, but he went into Cat's. She didn't want him in there. They were yelling at each other. It made Treasure cry, Kitty.'

'That's no good.'

'No. Then he came out and got his things and left. Will your boy mind?'

'No, he wouldn't care.'

Josh turned solitary. I was solitary myself, but a person who becomes solitary when they have not been before needs watching. A cause had given him shape and now that was gone. He wore his army fatigues and a football t-shirt or sweater. Sport or war, his clothing seemed to say, it was all the same to him. He could never belong here with so few people about. I thought he was a person of short-term purposes, good for a moment, a crisis – a house fallen, a gut overrun, a boating disaster – when his energy had a reason and a use. And now there was no point in him travelling to the main. But what would he have seen to upset him so? People see things differently. A storm is not entertainment or a leaking roof to some, but a falling world. That is the sort of thing I mean.

I saw it a few weeks later, such a simple thing: Cat and Luis and Alejandra squeezed together on their sagging porch sofa, passing the baby up and down. Treasure was trying to smile. Her tiny mouth wavered, and they were working so hard to help her. I was standing below laughing at it all. I don't know if the sun was shining, but in my memory it was. They were a family – that's what I saw. Cat said something and Luis laughed and their faces were lit up. They looked into each other's faces without hesitation. They held the world at bay; they dared it. I looked up the gut hoping Josh had been spared this. He was on the shanty deck watching, rocking from one foot to another. He leaped into his small skiff and rowed fast down to the landing. We kept an eye on him, pretending not to.

He came towards us.

'Do you want to hold her?' Cat said. 'Come on up.'

He ignored the question and looked along the line of them. 'I'm beginning to see it.'

'If you'd like to. She's your daughter.'

Treasure began to fuss on Alejandra's lap. Luis took her and held her to his front and patted her back.

'Sure. I'd like to hold *my* daughter. Thanks for offering *my* daughter to me. I wouldn't want Luis to miss out. You take your time, buddy.'

Luis peered over Treasure's head. 'She asked you. You only had to say yes. Here.' He held Treasure out.

'Yeah. Well. *Actually* I'm busy. Maybe another time. Okay if I use your computer?'

I said, 'Go ahead.'

He went the long way around by the bridge over the gut, perhaps so we weren't watching, but was gone when I returned to my house. I don't know where he went then. Afterwards, if I passed him, he could more or less meet my gaze, but there was nothing behind it. The next week, my season's makings were crated and taken to the main (everyone but me holed up inside for the day). I felt lost afterwards, as I always did. I didn't know what to think about. My hands were restless. I was emptied of ideas and new ones weren't coming in yet. I spent a few days bringing my notebook up to date – a good feeling – and not long after, towards the end of autumn, another visitor arrived.

Chapter 13

GIRL SAT UP, immediately and utterly alert. She gave her yip of alarm: someone was around.

'Girl?' I said. Down in the makings room I was cut off from the dock and relied on her. I set down the wire I was twisting and Girl made for the French doors that stared up the marsh road, the fastest route outside. We went into the day: tarnished silver sky and pewter sea. Girl rushed to the house corner and looked towards the dock, head to tail straight and glaring. She barked again and sounded a howl with nose raised – that would be for the other house. I hoped they'd have the sense to stay inside. I reached her. A man was striding our way and he didn't hesitate at the sight of us. Either he had a gun or was not right in the head. Why else so boldly approach a person and a dog he'd never met?

He was not the usual sort of hunter, and if he was one, he was not after animals. He was medium height and his jeans were in a dapper style, ironed and of a uniform colour. He wore a navy jacket and a blue silky scarf at his throat. He had the bristling pinkness of a fine hog, though he was in good shape. His hair was sandy and his moustache large and bristling, a shelter for his tight little mouth. In another setting he would have been unremarkable.

He kept coming.

'Girl,' I said. I didn't want her shot. My gun was on the shelf by the front door, and that made me the fool. She waited close by my side.

'Are you Kitty Hawke?' the man said when he was in speaking distance.

Girl took one step towards him and stiffened. The man stopped.

'I am.'

'The artist?'

'Some say. I don't sell from home.'

'Excuse me?' He looked uneasily back towards the Watermen. 'Oh . . . I'm not a buyer.'

'I still don't know your name.'

After the slightest hesitation he said, 'Harrison Andover.' That wasn't true. He wasn't as smart as he thought; he couldn't help giving himself away. 'Are you the only person on the island? That's what I heard.'

'No. I'm sure you know that. Only a fool would have missed the smoke from the other house.' He looked about, so I knew he hadn't noticed. 'Are you a fool?'

'I am not,' he said testily. Well, it's good to know the length of a person's fuse, I've always thought. He had a short one.

'I didn't think so,' I said.

'Who are the other people?'

'My granddaughter and her boyfriend, visiting.'

'What for?'

'Why would you care to know?'

He eased one shoulder inside his jacket. Girl and I were still. 'I'm of a curious disposition.'

'As am I.'

'Do they have any visitors currently?'

'No.'

'Or any visitors in the past?'

I shook my head.

'Or expecting?'

'Why would I know who they might be expecting?'

'Runners perhaps?'

I shook my head again. A long way behind I saw a movement, Alejandra running through the door, onto the porch,
down the stairs – I couldn't look directly – then another
person – Luis – leaping after and scooping her up around her
middle and rushing her back inside. Thank God.

'Harbouring fugitives is a crime. You would know that,'
he said.

'I have heard that. Not sure why you'd mention it now. I get
very few visitors. You're the strangest thing I've seen in a while,
but I suppose you're not a fugitive.'

'No.'

'You're a hunter then. Girl is never wrong. Why you would
want to frighten me is what I'm wondering.'

'Not my intention.'

'We both know that's not true. You can rest easy. It
didn't work.'

He blinked once. 'I'll look around if you don't mind.'

'I can't stop you, but I don't know what you'd be hoping
to find.'

'Nothing in particular.'

'And that's what you'll find. Good luck to you, Mr Andover.'

I went inside and watched from there.

He walked some way up the road to the point where you
see the sweep of marshland starting, the wind bending its

surface this way and that, the walkway, the tide-covered road, and the distant ruins of Stillwater, and thought better of it and turned back. He might have been considering coming in that way by boat, see who might be holed up out there. Well, let him try. He came back down the road and I kept abreast with him through the length of my house, with Girl going to each window to keep watch, making that rumbling sound deep in her chest. There was something about him that was worse than first appeared. I went onto the porch and leaned over and called to him. 'Hey, mister.' He turned and held his hand to his brow as if there were a burst of sun. 'Try the other end if you care to. But be careful. It can be treacherous. The name of the town is Stillwater. We have a backward sense of humour round here, so you know.'

'I've got a chart.'

'Good luck to you.'

'I will find them,' he said.

I had never met such a person before. Evil is not a word to use lightly, but it came to mind then. I didn't know where it was inside him, only that it was there in the flatness of his eyes and his hard, steady voice, his implacability. He turned away, done with me, and went on.

I grabbed my jacket from the door and the gun from its shelf and waited. Andover walked down to the harbour and around it without haste or delay and up the stairs to Shipleys, where he knocked on the door. Cat answered. From here, they were still and silent as makings, and stiff in their bearing, and therefore eloquent in their way. He descended the stairs, walked around the curve in the road, pushing at the doors of the tombstone houses, poking his head in and withdrawing at the sight. I could not determine his mood, whether rage-filled or thwarted or satisfied. He returned to his boat, a regular boat with a good-sized engine from the sound. He swung it around and puttered out, not too fast. Girl and I ran down the road and I banged on Shipleys' door.

Cat pulled the door wide, drawing breath to speak her mind. 'Oh, Kitty,' she said. Her face was bleak.

'Where's Luis?'

He came downstairs with heavy footfall, Alejandra in tow. It was as if he had been stove in, and all his worry and dread was exposed. He had thought himself safe here, and he was ashamed of that.

'Tell me,' I said. 'Who was that man? No one good, I'm sure. He wanted you.'

'Did he say that?' Luis said.

'Not by name. He wanted to know who's on the island.'

'You don't have to say, Luis,' Cat said.

'No you don't,' I agreed. 'I don't know who you are exactly but I know what you're like. I'll do anything to help. He's a hunter. He won't give up, Mr Harrison Andover.'

'Harrison Andover?' Luis said with contempt. 'Cat, would you mind Alejandra while I talk to Kitty?' Without a word she took Alejandra's hand. Luis and I went outside.

'I can't tell you everything. We have a connection with him that he wants to destroy, and he must destroy me to do that. He wants me.'

'Alejandra too. He said, "I will find *them*."'

He shut his eyes. I put a hand to his elbow and he righted himself. 'He, this Harrison Andover – which is not his name – is a department official we have crossed paths with. He was bad to my mother. They thought she was a no one; a mother, a cleaner, a common illegal. She had to pretend with him, like a game, and he used her. I don't know what he'll do. We know some things he did. He might suspect some things about us. He works for Josh's father, but I don't know how. I don't know why Josh's father wants us. Something political – about my father, because of my father. I am afraid they will use us or send us back to my country. I am afraid they will kill us.'

'Can you claim asylum?'

'It's the government that's trying to catch us. There is no asylum for us. We have to run before he comes back. He's on his own, so they might not know that he came; he might be acting alone.'

'Did he see you?'

'I don't know. If he tells someone—'

'You're not just runners.'

'Not exactly. But we must run again, and hope.' He looked weary, almost despairing, the way Tobe had looked one summer's end when returning to the main. I had let myself pretend he was all right. I failed him; I would not fail Luis now.

'Get me a jacket of yours, something you'd wear.'

'What?' he said.

'He wants a young man. I'll be one. And a hat. Quick.'

I pulled on his black puffer and twisted my hair into a knitted woollen hat.

I ran home, picked up my bike and gun, and rode as fast as I ever have to get to the walkway, and I started out along it. There was Andover's boat tracking the shore. He might have been heading around to Stillwater or looking for a way to come in by surprise. There was no reason to stay close to Wolfe otherwise.

I kept on, hoping I was right that Andover didn't have a rifle as well. It was hard to stand tall, to expose myself that way. Halfway along I shot above the bulrushes. A few geese lifted – not so many this year. I shot again, away from the rising birds, for a moment watching their lumbering take-off and the way they stretched and lengthened like Girl when she was pointing, the grace of them. The boat's engine dropped. Andover's head turned, scanning the island. I began walking, almost casually, and took another shot. If Andover had any sense he would have seen the trap I'd set. As if I had only just seen the boat, I dropped from sight behind the wooden slats. That did it. Andover turned the boat and drove it towards the shore. It looked pleasant from out there, I knew. Even though the sand beaches had gone, there was the inlet the walkway was supposed to bridge, and muddy embankments that a person might moor at. The boat kept on, fast. I turned away and then I heard it hit. I looked through the slats in the walkway. The boat was yawing on its base. Andover was slumped sideways. The boat heaved in the water, settling as it filled, as if with final breaths. He was still. I didn't want to watch anymore. The waves began lipping and rolling into the boat across the hidden jetties. There was nothing to be done now; a rescue dinghy was at least an hour away. The boat would be ground to matchsticks in a couple of days.

I felt strange, terribly heavy. The walkway was long. My legs were not mine, my sight was not mine, it was not this time. When Bette and I were small, a neighbour died and we heard she'd been laid out on her kitchen table – the table we'd drunk juice at when visiting with our mother. All morning we kept watch as people crunched over the shells of dead oysters to the kitchen door. We crept in at lunchtime when it was quiet. Her daughter Linda was in a rocking chair reading a novel, one finger playing with her mousy hair and smoothing a hand down the

front of her floral dress, easing herself in it. The cover showed
a swooning woman gazing up at a long-haired swarthy man.

Linda put her finger in the page, and said, 'Come on in, girls,
and take a look. You won't see her again this side of heaven's
gate. Come pay your respects.' So we went closer, wondering
how that payment was made. No one had mentioned money;
it would be embarrassing if we were beholden. Mrs Lacey had a
spotted kerchief wrapped about her head, but her slack mouth
hung open a little way and I could see her yellowish teeth. Her
eyes were silver and I knew they had been transformed and she
saw everything and knew everything, my darkest mutterings
of jealousy and hate. We flew through the door, letting it slam,
and all afternoon we washed our hands, washed them, trying
to wash that visit away. But it was too late. We knew death
was real now. It sometimes seems I've spent my life trying to
return to the day before, my final one of innocence. If only I'd
known the contentment of it. I felt hopeless now, saturated
in the dreary violence of what I had made happen. I had lost
something and I would never get it back.

Luis was waiting on the marsh road. 'You knew that
would happen.'

'Not for sure.'

'You saved us the day we arrived.'

'Yes. There are things out there waiting to tear you up. He
said he had charts. Old charts are worse than no charts, something my daddy told me, worth remembering. What will you
tell Josh? Alejandra saw him and she'll likely say something,'
I said.

'Tell him we had a visitor, Harrison Andover, who looked
around and went away.' He glanced at the swaying boat and
the slumped man.

We went back to my house. Alejandra was there. She climbed onto Luis's lap the way she used to. She pulled the front of his jacket over her face and hid there. I was shaking. I made some sweet tea and we drank it. Alejandra came out of herself when Girl came nudging for her dinner and went to feed her.

'Fathers,' Luis said. 'Josh's father is part of it. This "Andover" worked for him.'

'Parents are a mystery. I mystify my daughter.'

It was as if Luis hadn't heard me. 'I wonder about him, my father. He was home sometimes, sometimes not. He was the good guy, the hero, you know? That's what people said. Someone important, not only to us. Important in the political sense, I mean.'

'But you're not sure about him?'

'Why do you say that? I never said that.' His voice was harsh, which was a rare thing.

'I thought I heard it under your words.'

'Right, right.' He shook his head in confusion. 'I don't know. He *was* important, but there was something else, too. I would like to talk with him. I would ask him . . . I would ask him why my mother said to him once, "It will catch up with you one day. You cannot outrun the past. It will gather itself and find you." Why did she say this? Without him, without finding my mother, I will never know.'

'I don't like that man, Kitty,' Alejandra said.

'He won't come again, sweetheart. He has other things to do.'

When it was time to go, Alejandra ran down the steps. I took Luis by the wrist. 'Talk to Cat,' I said. 'We've bought some time, but we should leave, I think. Don't you feel it?'

*

The sound of a motorboat made me jump that afternoon. What if Andover had contacted someone before his boat was wrecked? We had been living in a fairytale world. Andover showed us that and I hated him for it. I forgot and remembered again and again, nauseous with it.

Next morning, early, I went on a preliminary scout along the coast looking for a body. I didn't want Alejandra coming across it. Nothing would make the pretended innocence of the first months come back, but I could spare her that. It was the dying days of the year, the leaves of shrubs that had only started colouring – when, a week or two ago? – were beginning to fall, and the grasses were turning brittle. We needed our jackets even in the sun. A small flock of birds circled and circled again, looking to gather up more of their kind. Some gulls, I think, were clustered, lifting and squabbling around the place the boat had hit.

Josh passed my house around mid-morning, as fast and purposeful as if he was running late. I presumed he was going along the marsh road and determined to follow him this time. I paused only to grab my collecting bag from the makings room – an explanation if we should cross paths – and also took an old salt-pitted camera of my father's. Once, I would have paused along the way to take shots of a heron floating above the marsh, its spidery legs trailing behind, and of the small birds that ran the road's tideline. If there was nothing going on with Josh – and I didn't know what I meant by that, only that I felt something was wrong with every bit of me – I had things to do and my own reasons for being out there. All those distractions. I needed some more now. I hadn't done an erosion check in months, and there'd been the storms, and from the dull smear of cloud on the horizon there were more to come. Things had already changed – the land, the barnacled road that the water mostly covered now, the tawny marshes – yet it was utterly familiar, too. The air was thickly salt, not so bad when the wind stilled, but chill when a breeze stirred. I looked towards Andover's boat. If it was there, I was not high enough to see it.

There is a way of moving and a way of dressing that I have learned. On a grey day I hardly exist. I passed the silent power station, which after its years of thrumming still seemed to gather quiet around it, and went on. By the time I got to the low bridge and climbed it, Josh had gone. The three tall, broken-roofed houses he had disappeared beyond were as flat as a picture slapped up on a board. I reached them, slowing on the road that passed between the houses on one side and shanties on the other, like a rider in a Western travelling a valley bottom. I felt a prickling sensation – only the past, I hoped. Girl's ears were up.

There was the muffled thud of something fallen from a height, and I peered around the corner of Nate Strudwick's house. The sound was coming from the next house along, Owen Jims's white clapboard with its shingled sidings breaking away. I crept along the sodden ground close to its porch, inside a cover of thick saltbush. Not ten feet away a box crashed to the ground and split open, books exploding from the cardboard. I edged forward. The wall had fallen away, leaving the second storey exposed. Josh, facing away from me, was flinging another box and watching his strange work. I saw when he flung it, heard his grunt of effort, and watched him disappear, and after a pause return to throw more things out, armful after armful: a chair, a saucepan, a box of clothes, which splattered on the ground in unnatural colours: tangerine, mauve, lime green. Three gulls watched from the writer's house, lifting when something landed and returning when things went quiet. Josh's behaviour seemed deranged, and for that reason I didn't call out to him.

A shot rang out. I made a sharp sound at that, and might have been discovered but for the two gulls that squawked and lifted. The remaining one fell broken-winged through the air, and landed flapping on the sodden grass between the houses, trying to drag away. I held Girl at the shoulder. Two more shots made us flinch. The gull sank, blossomed red and was quiet. Josh came to the front door and onto the porch. There was the shifting of his feet, his tread up and down, his loud breathing. He fired some shots at Owen Jims's big oyster shed across the road, randomly: a metallic hail. The bullets flew about, hissing in the bushes and skittering on the road.

He brought a container from the house and took it into the oyster shed. A few seconds later the smell of fuel wafted with the salt smell of the sea. He ran a short line of fuel along the road south and lit a match and touched it to the end. It was a bright day, though overcast, the flame was thin and the line of it burning was marked more by the shimmering vapour above. It trembled and raced, rising and falling and sputtering in places where the fuel line thinned. Josh watched intently, and when the flame approached the shanty he pulled behind the side of the end house. Seeing that caution, I plunged to the back of Nate Strudwick's house. The shed bloomed into light and sound, the air sucked and returned and crackling flames rose. Soon, the corrugated-iron sides were peeled and torn as an old pomegranate. Josh came out and stood before it and watched calmly. The first black smoke subsided. Old wood burns clean. What a waste. The tall salt-stricken fennel that lined the road had withered. It was a dismal scene. Life doesn't always happen in big shocks, in falling towers or tsunamis or epidemics, but something loud can make you notice the whittling things already happening.

This is who Josh made me think of then, though he didn't always: some boys from a school field trip that visited a few years back. I knew they were trouble from the way their teachers lagged behind. If they didn't witness anything, how would it be their fault? The boys looked around with excitable eyes. One of them, in fatigues and with a red cap pressed down on his wheaten hair, had something about him you couldn't help noticing. The other boys fell in behind him as he walked past me and Girl.

I found them trying to ride the last of the goats I used to keep, hitting them with sticks, which made a loud thwack, goats being hard and bony creatures, and chasing the kids till their eyes rolled and their mothers bleated. I told those boys to go and they did when Girl bared her teeth and advanced at them.

'We were going anyway, bitch,' that one boy said. He climbed the fence to avoid Girl. It made him appear weak. He saw that he'd lost some of his power then. People like him are sly and cruel and take a long view. They hold spite and humiliation close to their withered hearts.

Three months later, I couldn't shake a feeling of unease when I docked at Wolfe after a visit to the main, despite the warm afternoon and the pleasant smell of salt and grasses. The island was so silent. I ran past the house along the road to the goat run, which is marsh now. I knew before I knew. Carrion birds were scattered on the meadow, their heads low between their hunched wings, stabbing and pulling and raking at the bodies of the goats seeping red across the summer grasses, which were bright and quiet against the blue sky. Girl hung back.

I'm sure the boy got back his swagger that killing day. They smashed up the house too, but the poor goats had the worst of it. I dragged them into a heap and burned them. The smell of it hung around for days, drifting off the ground when the dew dried, and again after it rained. I thought it would never be done. The ground was gaunt all winter. In the spring I sowed flower seeds there, which grew brighter than the grass around. It was cornflowers and larkspurs that I planted – blue flowers, not red. It's turned to marsh now, as I said, but different things still grow in that one place.

That's when I built the Watermen. I used two cattle skulls with great curved horns. I joined pieces of metal I had flattened into sheets (from cans of poison and fertiliser and fuel for the most part), traced contours onto them, and attached layers of copper and brass with hundreds of rivets formed into outlines to mimic the sinuous lines of their horned heads. They were twice the height of a man: hard to connect and hard to stand. I thought of them as the island's guardians, but some folk read a curse or a warning in them. One of the old islanders who'd helped get them standing licked his thumb and crossed himself at the sight. I got them cake and a few beers and that seemed to reassure them of my Christian intent.

That night I dreamed that it was Tobe, not islanders, who'd helped get the Watermen standing. He came out of his quietness and his face was alive. 'Holy hell, Mother,' he said, and he let out a whoop when we stood back to look. In the morning when I woke it seemed like he'd left them behind to watch over me. Every evening for a long time after I went and stood by them and watched the sun drop and the darkness come, and I felt close to him at such times. Sculptures and makings of all kinds have their own life, even if they don't breathe.

I gave the goats' thoughts and feelings scant attention when they were alive. They were humorous animals and had friends and family. I didn't like to think of them watching those boys approaching and being trapped. I failed them and that part of Wolfe's history ended with me. That's when I started carrying a gun. It's why I nearly shot Mary Dove the day I met her. It's hard to stop that fear and anger once it's started in you. It's like an engine idling, waiting for fuel.

I crept to the road when Josh had passed from ready view. He was moving neither fast nor slow, perhaps with a little spring in his step. He'd put his gun away, unless he'd left it in the house for more of the same.

I found a spent shell by the water and pocketed it, and went into the house in search of the weapon, which I did not find. Boxes were upended and slippery long-ago dresses of nylon and polyester spilled free, as bright as one of the nets of spilled fish of my childhood. All the things people end up with in their homes: a folded wheelchair, a dentist's tray and spittoon, a drip stand, a perished oxygen mask. Someone had lived out their later years and maybe their last days here and I didn't know who. They might have been sitting here in the dark while I talked with Owen Jims and Nate Strudwick; they might have been waiting for me to visit. The sight troubled me, but not in the same way as a boy or a hurricane or a boat breaking apart.

*

There was no sign of Josh on my return; there was no comfort in the quiet of my house. I thought of the many-windowed Shipley house so close to shore and of the space around it and the view Josh had of it from his shanty. I could see the whole island, as if I was hovering above it, angling a wing to peer in windows, gliding low along guts to seek him out, swooping the marsh walkway and flying beneath its silvered timbers.

I put on my jacket again. 'Girl,' I called and we went along the road. The clouds were building higher, bulging ahead of us past the lit windows of Shipleys. I went up the stairs to the porch, knocked on the door and let myself in. Cat was feeding Treasure before the fire. Alejandra was drawing, but stopped for Girl. Luis was repairing the hole in the wall with a piece of plaster.

'Doesn't matter,' I said.

'Don't want to leave it like this, so . . .' he said and went on.

I invited them to dinner and didn't say more. Cat looked at me in a searching way. 'Storm's coming,' I said. 'I'm not sure when. Has Josh been by?'

'He went past a while ago,' Luis said. He jerked his thumb towards Tobe's shanty.

'I'll ask him too.' But when I shouted from the dock I got no answer. It might have been the wind that blew my voice away. There is that.

Dark was coming when they arrived. Each year I forgot and was reminded of the comforts of fires and curtains and locked doors and windows and a dog at my side as the winter drew in. The island fell quiet and the house closed against it. It made me think of other endings. Some rain began around the time the apple dumplings came out of the oven, and it didn't stop.

'You might want to stay the night,' I said.

Cat gave Treasure to Luis and came into the kitchen, stacking plates and rinsing things. 'Something the matter?' she asked quietly. 'You and Girl – both listening to what's happening outside.'

'I didn't know what to tell you. I don't want to alarm.' I told her what I'd seen.

'Oh shit. That gun, I should have thought. Maybe we will stay.' She looked over at Treasure asleep in Luis's arms and at Girl on her hearth blanket.

'She'll let me know if he's around,' I said.

'What am I supposed to do?'

'I'm worried about you all when he's around. He's dangerous. Would he be in trouble if he went back?'

'I don't know. He hasn't been caught for anything serious. I don't know what's going on with his dad. They'd try and keep it quiet. Like my parents.'

'I think it's time for us to leave. Did Luis mention it? I asked him to.'

'No. Who's "us"?'

What a strange thing: I didn't even know. They were so much a part of my life now. 'Things are closing in, don't you feel that? The birder with the drone – something about him. Wait, wait.' We drifted into the living room and I sat on the fireside stool, rubbing my hands along my thighs, picking at the thinning knees of my jeans. I shut my eyes, watched the birder come along the path, his boot feet crunching, his bright khaki pants. 'His clothes . . . equipment. All new.' I opened my eyes.

'Oh God,' Cat said. 'We should have—'

'No point crying now. We'll get going tomorrow.'

I got their rooms ready and took some quilts down to the sofa for Luis. Alejandra ran around saying, 'A sleepover. We're staying for a sleepover, Kitty.'

'You sure are.'

'And can we have waffles for breakfast? And can I stay up until midnight? Can Girl sleep in my room?'

'Yes. Yes, yes, yes, Miss Alejandra.'

'We're having waffles, Cat,' she screamed.

I put Cat on the other side of the landing in Claudie's room and for a long time the sound of Alejandra and Cat's voices threaded backwards and forwards, weaving a sound I had forgotten, and I didn't have the heart to tell Alejandra it was time for sleep. I wasn't in the mood for it anyway.

When I went to my room I knew someone had been there and knew who it had been and for what. The case I travelled with from island to main those years, up on top of my wardrobe, was askew. Inside, the box of shells had been opened and about half of them taken. That was a good thing in a way – he'd run out of ammunition, and it was the wrong type for his gun. He'd know that by now. But he wanted those shells for something, and what might he do without?

Treasure woke in the night with shrill and plaintive cries. I jerked awake each time. Once, I stumbled across the floor half asleep, moving through the room of a memory, and it was only the sharp pain of my knee colliding with a new chair that brought me back. I lay again with my hands across my front like a lady on a medieval tomb, listening to the rain falling away and Cat's quiet murmuring and the baby's sobs subsiding and turning to snuffling and gulping, and Cat's voice, 'sh, sh,' which comforted me too, reminding me of nights of my own, sitting and reading in the well of light, the darkness thick and pleasant around us, holding us safe, me feeding whichever baby it was, Hart snoring lightly at my side, his arm flung back behind his head.

I knew in those moments two things: the purest contentment, and that I would kill anyone who hurt these people. The things you go on discovering about yourself are interesting, I think, if you care to look at them directly. I've known for years that there was a murderer hiding within me, and somehow I'd gone on living, and often laughed.

Chapter 14

IT WAS ONLY the next day, early morning, late autumn, that I heard Alejandra's scream: 'Kitty, Kitty,' as urgent as a whistle. (They'd not long left for Shipleys to decide what to take.) I plunged into the fog – a smotherin' mist – and Alejandra came rushing out of it and ran into me in her haste. 'Kitty!'

'What? Tell me what's happened.'

'Josh. He—'

'Is he hurt?'

'No.' She buried her head against my front and sobbed: 'He's got Treasure. He's taking her. Because Cat won't go with him.'

'Wait here.' I ran back, grabbed my gun from the kitchen mantel, and we followed the road's white shell edges down the road towards the dock, almost blind in that uncanny white. There was only our panting and the crunching beneath, and, muffled in the cloud, sounds of distress.

'Oh, Kitty,' Alejandra sobbed, yanking my hand as we went.

'I'm here, sweetheart. I'm coming.'

We rounded the curve in the path and heard a scream from Cat – 'Give her back, just give her back, oh, give her to me, please' – and Treasure's shrill, curdled cry, which I never wanted to hear again. Josh was making a grunting sort of sound like he was pulling against something.

There was Luis's shouting in the mist ahead. 'What the hell? What are you doing?'

Josh bellowed back: 'It's my kid. Cat's mine. If she wants the baby, she can come with me.'

'Give her back,' Luis shouted.

Cat screamed: 'Let her go!'

They were slow blurs and then as close as if we'd flung open a door onto a shadowy room. Josh was holding the baby with one arm around her belly, and she was screaming and choking. Cat grabbed his arm, and Josh pulled from her grip and in his haste half fell into the boat, lunging its length as it dipped and listed to free the line. Cat grabbed its end on the dock, whipping it around the bollard twice and knotting it fast.

'Let it go now,' Josh said. 'Loose it, or I'll drop her overboard.' He held the baby over the water; he held her under her arms and dipped her foot in, and looked up in a taunting way. Treasure fell silent. It was unimaginably worse than her screams. He pulled her back up, and dandled her again above the deep grey water and she was still quiet but drawing juddering, hiccupping breaths.

'Oh no,' Cat sobbed, shaking. She leaped into the boat. 'Give her to me.'

Josh staggered, and gripped Treasure hard. 'Careful now.' He gave a sort of smile, like he was nearly done. He had Cat on board and they were almost free.

I had seen his determination. I said, 'That's enough, Josh. Give her back. Give her *back* I say.' I drew the gun from my pocket. 'I will shoot.' I have never felt calmer or more certain. The world had never been clearer. It was peaceful in a way.

'You'll have killed the baby then. That's on you.'

'I don't think so. I can dive faster than she can sink. I can shoot faster than you can move.' My voice was serene. I felt still inside.

'You won't do it.'

'I'm a good shot. And I'm a good swimmer.' I waited for a second. 'No?' I asked. I pulled the trigger and a splinter of wood flew at his side.

'You crazy fucking bitch.' A streak of blood appeared on his free arm. He turned it and pressed it to his leg and looked again. Treasure was horribly quiet, just making these jerky breaths inwards, 'huh, huh,' like that, like a runner who's almost run her race. Her legs went stiff and pulled up again as best they could.

Cat, poor Cat, after a first cry of horror was panting and sobbing, 'Oh no, oh no, give her to me.' I didn't think I'd hurt the baby. I knew that gun; I knew myself.

I aimed the gun again. Josh looked at his arm, at the red ribboning out. Treasure finally began to scream. He looked away from her strident mouth.

'Give her now,' I said.

Cat reached and dragged Treasure from him and passed her to Luis across the water so fast he fumbled in surprise. She clambered up, desperate, and took Treasure back and held her close.

I held the gun on Josh, who was looking dazed now, at his bleeding arm, at his failure. 'She all right?' I asked Luis.

Luis looked Treasure over around the edges of Cat's arms. He nodded and pulled Cat inside his coat so only her hair peeked out, hiding them both. Treasure disappeared. I had not noticed Alejandra still holding tight to my other hand and now I gave her a little push towards Luis and he drew her in and she was safe too.

'Better be going,' I told Josh. I untied the line and threw it into the boat.

'You can't make me.'

'I think I can. You're not staying here another night, I'll tell you that now.' I tipped the gun to one side and looked at it, and aimed and shot a little further along the boat. Chips of wood lifted and spun in the mist and fell again, splashing lightly in the water. I didn't want to hit him that time. It wasn't necessary.

'Okay, okay! Maybe I shouldn't have done it. But you fucking *shot* me.'

'It's a graze. And it doesn't matter now. You *did* do it.'

'I wasn't going to let the baby go. He *took* her.'

'He did not. She wasn't yours. *Look* at that. Do not *turn* from that. *Know* that.'

In his agitation the boat was rocking again. He planted his feet. 'If I leave now, don't bother wondering. I'll be telling my father about you and what you did. Who do you think they're going to believe, Luis? Did you think about that? I'm trying to look after Cat. You can't do that. What kind of life will you have?'

Luis looked at Josh. He didn't say anything.

'On your way now,' I said.

I'll give him this: he didn't beg, but started the motor and faced away and headed out of the docks into the mist. The wind was licking the water into small peaks and the mist was thinning. It wouldn't be much longer until it was clear. Storms came up fast, but he had time; he had a chance.

I turned away. We all did. He was cast loose and everything had changed. I always wondered why I wanted to see Wolfe to its end, or to mine, and why I didn't care which it was. The island was part of me as much as any other thing: a heart, a memory, a scar on my knee. But watching Cat in the rocking chair with Treasure at the end of that day made me see how the end of Wolfe was wrapped tight in a beginning. Things were already starting to gather together somehow, even while they were falling apart.

I thought about it quite a bit later, playing it through, and couldn't see it ending better if I'd done different. He said he could swim. I would take him at his word. There was a hole in the boat now, whether or not he knew it. Best that they didn't know or even suspect. That's what I believed.

Josh's boat dwindled until not even our eyes could trick us into thinking that we could still see him and he might yet return.

'That's the end for us too,' I said. 'We need to get going. Get your things fast, whatever you need. He'll do what he said.'

Alejandra's eyes were huge and black and there wasn't time to reassure. 'Come on now,' Luis said. 'Better get Luna ready.' She gathered herself at the thought of her doll.

We agreed on a half-hour from then. We didn't talk about what we'd do afterwards. I hadn't killed him; he was still alive, and I held on to that.

The wind was gusting in our faces already. By the appointed time it was buffeting louder and waves were sluicing up beneath the rear of Shipleys, like Barlows' ruin of long ago. There would be no leaving that day, and no one coming to search for us. The house was trembling, but they wanted to stay one last night; they were used to its strange movements.

The wind roared up louder in the dark, loosening shutters,

which thrashed the walls as if someone was trying to break in. There was no sleeping after that. The power had gone. I lit a lamp and went downstairs, where I stoked the fire and watched the flames, listening to the raging outside, thinking of what was to come, and trying to plan. Where would be safe? How would I know when I didn't know the world?

I drew the curtains back and looked out as best I could. It was black as pitch and filled with noise. I should have prepared better. I should have known better. Night and day flickered and repeated as if by switch. I could hardly take in what I saw: a slumped shanty, the dock disappeared, and to the south where there should be land, nothing but water. I strained to picture Shipleys and even peered from the landing window – no better there. Girl couldn't settle, walking to the front door and back in so intent a way that I looked through the window half expecting the gaunt and sodden figure of Josh to be dragging up my path, strands of seaweed trailing and drifting from him. Those childhood horrors, the thought of Baby, a puppy we'd once had, and Mrs Lacey and her silver eyes. But there was nothing but wild shadows, shattered light and flying debris. Girl whimpered. 'Good Girl,' I said, but she would not be calmed. I looked again. It was just a sort of moving density at first, a clot in the night, which I could only tell by the way it changed from one lightning strike to the next. It was them, coming along the road in the middle of the night in that weather.

I grabbed my jacket from the door and ran through the house and flung open the door onto the porch, and even though I was expecting something fierce the wind seized the door from my hand and smashed it against the wall. Girl howled and her fur plastered flat against her. I slammed the door closed, pulled my hood tight, and staggered down the stairs and along the road through the tearing wind to meet them. Lightning hit Shipleys. Its roof was gone, and its shingles blew about as ragged as leaves. Every lightning strike created a new image, as if the world was a gallery wall. Things floated by, catching and moving on, being swept away. They became clearer, Alejandra's head buried against Luis, who was holding her tight in his arms, Cat staggering, huddling Treasure beneath her coat. I reached them, much good I did, and though they shouted I couldn't hear. I turned and we went on, splashing through the water, which was flowing freely across everything, pushed along by the wind. The salt meadow and the low bushes leaned and couldn't right themselves, and for an instant I caught sight of the marsh walkway like a sea serpent rising above waves, and of all their ghostly faces beside me.

We reached the house and burst in. Girl shook wildly. Cat pulled Treasure, screaming, from beneath her coat. 'It's okay, sweetheart.'

'In front of the fire, all of you,' I said. 'There'll be clothes in the attic until you get yours dry.'

'Kitty, Kitty, I thought we would get drownded,' Alejandra said.

'Did you? I don't think that would happen with Luis and Cat around.'

'And you.'

'Yes, me too. I would definitely not let that happen.'

I went to the window. The world was lit again and it was made of water. I leaned against the wall. I felt through my feet and all through me, the way the house quaked and the ground seemed to quicken, and wondered whether the island would survive the night. There was nowhere better than our house on Wolfe, my father always said, but he had never seen weather like this.

'We have to ride it out, hope for the best. No point worrying about what we can't control. Bed first, and we'll get ready in the morning.'

Luis and Alejandra went upstairs. Cat stayed behind. 'Do you suppose Josh . . .'

'Made it? He left long before it got bad.' What else could I have said? I have regrets, but not speaking more plainly is not one of them. 'It's done now and that's the way of it. He had time, all being well.'

We waited through the next day and the next night. No one would go out on the water in this. Luis and I went down to Shipleys that first morning. It had sunk to its haunches in the night, its roof and back had sheared off and its front gazed towards the sky. We approached it gingerly, wading through the water and climbing the porch's end. The door stuck but we kicked and threw ourselves at it and it finally gave. The hall and the front room fell away. It was dry enough, the downstairs ceiling still being there, but sodden elsewhere. We turned off the power.

Luis nodded. Mostly they'd finished getting their things together the night before. We filled another bag, then had to battle up the road. That was the first run. What a day. The wind was not quite so bad by evening, though the rain continued.

'We should leave tomorrow morning,' I said to Luis at some point. 'The back door's jammed in my house. That's not good.'

'All your things.'

'No point crying. I chose this.'

We pushed against a gust of wind, the words blowing away so at first I wasn't sure if I heard him right when he spoke again. 'I heard about my mother.'

'Did you say your mother?'

He nodded.

'Pending deportation. I found out last week.' He leaned into his walk as if more than weather was against him.

'And you didn't tell us?'

'Because. *Because.* It's the end then. Just me and Alejandra and the next thing. I didn't want to leave Cat with Josh. She doesn't want to go to her parents.'

'No.'

Luis didn't mention his mother that evening. No one spoke of what would happen after we got to the main. That was stupid of us. Even now we were holding on to the island. I had some thoughts, but there was no point in getting people's hopes up when it might not work out.

The boat fought the old dock, which was mostly above water again and just holding together now the storm was dying. It was first light, sunrise was breaking through, and the wind was close to exhausted, kicking up in spurts but settling again. The churning water was the same strange green-yellow of the day they came. Luis and I took a rope at each end of the boat and hauled it close to the landing. Cat eased in, clutching Treasure; then Alejandra slithered from the dock on her stomach with Cat guiding her legs. Cat pulled her close and they sat together, the waves licking up around them.

'Now you,' I said to Luis, and when he looked like he might argue, I inclined my head at the boat and waited. He threw his rope in and crouched low and jumped. 'Girl,' I said. She leaped. The boat yawed, and even though things were not going well for us and the weather was still uncertain I thought that this might be the last time a person would be on Wolfe Island and looked down the dock to the Watermen, at their long shadows streaming back.

I jumped in and started the motor. We drew away. Waves rose and fell about us. There were the old posts in the waves, Tobe's shanty with water swilling in its doorway, Shipleys on its knees, the Watermen, and further away my house, with the water rushing along its front like a river, like a train. It is silent in memory. The water rose above the porch and the door stoop. A shirt caught in a pomegranate tree pulled free and billowed across the watery land.

'The Watermen,' Luis said.

'They've done their job, kept us safe. They'll have to take their chances. I might come back for them some day.' No one said anything. The gaunt creatures stared after us and I couldn't tell what their sentiments might be.

I kept watch for Josh the whole journey. Once I saw a long dark shape drifting on the water's surface, rising to wave tops and falling leisurely off the other side. It was just driftwood, but a big piece, and I thought I might be sick. I told myself again that he might have made it even after his boat filled with water, if he had got far enough before the weather got bad. He was a good swimmer, Cat said, a good swimmer. We didn't discover his boat or his body between Wolfe Island and the main.

I did not want to know myself a murderer again, like I didn't want to know that death was real. I had known Josh, though, and felt something for him – not only rage – and his death (if he had died) was close. I imagined his terror when the boat began to sink. He wouldn't have panicked, though. There is not a day since that I haven't thought of him and I think I will never be free. Cat was quiet, holding Treasure tight beneath her coat, smoothing the top of her head where it peeked out, and pulling Alejandra near.

Then the island, one moment so clear, began to blur.

'Just look at it,' I said.

'Do you love it more than my mother?' Cat said.

'What a thing to ask.'

'It's what she thinks.'

'Never. Never. I'll make sure I tell her. But I do love it.'

Wolfe was a thin line when I looked again. A moment later it was gone. What do you do when everything falls apart? You gather up the people you love and the few things you hold dear, and all the rest? You let it fall away.

Blackwater was quiet when we puttered into harbour, the sort of quiet that follows drama or precedes it. On the eastern shore trees had been torn from the ground and their roots reared in the air. Three people standing nearby appeared dazed. One man in a thick pea coat stared from beneath his fisherman's cap as we berthed. We climbed onto the docks. He might have been counting us, marking us, remembering our details. People notice the unusual in small towns. I made sure not to look at him too hard, and wished Girl was less memorable. Her belly was round with her unborn pups; perhaps it was on account of them that she seemed so wary. I wanted his gaze to slide away. Already I was thinking of how to become invisible.

'We're going to walk like we know where we're going, like we've just arrived in town for the day, okay?' I said. 'Look chatty now, like you mean it. If any talking to them is required, I'll be the one doing it.'

'Where *are* we going?' Cat said. She pushed the blanket from Treasure's face, and she looked around as alert as could be.

'We can't talk here. Come on,' I said. We loaded ourselves up and came down the dock towards the men. There was no choice about that. They watched with undisguised interest.

'Things are awfully quiet,' I said when we were closer.

One of them said, 'Where you been? Everyone's gone. Evacuated for the hurricane. Not a soul in town. Storm surges were predicted.' And then another narrowed his eyes and peered past me at all the others. 'How come you didn't know?'

'Came from Wolfe. Power's out. Haven't heard a thing for days. You think this is a mess, the island's just about gone.'

'No kidding.' He shook his head. 'All of you?'

'Grandkids visiting.'

'All of them yours? You got papers?' He said it so casually, the same way a person might ask for the time.

'Papers? Is this what we've come to that I need papers for family? God help us all.'

'Just being careful. "Vigilance *from* all, *towards* all."' Evidently he was quoting something or someone. 'Just being a good citizen. Something you should remember.'

'I remember it every day, don't imagine I don't.' This was the moment when Hart or Doree, had they been nearby, would have put a hand to my sleeve and said, 'Now, Kitty.'

'I heard of you, I think. Crazy hermit lady, right?'

'Crazy is in the eye of the beholder, as is solitude, I've always thought. I'm in better shape than you.' He touched his hand to his bloodied cheek. 'Good luck with all that,' I said, nodding at the fallen trees.

'Sure.'

I thought we were done, but at the moment we passed him the man threw out a line to Luis: 'Hey, son, what's your name?'

'Lou Patrick,' Luis said politely and without a pause. 'And your name, sir?'

The man didn't answer.

When the harbour was behind us and we were walking up the sidewalk over a carpet of sodden brown leaves, with water and more leaves showering from branches overhead, I asked Luis, 'What are you thinking? You need to head north?'

'First my mother,' he said. 'We'll try to visit her – I know the name of the place. Then there's another town further north where they help. A staging post. People move on from there.'

'Okay,' I said.

Alejandra took his hand and pulled it hard. 'We're going to see Mama?' He looked down. 'How, Luis? How will we find Mama?'

'We'll find a way. We'll talk to some of the nice people I told you about. We'll look that place up and start. Okay?'

Luis turned from Alejandra and said, 'Thank you for all your help, Kitty.' He nodded at me in that formal way he had.

'Wait,' I said. 'You're saying goodbye?'

But he was looking at Cat by then. 'Thank you.' And he looked away with some effort.

Alejandra touched Girl's shoulder and sank her fingers deep into her fur. Everything seemed to show on her face. She'd lost almost everything, found something good, and it was being taken again. And now all she could do was blink away her tears, as if to say: I'm okay; it doesn't hurt.

'What are you saying? Where am I going without you? And if you think you're going anywhere without me . . .' Cat said to him. Treasure spluttered and Cat began stroking her back. 'What are you thinking? We have to stick together.'

Luis shook his head. 'You stay here. You'll have a place here, with your grandfather maybe. We'll be okay.' His face was still and his voice plain and grave.

Cat handed Treasure to me, a step and she was before Luis; she put her knuckles to his chest and pushed hard, and he had no choice but to brace and take her weight. 'Don't be so fucking ridiculous, Luis. All that noble crap. Don't pretend we're nothing. What kind of shit is that after all this time? My God, I'm the only one who knows the way. You'd get picked up in two seconds even if you had a car. You haven't got a paper between you.' She stopped pushing Luis. 'I can't believe you.'

Luis's face twisted. 'The main thing is that you're safe.'

Cat looked disgusted. 'Oh my God. No, that is not the main thing. The main thing is to get you two to safety before that asshole ruins your lives. Who's going to hurt me and Kitty? Listen to me. We went roughly the same route on all our runs north. Josh'll expect me to go the same way. I know where to go – where *not* to go. We need Kitty to help drive – I hope you will, Kitty – and we need you two to lie low. It's just another run, only we'll go the whole way. If you don't do that, you might as well hand yourselves in now. We'll get some money from my grandfather.'

'He won't be there,' I said. 'The evacuation. We need to start being careful. I have some money and an idea.'

'So you *will* come?' Cat said. 'You would be perfect cover.'

'There's something at Hart's, if he hasn't sold it.'

187

'You have a car?' Cat said. 'Thank God. Stealing them is a pain.'

'I hope so,' I said.

Town was eerie, almost sinister. The traffic lights changed on empty streets. With all the bags, it was a hard walk to Hart's. I peeked around the corner onto Talbot, half expecting to see Doree waiting over the way. A boat was upturned on the road, more trees had been torn from the ground, windows were shattered. Finally, the blinking lights and distant blare of emergency vehicles approached in the distance. We veered onto a back way. Torn branches and fallen trees and debris festooned the roads there too. There was a scurrying movement across a window in one house. Looters already.

We reached Hart's place. The yard was scumbled with fallen leaves, russet and yellow. The hydrangeas still needed pruning. Hart was a person of habit, and the garage key was in its old place; I raised the door, and there was the big Silverado concealed beneath its tarp. The house key was back in its old place, which I took as some sort of sign or overture, as if I might come by one day or night. We visited the inside bathroom. I didn't see the harm in that. It was cool and dim inside – neat, clean, and a little musty, like the den of an old dog. I wrote Hart a short note expressing the hope that he wouldn't report the car stolen since so much of his family was involved, best wishes, Kitty. It seemed unfriendly when I reread it, but I couldn't think what else to say. In the garage we pulled the tarp back from the Silverado. It lay before us like a splendid olden time thing, a medieval charger, or a making bolted together from a half-woke idea. The fuel it must use – well, I had some money put by, and if not for this, then what?

'What a beast,' Luis said. I opened the back and we piled our things in and got in the car. I pulled down the visor and the key fell in my lap, and when I turned it, the engine groaned once and roared into life.

Part II

Journeys

Chapter 15

WE HEADED NORTH. Sometimes Cat said, 'Not this road,' or, 'Turn right here.' That's how often she'd travelled this way. We looked out for highway patrols, thinking of what happened with Josh. Luis and Alejandra didn't know where their papers were – maybe at their old family home. They fell asleep behind us, their faces and bodies falling slack, and we went on. Cat sat upright and alert. Sometimes she glanced back.

It was twenty years since I'd driven the Silverado, but it came back to me. I like the dull rhythm of highways and roads. They're like a heartbeat, like the cars bring the road to life, like that. We travelled a haphazard route, often on unfamiliar roads: barns stood in cold ploughed fields; houses – some almost castles – had fallen on hard times and been left to the bank by the looks. Others floated on the fields as stately as galleons before the dark stain of woods.

Perhaps those people felt as safely becalmed in their worlds as I had in mine, their fenced yards keeping creation at bay. Yesterday I had been walking home from Shipleys; now I was driving a carload of frightened people, half of them runners, and I was acting like it was any other day. That's how fast my life had turned. My usual turn-off to visit the young prisoner came and went. I resisted the pull of it, only looking along its grey length.

We turned onto another road and passed a church with a signboard that said:

SERMON THIS SUNDAY:
'ON THE RIDICULOUSNESS OF IT ALL'

A removal order had been slapped across one corner.

'There's a church I could get into,' Cat said.

All that time Luis had been quiet. Then: 'My phone,' he said suddenly.

'Give it to me,' Cat said. Swiftly, she dismantled it, throwing parts from the window at intervals into standing water. She asked for my phone and laughed at the sight. 'That's a collectible, not a phone, Kitty. Does it even work?'

She disabled it, calm and certain in her judgements. 'You can keep it, but don't use it.' This was her world and she knew how to be resourceful in it.

In the mirror I watched Alejandra rest her hand on Girl's shoulder. 'Don't worry, Girl.' Girl turned her head to her, panting and showing her big white teeth. Alejandra murmured on then fell into silence and looked out of the windows again at the tattered fields, the wires looping the roadside, the ruined and abandoned buildings, their old skin and thin hair and half-blind eyes.

While we were moving there was no reason for anyone to notice us, but when we stopped later we would need somewhere quiet, a house at dusk and the concealment of wolf light.

We pulled in to a McDonald's towards the edge of a town, which I will not mention the name of here since people are still travelling through that way.

'Not the drive-through,' Cat said. 'They'll see in.'

I parked the car. Luis slumped in his seat and pulled Alejandra down. They had their hoods on, which I thought would make people notice them the more. I said as much to Cat and she just said it was the way of things now, it's what people had done for a long time, pulled their hoods up and shut out the world.

We pushed the door and went inside and right away it seemed a mistake. I thought a town this size would let us go unremarked, but it seemed every person turned to look at us. If Cat and I had hackles they would have risen, and if I could not hear a thrumming growl in their throats, I could feel it. The people sucked their straws and pushed the yellow food into themselves, and watched with greedy attention. What kind of person would stop and come in if they did not live hereabouts? Why not drive through? Were we new in town? Say this was their island, their Wolfe, and people just came in and docked and marched up the docks and had a good poke around, how would I feel? I'd have my gun in hand inside my pocket. I'd be watching. And my clothes, my heavy fur-collared leather jacket, my worn-out jeans, marked me out as an eccentric or a strange lady drug dealer.

Cat pointed a thumb at the restroom and we went in – 'So they think we're here to pee,' she whispered. She might get us through despite all.

Afterwards, we crossed the plain between tables and counter to place our order. We passed a half-bearded and scrawny man sitting on a table edge swinging his one flesh leg like a boy, though he would have been forty or a life-blasted thirty, his khakis rolled up to reveal a metal limb, clean as a butcher's hook. The walker at his side somehow put me in mind of a child's playground. He was jaunty and menacing, childlike and vicious. He narrowed his eyes and grinned his large armed-service teeth at Cat by way of flirtation. (Tobe's teeth were wonderful too, much good they did him.) This man was king here and this was his court. He was like Owen Jims at the Fisherman's Confederation Hut.

Cat gave our order.

'Something else with that?' the woman asked.

'That'll be it,' Cat said.

'And you, ma'am?' She looked at me directly, so I couldn't pretend I hadn't heard.

'I'm fine, thank you.'

It was like she woke up. She looked at me with all her attention. 'Excuse me?'

'Mmm?' I said.

'I couldn't help noticing your accent. If you don't mind my asking, where you from?'

'Not here. From south. Sutters.' I checked her name badge. 'Silvie.'

'I knowed you was from somewhere different. Ain't Sutters gone?'

'It is. And it's where I'm from.' I smiled.

Silvie stared at me, her eyes moving across my face as if I was some sort of apparition. 'You stopping here?'

'Passing through.'

'We get a lot of that.'

'You do?'

'Sure. People washed out mainly. You washed out?'

'Yes.'

'That's bad luck. How many of you?'

I felt some misgivings about her curiosity, and glanced at Cat to see what she might be thinking. She was frowning.

'Does it matter?' Cat said.

'Two of us,' I said.

'A lot of food for two.'

'Something for the dogs. They love a burger.'

'Well.'

I got my wallet out. I felt the prickling of people's gazes at my back, and didn't turn. It's a way of making yourself strong.

A supervisor called out, 'Silvie, some kind of hold-up?' and she said, 'No, sir,' and began to bustle, bagging up our things and letting us go. On the way out a chunky yellow-haired woman sitting at the door-side table said, 'Don't mind her.'

'I wasn't bothered,' I said.

'Just there's so many these days. Not enough jobs here as it is.'

'A few empty houses around.'

'Yep, that's so.'

'We're passing through,' I said. 'Not taking anything we're not paying for.'

'I hear you. Safe travels.'

We went outside. I couldn't get that not-belonging stench off me. People smelled it and saw it, and who wants to imagine such a thing could happen to them?

Outside, Girl was yipping her alarm call and her head was out of the window warning a beefy guy standing nearby, staring. Luis tried to pull her back without showing himself. Alejandra's face loomed at a window like a goldfish. The man's legs were spread wide and his hands were deep in the torn pockets of his jacket in a way I didn't care for, having deep pockets of my own. He had the wornest-looking boots I'd ever seen, the sides busting out and the toes almost through. I wondered what it was his job to kick. More scuff than surface, my mother would have said.

I said, 'Girl, stop that now.'

'Wolf?' he said, turning his weathered face.

'Malamute husky,' I said before he could start talking about the rights and wrongs of wolfdogs.

'That so.'

'It is, and we've got to be getting on. Got a way to go yet.'

'You got some company in there.'

'Grandchildren,' I said. 'If you'll excuse me.' I had to pass closer to him than I cared for to get to the car and he had a rank smell close to. He did not have any scars but he was the kind of person in whom that seemed surprising. We got in the car and I locked it. The man stepped closer and through the window I watched his mouth move. He rapped the window.

'Hey,' he said. 'Hey, I'm talking to you, ma'am.'

I let the window down two inches. 'We're heading, mister.'

'I want to see their faces.'

'Whose?'

He jerked his head at the back seat.

'My grandkids? What for?'

'Just making sure.'

'We don't have to show you anything. Just step back now. Wouldn't want to hurt you.'

'They're not yours.'

Maybe it was Luis or maybe it was Alejandra who lowered the window. Suddenly Girl's entire head and a good part of her shoulders were outside the car and she was snarling and snapping. The man jerked back.

'That's a fucking wolfdog,' he shouted.

'Quit it, Girl,' Luis said.

I pulled out and I did not care too much about his toes, and we were out of there in no time. I saw him in the mirrors shouting and pointing his finger at us. Oh Lord, what a mess it was. But we got away. Girl sat panting, looking like she'd seen him off and was pleased about it.

'Alejandra,' Cat said. I glanced around. She was shaking all over and had her hands clapped over her eyes.

'It's okay,' I said. 'We're all okay. Girl's there. Feel Girl next to you? She was looking out for you.'

She nodded and smudged the tears away. When I looked again after rounding the next curve Alejandra and Girl were leaning against each other. Cat passed the food around. The smell of the cooked meat and hot oil and coffee was homey and gradually things began to feel better.

We continued on through a couple more towns and turned off the highway when it began to get dark, and drove down an empty road. The light had turned strange, glowing and filling the space above the road between long stands of tall black pines.

We wanted somewhere not too close to the road, but the places we saw made us think that there might be something better further on and we kept going until we began to see faint stars pricking the sky. Alejandra had curled up to sleep with Girl as her pillow. One good thing: in that light we could not see the houses' brokenness. The road narrowed and on either side, hard up against the road, wide ditches were filled with standing water and cattails that were tall enough that nothing could be seen beyond. There could be no turning on the road until we came to a fork or a driveway or a set-in.

A mile or so further and we found it: a short bridge across the ditch, and a gravel drive between long arms of fence. Further along the wooded drive we came to a white house, which loomed in the thickening dark. We felt the cold breath of the trees when we stopped and got out of the car, the doors loud in the enormous quiet. It was like a memory of a home. That was enough for me. It was the first such place we stayed at and it might be that I took more note of it than the other places we stopped in. We climbed the steps to the empty porch.

It was locked. Luis went around the side and prised open a window – there was a screeching of tired wood in its frame – and came through to let us in. All we had was my phone and Cat's to light the way. It wasn't so bad inside. There was a hallway with doors to either side and a few leaves that crunched and scuffed at our feet, and a half-damp smell like the outside had come in some way but not taken over entirely, and a whiff of dead animal thrown in too. Wallpaper peeled away in buckling tentacles. The owners on some whim had chosen a meadow design with daisies and fawns nestled in circles of – I raised my phone to see better – dry grass, as if there weren't enough of that outside. It needed airing but it was too cold to let a breeze through. The light held some of the darkness at bay, though it pressed in softly, close around and between us, separating us from each other. There was a skittering, something small, but enough to make Alejandra squeak and bury her head into my front so she had to walk backwards while I walked forward holding her there. We passed a bathroom with its toilet pulled clear off its base, and a kitchen with its fittings torn out and the ceiling fallen and a tap hanging loose. Without a word we turned back and looked through the other doors and came to a room that smelled drier than the others. It had a fireplace and an old sofa pulled up to the cold stone hearth.

'Wood,' Luis said, and headed out again, leaving Alejandra

behind. Cat looked after him and back to Alejandra. She gave me Treasure, who was sleeping, and left the room.

'Well,' I said, 'this is an adventure.'

'I don't like it,' Alejandra said.

'Get busy, that's the way to deal with it. Doing something helps you forget your troubles.'

'We could sweep?'

'There you go. Think about what's important right now.'

'Something for Girl to eat?'

'That's the way. Good girl.'

By and by we put a little of the house to rights, found a broom outside the back door and swept the living room and hallway by phone light. I laid Treasure on her quilt in the corner of the sofa and built a fire with the leaves we had swept up and some wood and kindling from a heap that Luis and Cat had found. Things began to seem not so bad. The quilts we'd brought, draped over every part of the room to air and warm, made it seem almost cosy. The water from the kitchen tap, after a groan and rush of water of unappetising colour, cleared and tasted okay. I filled a saucepan with it and rested it on the fire coals and it began to steam. The yellow light of flames scattered across the room. We were like cave people; a little warmth and something hard at our backs was enough to make us feel safe, except perhaps from our thoughts, but I should not generalise on that score. Even the house's emptiness was reassuring. Who else at such a time of day would pass by at a moment's notice? It seemed as old as time and in this way I felt that life, which is transitory, would continue in the same way. Food, shelter, warmth, safety; what else could a person need? Love was a luxury. Hart would be welcome company in this room. I would have liked to feel his hand in mine or to rest my head on his chest. I'd sent a boy alone onto a heaving grey sea. I imagined the boat failing and wallowing, and the boy striking out as solitary as could be. It was a lonely thought, a lonely cold way to die, worse than for Harrison Andover. A person like me did not deserve love.

Luis and Cat dragged another chair in, and went upstairs to see if there was anything else worth bringing down, as if we might stay here for a while and see what could be made of this place. I mapped the place in my mind, counted the rooms on the first floor and what was likely to be upstairs, one for each of us, and I even thought about a stove, and whether getting the power connected would be a problem or cause suspicion, just for a while. Papers – they would be the problem. Well, cooking over a fire wasn't so bad. A trivet to hang things on would be needed. So my mind went. Presently Luis and Cat returned. They were quiet and when I said the house could be fixed up a little and maybe we could stay a few days, just lie low, they didn't say anything when I thought they might and I didn't like to ask any more with Alejandra there, thinking about her mother and her sister and whether she'd ever see them again.

Thank fortune I had packed some bread and butter and vegetables – carrots, onions, potatoes, the last peas in their drying pods. Shelling them gave Alejandra something to do. She gave the empty pea pods to Girl, who nibbled them politely and dropped them between her paws. She stared at the fire, her ears pricked, moving at the sounds the house made, and whined and went and scratched at the door. Alejandra let her out and came back. I hoped Girl had not gone to whelp her litter. Her time was getting near by my calculation, and what would we do then? We'd have to stay still for a few days. Girl wouldn't let us near those pups.

I chopped the vegetables on a plate and tipped them into the water and when they'd cooked through I mashed the potato against the side of the saucepan to break it up and thicken the broth and added a little salt and it was done.

From the darkness there came a screaming, shrill and womanish. I looked at once for Cat, but she was there on the sofa near Luis, her face stark in alarm. Alejandra was on the edge of the sofa looking like she was about to scream herself.

'Girl!' I ran to the door and down the hall and outside, the door bouncing behind. I heard people run after me, all of us hurtling into the open mouth of darkness, the ink-black trees, the soft needle fall, with nothing to guide me but that dreadful sound coming closer. 'Girl,' I called again. 'Here, Girl.'

The screaming subsided and then low crooning growls began to pulse into the night. I lit up my phone and held it aloft and moved the light around, and there she was at the base of a pine, its scaled trunk strangely white behind and her mottled black and insubstantial as fog, crouched over a creature, biting and squeezing it in her mouth to make sure of its death. Her eyes glittered, uncannily fixed in the unsteady light. She growled at me, which made me stumble as I halted my headlong rush. And then Luis and Alejandra were there.

'Girl,' Alejandra said. 'Poor Girl, what is it?'

Just in time I grabbed her arm as she went past, swinging her back. 'Stay here. She doesn't want company. She's caught something. We need to leave her be.' Girl continued her biting and tearing, taking the furred creature apart. 'She'll be back when she's ready, when she's done.'

'What is it?' Alejandra said at my side.

'Squirrel maybe.'

Girl's soft song of satisfaction and warning was unnerving. Luis held his light high so it shone on her. We could see the red about her mouth. 'Bigger than that,' he said.

'Well, never mind.' I started back, with my hand on Alejandra's shoulder so she had to come with me. I felt her reluctance to turn from the sight, and her revulsion in the shiver that she gave. She looked over her shoulder. Girl had surprised her and it made her uneasy.

We left the door open and returned to our meal, dipping cups into the soup and drinking from them. Then we took turns holding turkey patties over the coals using a toasting fork that hung at the fireside.

Girl slunk in later, head down between her shoulders, as if she was still stalking her prey. She did not seem one of us, neither approaching nor really taking us in. She sat by the fire apart from us all and commenced to clean herself, licking the blood from her paws where she had held the creature down. There was blood about her mouth too. The thick fur about her neck and shoulders looked rough and yanked around, as a forest does after a storm. Alejandra watched her and looked at me as if she was asking a question. I could see that she understood without being told that Girl was not one of us yet. 'In a while you can pet her again,' I said.

'I don't want to.'

'You will. It'll fade from your mind. You just need a little time. You both do.'

Much later I stood by the fire and Girl touched her nose to my hand. 'Hey, Girl,' I said. And touched the back of her head and felt down her neck. There were long hard dried clumps in there, of blood that had run down the fur and stuck it together. So the creature had given something back before it died. Her muzzle was scratched too and there was a gouge over one eye. She'd been lucky.

We were tired by then, and person by person – Cat taking Alejandra – we went out to relieve ourselves behind whatever bush we found. Cat changed Treasure and fed her and we chose our places to sleep: Alejandra sandwiched between Luis and Cat, and quite late Girl came and lay alongside me. And so we passed the night.

It was still on the dark side when I woke next morning, shadowy dawn just stirring the sky, and the trees separating from the dark mass of night without yet revealing their colours. Alejandra was snoring softly and she was curled on her side with her hands to her mouth, like she was praying. Cat and Luis's hands formed an archway above, barely touching as if they had gone to sleep clasping them or were reaching for each other in the night. I pushed back my quilt and stepped quietly to the door and eased it ajar. Girl came with me on her soft hunting feet. We went outside and came back in, still moving softly, and seeing the stairs before me, and wondering what might be up there and whether there might be anything useful, moved upwards through the guts of the creaking house. Near the top, I felt a prickling misgiving. The smell was worse here, bad meat. Girl faltered at my side.

It was not a big house. There was a landing up there with a window looking out over the woodland and the clouded dawn and a short corridor with doors off it. In the first room, the door already open, was an old bed with a curved bedhead and tall posts of brightly varnished pine and a sagging mattress halfway across the floor, as if it had run out of puff while leaving. The other doors were closed. In one, a dark jacket hung in an opened cupboard. The next had another bed, a packing crate by its side, a bong and burned-out cigarettes and ash that had overflowed a saucer and scattered to the floor. A patch of its aqua-coloured carpet was scorched black and I wondered if that was the smell that I didn't care for and which was making Girl uneasy. By then, I think I was hoping that was all it was. There was just one more door, and I wish now that I had turned away from it. Girl wanted me to, I know that. She whimpered and hung back. Anyway, I had to know by then. Curiosity can be an evil curse of a thing.

'Okay, Girl.' I opened the door. It was a pitiful thing, which I felt as much as saw, being so overcome by the smell and the horror of it. I retched into the crook of my elbow and pulled back. A window, a mattress beneath, a thing, a person curled beneath a blanket. The blanket moved and I thought the person was merely ill, but a rat shot out and disappeared through the fireplace. I grabbed Girl's ruff before she could lunge, and looked: grey hair like dead grass, stubble, the body sunken, the carpet dark all around. His yellow teeth were bared and the flesh was gnawed and the bones beginning to show. The room stank of everything you could imagine, and we had spent a night below. There was a plate and a cup by the body. I backed out, not wanting to turn from it, to feel death at my back, and pulled the door closed. Girl was waiting at the top of the stairs, wanting to run.

'Wait.' I turned back and pushed the door narrowly ajar.

Cat was dragging herself from her bed when I returned – Luis had gone out for wood, she whispered – and Alejandra was moaning and stirring.

'We should get going,' I said to Cat.

Her eyes moved across my face; she knew what I had seen.

'Yes,' she said, and she put her hand to Alejandra's shoulder, very gently. 'Come on, honey. Let's get you up now.'

Alejandra rubbed her hand to her eyes and sat up. Luis came back with an armload of wood and we stoked up the fire and boiled the water again.

'Will we see Mama today, Luis?'

Luis shrugged. 'Maybe. We'll see – if she's where she's supposed to be, we might be lucky.'

Luis made coffee, Cat and I put things in the car, Alejandra and Girl went poking about in the garden. She came back with two russet apples from a tree down the back.

'Any more there?' I asked.

'I can look.'

I found her a bag and she went out and came back with five more. Something or someone must have pollinated them. Maybe it wasn't so long ago the people left. They might have meant to come back for that old man. I made sure to leave the back door open, to let every spirit depart from that house that wished to do so. I'm not sure I believe in that sort of thing. Still.

That was the first place we stayed.

Chapter 16

WE TREATED GIRL with caution for a day or so after. She kept her distance and waited. She was not what everyone had thought she was. I knew the feeling of mistrust. It would take time for her to be Girl again to them, rather than the wild creature we'd seen crooning in the darkness. Cat drew back from her, though, and was careful never to leave Treasure near Girl. I understood. We look after the thing we love most, that we are designed to protect. Cat was so certain she'd be able to keep Treasure safe. It's not so easy when your child sees the world beyond your arms. But they are what they are too. What if they don't care to be kept safe in the way you have in mind? I had only to think of Claudie setting her life on other tracks than mine, or to look at the way Cat had broken free of her parents (or Josh from his), to know that. Sometimes we fail, as I did with my children. I couldn't help thinking, then, of the young prisoner on death row, wondering whether someone – or life itself – had failed him, or he had seen some excitement that he couldn't resist? What thoughts filled his mother's mind? Did she wonder what she might have done better, as I did with Tobe and Claudie? I didn't know a thing about her, but sometimes she didn't feel so far away.

*

At a gas station in a nearby town we stopped to fill the tank and ask for directions.

'Don't see many of them round these days,' the till lady said, nodding out of the window at the Silverado. She might have been a grandmother, a different style of one from me, cushiony, comfortable, powdery-cheeked, but she was nice.

'Fortune to run.'

'Yuh. You're the first millionaire through this morning.'

I let out a short hoot. 'That tank should just about get us through to the next town.'

'Where you heading?'

I told her the name of the town near the prison where Luis and Alejandra's mother was incarcerated.

'A two-tank journey I'd say.' She chuckled at her joke.

I asked her the route and she showed me an old map she had tucked away under the counter. 'Here.' She shut the cover and pushed it across. 'You take it. Cluttering things up. Roads have changed anyway. If it's any use to you.' Someone came in behind me.

'Thank you,' I said and she gave a little nod, as if she'd embarrassed herself now, overstepped some mark.

It was a fair way to the prison, as she'd said, a whole morning's drive east. Cat spelled me once. Luis and Alejandra sat behind, as usual. It was easier for them to hide there, Cat said. She was right about that. The first police we saw were flagging people in at a roadside stop ahead. I slowed right down. 'On the floor quick,' Cat said without looking back. 'Both of you. Put everything on top.' They moved fast. Cat reached back with a couple of coats from the floor and they disappeared. Girl wanted to join them. I told her to sit still, and she did. It sounds slow, written, but was a whirl at the time, believe me.

Treasure squawked and Cat pulled her top up to feed her. It was a good distraction when it came to our turn to open the window. The trooper peered in and then stepped back fast.

'Excuse me, ma'am,' he said.

Cat shrugged and smiled. 'She's a hungry one.'

Girl filled the window as she stared out. I thought the trooper at my window might mention her, but he merely complimented me on the truck, asked where we were headed, tipped his cap and sent us on our way. I was calm at the time, but shaking afterwards when Luis and Alejandra came out all flushed and their hair mussed. Luis's manner reminded me of the way he was the day they arrived on Wolfe, when he was running and felt danger coming behind. It looked like it had been a game for Alejandra. She practised diving down and covering herself as fast as she could. 'Time me,' she said. 'Time me again.' It seemed like we'd got off lightly until the shrillness in her voice made me look back. Her eyes were bright with waiting tears. 'Kitty, again, again.'

'Luis, your sister,' I said. He pulled her onto his lap. 'Sweetheart, listen to me,' I said. 'No one will get you. I won't let them. I'll get them first. I promise you that, do you hear?' I looked from mirror to road and back.

She stared at me in the mirror. 'But I *was* fast,' she said.

'So fast. No one could catch you.' Finally she quit her game.

Cat told me one or two stories from when she and Josh were 'railroading clients'. She usually concluded by saying 'assholes' or 'fucking assholes', meaning any person they came up against.

'You miss it,' I said.

'No, I don't. It was not the excitement. That was Josh.' Treasure, sitting on Cat's lap, grabbed Cat's hand and gnawed at a finger. Cat stroked her cheek. 'It was doing something because it was right and the opposite was wrong. It was interesting, though.'

Outside, it was turning to winter before our eyes. Frozen rain splintered on the windows. It made me think of my mother, of a story of hers that is part of me now. I don't remember a time I didn't know it. She told it to me in snatches, as if it was a piece of art or a making that she added to and looked at and put a little more on, bit by bit, as I got older. Perhaps in the beginning it was no more than: 'My mother died one cold winter when I was just a girl.'

'My God, it's freezing,' Cat said when we got out to stretch our legs around mid-morning. Our breath sent more white into the world, standing stark and disappearing, and driving flecks of ice stung our cheeks. Girl went romping and bounding into the trees, though slower now she was so heavy with pups.

'Cold,' I said on my return. 'This is nothing.' We got back into the truck. The falling ice needles grew larger and began to slow in their descent, the flakes drifting like spiderlings across a meadow.

As I got older I asked my mother more, I remember that, and perhaps my imagining has added to it so it's not clear which parts are true, or which happened, which is not the same thing. It is all true to my mind. I can't remember now how much of it I passed on to Claudie – some of it, I think. I hope enough for her to remember. I suppose I thought of it then also because of the cold of the first house we stayed in and the dead man and the ground at the roadside turning white with snow. I squatted and began to form handfuls of snow into balls.

'What are you doing?' Cat asked.

'Making a snow lantern with the first snow.'

'Because?'

'Superstition. To light the way home for travellers in a storm probably. Makes sense. Like putting a lamp in a window.'

They made snowballs and passed them to me to place. I built a low igloo with chinks to let the air in. The soft snow matted on my mittens. When it was done I eased one of the bottom snowballs out a little. 'Now a light.' A phone flashlight would be something, at a pinch. 'Cigarette lighter in the car,' I said. I got a handful of twigs burning and poked them carefully inside, with a few more sticks on top, and pushed the snowball back in place. The snow glowed pale yellow and the light flickered. It came alive from nothing.

'Water is perilous in all its forms,' I said. 'Never forget that. Something my grandfather used to say to my mother. She passed it on to my sister and me. It's your job to remember now.' Even if water did not now freeze as it used to (usually for shorter times, and the ice not as thick or strong), the story of my grandmother dying still mattered. It meant more than it said and its meaning seemed to change for each person. Some stories have weight in them and require a voice. So I told it to them, and have included it in my notebook for interest's sake.

When my grandmother died

Years ago, one icy winter, my grandmother was caught on snow-weighted ice-bound Wolfe Island, her home, while in labour. Things were going badly for her. No seaplane would chance a landing because of the wind and the building ice, there was no rescue helicopter at that time, and the only boat powerful enough for such icy waters having been frozen in at the docks, the strongest men on the island, my grandfather among them, went down with pickaxes and shovels and crowbars and any other bit of equipment that they felt might work to try to free it. Their white breath hung in the air. Despite the cold, their work of raising and driving their tools made them sweat and their clothes steam. Their tools chimed and bounced against the hard ice, and its cold smell, clean and sharp, in other circumstances almost delicious, began to rise around them. Chunks of ice flew and cut them on their high-coloured faces until the blood mingled with their sweat and caught in their stubble and gave them a wild and dangerous appearance above their soft fur collars and thick plaid jackets. They were mad with it and cursing, and their shouts and grunts travelled inland quite some distance, my mother said.

She heard it all from the gate, including her father's shouts of desperation and urgency. She stood and waited in the bitter cold – too frightened by her mother to stay in the house – for her father to run back to see how her mother was faring before stumbling and sliding back down the icy paths to the harbour, waiting for fate to have its way and doing all he could to prevent it. But as fast as they chipped a hole through one section of ice and the piles of ice shards were shovelled away, the ice formed again behind them. Not a mother on the island would let a child close to look, much less help, or they might have kept the dark water moving freely about the boat so it could get away. But what mother would allow such a thing when everyone knew of people who had slipped into the icy holes made for oyster tonging and who were not seen again until spring, if ever.

Sometimes I couldn't sleep for the thought of that moment: the fall into water, dark from above, green from below (I imagined), the thick ice as lovely as my mother's chrysoprase ring – that soft opaque green which was also somehow clear because of the purity of its tone. That light would be the last thing I would see before the cold and the water poured into my lungs. Would I lift my hands to that under-surface, or goldfish for a pocket of air? Would time be slow or fast? Would I see people above foreshortened, obliterating the light as they looked down? And would a person looking down see a shadowy shape, me, beneath the ice? I thought of the currents below and where they might take a body, and in bed left my arms and legs uncovered until they were icy cold to the touch, seeking an epiphany. I always weakened before enlightenment arrived, to save my precious flesh.

After my grandmother died the same cold that had prevented her rescue now preserved her. Since the ground was frozen, her body was placed in the family's storeroom, where hams and meats and sausages and dried fish had been hung, and where root vegetables had been stored in darkened bins, and dried fruits, sweet apples, corn and grains had been kept clean and dry for the long cold winters of centuries. (It's gone now, demolished on account of the sad memories it held for them all. I knew where it had been, though; there was a square depression in the land, clearly marked in dry weather. I used to stand in it, as if in a half-dug grave. One warm summer day I gathered my courage and lay there, draping a silk scarf over my eyes to hold off the sun.)

My mother, who was eight at the time of her mother's death, would creep out, her boots creaking on the snowed pathway, and she would lift the little hook latch on the weathered door, icy on her bare fingers, and go in and take her mother's cold hand and stroke it and hold it to her cheek to see if she might be able to coax her back to life. It was dark in there, not true night dark, but dark just the same, with only a milky light drifting from the high-set four-pane window. The shadows were blue in the corners and a darker blue beneath the bench that her mother lay on, as if she was suspended above the grave that would be her final resting place. The sun cast a pale lemonade light over everything as it rolled the rim of the horizon, glowing through the winter basketwork of the wooded lot that edged their house at the time (trees long dead now of salt, or beetle damage, or drowned and felled and burned), and being so low it illuminated a path across the room above my grandmother's dead body and struck the opposite wall in a clear patch of light intersected by what looked like the mark of a cross from the window's form. Jesus was with her, someone said when they saw this sign, as they called it, when they'd come to pay their respects. I would suppose my grandfather didn't agree, though his response isn't recorded, since he declined to set foot in a church again.

'She didn't look so different. Just like she was taking a nap,' my mother told me once. 'She *was* cold, though. I took out one of her quilts – the pink and red maple leaf one, you know – and put it on her to keep her warm. She really looked like she might be asleep. No one believed me.' Her voice was wistful, as if she wondered yet why the quilt had not revived her mother, and whether one more day or a little heat might have done the trick. 'I thought if I could get everyone to believe at the same time and to pray for it, it would come true. I prayed for a miracle. Fishermen come back to life every couple of generations, though it is unusual, and in different circumstances. Drownings.'

It seemed an old-fashioned way to die. As long ago as it was, it was still uncommon. It's a beautiful old quilt. I suppose

215

it was too fine to bury or to throw away, one of her best, people said, and she was a known quilter and needlewoman. I still have it, but not in my room. (If I ever get back to the island and it hasn't washed away, I'll rescue it.) It has something of a blue shadow hanging about it still.

I visited my grandmother's grave often and always left a posy of flowers – red and pink like the quilt. The baby never had a name. There was just my grandmother's name, Suzannah Hawke, on the gravestone, and the dates, and below that *BABY* with the date of its birth (if it was born in the end, which my mother could not remember or had never known) and of its death. For a long time there were just that gravestone and the gravestone of my own parents remaining. My mother didn't want her bones or my father's or her parents' getting mixed up with other folks', so I did not permit their removal during the relocation. Let them wash away if that was what the world meant for them. I felt different when they began to show – and made some arrangements. I must tell Claudie where they are.

When I finished the story, leaving out some of my own wondering about it and other matters, Cat and Luis and Alejandra were quiet. Snow was as thick and slow as feathers now, landing softly on the windscreen and being wiped away.

'I think my mother told me about this,' Claudie said. 'About her great-grandmother dying on the island. She said it wasn't going to happen to her and it wasn't going to happen to me. She said it was irresponsible.'

'It must have frightened her. I didn't know that. She's a practical woman.'

'Is she? I never thought of her like that.' Cat said. 'I never saw any graves. I would have taken flowers.'

'The place where they used to be is mostly underwater now – the church too,' I said. I didn't mention that once, passing that way, I'd come upon a skull peering towards the sky, and another time what looked like a leg bone washed up on the shore. 'My grandfather and my parents – your great-grandparents, that is – were the only ones left for a long time. They moved everyone else when the sea reached them. That was before my mother died. People didn't like to see the bones poking out so they took them to Blackwater. It was part of the package when everyone left. "Documented removal and relocation of all buried human remains." What a fuss there was. My mother was superstitious. They muddled the bones, which she said would confuse their spirits, and there'd be no end of trouble after that. I've always wondered about her people, whether they'd been on the island for longer than she said or knew.'

'Where are their bones?'

'I got a private contractor to move them and the grave-stones. All the Wolfe folk are lined up as neat and straight as if they're about to have their photograph taken. Chudleighs from the north end muddled with Jimses from the south, which they would have had something to say about if they were still living, that I can tell you. I got them to put the stones for our family the way they'd been on the island, turning into each other, sort of cosy, like they're having a chat.'

'I don't like bones,' Alejandra said.

'I remember that.' I turned the wipers up. 'Not everyone does. They don't mean any harm. It's people do that, not treating each other right. *Some* people. The Watermen were just looking out for us. Guardian angels. We could use some of them now.'

'What are angels?'

'Beings of protection everyone needs more of, wolfdogs *and* people.'

I would tell them about our wolfdog cub Baby another time; it would be too much for one morning. If you call something Baby it seems like you're asking for trouble. Maybe if we'd called her Lady or Madam or something like that she might have survived. She was like a baby. She liked to be carried, which is not usual for a wolfdog. She licked our cheeks with her pink tongue and made the children shriek. She was a dangerous combination of wicked, funny and sweet. Claudie and Tobe would make beds for her and fight over her and give her treats for no reason, and I let them because of the rareness of them sharing something. It spoiled her. She didn't learn any sense or pay attention to us. She thought rules were nothing to do with her and that was our fault. It was winter and just the once she walked out on thin ice and broke through. It wasn't even deep enough for her to drown – just enough to hold her there while the cold did its work. We were inside and didn't hear a sound.

She turned from her wolfish nature because of us. I have taken care since not to make the same mistake. A wolfdog is not a person; bending their nature is a sin, I believe. My mother used to say I was a quarter wolf at least. She told Hart my nature would not change. He said that suited him fine and my mother said, 'As long as you know, as long as your eyes are open.'

I didn't tell the story of Baby and that was a lesson lost and someone would have to suffer again to learn it. I will try to tell it if it comes to mind another time.

The sign to the prison came into view then and took all my attention.

Chapter 17

EVERY TIME I see a prison sign it feels as if officers might make a mistake and detain me, believing me to be someone else, and as if there's no choice but to obey. And now I had done something wrong and deserved to be in prison. I could almost imagine they knew about Andover and Josh and were waiting for me with a verdict and sentence, and that gave me a sick feeling.

There is a silence around a prison that is hard to understand or explain. They hollow something out of a place, as if a bomb has gone off and every creature has disappeared apart from the ones that have been hit, the ones with their wings burned. This one reminded me of the one Hart and I passed by once, with its double layers of mesh fencing, the barbed curls of their tops hunching inwards like buzzards over meat. Orchards ran alongside to the south in their own high-fenced compound, which in summer would be swarming with inmates, all of them waiting to be sent somewhere they didn't know any longer, if they ever had, no doubt some of them doing the work they used to be paid for. We drove to the visitor car park. Security cameras were all around.

'I'll ask,' I said. No one replied.

There was a low grey concrete and metal box room bolted to a concrete base, and a place where visitors had to make themselves known, a grille and thick glass that was foggy and scratched, and a small, dented microphone grille to talk into. A sign said: *Attacks on government property are prohibited and punishable with a fine.* I peered in and spoke to the woman.

'They the inmate's kids?' she asked, nodding at the truck.

'No,' I said. 'She's an old friend.'

'What time's your appointment?'

'We don't have one. I didn't know we needed one. Is there any other way?'

'No cancellations today, ma'am. Could put you on a list?' I told her okay and she looked at her screen and there was a faint tapping. 'Name?' she asked and I gave her one, which I will not mention here. 'Address?'

'No address. We've just sold up, moving north.'

She tapped a few keys. 'Phone number?'

'I lost it.'

'Ma'am,' she said, 'how would I contact you?'

'What if I came back tomorrow? Would you put me on the list for then?'

'Tomorrow?'

'What number would I be for tomorrow if there's a cancellation? What chance would I have?'

'You would be —' she looked at her screen again '— number seventeen.'

'Excuse me?'

'Your place on the list, ma'am. You asked.'

'Have you ever had that many cancellations?'

'No, ma'am.'

'I see. What's the wait for an appointment?'

'Six weeks.'

'Why—'

'Ma'am?'

I looked at the sign, the scratched screen and the dented microphone plate. 'Thank you,' I said.

'You're welcome.'

I returned to the car. 'Six weeks,' I said. 'That's the wait. I'm sorry for that. Should have thought. I had no idea.'

'We can't see Mama?' Alejandra asked.

'In six weeks. Not until then. I'm so sorry.'

Luis put his arm around her, curved his hand right round until he was stroking her forehead.

I drove, trying not to think of the cameras, wishing I'd covered the plates, listening to Luis's soft murmur, Alejandra's hiccupping breaths. At my side Cat held Treasure against her front. 'We should get her a what-do-you-call-them – baby carrier,' I said.

'Yes,' Cat said and stroked Treasure's hair over her temple, the top of her head, all the soft places of her skull.

The road curled away and ten minutes later, maybe more, over the crest of a forested hill we came to a straight section of highway and a road crew truck and a band of prison inmates in bright orange picking rubbish from the wooded roadside. A guard in the truck cabin nodded to some music, a booted foot up tapping the windscreen; another stood on the tray holding a gun. They looked bored, all of them, and we slid by with hardly a one looking up.

Luis lunged forward. 'Stop, go back. That was Mama. Mama, I'm pretty sure.'

'Mama,' Alejandra screamed and in the mirror I watched her kneel on the seat and peer out the rear window. She screamed again, 'Mama,' and scrambled through and banged at the window.

'Go back?' I said, gripping the wheel tight. 'How? What would the guards do? They'll see you then.'

'We have to,' Luis said. 'So she knows we're okay.'

'Kitty, Kitty,' Alejandra pleaded. 'Turn around, Kitty.'

I pulled in and we cooked up a scheme that we thought might work; it was at least worth a try. And this is what we did. It was a sorry story, don't think I don't know it. We doubled back and parked a little further down from them and Alejandra pretended to pick something from the ground. Luis couldn't leave the car, we decided on that: too risky, too easy for him to be shot. That was hard for him, though he agreed. Alejandra and I walked along the concrete shoulder towards them.

Casually, the guard on the truck tray eased his rifle around and aimed it at us. 'Ladies,' he said. I tucked Alejandra close up behind so she was peering out from under my arm. Her eyes were huge. 'Stop right there.' The guard jumped down, his belly giving a soft bounce, and hitched his pants up snug beneath it and smoothed his plump fingers over his buttons. 'Show me your hands.' The inmates bunched up like fish do when something big is sweeping around.

I held my hands up. 'The little girl here saw one of your prisoners drop something when we were passing. Can we give it to her?'

'Oh yeah? Which one?'

Alejandra pointed.

'You drop anything, three-eight-nine?'

A thin black-haired woman looked up warily and shook her head, and looked again, seeing Alejandra. That poor woman. It was not kind, what we were doing.

'I guess,' the guard said.

Alejandra began walking and I followed, not many steps. Then they were standing close together. 'Mama,' Alejandra whispered.

The woman spoke to her fast. Alejandra blinked very rapidly, which I knew meant she was getting upset, but she managed a few words in reply. She needed Girl at her side. I put my hand on her shoulder. Alejandra held out the thing we had thought of.

'Wait, show me that,' the guard said, coming up. Alejandra held out the little hairclip that her mother had given her a long time ago. The guard took it and looked closely and threw it to the ground in disgust.

'It's a kid with a hairclip,' I said.

His fingers moved on his rifle. I should have stayed quiet. I gave Alejandra a tiny nudge, no more than a little pressure. He would not have seen it.

Alejandra picked the clip up and gave it to her mother.

'Thank you,' she said, looking at it, stroking the head of the Virgin Mary and a rose and a small cross and a sweet skull all lined up and the thumb of the hand that held it. 'Oh yes. I would be sorry to lose this. My daughter gave it to me.'

'Hold it there,' the guard said, his glance moving from one to the other. I hadn't realised until we came close how alike they were, mother and daughter: their high cheeks, the kink in their hair, the little turn at the outer corner of their eyes, the way they both blinked so rapidly in this moment. 'Okay. I'm going to ask something. I want you to think carefully before you answer. Understand?'

Alejandra's mother nodded.

'Do you know this kid?'

'I have never seen her before in my life,' she said.

I curled my fingers about Alejandra's shoulder. She was as stiff as a board, vibrating, just holding herself together.

'Thank you for stopping for me. I would not like to lose it,' she said to Alejandra, and to me, 'Thank you for your kindness.'

The sound of the truck cabin door opening came from behind us. 'Everything okay back there?'

'Just moving on, isn't that so, ladies?' the guard said.

I was obedient, but Alejandra lingered and I think she might have said something else to her mother, and the guard might have said something to one or other of them, but I didn't hear it. Alejandra's mother turned with the guard and they walked away towards some trees. Alejandra came to my outstretched hand and held it tightly and there was nothing for us to do but leave.

I drove blindly after that, not thinking of direction, just of Alejandra and Luis white-faced behind me. We weren't going home; nonetheless, some homing instinct sent me towards the coast and after an hour or two we came to the beginning of marshland, and dead and dying pines standing stark and white-trunked and bereft of branches and almost any green, and entered it. It was a serpentine road that slithered along the flatness and canted around bends through slow-moving cattails and shivering grasses at marsh edge and more pine forests, some living more or less, and stretches of water like lakes, utterly still and reflecting the pines and sky above so the water appeared black and deep. There was no shoulder to the road: just two narrow lanes, then water-filled ditches and then endless marsh.

We came upon a truck with a big-headed white-and-tan dog sitting bolt upright on the tray. Everything slowed from the surprise of finding it and the lone dog, and us watching and the dog impassively watching us. Girl was quiet at the sight. She and the dog stared at each other. I could not discern their mood. There was not a sign of a person on that stretch of road and no way for them to leave the road except into marsh, yet the grasses along that stretch were not broken and the reeds stood tall and the line of them was unblemished and we saw not a soul and the road stretched and stretched before us and behind. But even despite that dog, which I would not wish to see any harm befall, I didn't stop to see if help might be needed. I slid by and pulled away and was half surprised that no gunshot came and no bullet hit the car. I didn't turn in case it would provoke such an action, as if there was no difference between a turned head and a pulled trigger. 'Don't look back now, honey,' I said to Alejandra, and she was so well trained to flight and terror by then that she obeyed me.

Further on, raggedy weeds wavered along the fields' salt line, the rime of white dusting the brown on its other side. Say you found a watertight house; you still needed a way to live, something to eat, something to wear. Shelter is only one thing. I kept playing over in my mind what had happened with the prison guard and whether he liked his job, the way he was with Alejandra and her mother, and with me too. He considered us as if something was nudging his mind; he might have seen the resemblance between them. What if he was a decent man whose farm had been ruined with salt water like the places around here? What if his wife worried about his work and the way it troubled him and ran against the grain of him, but he did it anyway to keep a roof over his family and food on their table and make sure they had clothes to wear? What if his wife felt bad about that, wishing she could leave her children in someone else's care and go out to work in his stead, or couldn't find a job or child care but chafed at him anyway about getting a less troubled job? What if that was all there was for them and they were grateful for it? What if he went home that day and said to his small daughter, about the same age as Alejandra, 'Honey, I met a little girl today almost as sweet as you.' And she said, 'Did you, Daddy? What was her name, the little girl?' And he had to make something up or tell her he didn't know, and then she would wonder how he would meet a little girl without knowing her name. For years she might wonder about that strange day her father came home and told her that. What if his children had friends from other places and they kept their father's work a secret from them? What if he kept his work a secret from his family? What if he'd treated us as decently as he could when there were witnesses? What if he was bad? There were so many ways that could be true; I tried not to think of them.

Do you see what I mean? I've teased at the edges of that encounter and the people who made it up, wondering what it meant, and none of the meanings can explain why I couldn't get away from that convoy fast enough. When we drove away, Luis was pure rage; as if rage was something that could be carved out in the shape of a young man and Luis would be its truest form. He didn't look back, he wouldn't allow it in himself and I don't know if he thought that would be weakness, or whether he was frightened that the rage would then run free and he wished to protect us from that. Alejandra was merely misery, and the danger of that is slower. Twice she looked back, and when they were beyond sight she stared in black-eyed sadness for mile after mile as we drove, the car slithering on the road's edge when I accelerated too fast, which

I couldn't help doing. There was some badness in it I couldn't understand.

Ruined houses reared up in places, or rested in ancient disintegration, broke-backed or droop-faced, more eloquent than the few ragged people we passed walking the roadside's edge, their stares so frank and direct. Who had lived in these places? It seemed my leaving home, even if it was for a different reason, was a common thing and a piece of me resented the commonness of that. What did it matter, though? The result was the same. I had nowhere to call home and neither did they.

The road followed queer pitches and tilts in the marshland. The gas station attendant had been right: the land had changed since the maps were drawn. Roads dove into marsh and reappeared ahead past a stretch of water. Thick grasses and reeds encroached along their edges. The roads, like the trees, were dead or dying, and haunted the landscape with the world that had been. With no way to test water depth there was nothing to be done but turn and try another road back along the way we came, feeling our way along, and doubling back, again and again, as haphazard and bumbling as an insect in a flood.

Finally we came upon a town, by chance more than design. It was like Blackwater, all prettiness, each dollhouse down the main street a different colour and trimmed in white. A few stores had hopeful stands of clothing out front, and souvenirs and paintings of sunsets in their windows. A big sign out front of a diner said *Crab Cakes and More!* We should have kept moving, but I wanted something good to happen that day and I slowed and made the next right and parked down a quiet tree-lined street carpeted with sodden leaves and a scant covering of snow.

'What are you doing?' Cat said.

'Getting crab cakes. Who knows when we'll get another one? You want to come, Alejandra?' I was hoping to lift her spirits.

'No thank you, Kitty.'

'Sweetheart,' I said.

'Kitty, you shouldn't,' Luis said. 'People are going to notice.'

'No they're not.'

'People always notice you.'

'No they don't. Anyhow what would they say? This lady came in for crab cakes. Great story. Come on.'

'You stay here, Alejandra,' Luis said.

She looked at me and she looked at him and said, 'Okay.'

'You too, Girl.'

Girl was so heavy with unborn cubs that she didn't care, just curled up in a patch of sun shining in.

I got out and walked away from the sadness of them, trying to walk away from my own. What would their mother be thinking now? She'd looked into my eyes; I didn't mention that before and I kept thinking of it now. 'Thank you for your kindness.' I kept walking down the road, pulling my jacket tight against the chill, covering the ground fast, trying to put that out of my mind. Crab cake, how hot and fragrant and melting it would be in a soft white bun.

One house on the left I felt before I saw. It was small and low, a dirty white and grey with one mean little dormer poking from its roof. The yard had not been raked clean for some time; sodden leaves lay thickly on the ground and nothing but a single leafless shrub and the tree that had grown the leaves grew there. Even on a bright day with the tree bare and the sunlight reaching the ground it still appeared shadow-filled and watchful. The neighbours had tried their best to conceal it with thick bushes along the boundaries. The shrub was hung with enormous fruits, though the time of year was wrong, and the way they hung was wrong, and their colours – browns and greens with flashes of muted orange or blue – were wrong. Slaughtered ducks, not fruit hanging there to ripen. Then, from the angle of their slender necks and the way their bodies hung against the world at a queer diagonal, and from the stiff way they moved, like pendulums counting out the wind, I saw that they were only wooden decoys. Yet their lack of life, their never-life, seemed threat and nightmare both. My heart pounded as much as if I'd been a child. I wished I'd crossed the road.

I held my breath while I rounded the corner and only let it out near the shop. The door had a jaunty old-style bell, which startled me, and for a half-second I was stopping at Patty's for ices after school. The woman behind the counter was young and soft and slumped-looking in her pale blue polo. Her light brown hair was lank and pulled back. Her skin had a sheen of grease. She didn't smile.

'Afternoon,' I said.

She nodded.

'I'd like crab cakes with coleslaw.'

'Slaw?'

'Yep. You think it's a bad idea?'

'I do.'

'What would you recommend?'

'Lettuce, tomato, mayonnaise.'

'No slaw?'

She made a curt motion with her head. 'As a side.'

'Slaw for one. Five of everything else. And fries.'

'For five?'

'Is that okay?'

'Sure. It'll cost ya.'

'I've got money.'

She made a note on the little paper pad she had and put the pen in her pocket and phoned the order through to the kitchen. She kept an eye on me while I poked around the shop to see what else we might need: a couple of cans of soup, a box of Rice-A-Roni, a bag of dog food, milk, juice and took them to the counter.

'Where'd you say you were from?' she said.

'I didn't. South of here. You know how long it'll be?'

'Ten, fifteen minutes.'

'I'll just step out. I saw something in a shop down the street. I'll be back.' I went out and the doorbell rang behind me again. Further up the road, past all those quaint and pretty shops, I turned the corner and walked and turned another corner and walked and turned another corner and I was back on the street where the car was parked. There it was, fifty yards ahead maybe. The yard of the corner house was open at the back, and piled against a shed were stacks of the slat baskets that people used to use for crabs and oysters, and some oyster tongs, long and rusted, and dredges and crab baskets, most of them neat – someone had expected to use them again – but some rusted, and all grown through with weeds. It was like Wolfe. I kept walking and had a strange sensation of alertness all over my skin, but didn't turn or look about to see where it was coming from. An old man came out of his front door and stepped onto the porch over the road from the car. He didn't do anything, just looked at the car. I got in, paying him no attention.

'Where are the crab cakes?' Alejandra said.

'They're cooking now, sweetie. Just going to move the car.'

'Why?' Cat said.

'Someone paying too much attention to no business of theirs. Don't look now.' But of course it was too late for that. They flung their heads like windvanes in a changeable breeze. 'Stop that now.' I eased away up the road. There was no rush – no, nothing at all worth noticing.

'We should go. I really think we should, Kitty,' Luis said.

But I wouldn't. My stubbornness used to drive Hart crazy. I circled the block to the next street and parked beneath a tree so the car was in shadow and walked down to the main street and around the corner. There was a police car near the diner, no lights going, and two police going in, one feeling his holster, the other holding the door. Oh, my heart. I stopped at a stand of sweatshirts, and began flicking through and over the top of the stand saw one of the troopers come back out and peer up and down the sidewalk. That was enough for me. The minute he went back in I turned and was at the corner and around it so fast. Any minute, any minute, they'd be at my side hauling me in, but if I broke into a run someone would notice for sure. I took my jacket off, as if I'd got a little warm out walking, and tucked it under my arm, and when I got to the car I threw it in and started it up.

'You were right,' I said.

'What happened?' Cat said.

'We shouldn't be here. I don't even know. It's like this whole town is watching for something.'

'What about the crab cakes?' Alejandra said.

'Another time. Might be a coincidence. Those cameras at the prison, those guards. What if they're looking for the truck?

What if Josh . . .' I turned on to a street running parallel with
the main street and headed along. Every bit of me wanted to
press hard on the accelerator, but I didn't. My foot was shaking
and my hands were trembling. 'It didn't feel right. Police
looking for something or someone. Probably a coincidence,
probably not us.'

'Go faster,' Luis said. His head filled the mirror as he turned
to look behind.

'No.'

I went along every back street I could find that kept heading
out of town and when there was no other choice I rejoined
the highway, and got off it as soon as I could, back on to the
byways that ran through woods, even on ones heading south
if they presented themselves, steering clear of any road with
a name that included 'point' or 'pier' or 'dock' – they went
nowhere – heading away from that pretty and dangerous
town. The whole world could trap you at the end of one of
those roads. There'd be no way out but by boat. I gripped the
wheel so hard. Driving through those places, doing our best to
stay unnoticed, it seemed like everything, every thing, made
me angry. A tree felled, a hunched cat crooning over a bird,
a salted field, a bug-eyed and lank-haired man who reminded
me of the creature who'd touched me in an oyster shanty, and
another, a town teacher who made Claudie cry when she stood
up to him. I went and told him what I thought and it didn't
happen again. Wolfe had contained me, it had held me in
place, and seeing all this, people, places, there was nothing to
hold me together. I don't know what it was. I felt like I was
running loose, and now I understood running.

Chapter 18

IT WAS THE relief at being off those slippery roads and the feeling of having been trapped within them that kept us at the next place we found for two nights. We went through a fair-sized town beforehand, which Cat knew from other trips with Josh. She directed me towards a big supermarket and went in and did the shopping herself while I minded Treasure. A small woman from somewhere in the far south knocked on my window. I let it down. She didn't have any hopes of me. She looked so tired, but she would do this anyway because what choice did she have. She said something, and held out her hand. Reluctantly, Luis involved himself. 'She would like some money,' he said. 'Her family is hungry. There is no work. They left their farm from many seasons of drought and now they are hungry.' I gave her some money and she bobbed her head and tucked some strands of hair behind her ear, and bobbed again.

Alejandra leaned forward to watch her go. 'Who was that lady?'

Luis looked terrible. He looked out of the window, staring until she'd turned a corner. 'I don't know.'

We had to leave the first house we tried in a hurry. It seemed empty – no smoke was rising; blinds were drawn;

leaves tumbled across the lawn; we couldn't see a car. But no sooner had Girl leaped down and begun her sniffing than a second-floor window went up and a man put his head and his gun out. 'Anything I can do for you folks?' he asked in a scornful voice, as if he was playing with us. I made up some excuse about the wrong address.

'What address would that be?' he said.

I didn't reply and he said, 'Thought so,' and waited until we went.

The next place we found was a couple of miles further on, just another farmhouse down one side road and another, and along a drive set into a wooded lot. Cat went and knocked at the door first to make sure no one was there. (She'd prepared a story about losing our way in case someone was home.) A few toys had been left behind – a small car on a windowsill, a rattle behind a door, a child's bicycle in a lean-to. Alejandra rode around on it in the ghostly light. We boiled some water and sterilised the rattle and it amused Treasure for a while. There was an old-fashioned wood-burning stove in the kitchen and a little furniture. It was a good house. It hadn't been let go. We got half comfortable and settled for a couple of nights; that was a mistake. Somehow I couldn't stop making them. It's when you start to relax that things happen.

In the half-light of dawn on the second morning Luis and Cat went outside for more wood and kindling. I sluiced out the dishes from the night before and got the breakfast box from the kitchen. Alejandra's eyes were open when I got back. She moved to the sagging sofa and watched while I got the fire going again, putting one little stick on after another and blowing the basket of twigs until they spurted into flame and the basket fell and crumbled and became the bed for larger pieces of wood. The room flickered into life and I could imagine how it had been once, with maybe some photos and knick-knacks on the mantel and a lamp in the little window on the cold north wall – who knows, maybe flowers even. I poured some cereal into a cup for Alejandra and she picked at it with her fingers, dainty as a lady.

'We have to go,' Cat said, banging the door open. 'Right now.'

'Why?' I said.

'Sun's up. A car slowed coming past here. We need to get going. Could be anyone around here.'

'Right,' I said, and put the cereal, the cups, the juice, in the box.

Cat grabbed it from me and headed out the door. 'Luis,' she called, 'Get the quilts. Come on now, Alejandra.'

I forgot to pay attention to Girl. She was warning me, standing beside me with her ears up and sounding soft whines in her throat. A shadow passed the living room window making for the door. Alejandra stared at me, her mouth pulled back until I could see her clenched teeth and her clenched fists. Bad things had happened to her and her body was braced for more. I crept down the hallway to the front door, Alejandra behind me holding my jacket and tugging, weighing me down. (Oh, children, it's what they do, they can't help themselves; it's wrong to expect otherwise.) I pressed my ear to the door and imagined someone doing the same on the other side, each of us wondering and fearful in our ignorance of what lay beyond.

Girl, behind me, gave a terrible growl and I swung around. An old sort of man, with a white beard and a fat under-chin, stood at the end of the hall, gun in hand hanging at his side.

The thumb of his other hand was tucked into his belt as if he imagined himself standing in the swinging doors of an old saloon. He tapped the muzzle of the gun lightly against his faded jeans and considered us both with interest and an eye to performance, glancing sideways into the kitchen and down the shadowy hallway at us. Alejandra pressed up against me, burying her head into my jacket front and I put my arm around her and shifted her around behind. Girl stood before me, close to the wall.

'Can I help you?' I said. 'Who're you?'

He said, 'Say that again?'

I said it again.

'I thought so from th'other day when you came by my house. Wrong address? Remember that? You one of them islanders?'

'I don't know which islanders you mean, mister. I'm from an island if that's what you mean. Can I help you? Is this your house? I'm sorry if it is. It was empty when we came.'

'Well—'

The front door burst open behind me, cold air rushing in with Cat.

'Who's—' Cat stopped and said softly, 'Come here now, honey.' Then she hissed, 'Alejandra.' The little girl's grip on my coat and her warmth were suddenly gone. (I will note here that even though a child will likely not be able to protect you, there is something about them that seems to wrap around and protect a person's spirit. Who would attack a child knowingly? I know that people do, but it is a shock each time to hear of it, and with Alejandra gone I felt less safe.)

'We were just here for a night taking the kids back to my daughter,' I said.

'Two nights,' he said. 'Can't both be hers unless she's a whore.' He chuckled at that.

'No need for that talk. Cat here's the other one's cousin, and there's one more. The two of them my son Tobe's. They live with my daughter, all of them together. We didn't think anyone would mind us staying for a couple of nights. We keep things clean. We don't steal. We treat places right.'

'Not my place, but I know whose it was, which I am guessing you do not.' He put his gun into his belt and came bandy-legged towards me.

'Right.'

'It's been empty since summer. We keep a lookout around here, a few of us. Make sure no one's moving in on a place they've got no business with. Watch out for runners, dealers, burners, grifters, squatters. Only ones we approve are owners, renters and friends. Are you one of them? Don't lie to me now.' He came a little way closer – I touched Girl at the neck to steady her – and with his forefinger pushed the door open onto all the bedding pushed roughly back and the evidence of cooking from the night before. 'Looks like a regular infestation. How many?'

'Just me, like I told you, and my grandkids.'

'I see.'

'And we're leaving today.'

'Which island you from?'

'Sutters.' I thought I'd keep my story straight. 'I've been on the shore a while now. Years. You have some problem with islanders?'

'I don't suppose I do. Just seem to be sniffing around for work, what I've heard, what I've seen. Don't belong round here.'

'Not me. I'm not looking for work.'

'I'm not saying I'm not sorry for you all the way things are going,' he said, 'but you're not my business.'

'That's right, we're not. We're not doing harm and we didn't ask for your company.'

He paid no attention to that. 'I turn on the TV, see a donkey stepping through a minefield, ain't a damn thing I can do about it. Do I want it to die? No. Can I do anything? No. Should I? Why would I? Not my business.'

'Seems like you've got all the answers.'

'I'm saying that's all you are to me.'

'Donkeys in a minefield?'

'More or less.' He hunched his shoulder and allowed it to drop again. 'Well,' he conceded, 'not you maybe, but her?' He nodded towards Alejandra, some way behind me, Cat's arm about her shoulder, holding her tight. 'She don't belong. She can get out of here.' Luis came in the back door. The man swung around and stopped to get a good look. 'Him too.'

'They've been visiting and now I'm taking them home.'

'Bullshit. You're a poor liar, ma'am, I'll tell you that now for your own good so you don't try it again. They're from down south. That so?' He appealed to Alejandra and Luis, as if his pleasant tone would make them trust him.

Alejandra was frozen, her face half-buried against Cat's side. He was just a shabby man trying to feel big and it made me mad to see what he had done to a little girl. I should have held myself in at that moment, not let the anger in me find a pathway out.

'I'll be the one to tell you. This here is Cat, and these two, like I said, are my son Tobe's children, but they're not runners or anything like. Born here, same as you, same as me, and their father too, my son.'

239

'They going to change that rule, don't worry about that. That one-parent rule's a piece of shit anyway, so they got nothing.'

'They haven't changed it.'

'Yet. Some of us are expediting the situation, ma'am, around here and other places and have been for some time.'

'We've got the law.'

'Hell, darlin', the law don't even care about the law these days. Where you been?'

I did not move or shift my gaze from him. 'We'll be moving on now, if you don't mind. Could you start getting things in the car, Cat, Luis? You go on then. You too, Alejandra. Outside now, quickly. Understand? Get in the car. Wait there.'

Cat nodded and threw open the door and they ran into the dank and clouded morning, vanishing into its drift.

The man shifted uneasily. 'I didn't say they could go.'

'I wasn't asking for permission.'

He looked behind – I don't know why; considering how to retreat maybe – and then he faced us again and took a step towards me and jabbed his finger at me. 'Don't let me see you round here again. I'll be talking to a few people about this, don't you worry. I've got your plates and one of us'll be seeing you again somewhere along the road.'

Girl leaned into a crouch and her teeth showed white and a humming sound started deep in her chest and her throat.

'I hate a wolfdog,' the man said. 'Can't be trusted. Never turn your back on one. Asking for trouble.' And he raised his gun, Girl leaped, and he shot, the bullet hitting the side of her chest. She hit the ground hard.

'Told you,' he said.

Girl set up a screaming howl, her paws scrabbling.

Then I pulled my gun.

'What the hell, lady? Put that away.'

'Drop it,' I said, and when he didn't I shot the gun in his hand, which flew up so sharply he might have been burned. He shook his hand from the sting of it.

'Shit, what are you, crazy?'

'Now get out. Run now. You better,' I told him. I glanced at Girl, who was hardly moving now. There would be no saving her.

He turned and ran, and I followed and the minute he was outside I aimed at his chest and thought better of it, though it was an effort, and pointed the gun lower and shot his leg instead, feeling nothing but the rightness of his pain and a moment's satisfaction, and he fell like he'd been tripped by fishing line, straight down, smashing the ground. The back of his thigh bloomed the brightest red, like the old Abraham Lincoln rose that grew over our broken shed, and a sobbing caterwauling poured out of his mouth. He looked back and seeing my gun still raised lumbered to his feet and limped-ran to his truck, one hand clutching his ruined leg, which dragged behind him, holding just enough weight to throw his good leg forward. He was fast. Adrenaline will do that. I've seen it often in creatures in fear of their lives. Look what it had made me do. He flung the truck door open and heaved himself in, sobbing and screaming all the while – 'Shit, fuck,' and so on. The truck was moving away before the door closed. It wove up the drive away from his trail of blood, which stood stark as a lit fuse running along the dirt to the point of his departure. I wasn't going to let him win – I'd save those pups even if there was no saving Girl.

I ran back into the dark house, grabbing the sharp knife on my way through the kitchen, to my poor Girl. Hardly a minute had passed, but Girl's eyes had stilled. Her blood was everywhere, seeping along the hallway, crimson and thick against the dark wood. I had not been at her side telling her I was with her to the end. There was no changing that and I knew I would regret it always – one more regret, and one of the worst. I crouched at her side and heaved the soft warm weight of her, spoiling her fur in her blood, onto her back so she was braced against my knees and drew the blade down her belly, a strong cut before I lost my nerve. And there, rummaging gentle and desperate in the meat of her belly, I felt some slight movement, and pulled aside glistening flesh to expose the lumpy pouch where the pups lay. A cut and there they were, little wet things, five of them, still but for one of the bigger ones, which twitched a paw and flexed its neck – just enough to give me hope. I pulled it free, wiping the goo from its nose, sucking with my mouth and spitting to one side, rubbing its little body. 'Come on now, sweetie,' I said, and sucked and spat again, and rubbed its body. 'Come on.' And when it began to move its four feet more strongly and to bob its head in a searching way, I took the knife again and cut the cord, and pulled the bottom of my sweater up around her to keep it warm. What on earth had I done? It was alive now, but how was I to keep it that way? 'Don't you die on me now. I have you safe. We're going to be all right.'

'Kitty.' Luis was at the door again with Alejandra and Cat. 'What happened?'

'He shot Girl,' I said. 'She's gone.'

'Girl. Oh, Girl.' Alejandra's face was wet and pale; she was panting with her sobs.

I rolled Girl back on her side and smoothed her flank. There was nothing I could do about her insides. 'Stay on that side,

Alejandra. That's the way. You pat her if you want. She won't mind. She'd like it. There.' She knelt and stroked Girl's fur, and between her ears and her forehead, so soft there. I touched her ears and brow and gentled her eyes shut so the death of her was hidden. I wiped my face. Alejandra howled. She threw herself into Luis's arms.

'It's okay,' he said.

'It's not,' she wailed. 'Girl. It's Girl, Luis.'

'I know.' He held her tight.

I stroked Girl again and got up, holding the little pup close, and stepped over the bundle of fur that Girl had become. 'Look, Alejandra, look what I saved.' She flinched at the sight of me, all blood-spattered and blood-soaked and sticky. I knelt before her and drew a fold of sweater back to show her the fragment of living fur, nosing blindly, hunting for food. I was in trouble now all right.

'Oh, little puppy,' Alejandra said, still sobbing. 'What's its name? What's it called?'

'It hasn't got a name. I don't even know what we have here.' I took a peek and her tiny paws paddled the air. 'A little girl. We'll have to think of a good name. And something to keep her alive.' I don't know if it was my place, it probably was not, but I wanted Alejandra to know this: that something – someone – she loved had died, but there was something else that could give hope. There was no time to pause.

Somewhere far away a horn sounded and did not stop. 'What now?' I said.

Luis went down the hall and through the door and was gone. The horn went on. A minute or so later Luis came back. 'That guy,' he said. 'He's gone off the road. Into the ditch. Just . . . drove off the edge.'

'Dear God,' I said.

We went outside, the tiny pup bundled up close under my sweater, moving a little, and half ran up the driveway, over the ditch bridge and turned onto the empty road. The woods had fallen silent – any living creature had made itself small and quiet and scarce and every bit of me screamed out to get into hiding with them, to conceal myself from anything drawn to that mechanical blare.

A short distance ahead was the truck – stark white against the dun-coloured grass – nose and side into the wide water-filled ditch like it was taking a sideways sip at the water. The man's head lolled against the steering wheel. Luis ran ahead, making for the far side of the car where it was listing on the road, but the door was locked and as I reached the car, my breath puffing out like a locomotive, he stepped without hesitation, though he did grimace, thigh deep into the cold water on the driver's side and began beating at the window and worrying and heaving at that door too, which was also locked, the water swilling around him and washing back against the car as it rocked with and against the water. The water stirred up muddy and the miserable rank smell of rotten flowers in a forgotten vase lifted. Luis gave one last desperate heave, grunting, and the man's head slid off the horn and there was silence again, which seemed now as loud in its own way as the horn had been. Nothing would mask the noise that we made now. Anyhow, there was no way in.

Luis scrambled out of the ditch clutching handfuls of reeds, which tore free in his hands, and gouging fingers into the mud. On the road again, water streamed from his pants and pooled beneath him. Neither of us spoke. We looked in at the man, at the queer angle of his head and the limp splay of his arms at his sides. We didn't need to touch him, to feel for his pulse or pound at his heart to know that he was as gone as Girl.

'A rock,' Luis said. 'We can break the window.'

'No point.'

We stood together, breathing, air in and out, life.

'What now then?' Luis said without turning his head.

'We wipe the car down. Every bit, any place you touched. We don't want to have been here. And fast. We need to get going.'

'I think you'd better,' he said. He held his hands out, palm up. They were all over blood. He wiped them on his wet pants, and showed me again – all cut up in stripes from the grasses, the blood beading up, seeping across his wet hands like watercolour.

'Here,' I said. 'Hold this.' I pulled off my sweater and handed him the pup wrapped up in it, then got a handkerchief from my pocket and wiped the car all over, any place Luis might have touched. 'Watch me now,' I said. 'Tell me any place I've missed.'

He shut his eyes for a second or two. 'Upper back left bonnet, rear catch, door handles, windows, roof above front doors, all around the trim.' I stepped into the ditch, feeling the mud slide underfoot, the cold of it, trying not to hold on to any grasses, (that smell again – I thought I might be sick) and lunged about, pulling my feet from the sucking mud. I looked around for any of his blood on the grass and with the bottom of my sleeve about my hand for protection tore the stalks of bloody grass free and pushed them under the water and swirled them until they were clean.

'That's good,' Luis said.

I held a hand up and he heaved me out. The water eddied behind. I thrust the handkerchief away. 'Better see to your hands.' I took the pup from him and we made our way back towards the house.

Cat was waiting by the door. I shook my head at her questioning look. The cub-pup was mewing. I freed its head, which moved like a searching caterpillar, desperate. I looked at Cat.

'Don't look at me like that,' she said.

'Like what?'

'In that way you do, like Girl. Stop.'

'Cat,' I said.

'What the hell,' she said. 'This is not some old-timey fable we're living. This is not *The Grapes of Wrath*. I am not fucking feeding it.'

'Not directly. I'm not saying that. Cat, this is the last wolfdog of the island. It's Girl's.'

'Let it be the last then,' she said. 'This family.' But she turned some way towards me. 'I have an actual baby here, in case you haven't noticed.' She held her out to me, practically brandished her. 'Get me a cup or a jar or something then. I'll see what I can do. For Girl. She would have fought.'

I found her something from the breakfast box, a favourite cup of Claudie's with a little yellow chick that I couldn't leave behind. 'Here you go. Shall I take Treasure?'

'Nope. She can come with me. It'll help.' She took the cup and held Treasure close. 'Don't you follow. Leave me be,' she said. 'I can't believe it . . .' Her words faded as she went into the house.

I got busy tidying the car, which was a mess from the haste of our packing, and Alejandra held the cub and stroked its forehead, and between its eyes and down its back. She felt its tiny claws, sharp as broken shell.

'What'll we call her?'

'Niña,' Alejandra said. 'Little girl Niña.' She touched a finger to her lips and then to the pup's forehead, between her eyes, like a blessing.

Cat came back with a little cup of milk and by dipping a pinkie finger in it and putting it to Niña's mouth again and again we were able to get some down.

'You could sit in the truck,' I told Alejandra, 'and mind Niña. Could you do that? Don't let her fall now.'

'No, I won't.' She took Niña and walked solemnly towards the car, her head bent over and her arms curled around the tiny creature.

Cat stood to one side holding Treasure, pulling the covering back from her face, tugging her beanie down and smoothing it there. The baby's mouth trembled at one corner – some dream she was having. Cat smiled too. I stroked her shoulder.

'Sorry,' Cat said, and lifted the baby an inch in some gesture, reminding me of her. I hadn't forgotten her. But I had not properly remembered how a baby or a child is always there even if they're in another room. They cannot fall from your mind. And where we were, I knew that Cat would not let her go except into another's arms. This place was not safe now.

'She is beautiful,' I said. 'You could wait with Alejandra.'

But she worked one-handed, getting things into the car, while Luis and I dragged Girl, grown stiff and cold, onto a blanket and outside. I didn't let the tears stop me. I didn't like to think of her out in the open, but there was nothing around to dig with. We pulled her over the lumpy ground and the fallen leaves to the edge of the wooded area, and wrapped the blanket about her and piled dead branches over her and that was all we could do. We changed out of our bloody, wet and stinking clothes, wrapped them up tight and put them in the truck. I thought it better to throw them away in a big town. Anyone could have bloodied clothes in town, couldn't they?

Then we left. Driving away in the cold morning, the sun not yet broken through but the white cloud glowing, the wet tracks that Luis and I had left were still plain along the asphalt. Whether they would dry to nothing or leave ghost footprints I wouldn't know. There was nothing we could do except hope for more snow or rain.

Girl, Girl, Girl. All those years on Wolfe together. I had lured a man onto rocks. I had shot someone, and there was Josh, who I as good as killed. Three men. I was alert to threat now. I was dangerous. My world had changed, and I had changed with it. I looked at my hands on the steering wheel and didn't recognise myself. I was silent unless someone spoke to me, and my hands shook unless I held the wheel firm. I tried thinking things through. Did I have a choice or not: that sort of thing. What else could I have done? Nothing, nothing. A small insistent voice inside me was saying, Who are you? Fool, murderer, you're not deceiving me. I know what you are, I know your like. And I could go on despite that, despite what I had done.

I thought of the prisoner on death row. He seemed close just then. He'd only killed one man. For the couple of years that I visited, he would tell me about his innocence, how he had not done the thing of which he was accused, and how one day the truth would come out and he would be released. I never said anything about that. What would be the point in quarrelling? If there were raised voices that would be the end of it and by then I wanted to be there when he stopped lying or when he said something that made me think he truly had been unjustly accused. I didn't think that would happen. Sometimes I wanted to kill him. Then one day he said, 'What's it like out there today?'

'How do you mean?'

'The weather, the sky, is it blue? Or raining? I liked the rain.'

It was late in spring and I had driven up through fields that were shooting bright, the great bowls and stretches of soybean and corn scooped out of stands of dogwood and maple and pine. 'Sun's out,' I said. 'It's warm, almost hot. The sky's pale blue – high, you know? I saw an eagle on the way, circling round.'

'Yeah?'

'Yeah.'

'I like an eagle. I never seen one except on TV.'

That was all he wanted, a taste of life. Something about him made me porous and he seeped in. (It should have been a relief to leave him behind, to drive away free and clear, but from experience I knew it would take days to break free.) Later that very same visit, like something had loosened in him, he said, 'I didn't do it.' I didn't say anything, same as usual. But this time he went on in a heavy way, like he was putting something down. 'Didn't mean to. It was a accident. I just was falling. I tripped is all.' I didn't say anything about that either. He said, 'It was a misunderstanding. That guy, I don't know, he was trigger happy or something.'

'He had a gun?'

'Yes. I thought I saw it. He might have.'

And the time after that that when I visited he said, 'He gave me a look, right at me. I thought he was coming at me. He had a look on him. He was going to get me. I knew it.'

'I heard he was saving someone.'

'We were okay.'

'I heard different.'

'A little shy, you know?' He giggled as if it was an old joke, then remembered who he was talking to, a visitor, a woman, and instantly stopped. 'She was coming round.'

'So you shot him.'

'For my protection. What else could I do?' He had a simple look on his face, like he'd thrown down his last card and was begging for mercy, as if admitting this might give me the power to arrange his release. I thought it was my release he'd arranged.

I said, 'That was my boy. Tobermory Hawke Hartford.'

'Oh shit, ma'am,' he said, 'oh fuck,' and he dropped his head and his hands jerked up, trying to hide himself, before they fell back. He had to let the tears run free down his face. That was all the freedom he had. I didn't feel much about that then. Some curiosity. He was a real person. The tears were evidence of that even if I wasn't sure who they were for.

I watched until the tears reached the corners of his mouth and his tongue came out and licked them away. 'I have to go now,' I said.

Chapter 19

WE SAW POLICE cars and heard sirens wailing. Twice, I saw people being questioned or dragged in the street. I was frightened of the Silverado being recognised or photographed or having been reported. There were the tyre tracks we'd left at the house, and the man's body and his car, and always the thought of Josh, who might be somewhere. We passed a golf course with its fence torn down, and tents all over. *Tee Up A Tent – Human Rights For All*, a banner said.

When the fuel ran low I parked around the corner from a gas station in a town and filled the spare tanks and Luis and I lugged them back to the car. We emptied them into the truck on a quiet back street.

'Run out of gas?' a man passing said. 'That sucks.'

'Yeah,' I said, slopping some in my surprise.

'Need some help?'

I kept pouring. I didn't want him too close. 'All done.' I smiled and he went on.

We found a vet in town, a young, tired woman with a pleasant manner. We struck it lucky there. She sold us some puppy formula and told us: 'Little and often. It really matters to keep everything clean. Remember, she hasn't got her mother

to lick her or feed her or keep her warm. That's your job.'
She gave us a box of pipettes and a couple of bottles for when
Niña was bigger to help feed her.

'Are you going to help with the little cutie?' she asked
Alejandra.

Alejandra got chatty. 'Kitty's going to show me how and
then I can do it. I'm big enough.'

'Are you really careful? Because you have to be really careful
with such a new puppy.'

'I am, aren't I, Kitty?'

'You're my right-hand girl,' I said.

'What happened to her mother?' the vet said. She sort of
slid that in, not looking at us, while she was searching for
something in a drawer.

'Whose mother? Alejandra's?' I nearly told her out of
surprise. 'Oh, you mean the cub pup.'

'She got shot. Girl got shot,' Alejandra said. Then she was
stricken and didn't know where to look. There were so many
secrets in her and this one just spilled out. She couldn't help it.

I put my arm around her. 'It's okay,' I said. To the vet I said,
'It was an accident. This little one was the only pup that made it.'

'You got her out?'

I nodded.

'You must have been quick.'

'I was,' I said. 'She was something special, her mother.'

We were both quiet after that, thinking of Girl, and
watching her baby bumping her head around on the examina-
tion table, looking for shelter. It was warm in there, but metal
is not cosy. I picked Niña up and held her in close under my
chin and she settled.

It might have been the strange story that alerted her. I had

Alejandra with me, it's true, but the car was down the street. Or it might have been how shabby we were, and how dirty. We probably smelled. Yet we had enough money. They made sure of that at reception before we went in.

'If you don't mind my asking,' the young woman said when we were done, 'might you be on your way north?'

'I'm not sure why you would want to know?'

'I wondered if you might like some advice about . . . that.'

She was so gentle and pleasant with Niña – with Alejandra too. I examined my feelings and decided to trust her. 'If you know anything you can pass on, I would appreciate it,' I said.

So she told us the best road to take, and when to leave the car to cut through a wooded area. She drew a small map. 'Don't try driving across the county line,' she said. 'Local armed men, vigilantes, whatever they call themselves, patrol that road – not all the time, but enough.'

'What are they looking for?'

She looked patient. 'People who might be heading that way instead of south.' She glanced at Alejandra. 'The same is happening in a few towns – anywhere close to the county border. It's the off-season now. Not a good time for travel. Longer days and warmer nights make it easier for travellers, but more comfortable for people hunting them. They can't touch you after you cross it and mostly they don't. But there have been some shootings. You can come back for your car later.'

'I don't know about later.'

'Get to Freedom first. The camping store's over the road. If you want.'

Freedom. It had another name on the map. It was the last stop before the county border to the far north and true freedom. People talk about the kindness of strangers, and I have found that to be true some of the time. I wouldn't risk anyone else wondering about Alejandra. I took her back to the car and went to the camping store alone.

We stayed in an old cheese house of silvered wood that night. It smelled of wild animal and rodent. We left the door open for as long as we could and I made a broom of loblolly branch, tying some extra needles at the end the way Doree and I had done when we were girls, and we swept it out pretty well. Luis brought everything in from the car. I put Niña, wrapped in a soft bit of blanket I'd torn off, on Alejandra's lap. It suited them both. The puppy stayed warm and it gave Alejandra something to do. She stroked Niña's head with her forefinger and when she woke up I prepared a little cup of warmed milk and showed Alejandra how to draw milk into the pipette and hold it to Niña's mouth and squeeze it in. 'Not too fast,' I said. 'Kind of drip, drip. Give her time to swallow.'

I watched to make sure she had the knack of it. She curled her head over the tiny creature, intent as if each single drop of milk was the breath of life.

We went through everything, dividing into two heaps: take and leave behind. At the camping store I'd picked up a tiny saucepan, which I got out then, and more matches and firelighters. We had a bigger saucepan we'd found at one of the houses we stayed at. I was using it at the edge of the fire Cat made.

Cat said, 'Why not the big one? It's not that far, is it?'

'Feel the weight of it. Awkward to carry. As long as we're warm enough or can get something warm inside, things won't seem so bad. Niña can't have cold formula.'

'We don't need the potatoes,' Luis said.

'We can carry them for one day. *I'll* carry them. I'll roast them in the fire,' I said. 'I think we'll be grateful for them.'

'How about the apples?'

'I'll cook them tonight.'

'A tent? You got a tent, Kitty?'

'Only a pop-up. Hardly weighs a thing. If it rains, we can all squeeze in.'

In this way we proceeded, whittling things away until all that was left was warmth, food and shelter. An insulating mat and four space blankets came. We took as much dehydrated food as we could, and packed the bags. I gave Alejandra the job of carrying Niña's things.

We dumped the car behind a ruined barn the next day, and walked along the edge of a field of corn stubble. We were close to the county border then, but 'close' when you are on foot and have a puppy and a baby to keep fed and a child to keep going is still quite a way. We stopped often to feed small creatures, and to ease the weight on shoulders and the cut of bags into hands, and slept that night in a shed shrouded in dead honeysuckle in the middle of a field of sprouting grain. After dark we kindled a small fire and cooked some of the food we'd bought in town. I put those potatoes, which I had more than once considered dumping, into the coals to give Alejandra something to poke at and think about. The fire lit up her face. I boiled water in the pan to sterilise Niña's things. Somehow I remember that, making things sterile for Niña and keeping her fed, not the walking and carrying, as the worst bit of the journey's end. She was a tough little thing, though, she wanted to live, and I wanted to make that happen for all our sakes, not only Girl's.

We walked through open country next morning, and stopped near the edge of the woods marked on the map, across the county line by our estimation, aiming to cut back and meet the road after the checkpoint, not that we knew for sure where it was or what it looked like. Between wood and road lay swampy marshland, not so bad at the edge where we were. Alejandra was weary enough to stumble and lose her footing by then. Luis took her hand and lifted her back to her feet, neither saying a word, and she went on in the way of children and puppies. Complaining would make no difference.

We came across a fallen tree and a pool of speckled sun and sat for a few minutes, and I let my mind empty of everything but sensation, the way I used to on Wolfe. I was glad I still knew the way of it. Cat fed the baby, who kicked out her legs and wriggled. Luis watched and looked away. There was rarely any telling what he might be thinking or feeling, so there was nothing unusual in that. But he'd become more distant from Cat, too, in recent days, when they'd been so easy with each other on Wolfe. It was as if he was always preparing to lose her, expecting to. He held himself aloof and didn't talk to Cat or anyone a great deal. He was carrying a lot, another whole person. He was not alone in that, I know. Alejandra sat at his side on a fallen log, stroking Niña, whispering to her and nodding as if she understood well what Niña was thinking.

We all drank a little of the remaining water, passing the cup along the line of us. Cat handed the baby to Luis and took off her jacket, which she laid on the ground, and took Treasure back and laid her there, kneeling to change the baby's nappy – she shivered at the air, straightening her legs and drawing them up.

'It's okay, sweetheart,' Cat told her, and Treasure began to kick her legs up and down, her heels drumming the jacket she lay on. She was a good baby, listening as keen as any other creature to the thing that kept her safe. Cat wrapped her again and held her tight, kissing her neck and blowing a bubble into it until the baby laughed. Here is the truth that I feel in such moments as watching my granddaughter feeding her baby, watching the light on the water and the wind in the bare and blushing trees and the turn of a cheek: I love life, which I haven't always, despite everything.

When it was time, Luis stood up. Alejandra didn't say a word, just followed into the reeds, holding his hand. I heaved on my pack and picked up Niña and a bag. Cat carried Treasure.

Late that afternoon we chanced upon a small farmhouse not marked on the map at the back of a cornfield. Its porch roof was caught mid-blink over its two front windows, part of it resting on the porch railings. A woman in jeans and a puffer jacket came out, ducked beneath the roof and jumped to the ground. She stopped at the sight of us and looked back, calling out to someone, and kept her wary gaze fixed on us. Another woman and a man came out, and three children, a girl and two boys, all younger than Alejandra. We could have kept on, but we needed water and there was a tap outside I had hopes of. I held my water bottle up and waved it and we kept on towards them. They were worn down. We filled our bottles. They didn't do anything, but they didn't stop watching.

Cat said, 'It's okay. We're running too. Not much further.'

Luis said something too, and they spoke a little.

I said, 'Good luck to you all.'

One of the women nodded. A little boy burrowed his head under her arm and stared. They kept staring as we left, following an overgrown farm track, and were still watching when the path curved into the woods.

Darkness began to spread. We stopped and lit a small fire under cover of trees to boil water and clean Niña's equipment. Sparks crackled and spun in the darkness. Alejandra sat on my lap. 'I want Girl.'

'Me too,' I said. 'How's Niña?'

She unwrapped her. Her tiny legs paddled and she began her blind searching.

We spent that night in the tent, which we were glad of. I thought I heard shouts and whoops and screams once and then thought I might have been dreaming. I got up twice to prepare milk for Niña. The second time I could swear I smelled smoke, but perhaps the wind had shifted and it was our own small campfire. I got everyone hurrying next morning. Something didn't feel right.

It was a relief to get going. Thin daylight began to trickle into the dense wood, then flow, diluting the darkness until it was mostly light that we saw ahead. We came to thick reeds and bushes, and pushed through them, and as quickly as that left the forest behind. Before us was a stretch of straggly marsh meadow, dry enough to walk on, and past that, not far, a banner dangled above the highway: *Welcome to Freedom!* It was caught between electricity poles propped up like drunks in the grasses. Its colours – red and yellow and green – were faded, and the limp balloons that dangled from it moved. The breeze was shifting about and I caught another whiff of smoke, of something burning somewhere. A dense plume was rising above the woods.

'Would that be our fire?' Luis said.

I shook my head. 'Further away.' I thought of those screams and wondered if we should go back but didn't say it.

We walked parallel with the highway inside the line of the wood. A few cars went past, and a fire engine, sirens going, and police and, some minutes later, an ambulance. We stopped in shadow at each one. When we'd passed the sign by a good margin and came to drier ground – a winter-sown field just sprouting – we cut across. The soil clagged our shoes until we grew taller and had to pause and bang them clean, the way we used to with snow on our boots. We reached the road a hundred or so yards further on. We were too tired to rejoice. A car went past and didn't slow at the sight of us. Then tall buildings – skyscrapers I suppose you'd call them – came into view, appearing like a lost kingdom or a mirage.

Chapter 20

I DIDN'T FULLY understand what we had become until we began the walk into the city, which, like us, had fallen on hard times. We walked down canyons of abandoned factories and warehouses and apartment buildings with hollowed-out windows and boarded doors covered in graffiti: writing in many languages and fantastical images of flowers and crosses, skulls, chains and manacles, hearts, and screaming faces and laughing faces. The side roads were lined with overgrown empty houses – some with their sidings stripped away, some burned. Behind us was that low smudge of smoke and a long way ahead dull-windowed skyscrapers. I could imagine it whole and lived in, pulsing, people on their porch swings, children running or climbing those trees, people falling in love and people dying at the proper time, every neighbourhood its own world. Every bit of dirt, every chink in a paving stone, every vacant lot, every yard, every traffic island was tall with winter grass, and the roadsides and roads and asphalt turned to crazy paving were too. Ghost gardens were all around us, if a person knew how to see them: the seed heads of tall flowers (lilies and Queen Anne's lace and thistles, other things I couldn't tell), fruit trees, hydrangeas with papery flower heads bobbing stiffly, giant oaks, ivies that had broken free. It was beautiful actually, soft, and quiet, but uncanny too, and mostly empty. A car travelled the highway we walked the edge of towards the city, and a minute later another one, and at first there was not a person apart from those in the cars.

Then there began to be more: a child riding a bike, a father walking a pram, a couple of laughing teenagers with linked arms heading somewhere (but where?), a middle-aged woman with a shopping cart like mine, a boy with a dog. (I am frightened of the way my face might change at sight of a boy and a dog. Do I look longing or bereft? Either might be creepy.) A few leaves trembled still on roadside trees, the dew had dried and the air was textured with it, the sun had had its way and goldenness bounced from the leaves and the sandstone buildings. Things changed again. Grass had been mown around a house, and an expanse of land had been turned into vegetable gardens bedded down with straw to sweeten the soil for spring.

In the space of a block we were in town. Menu boards were out on the sidewalks. I couldn't help reading them. I'd lost count of the days. It was Sunday by the look of it. A sign in a front yard said, *Welcome! Help Yourself to Water!* and a large arrow pointed to a tap and a dog bowl brimful with water at its side. We filled our bottles and drank. Cat sat on the sidewalk against a low brick wall and fed Treasure, crossing her legs comfortably and making a little world around her. I mixed some formula for Niña, warmed it against my skin and did the same with Niña. She was getting wriggly and nosing around. Luis opened a bag and shared some chocolate. We didn't care what people passing by thought, if they thought anything. We would have been a strange sight – a middle-aged lady, a young woman, a young man, a little girl, a baby and a puppy, all worn down and in need of washing, and there because we had no place to go, not yet – but people hardly spared us a glance. We were in our world, which was real and solid. Other people were nothing but legs passing by. Only children looked twice, especially at the sight of Niña dozing at my neck. We were islands and they were boats.

Luis stopped a woman running past. She jogged on the spot in her slippery black clothing. She looked at us as if we came from some remote pit of hell, a clay mine, a slave farm, a place of horror, but she adjusted, pulling a smile from somewhere, and before he could ask a thing she said, 'Straight on at the lights, second right after the park. Charlotte Street.'

'Okay,' Luis said. 'Thank you, ma'am.'

'Basketball courts. Cute puppy. Anyway, welcome to town. Hope it works out.' And she pumped her fist and yelped, 'Freedom! Woo!' and went on her way.

We came to a Burger King and I went to buy fries for us all and realised my wallet was outside packed away – I hoped it was, anyway. I couldn't remember. I had nothing but a few dollars and coins in my jacket pocket, enough for the fries. My worry must have shown on my face.

The cashier looked me up and down, what she could see over the counter, and peered out the window. There they were, the wind buffeting them and pressing their coats to their bodies, standing bunched together like they were holding each other up and waiting for someone new to knock them down. 'They with you?' I nodded. 'Wait a minute.' She came back with another big bag. 'Burgers,' she said.

'Thank you.' I wiped my face clean of sudden tears (they'd been coming up from nowhere since Girl died) and picked up the bags. Fifty miles down the road my dog had been killed. What made people so different?

'Have a nice day.' She looked past me to the next customer.

The stadium was a white and grey circular monolith with a red-lettered banner – *GOING SOMEWHERE? WE'RE HERE TO HELP* – swagged above the entrance. Clustered beneath, people dragged on cigarettes or hunched against the wind with phones tight to their ears. Cigarette butts lay like old snow, softening footfall, thin and worn where people walked, thick and driven against the building's corners. Some kids ran about kicking a soccer ball. It was a small space they had and they used it all. They wore their thin clothing layered up. Their breath steamed and they wiped their noses on their sleeves and the running seemed to keep them warm. We edged past the people, whose eyes moved over us economically, pausing on one face or another, building a story about us that made some kind of sense. It's what I'd do, what I thought they were doing, but I don't know if I was right. We might have been nothing but competition: five more people wanting the same thing, a passage to somewhere safe. They didn't prepare me for the inside: desks with big signs – *Documentation, Food Stamps, Bedding, Legal, Medical, Missing Persons, Transportation* – swaying above, and rows of low cots, people sitting talking on them; people lining up; people shooting hoops – muffled yells and laughter when the ball went skittering among the cots ("Scuse me, ma'am,' a young giant said, squeezing past after a ball); a makeshift playground crawling with children, parents and people whose eyes were seeing things far away, as I was. I'd seen rooms like this online after hurricanes or earthquakes or revolutions. All around us, other disasters were playing out, each as outlandish and ordinary as ours. We were nothing special. No one was about to pick us up and comfort us. I count that thought a revelation (to me, I mean), though it's one I'd edged up to a couple of times. We are each the centre of our own lives and now all these lives were humming up against each other, their voices overlapping like our singing in the revival tent. I thought of my mother saying: Everything has a tune. If that is so, I wonder what tune people create together in the world – unthinking contentment or discord and misery shot through with rare and piercing notes of beauty?

There was some kind of buzz around, of people passing on news they'd heard. The murmuring rippled out and finally reached us through a worker filling out our forms. A family of runners had been shot and the abandoned house they were in torched the night before, just south of town. No survivors, she said; vigilantes from south of the border everyone supposed. It was not usual for them to come so far north, and it had spooked people. I said we would have stayed in that house except they got there first. She said someone must have been looking out for us. I said it was no such thing, nothing more than luck. There's no justice and no pattern to the world. How could I be grateful it wasn't me? But I was thankful for the others, and glad that Alejandra did not have to suffer that terror.

I had thought Wolfe small and the world large. It was the opposite. The whole of Wolfe had been mine; here, I had the space of a single cot and room for my feet when I sat up, and a safe night's sleep. But if I wanted to leave that, go for a night walk, I had to be careful, watch my back, be alert, make sure I had my gun with me, and yet I should be grateful. I was for Luis and Alejandra most of all, and for Cat if she wanted to be with them. I wouldn't try to stop her in that. I'd explain it to Claudie as best I could, or leave Cat to speak for herself. I was glad for them. As for me – no one would throw me out of my country or imprison me for the crime of not belonging; murders were a different matter. I was in my own country yet I had become – I don't know what other word to use – a refugee. And I supposed I was an outlaw, too, if that was possible when my crimes remained undiscovered.

On the second day I learned that I was merely homeless. No one would imprison me for that or deport me. No other country would take me in.

It was a mistake of habit I made at the documentation desk. They asked me for my papers and I handed them over, as obedient as a child. It was a nice young man there helping, a rosy-cheeked lawyer volunteering his time to help right wrongs. 'Are you in danger? In fear of your life? Are you being persecuted?'

The things I could have said: I have committed grave crimes, I am haunted by memories and the thought of my failings and the murders I have committed. I said, 'No.'

He gave me a gentle, pitying look and opened his mouth to explain my mistake. I held up my hand to stop him. He told me he was sorry. 'I'd look the other way, only it's life or death for some.'

'Can I at least stay until the others go?' I asked. Busloads departed each day, heading north to the border, where they had to walk over a snowy pass to safety.

He moved his eyebrows and mouth in a sort of shrug. 'That's a different department. I'd have no reason to talk to them. So . . .'

'So,' I said.

It might have been three weeks we were there. I mostly kept to my cot by day. I brought my notebook up to date, told the truth as far as I could. If others saw it differently, let them set the record straight. I slept poorly in the midst of the murmuring and snuffling and coughing and sobs. There was nothing to drive me on, only this dull waiting, and the thought of sadness to come. I might not have concealed my feelings as well as I thought. Even Cat noticed. I'd finished my writing one afternoon, and made my cot and Alejandra's, smoothing the grey blankets, folding the tops over so the red trim showed nicely, fluffing the pillows. Then I lay back with my hands folded on my belly, and stared at the stadium ceiling. A few birds twittered around up there, like the pigeons in the old revival tent. Did they ever go outdoors? Perhaps they were accustomed to this; perhaps I would be too in the end.

'Posing for your tomb?' Cat said. She laid Treasure by her side on Alejandra's cot, patting her tummy and catching her feet when she kicked them up, a game that made Treasure laugh.

I couldn't break a smile.

'Do you regret things?' she asked.

'Regret things.' I turned my eyes on the roof to protect her from my feelings. 'You're asking me if I approve my own actions. I ask you: what choice did I have? I had responsibilities. I had to keep you safe. How else would I face Claudie? How would I live with myself? I haven't always done that with people I—. I did this time. Are you sorry Luis and Alejandra

266

are alive? I am not. Doesn't mean it's comfortable living in my skin.' My voice was harsh.

It was impossibly rare for Cat to back down, but she did then. She stopped playing with Treasure. She paid attention to the moment. 'I'm sorry.'

'No need. I know that. I still have to live with it, though. The rightness of an action doesn't set you free from it; it only sets you free from the danger.'

She nodded.

'There's not much here to distract me.'

Gradually, Alejandra took over with Niña. She did a good job; I kept an eye on that. Luis and Cat disappeared for hours and came back quarrelling. They'd lost the way of being comfortable together. The best of that time was hot water and the Goodwill. I kept my jacket, got new jeans, thermals and fur-lined boots, and did the same with Alejandra, thinking of the deep winter of the deeper north. There was a lucky find too, a travel basket that could hold Niña, if necessary, for a few more weeks at least.

Freedom was nothing but a way station. It could never be home. People didn't mind newcomers as long as they understood it was only passing pleasantness and support being offered. They had space but no jobs, and who could trust that the creeping sickness and discontent in the country wouldn't spread this far north? People had believed that before and been wrong, and there had been that house burned down. It wasn't a bad place, not prettied up, ruins, a few nice old buildings, several schools in the area, the things you would expect of an old city, and yet the people here were not the same. They went out of their way for others. How had that happened? I went walking, learning to be alone again, as I knew I soon would be.

Night seeped in early. The soccer games finished before dinner. Parents called their children inside, worried at what the darkness might conceal. It was cold out. By night Freedom was another place. A building was burning nearby. It made some folk edgy and inclined to stay indoors. Others clustered in the smoky half-light of streetlights looking at the glow and the sparks flying, and it seemed like they were looking at places far away. There's smoke from fireworks and explosions and flames and a lingering haze in the aftermath of each, and there are the crowds and heat and sirens that go along with these things, moving through them like ghosts. Sometimes there's beauty in that, and sometimes violence.

The centre was stifling after the cold. I checked Alejandra and Niña and went to bed myself, listening to the many sounds people made. Later I woke to a hissing conversation between Luis and Cat.

'What are you talking about?' That was Cat. 'I'm not going back to my parents.'

Luis's voice was lower, and strained. He said, 'You have to go home. There's no need for you. There's nothing there for you.'

'There's *you*. Both of you. How do you leave your family if you don't have to? And there's Josh. What might he say? How would I forget that?'

'Yeah.' He sounded despairing, the words meaning something different to him.

'Luis,' she hissed. 'Listen to me.'

But he rolled over to face the brick wall.

They hardly spoke for days. Alejandra fluttered between them, trying to draw them together again. I was drifting, and drifting away from them, waiting for the time to be done, maybe even looking forward to it, even though it would be hard, because at least then it would be done. There was nothing I could do except stay until the end and mind Niña if Alejandra wanted to join one of the games. I created a few makings and gave them to children. I emptied my pack.

Contents
- *Clothes: one change of everything, extra socks, fleece sweater*
- *Utensils: 2 spoons, 1 paring knife, 1 fork, 1 small saucepan, 37 rounds of ammo*
- *2 packets soup mix, dried hunk of bread*
- *Silverado keys*
- *Makings things* (I hadn't realised I'd collected so much)*:*
  - *roll of thin wire*
  - *5 paperclips*
  - *3 buttons*
  - *1 reel of cotton (black)*
  - *11 small sticks, various lengths* (I wondered about them, and put four aside to throw out, but I passed them later and liked them so much I took them back)
  - *1 cardboard tube*
  - *alfoil, pieces*
  - *assorted bottle tops*
  - *a plastic cereal figurine – a tiny freckle-faced creature with yellow hair – from long ago* (easy enough to date online, but competition for computers was fierce at the transfer centre)

One night late in that time of waiting, lying awake in the darkness worrying about possible futures, I watched Cat delicately lift herself away from Treasure and cross the narrow space. She lay alongside Luis, along the curve of his back, and put her arm around him and her face against his neck. His arm reached back around her waist and pulled her over, close, and their arms went clumsily around each other. 'Idiot,' Cat whispered and touched her mouth to his. I shut my eyes and went to sleep.

His mood was lighter after that and we were all lighter because of it. They were nearly there, nearly there. They assumed I was coming with them and I couldn't bring myself to tell them I could not. I thought they would try to fight it and things might go worse for them. The pretending was not so bad. Picking a scabbed wound leaves stinging tenderness in its wake. There was no time or room for us to heal free of each other in this place. I thought it easier to do that on my own, and they had each other. I saw the way they held together, and it seemed as if each day I was seeing them from a greater distance. I packed my bags when they did. I put my gun in my pocket. I was ready.

On the day of their leaving, when people were gathering themselves, I told them. I don't remember the words, only that Alejandra became again the tiny shell of a creature she'd been the day we met. She buried her face in my front, and her words came out in growling sobs. 'Kitty. Kitty. You have to come.' She butted her head against me like a battering ram. 'Come with us, Kitty. Please, Kitty, please.'

I squatted and held her. 'I can't. They won't let me. They say I have a home here; I'm not in danger. I've got a home and you're going to a new home. Cat and Luis will find one. Plenty of people don't have that. That makes us the lucky ones.'

'No, you don't have a home. That island's all broke.'

'Maybe it is. I'll find that out and let you know. I've got friends in town. Don't worry about me. I'll be okay. Except I'll miss you, I will.' I stroked her hair. 'My heart will just break. But you'll be fine without me.'

'I won't. I need you to come *with* us, Kitty.'

'I wish I could, sweetheart.' I brushed her hair back and pushed it free of the tears on her face and held her face, a hand to each cheek so I could look into her eyes. 'Listen to me now. I want you to do something. It's important, a big job, okay?'

She nodded.

I smoothed the tears on her cheek with my thumbs. 'I want you to take Niña, have her for your dog, you know? Take good care of her. Will you do that?'

'Niña?'

'Yes. She's your dog; you named her. That person's the one who has to have her. It's like a rule. No one knows her like you.' I took Niña from her travel basket and handed her to Alejandra, who held the ball of fluff in her arms. I touched the pup's forehead and her nose, and she bumped around with her tiny wolf head. 'She'll be hungry again soon. You've got her things? You know what to do? Better take the basket so she doesn't scare people on the bus.'

Alejandra nodded. A keening sound came out of her again, her mouth stretched wide. 'Kitty. Kitty.'

'Careful now. Don't want to squash her, don't want to frighten her with your wolf mama howling.'

Alejandra made a snuffling sound. I stroked her hair again, which I'd brushed smooth that morning.

'I promise I will come visit if I can. I promise that. And when you're older you can come visit me. Nothing can stop you if you want to do that.' I hoped that would be true when the time came.

Cat had been waiting with a look of judgement, as if I was after all what her mother had warned her about: a person who would fail you. I'm not saying she was wrong. Treasure, in her arms, looked around imperiously.

'I should have told you before.'

'Yes, you should.'

'I'm sorry. I thought it was the right thing.'

'We can fight this, Kitty. Why?'

'Because you shouldn't wait. You have to take this chance: Alejandra and Luis do, anyway. They're not safe here.'

'I have to go with them.'

'I know, so go. Don't make them wait. They'll do it if you ask, and they shouldn't. Don't put them in danger, I'm saying. You don't know if things will close up. Anything could be coming up the road behind us.' I took her by the arm and pulled her closer and spoke quiet enough that no one would overhear. 'What if Josh told his father about Luis?'

'I don't know what you know.'

'Don't talk about it. There's what you and Josh were doing too.'

'The fires were Josh.'

'He might say different . . .' I glanced at Luis.

'Why didn't you say before?'

'Because acting normal is the best thing you can do. Easier to do that if you're not jumping at everything. Your chance is here now and you've got to take it. Only a fool would let it go.'

'What about you?'

'I'll go to Doree's.' I gripped her arm tighter. 'It's not the end. We'll see each other again. If you need me, ring Doree, or write, whatever, the minute you've got a base. I've got money put by – I'd like to help you out, make sure you've got a home. We're not lost to each other. This is just now. Now is just something to get through. I could die of pride looking at you.'

'Kitty.' She stared into my face as if she was trying to decipher the words of another language. 'How are you even going to get back?'

'Same way we came. I'll pick up the Silverado and drive. Easiest thing.'

She nodded as if now she understood something or we had agreed to a plan.

We went outside with the others to the bus in the lot. There was a jittery buzz around – people smiling and talking and children running around and being called back – of hope and the prospect of safety and some fear too. Niña wriggled and was hard to hold. She nuzzled Alejandra's ear and her face and briefly made her giggle. We put her in her travel basket and she peeped out from there. A dog and a person is a family on its own. I've always said that. I hugged them, and then suddenly I didn't belong with them in the line and wished I'd put it off a minute more so there was still something good to come. I stood over to one side, not far away.

Luis stood with Cat looking very serious, and she very serious at his side, as solemn as the day they arrived on Wolfe. They were husband and wife in the ways that meant anything, despite being so young, and it suited them. Luis glanced across and gave me one of his faint smiles, this one tinged with dry humour and awareness at the strange turn their lives had taken. Here they were again, he seemed to be saying, but at least they were together and in the end did anything else matter? (I felt he understood me in that moment; my life had changed trajectory too, and I couldn't make sense of it.) I smiled back, trying to convey my many feelings. Alejandra looked at me too, expressionlessly. She was wound so tight.

Every other leave-taking of my life was behind this moment like cards to be shuffled through: Tobe staring from the skiff with imploring eyes, Hart all anger and pleading at the Blackwater docks, Claudie simmering with resentment and rage on Wolfe, even Josh in his sinking boat, and the prisoner farewelling me at the edge of his foundering life. My parents too. And now this. I had let them in, the quiet in me was gone, and I would have to learn to live again on my own. I dreaded that.

Sometimes after returning to Wolfe from a visit to the main my spirit had sickened; even the island could not save me. I felt empty at such times. The island seemed to die a little in my absence and it was hard bringing it to life again.

I'd shut the curtains and trawled the world online. I didn't like what I saw but I couldn't look away for the strangeness of it. I looked at people who scraped mud at the sides of tidal rivers for ancient treasures, people who stalked remnant birds through wasted landscapes, people who gardened and cooked, people who sold houses or adorned them, people who made things to fill houses, people who grew vegetables and flowers, people who embroidered pictures of those things, people who danced in shanty towns and had only their own arms for pillows, people who cooked and ate in shanty towns or cities, people who took pictures of themselves in many places, people who dressed tribal to get in touch with their roots, people who climbed buildings and sometimes fell to their deaths, people who climbed mountains or dove in the sea, people who cut fabrics and made clothes or knitted yarns, people who refashioned junk into art or food scraps into feasts, people animated by the call of some hunting past who shot lithe animals they'd never eat, people who cut off dogs' ears and laughed, people with earless dogs who hated women, thin people with painted faces who lay on sandy ground, people who wanted to be thin people lying on sandy ground, bears moaning out their caged and painful lives, sad people who watched sunsets and moons and planets, staring as far away from the world as they could get. Sometimes all I could see was the ugliness of the world.

People kept their distance from me later on that night in Freedom after the bus had left. I stayed out in the darkness. It was a clear, cold night. The stars were faint pinpricks, dulled by the city lights. The cold pressed into me and I waited for the epiphany it might bring to make sense of it all, the way I had when I was a child. But the cold was just cold and loss was loss. I could not soften one with the other.

Chapter 21

Winter

I GOT A ride south the next afternoon. The driver's hands are the only bit of her I remember: her manicured nails, her big diamond ring on the leather steering wheel. She was a rich volunteer at the centre and she could have bought the car the day before, it smelled so clean. My tattered pack rested on my lap. The travel stink of it, the smoke and grime and filthy clothes worn deep into its pores, swelled and lifted richly in the warmth and filled the car, and the memories of the miles we'd walked were all through me. Girl was there for a moment and gone anew. The woman didn't flinch from my tears or the new stains on my clothes, and if she saw them she didn't pry. She would have heard things I suppose. One hand was loose on the wheel, and the only sign of disquiet I caught in her might have been a fingertip of her free hand softly scraping her knee, and the pause in her conversation, but the pleasantness of her voice when she resumed talking about the weather and her children didn't fail.

We crossed the flagged line between the counties, which hadn't changed to speak of, except for the two men sitting in their truck on the roadside beneath the sagging balloons. They waved us through with lazy hands. We hardly slowed and it wasn't long before we reached the turn-off which I remembered from a fancy white pavilion in a farmhouse yard. It was hard to credit the days it had taken to cover that distance through back ways and woods. The lady offered to take me further in to help find the truck, but I told her I'd walk it, that I wanted to stretch my legs and clear my mind. The truth was I didn't want her to see what I would be travelling in and to know it. I knew she wouldn't forget. The old unease was creeping back, as if it mattered whether I lived or died. What if she was one of them, or knew someone, or had beliefs that she concealed? What if she wanted to know how I, a known sympathiser, was travelling and where I might go?

I walked away from the highway and pushed the gate of an abandoned house and went in and drifted around the ghost garden to pass the time until I was sure she wasn't going to drive in after me. Out back were two rows of fruit trees in need of pruning, a chicken house with its wire sidings staved in, vegetable gardens gone to seed and abandoned, allium flowers leaning stiffly in the breeze, bean frames grown over and the plants died, and several tall, stricken sunflowers, their enormous heads facing every which way, as hopeless as forgotten children. I took out my notebook and did a sketch, and pulled three leaves – they had more give in them than I thought – and a few seeds from the sunflower plants, wrapped them carefully in a t-shirt and put the parcel in my pack. It would have been lovely once, green and insect-filled, humming with life, the scattered chickens pecking and fluffing their feathers in the sun and the dust. That's how it lived in my mind, whatever it was like now in the cold of winter, all faded browns and withered leaves and still.

I sat on the back steps regarding this world, trying not to think too far ahead or to recall what I'd left behind. After a while I returned to the gate and looked out to make sure the road was clear, and went along the roadside until I came to a curl of woods cupping a field and a corrugated tin barn scraggled with dead vines. The truck should be beyond, but before I rounded the barn to cross the ploughed furrows I spied a burned patch, and a little further on saw the blackened truck down on its haunches, windows blown out, tyres burned to nothing, a black circle in the dead field around it, and patterns of burn all around where fragments had blown off and spot fires had lit. A summer fire would have gone for miles; it might have finished those woods, so there was some mercy there. Maybe it was the Silverado that had set gunmen in pursuit through those same woods. I thought of those runners in the droop-fronted house thinking themselves safe, and the way that blunt danger had hit them, not us, and how we'd envied them their shelter for a few hours. I hoped we'd had no part to play in those events.

I approached the Silverado as if there might be an unspent explosion there yet. Every bit of the car resisted me. The door handles had melted down the car's sides lazy as candlewax. I tried for a while to prise one off, but it had become part of the other metal, a solid join that I had to respect. The doors declined to open, but wanting something I could take back to Hart, and looking for distractions, I found a rock by the roadside and used it to bash out the remaining glass from the driver's window, scraping it back and forth to be sure there was nothing jagged there. I wrapped my coat tight and doubled across my front and leaned in until the window cavity took my weight, and reached in to the black space and its vile wet burned smell. The stick shift snapped off so I tried for the indicator arm, but the charred knob crumbled and the arm broke off short. There was nothing there but seat frames and springs. I pulled one and it came out, an ossified snake thing with its skin all roughened and ruined. It would destroy every other thing it came up against. I pulled a few more springs out and lined them up and beneath them found a square chunk of metal – the seat belt clasp; still, somehow I couldn't leave. It was good to be busy. It stopped me thinking so much.

I went back to the farmhouse and pulled chicken wire from one side of the chicken house, and looked around for some other things – timbers, big spent cans of herbicides and pesticides and fertilisers, a broom head, three rolls of wire of different gauges hanging by the back door for convenience – and dragged them back using the chicken wire as a sort of stretcher. I hated myself for not moving on and built something anyway, a creature to mark this place, a wild thing with poison inside that I affixed to the roof of the car so it could survey this world and tell something about it. It was the first making of the journey south. I felt less jagged afterwards, and poked around for a while collecting more things I might use.

I thought about retribution and atonement and whether the world intervened in such matters. On the whole, I thought not. I was still alive and that made no sense at all. Still, I wasn't surprised at the car. *Of course*, I thought. It seemed almost right after everything that had happened as if I might be able to walk out the wrongness of my actions and the badness of the world, which I didn't believe possible. I'd worry about what to tell Hart later, and I would try not to think of the bus driving away.

My clothes were warm, and I had a little water still. Not enough for the three days advised in the nuclear flyer or the longer time I knew it would take, but enough to keep me going for now. I'd walk back to the highway and hitch one ride and another, keep going, just move along in the little patch of world that was always around me, and not think ahead or behind. What choice did I have? Even then, despite everything, I proceeded. I was alive and I tried to start walking.

I put on my pack, and looked along the road to the highway and the cars flashing past. I couldn't take the first step. There was no leaving behind what had happened in Freedom. I had to write it all first, and then see if I could go on. Time rots down. What happens today or last week or a month ago in one way is nothing but fallen leaves building up in layers, soon to become mud and muck and silt. It would take a long time for the events of Freedom to feel like that.

I hadn't been paying attention at the bus stop in Freedom. No one had. The worst of their worries – life and death, I mean – were over. Girl would have felt it. Her hackles would have prickled and her body throbbed with disquiet. I was watching Niña poking her tiny wolf head from the basket and Alejandra wiping her face with her arm, Cat holding Treasure and keeping Alejandra close around her shoulders, and Luis with several bags, looking ahead, almost buoyant now, straight and true. I was hoping people would be kind and they'd find seats together. A small crowd of volunteers and workers at the centre and a few townspeople gathered waiting were calling out: 'Good luck, guys', 'We're going to miss you', 'You think it's cold here!' – things like that to lighten the moment, which, despite the promises to phone and write, did seem final. Crossing the border: the words were in my mind. I was waiting for it to be over.

Someone called out, 'Hey, Hugo Galves! Hey, Hugo! That you, man?' The accent was heavy.

Luis turned fast, his eyes darting around, and tried to still himself before his reflex was seen. No, I thought immediately. I understood it so fast. I saw an arm lift, and a flash, and Luis drop. Then he was a crumpled thing. I don't know if I saw or imagined in him a glimmer of surprise, if that was the last thing. He was on the ground before Cat had even turned. 'Mariana,' the man called, but when Alejandra looked, which she couldn't help, though Cat held her tight, he hesitated. She was so young. Even a person who will kill like that has something inside that will make him hesitate. Nonetheless he lifted his gun. 'Step away,' he called to Cat. 'It's not you I want.'

Cat turned away from him, shielding Treasure, who was screaming, and Alejandra, who was gasping for air, shielding them both as best she could. I pulled my own gun – people were screaming and running by then – and shot from the hip and returned the gun to my pocket. I don't remember the sound of gunshot, but the man fell hard. His head bounced on the sidewalk.

'Call them back. Get them on the bus! You've got to get going now,' I shouted.

The official at the bus steps looked at his binder blankly, as if it might contain instructions for what to do after a gun attack. He was a young man running to seed, with his jeans pulled high, the belt digging into his softness and his baseball cap digging into his thick neck, but he was giving a bit of his free time for others to do this simple job, which had become so difficult.

'Hey. Hey, sir,' I said.

He stared and backed away like I might shoot him now, so I knew he'd seen me.

I looked at his name tag. 'Warren. They could be in danger. Get them moving. Do it now, Warren. Now.'

He began calling, weakly at first, and then stronger, and people began rushing back. Folk were streaming out of the centre as well, the lawyer I'd handed my papers to among them. He took charge. 'Come on, come on, before the cops get here. You want them going through your papers?' he yelled at a lagging woman looking through her bag. She scuttled.

People averted their eyes from the two bodies, and from Alejandra standing so still, and from Cat who had dropped to Luis's side. She touched his grey face and peeled his coat back and saw his smashed chest. Alejandra's head was tipped back and her eyes were closed and her mouth was open. No sound came out. Somewhere sirens were sounding. I went to the man I'd shot. He was just a guy in jeans and a padded denim jacket, a wispy moustache, short black hair covered by a knitted hat that was askew across his forehead. There was the outline of a small blue tear tattooed beneath one eye, like Tobe's. He looked young lying facing the sky with his legs kicked out almost carefree, like a child being swung around. He was dead but I spoke to him anyway: 'You got the wrong person. It should have been me.' I wanted to kick him. I wanted to smash him and worse.

I went to Cat and pulled her to her feet. I took Luis's scarf from around his neck and thrust it in her pocket. 'For later, so you have something,' I said. 'You'll need it.' I pulled the leather thong bracelet from his wrist and tightened it over Alejandra's. 'For later, so you have something,' I told her. 'I'm sorry you have to go, but you have to, for him.'

I hugged them – they probably wouldn't remember that – and told them I loved them more than life and pushed them up the stairs and threw their bags up. Warren checked their names. A man helped them. I tracked their progress through the smoked-glass windows. They moved dumbly to their seats. There were three more people – two women and a child. Warren banged the bus doors which hissed shut and the bus drew out. I watched until it swung onto the highway and disappeared.

I waited by Luis's body with my hand resting on his chest. It seemed like he was cooling already. Would it happen so fast? I put my fingers to his neck. It was still warm, but unmoving. The fluttering of blood was in my own fingers, my own body. I stood when the police arrived and saw that some of Luis's blood was on my jeans now, from kneeling in the run-off, I suppose, and my jeans stuck to my knees and I had to keep pulling the fabric loose. Luis's soft black hair was lifting in the breeze. I stroked it and it felt the same as Alejandra's. It made him seem alive again and the breath caught in my throat. What would I know about life and death and the signs of them? The police looked at him, lifting his sweater, pressed fingers to his neck. They draped a sheet over him, tucking it at head and foot so it didn't blow away. So he was truly dead now. They looked at the shooter, lifted his jacket, felt his neck – it was nothing but routine to them – and draped him too.

They asked for witnesses and a woman in her thirties told them about the shooter, and the names he'd called, which she'd forgotten. She asked me if I remembered and I said I didn't. Warren looked away. A few others drifted around for the drama. The woman whispered to me, 'I saw what you did.' I didn't reply. She said, 'It's okay.' If people had seen anything, it was Luis falling, and if they weren't running from that, the other man falling. No one else mentioned me or my gun, but my gun was in my pocket and I had used it. I told the police what I'd seen of the shooter, and said I hadn't seen who shot him.

'Assholes,' the younger policeman said in a flat voice. His face was hardly touched by life.

'What were you looking for on their chests?' I asked.

'Tattoos, their membership. One isn't marked.' He pointed towards Luis. 'Must have really pissed someone off.'

'Got him in the end,' the other said.

I gave them a name and number, false ones, in case they needed me, and I walked away. The man had known Luis and Alejandra's true names, but the names I have written were not the names he called, which I can't remember. Maybe it was Hector. I'm pretty sure it was H and G for Luis and M for Alejandra. They came out like water running. I've dreamed the moment and heard the names again, but they're gone by the time I wake. It might be better that way.

It is a dark moment leaving the people you love. It leaves a hollowness at your core, and life billows, buffeting and changing shape, shrinking sometimes until the idea of it is lost over a horizon. Other times the hollowness consumes. Likewise, no one can explain what it's like to leave a place they love, that has held them and their family safe for as long as memory. Would I have left Wolfe if I'd know what was to come? Would I have sent them up highways on their own with nothing but the Silverado, a little money, a tin whistle (my father believed one essential to any journey from home) and a penny hug? In that life I would still have Girl; I wouldn't know of the storms to come. Nothing new in that. Life is good and bad together: everything mixed through and all the parts growing in and out of one another: no sunrise without the sun setting; no future without a past; no redemption without a sin. I used to imagine the waters rising high. I was finding things out. Would I have done different if I'd known about the journey home?

Chapter 22

I MOVED IN a dream on the roads heading south. It suited me that way. I didn't want to be thinking. People in scattered numbers moved steadily along highways and down roads that led off them and on streets in towns, looking for places to stay for a night or places they might settle for a little longer to catch their breath or evade violence or wait for kindness or food or warmer weather. A tide of people was heading north, which I hadn't known when I was in the stream of them. It was disconcerting being on my own after a year of company, like my return to Wolfe Island when I left my family behind – that walk up the road in the soft darkness, the aloneness of it, not a soul to watch my back or decide a single thing. It had been by turns a rapturous and fearful freedom. In the days and weeks that followed it came at me sometimes like a vicious animal darting in, biting my arm or stealing a finger. My heart leaped and I trembled and sweat prickled at my hairline. Wherever I was, I stood still and shut my eyes and waited to settle. I would not look behind in such moments or I'd forever be looking back, but it was not easy.

Now I became accustomed to quiet again, to my mind roaming undisturbed as it used to on Wolfe Island. I'd forgotten.

I heard everything there as clear as if I'd been half deaf before: the thin call of a gull, the whistle of a kite, the wind sounding like rain in the grasses. I might sit for a morning, watch the clouds, feel the wind on my left cheek, and how it shifted by noon, the way the clouds shadowed the sun and I shivered, insects going to ground, birds plunging to trees, everything but weather growing still and watchful, and without a thought I went into the house with Girl at my side and secured the windows and watched the storm. This was my world and I was its. I wished for nothing else. But life does not go on in the same way. Sometimes the world is a blizzard-filled snow globe. Things happen in the shaking and the settling.

Some people I passed

I saw a man travelling the same direction as me, though slower. His shabby-elegant pinstripe suit hung loose on his skinny frame, and he carried his hands before him, wrists close, as if the remembrance of shackles and trying to break free ran deep inside him. I caught up with him by degrees. Eventually he sat on a fallen roadside tree, removed his shoes and shook them out – a courtesy to show he was no danger to me – and waited till I was well past before putting them on again. There is etiquette on the road that any new vagabond such as myself must learn. I count this man one of the most courteous I met.

I passed a swarthy man with a red cap and blue jeans frayed at heel and a leathery old rocker man with a long sparse grey beard that drifted over his shoulder in the wind. I crossed the road to avoid him. He watched too hard and glanced around to see if we had company. I let him see the blood that stained my clothes and he thought better of whatever plan he was hatching.

I passed two women and three tired children. The smallest, a boy, was crying hard. One of the women looked around and went back to the child. She knelt and he walked into her arms. She rocked him, passed a little cloth over his face, and smoothed his fringe out of his eyes. I had reached her by then and stopped to tell her about the man with the hard look and she thanked me. She stood and held the boy's hand and they went on.

I entered a region of low hills and forests – maples and beeches and dogwoods with an understorey of holly. A truckload of gunmen came over a hill and down the road. There were nine or ten men swaying in the tray, their guns sticking up, and no time for me to hide, so I waited, thinking they'd pass, because what would they want with me? They pulled up alongside. They were young and dumb-looking – costume warriors in hunting store fatigues, a couple with those ridiculous bandanas tied around their heads. They already had two handcuffed runners – a small woman and a beaten-up man and a little sobbing boy who reached his arms out stiffly and cried, '*Mami, Papi, Mami, Papi,*' over and over.

One of the vigilantes was truly mean. He pawed through my bag, then emptied it on the muddy ground, shaking it joylessly. I began picking things up. Before I'd straightened something behind me caught their attention – a new plaything; a silent, slight, ragged young man I'd just passed, I guessed. The truck reared forward, the gravel spitting up and smacking into my legs and jacket, leaving gritty mud on my lips.

Evidently, the young man had slid into the woods. The truck came to a skidding stop and the men shot after him, haphazardly, it seemed. (The gunfire made me shake.) They went on their way. Perhaps the man was dead; perhaps he was wounded. I went back and plunged into the misty trees. It was quiet in there and still but for the drip of water from leaves. I called, 'Hey there.' My voice was an explosion. My heart raced. I lowered my voice to a loud hiss, 'I'm the lady you passed before. Remember me? Do you need any help?' But the man wasn't there, and after some stumbling around I returned to the road, heading south again. At the churned section where they'd stopped me I slowed, looking for anything I might have missed and there was the man, a shadow between the trees, as quiet and still as a making.

'*Señora*,' he said. He had a desperate look about him, and a grey sheen to his young face. His hand pressed his side beneath his jacket. He swayed and took his hand away and turned it over to show me, as if he was giving himself up to me or to death. His hand was red.

'Oh God,' I said. I wanted to turn and run from him – more blood – but I skidded down the short embankment to his side and pulled up his jacket to see his wound, a deep welt sliced into his scrawny side. The bullet had not reached his guts. 'No, no, no. You're all right, honey,' I said and made him look. I staunched the wound with my spare t-shirt and cinched it in place with his belt. He winced, then vomited, or tried to. His stomach was empty.

'It's okay,' I said. 'I know it hurts, but it's not deep. You're okay.'

'*Gracias*,' he said, and kept on talking. But I didn't understand. I wished I'd picked up some Spanish in Freedom.

'You need stitches,' I told him.

He didn't understand, so I mimed sewing and he shook his head wildly.

'No, no *doctor*.' Tears turned his black eyes lustrous.

'Okay,' I said.

He sat abruptly and shut his eyes and retched again. He had a drink from my water bottle. I listened to his shallow breaths. I gave him two dollars and was ashamed I didn't give him all I had. When he was ready, I helped him back to the road and gestured south – would he like to come with me? He shook his head and pointed north.

'*Gracias*,' he said.

'Be careful,' I told him, and we parted. I turned back to watch him a couple of times, wondering if he might collapse, but his line was steady enough. People pass through your life and it can be hard not knowing what happened to them. I hope he made it, but I could not picture it. I could see a fever infection and hunger and fatigue setting in, him leaving the road to rest against a log, a cold night and an endless sleep. But people do surprise.

Later, it began to snow, falling randomly at first, scudding across my vision in flecks of light. The sky was so heavy and low it seemed it would fall. The snow began in earnest. I needed shelter before dark – perhaps one of pine branches, like the ones we'd made on Wolfe when we were small, or I might get lucky and find a hollowed-out tree and it would be enough if I could just stay dry till morning. There was an opening between the trees down the embankment and I headed into it, stumbling and slipping, anything to get out of the wind. I trudged up a wide path – a fire or maybe a logging trail. Ahead, bare trees ran the ridges of the hilltop like a fine lace. The snow blew across them but I had my path.

Oh, but I was cold and there was nothing to do but keep going and keep going, hoping I'd find something. I shivered till it hurt. A whiff of smoke came from somewhere, good wood smoke from a fire. It blew away. I thought I might sit for a minute or two and gather myself, but didn't. I stopped, looked ahead, pulled my woollen hat low. A dark shape came towards me.

'Ma'am?' The voice drew closer. 'Ma'am, are you lost?'

'I think I might be.'

Then the person, a young man with a light pleasant voice, was beside me. 'Better come. Not the weather for it. Just heading home.' He turned around and I made myself follow.

It was a bad storm. I would not have made it without the kindness of Eddie, the young man. His home – part cave, part shack – was worked into the entrance of a sheet of overhanging rock, and was as snug as a gypsy caravan, lined with straw bales right up to the tarpaulin ceiling. He was a scarce-bearded, gentle, willowy sort of person; he had to stoop here and there so he didn't knock the ceiling, something he did with the grace of familiarity. He'd crazy-paved the floor with pieces of slate, and wisps of straw were scattered across it as if it was a barn floor. More straw bales became benches, topped with tablecloths, wooden planks, and jars and saucepans all lined up neat. Two jars of honey stood in a pan of water. An old wood stove kept his home warm, and warmed me. I turned myself around and around, roasting one side and another of my chilled body, taking it all in. He'd pegged a pair of drying socks to a singlet-clad wood block pulled up to its side, and it seemed halfway to being a making. At the foot of a narrow bed covered in rich brocade (a curtain, perhaps) he'd fashioned shelving filled with blankets and clothes and books.

Low-watt lamps hung from the ceiling (a generator ran from a nearby stream), and pieces of paper in plastic sheets pegged to fishing lines crisscrossed above, rustling and shifting like roosting birds as we moved. They were drawings and paintings of things he'd seen: intricate observations and notes of creatures taken from unexpected angles, the profile of a dead nestling, a raptor's skull, mosses and toadstools and lichens, leaves and branches, spiderwebs, moonlight, constellations. (He didn't mind my looking at them. With the storm outside there was time.) He paid attention to his world.

One picture was of his dog, Captain, a retriever, drawn with a bulge on its neck: *Captain: rattlesnake bite*, the caption read.

'Nice dog,' I said.

'He died.'

'Oh no. I lost a dog not long ago. Nearly killed me.'

He shook his head. 'I'm sorry.'

I waved my hand to shoo the thought away. 'I'm sorry too – for your loss.'

He shrugged, as if a shrug could dismiss a broken heart. We sat in the lamplight, each of us knowing that it couldn't, that we were just agreeing not to sink into it. The storm got louder. He was unperturbed. He sat on an upturned bucket at a lower section of bench, one bale high, that contained his drawing and painting things, and began adding to a picture. He was comfortable with silence. He looked up once and said, 'It'll be a couple of days.'

'Pardon me?'

'The storm.'

I believed him. I was getting used to his way of speaking. I thought he was taciturn at first, but I came to believe it was lack of practice. I wondered what I was like after a few months alone, getting my conversation going, taking a while to catch up with the way other folk talk and the directions their minds travel.

Before dark fell he showed me an outhouse down the path (not an expedition to undertake lightly) and insisted I take his bed, which from the feel of it was more straw bales. I slept well for the first time since I left Wolfe Island. I felt safe there in that living space, as if I had some kinship with it.

We fell into sporadic conversations like quick flurries of snow during the days of my stay. They left me somewhat breathless. I told him that once upon a time I had a husband and two children – son and daughter – and now I had only a daughter; I left the details vague.

'How old are you?' I asked.

'Twenty . . . wait. Twenty-four.'

The same as Tobe.

Six years older than Luis and Josh.

Six years younger than the prisoner on death row.

Perhaps twenty years younger than the man who wanted to get Luis and Alejandra on Wolfe Island, who died on its sunken jetties.

Forty years younger than the man who killed Girl, and who I killed in turn.

Younger than the man who'd killed Luis and wanted to kill Alejandra, and who I killed to save her.

I couldn't breathe. All those people. What was I these days? Eddie looked at me like I was clean out of my mind. He probably was right. I was panting, *huh, huh, huh*, like that, as if I was giving birth. It was that terror I used to get about what was behind me. 'Don't look back.'

He was alarmed. 'You okay, ma'am?'

I shook my head. 'Some people.'

He brought me a glass of water, about the best water I've ever tasted. Sipping it, I slowly began to put my feelings back, to smooth them.

After a while I got out my notebook, and began to feel better after some work. It took me out of myself. I drew a couple of things that I liked about Eddie's home – the connection techniques he used which I considered original and pleasing. I drew a picture of the young runner who had been shot, and wished I'd helped him on his journey north, for a few days at least. (It was Luis who had been on my mind, the thought of him lying in a parking lot, a shrouded thing.) By the time I thought of travelling with him it would have been like searching for a shark tooth in marshland.

Things I wished I'd brought with me
- *Bandages and bandaids*
- *Adhesive tape*
- *Antiseptic ointment*
- *Painkillers*
- *Tweezers*
- *Space blanket*
- *Waterproof matches / a lighter*
- *Firelighters*
- *Jelly beans, chocolate, energy bars*

Eddie began to cook, standing at his bale-and-wood kitchen bench, dicing dried apples and putting them in a pan with vanilla and some water. A sweet spicy smell wafted about.

'Mmm, cinnamon,' I said.

He gave his diffident half-smile. 'My mother liked cooking with it.' He was getting his words going now.

'And the straw.'

'Yeah. We had a farm. Drought got it. Ended up walking. I went through some times until I set up here.'

He began a pastry. The pictures moved in the breeze that he made, depending on him for their life. I could use that in a making, get people to walk past or through a making so it moved and they were helping it become itself and becoming part of it themselves.

We ate his apple pie in the middle of the afternoon because we were hungry. I considered the way he lived refined, and the place he lived as fascinating as any art I ever saw. I told him I liked his work, mentioned my line of business and asked him if he considered himself an artist.

'I don't know.'

'I wondered why you store your pictures in plastic.'

He shrugged.

'And why you hang them.'

'I don't want to bend them and I don't want to lose them. I don't want them getting wet.'

'So, *for* someone? One day?'

'I don't know.' He sounded sharp then.

'My daughter Claudie would say, "God, Mother," right about now. I didn't mean to be nosy.'

'Yes you did.'

'Yeah, I did.'

He smiled then.

'But it is very good. I want you to know that.'

He looked pleased, shy-pleased, and then gave that shrug, like he was saying, So what? What do I care what people think?

I told him about the Watermen calling. I found a picture I'd drawn of them early on, after we left Wolfe Island, as if they might be able to watch over us from there. 'I didn't know I wanted other people to see my work.'

'I wouldn't mind seeing them.'

'Yeah, well, come visit sometime.'

He stared at me hard. 'What happened to your son?'

'Died a few years ago.'

'I had a feeling.'

'He had a place something like this.'

'Oh yeah? Did he like to draw?'

'No. He liked the water. He was a waterman. How about your mother?'

'Car accident when I was fourteen. Didn't like my dad's new wife. She didn't like me, so—'

'How long you been living like this?'

'A while.'

He looked at the ground furiously. He hated himself then, and he hated me because I'd asked and he'd told and felt something about it again. It was pollution in this pure safe place. He got up, flung on his jacket, threw the flap door back and went out. All the hanging papers swayed wildly in the wind he'd made and the breath of the outside and began their strange whispering. I heard some chopping sounds – plenty of dead trees around to be going on with. I looked through a couple of his drawings and wrote in my book, and worried about Cat and everyone, and wished Luis was here in this safe place. Tobe too.

Eddie came back in. The cold came off his clothes in avalanches – a good clean hard smell. Sweat beaded on his forehead. 'I don't need anyone's pity. I'm not looking for a mother.'

'I'm not looking for a son. Your age doesn't mean anything. I like your work. It's interesting; you're interesting. I have connections that might be useful for you – with your art.'

'I'm not sure I want—'

'Connection.'

'No.'

'The world?'

'What's the word? I've got enough . . .'

'Charity.'

'Yeah.'

'Got it. People acting like you're pitiful. Never mind the money. If you want people to see your work, you've got something to say, you'd like to talk to people about it, as equals – that's what I mean. You'd be welcome as a friend.'

'Well.' He wouldn't say thank you because he wasn't grateful and he wouldn't lie, but I think he understood that I meant well. He lived by rules I didn't know, the way I had on Wolfe. I wondered what his were. 'Be sure to welcome strangers' would be one of them, some ancient frontier habit, maybe something from his mother. I had disturbed the stillness he lived in with my clumsy talk. I hoped I had not ruined it. What could the world do for him? I didn't consider myself lonely at the time Cat arrived. The subject didn't come up again. We were quiet after that for some hours. I caught up with recent events in my notebook.

Here, writing now, the past seems as close as the present. The straw prickles under me, feeling not so different from the dry saltmarsh we lay hidden in when we were small. I pull a little piece from the side and stick it in my mouth, nibbling the end. It doesn't taste a lot, but it's a pleasant thing to do. Eddie seems to find it amusing. 'Hayseed,' he says. It's peaceful being around him. It's the quiet of him, and the unhurried way he inhabits his world. I can't help thinking about the sadness of his past and how he came to be like this. He has kept going despite all he's lost, and his world is as filled with meaning as Wolfe Island was for me. He doesn't seem lonely, merely alone. It suits him. He has lost everything and made something. Tobe lost things too, but not more than Eddie or Luis. He hadn't finished with trying and searching for a new way and a new place to live. It was circumstance or fate – whatever you want to call it – that got in his way, as unstoppable as a weather system sweeping through. There is no controlling some things. What I mean is that what happened to Tobe is not all on me and, for the first time, I feel that.

What else can I do but move forward, persist, homeless and grieving though I am? I've lost almost everything, as Eddie has, and will have to find a new place to be. Who will I be without Wolfe Island? I don't know, but Eddie gives me some hope.

On the second afternoon Eddie lifted his head. 'Smell that?'

I lifted my head and sniffed. 'No.'

'Snow's slowing.'

'You smelled that?'

'I might be wrong.'

I peeked out of the thick vestibule plastic. 'You're right.' I poked my head out. The snow was unblemished, blue in the shadows of trees, and beautiful. 'I had a place I knew like you know this.'

He looked up from his watercolour. 'That where you're going?'

'As near as I can get.'

I gave him my name and Doree's contact details on the final morning. He gave me some cookies. 'Thank you,' I said at the road. He ducked his head and turned back. Ten seconds after I started he'd disappeared.

*

Everyone I passed in that forest region warned that militias were about, and I spread the same news to anyone I saw. When danger is running loose, people begin thinking in old ways, more like animals. For two days I veered along the sparse edges of woods, the ridges of hilltops, old dirt roads that curled around hills, the threadbare edges of marginal farmland. One night I pressed into the corner of an old hunters' cabin on a sleeping platform of hewn timber, fearful of every sound in the darkness. Finally, the road curved and descended at the edge of the forest and the hills made way for open farmland with grids of roads, asphalt and dirt. The white stubble on fields looked like new snow. I walked down into it, breathing easier now I could see into the distance.

I walked through Ruston and Edmore and the undulating farmland between. Signs on the scrawny outskirts of each announced their thoughts on people running and searching and escaping. In Ruston they said *Welcome* and bore directions to a centre where food or water or advice or warm clothes could be found. Another town had *No Strangers Here* and *No Room Here* yard signs stabbed into their lawns. People stared as I went past, unsure what abuse to hurl since I was heading the wrong way.

A man and his son drifted with me on the other side of the road. They were clean, their hair was cut neat, and their clothes were warm. They were bored and angry, each feeling diluting the other, but they threw some stones at me anyway and one hit my coat. It gave me a bad feeling. Finally the man summoned some dogged remembrance – 'You can get on out of here, bringing disease' – as if the words were his civic duty.

I was tired after that and rested in the lee of a highway wall just out of town. Three skinny teenagers, two girls and a boy, their thin legs stretched out, hands buried in their pockets, were already in occupation, but they didn't mind me. One girl's hair wisped about like thin smoke. She reached into a raggedy plastic bag and pulled out a tough old baguette, and broke it over her knee as if it was kindling, and handed the shards around. It tasted good. The traffic droned past, a strange experimental music. There are many ways of living.

Chapter 23

ROSE WAS SMALLER and older than me, like a colourful bird – an oriole, say – with her short grey and pink hair. She'd picked me up on a curved stretch of highway bordered by fields and distant long-dead pines still standing and as white as bone. (One lone loblolly put me in mind of the tallest tree on Wolfe Island and the time years ago that someone took a chainsaw and cut it down. People had looked for it out at sea for as long as anyone knew. Wolfe's Pine, gone.) I was glad to be inside a moving vehicle for a while. The outside of Rose's camper was covered in stickers of places she 'hearted'; inside, the seat springs were gone and they squeaked as we bounced. She sat forward in her seat with cushions beneath and behind, almost pecking the wheel in her need to see out. She rolled the sleeves of her plaid shirt, which spilled loose immediately until she looked like a dishevelled child. I picked at the vinyl piping of my seat, poking back the grey stuffing that was nosing out.

Words rolled out of Rose. She'd been working up north, seeing her daughter, but her dog couldn't get along with her daughter's boyfriend's dog and she couldn't get along with her daughter's boyfriend and he said it was between him and her and if she didn't move on he would, so her daughter told Rose goodbye. Not to worry, Rose said. She got it. Her daughter's man was the future, and her mother was something from the past. She, Rose, had places to go and friends to catch up with; right now she was heading south for a regular gig at a factory warehouse pulling stock, only the hours were long and she had the dog. The dog, a scrappy scruffy thing, condescended to sniff my hand.

'She likes you,' Rose said.

'You can tell from that?'

'Well. She's slow to warm. Isn't that right, Hurtle?' The dog panted lightly and stared ahead. 'She's not really my dog.'

'You don't mind moving about so much?'

She lifted her shoulders and let them fall. 'I don't know why I would mind. As long as I can, I will. What else would I do? It pays the bills; I get to see the country. If it gets too much, though – well, I'll worry about that when the pearly gates come into view. Ha!' It seemed like an old joke. Perhaps it held the truth at bay. 'How 'bout you? Looks like you've seen some times.' Her eyes flickered to the dark stains on my knees.

'I took my daughter north. My car got burned out. I'm walking home instead.'

'That sucks.' She tapped the top of a floral-patterned thermos and glanced at me. 'Coffee? Help yourself.' So I did, holding the cup in one hand, popping the top of the flask and pouring. A few clumps of undissolved milk powder came out along with the coffee. Rose looked at them. 'Cheaper than fresh and no waste.'

'Have you got another cup?'

'Nope, just the one. Pour me one when you've finished.' We jounced along for a bit and then she said, 'I heard there was a big storm down south a couple weeks back.'

I had lost the way of keeping up my end of a conversation so fast. I said, 'Really?'

A while later she said, 'I heard we're in for an early spring.'

'Is that right?'

'I heard vigilantes been killing more folk.' She looked at my knee again.

'That's no good,' I said.

'I guess not.' Rose darted me another look, assessing me for my political leanings or maybe my temper. I didn't look back so I didn't have to add anything to the space she left. Finally she quit her meaningful glances and said only, 'I heard avocado is good for your skin – like I've got the spare change to put food on my face.' She laughed.

It went like that, avocadoes and death mattering about the same. I guess that was right where she was coming from. Her van was a cocoon – her world – that kept her safe. I was sure it wouldn't suit me. I wanted to see more of Claudie, if that was possible, if she was willing. Where would I put my makings things and my tools? Where would I store makings once made? I wanted salt meadow, a watery sky and a familiar sea. I wanted to put some roots down. Rose's life seemed like a stone skipping across still water; she could never pause to see beneath . . . She could depend on no one and no one could depend on her. It made me shiver, thinking of it.

We stopped at a highway gas station and I went into the restroom and when I came out she was getting into the van.

'Hey!' I called. 'Hey, Rose.'

She wound down the window and pointed. 'Her name's Hurtle.' Hurtle was tied to a post with my pack, a big bag of dog food and a bowl at her side. When I looked back, Rose was accelerating away. Hurtle was trying to reach a fry just beyond her nose, making a hacking choking noise as her collar cut into her throat.

I approached Hurtle cautiously. She thought I was going to battle it out for the fry, and growled and snapped. I kicked the fry towards her with my foot and untied her gingerly while she was busy with it and searching for more. What else could I do? I was nothing but an anchor at the end of a lead to her. I kept her tied, though it would have been easier if she'd run off. She had wiry fur of many lengths, was no more than knee-high, and solid in her body without exactly being stocky. She kept a sideways eye on everything. She had a mean streak and had been looking out for herself for a while. Her growl came from deep in her body. She hated other dogs and didn't like to be touched, but could abide lying along my outstretched leg if we stopped for a rest. But these were discoveries for the next couple of days.

In your mind you might be thinking it's because she wasn't a wolfdog that makes me show her in an unflattering light, and thinking that she might turn out to be one of those chipper movie dogs with a bright eye and a cocked ear and a tail raised and a speaking look, like if I said, 'Would you mind getting me Mama's old recipe book?' she'd trot to the breakfront, pluck it from its place with delicate teeth, return it to my lap and settle at my feet, her head resting on her front paws, and sigh, content that her job of loyalty and utility was done. She was not like that.

Even a dog that doesn't care about you is better than no company at all. At the time I thought I'd taken her up and saved her; she might have thought the same.

There were no more rides after that, not that I'd ever caught many. Hurtle wasn't a dog who'd add lustre and respectability to a foot traveller. After a long morning standing on a raised section of highway on the outskirts of that town, where I reasoned that I might be seen from the distance, I realised my hitching days were done. I had no clear idea how far I had to walk. The road signs didn't mention Blackwater or any place I knew. I didn't know places. All I knew was to keep heading south.

I couldn't think too far ahead, I just kept moving forward. It was me and Hurtle, staying alive, safety and danger, hunger and wondering and searching, walking. That was all. It is a lot, put like that. And I got off lightly.

It's harder to write on the road. My hands are often cold, or it's too dark to see. But sometimes there's a fire, or I find a sheltered patch of sun – the edge of a highway or a house porch – or I'll wake at dawn and stay still for a while, Hurtle keeping me warm, and get out my notebook. It holds my worries at bay even if I'm writing about those very worries.

Right now, for instance, I'm sitting on a wooden staircase down to a river. The river is black and its surface is fissured with currents and slick – cold looking. The air is milky. The whippy saplings growing along its banks are grey-white, pale orange, scarlet and still. There are neither wind nor clouds. The sky is white – yellow white at the low sun. Hurtle has gone to explore. She looks back to make sure of me, frightened I'll run. 'Hey, Hurtle,' I say. She has resumed her snuffling now. My hands are not too bad, so I am writing, and also thinking about some of the things I've picked up for makings, and the things that have been a wrench to leave behind. I take what I can and every couple of days do a making or a cull and keep what I like best.

Makings things
- *Ploughshare, found on a windowsill*
- *A length of fairy lights*
- *Weathervane*
- *Old cracked boot*
- *Antlers, from a shed*
- *A squirrel skeleton, found curled under a mossy rock ledge*
- *Acorns*
- *Feathers*
- *A tiny toy excavator, found behind a curtain*

I thought about Irina in Essex, who moved about for so long. I felt closer to her now I was without a home, though my troubles were nothing compared to things she endured. She had been broken and was yet together. She was her own making – what a thought. Sometimes I put together a making with the things I was leaving behind. I mostly used grass to hold them together. They'd fall apart by spring. I liked to think of that happening – they were like living things in that way – and drew quick sketches of them and things that caught my eye in case I forgot.

I stopped beneath a bridge a little further along that afternoon. A woman had a hubcap over a fire and someone else had stolen a chicken and someone had killed and plucked it and more than one person ate it. (Hurtle had the backbone and the gristly bits at the joints.) Sometimes we talked. The roadside wood-edge life cut off the rest of the world. It was a ribbon that carried me. One place after another passed by and the ribbon remained intact. It seemed like no one else knew about it except the people who needed it. It was ours. People thought they could see us, but they were wrong. They had no manners, looking into our wall-less homes, sometimes staring. They couldn't see the courtesy, the many courtesies that we lived within. We had our different reasons, but etiquette prevented us from asking each other prying questions. If you waited, a few words or a scar or a crooked leg might tell you something of a person's life.

Some people had been on the ribbon for years. It was different from Rosie's skimming way of living. People on the ribbon felt the land around them. They were part of it and did not pretend otherwise. I asked one lady what was her thinking. She said, I am here and I am alive. Pickings are not good, but it is the time of year and things will improve. I said everything tastes better outside and she agreed. Everyone did. It was hard getting the food to eat, and I was hungry and Hurtle was too. I was rationing the dog food. I found some young shoots somewhere, and picked them and ate a couple and put the rest in my pocket and ate them on the way. I learned to look out for rosehips. They weren't bad. Hurtle wasn't sure but she tried them anyway. Beggars can't be choosers, my mother said. Remember that.

Sometimes I'd watched cooking shows on the island. Animals would get killed – fish and goats, cows, octopuses, crabs, enormous lobsters, rare creatures: eels writhing while their bodies were being split, lobsters thrashing and banging while they were boiled alive, pigs struggling as they were bound for slaughter, their eyes looking out of their basketware cages as their bodies shivered with terror and then with the loss of blood, when their lungs could not fill with air. Every one of them tried to get away, understanding well what was happening and fighting with no expectation of winning. Yet we hold our own life so dear. I enjoyed the chicken and didn't lose sleep over the chicken's lost life, though I don't like to think of its death: the way the man laid it on its back and stood on its spread wings and held its head and sawed its neck with a blunt old knife; the way a woman held a margarine container beneath its neck to catch the blood; the greedy horror of the people watching. I don't excuse myself. I was hungry. I watched.

Chapter 24

WE WALKED ALONG the black lace edges of deep woods and fallow fields. Winter crops were sparse; a few geese moved about on them. It was cold. Another time, I'd make sure to walk in summer. There would be fields of corn to lie within and watch swaying overhead. I would reach up and pluck a cob and peel its taffeta husk and eat its milky kernels, and pass one to Hurtle who would be appreciative. I came upon a reserve, with signs pointing to marshes and swamps, and boards explaining how people had been getting lost there for hundreds of years, by accident or design. I half expected to find bones laid neatly to rest, arms folded across chests and trinkets about bare skulls, a stone at head and foot to hold a body in the open space, or to come across a person curled against a log with their knees drawn up and their clasped hands to their chins so they had something at their backs when exhaustion and hunger defeated them: a prayer, a baby, a dead body. I was not at that point yet. I thought I was getting closer to home judging by the flat, watery land, the standing pines, and the hummocks out on open water.

I didn't know how far we'd have to walk, or even if I'd find Doree or Hart at the end, or how I'd feed Hurtle after the bag of dog food Rose had left behind was finished. I kept heading south as best I could, following the coast, looking out for signs to make sure I didn't roam onto one of the tendrils of land that jutted into the sea, which would likely become islands in due course. There are many similarities between people and land.

I thought of Doree on her dock, the water rising around her spit of garden. It might see her out. I thought of Cat and Luis and Alejandra, Treasure, even Josh. It was like they walked into one side of my life and walked across it and out the other side taking a little bit of me with them, changing everything.

The next day in heavy woods – a shortcut, I hoped – I came across two hunters, fit-looking, younger than me, one with a goatee, their ears sticking out like sycamore seeds beneath their caps, and wearing combat fatigues. They were as startled as I and threw their weapons to their shoulders. Hurtle rushed at them, barking. 'Hurtle,' I said. I held my hands up, though I had my gun in my pocket, right there; I could feel the drag of it. 'Hey,' I said.

'You doing out here?'

'Passing through, heading south. I'm looking for my wolfdog. She ran off the road.' I called out, 'Girl,' and looked about to make it feel real, to me as well as them. Hurtle came over as if to say one name was as good as another. 'Where's she gone, Hurtle? Where?' Girl would have lifted her ears and tilted her head. Hurtle looked at me and sniffed at the ground in case I'd dropped something there for her to eat. 'She headed after something. Might have been the noise you were making. She's a good hunter. You didn't see her?'

'Ain't seen a wolfdog,' the older of the two, the one with the goatee and the growing-out side-whiskers said.

Hurtle barked again, hoarse and random. 'Well, see ya,' I said and lifted my hand and we went on. Finally I looked back and they were gone, I didn't know in which direction. I thought I heard a shout, and then I did for sure.

'We're coming to get you' – a singsong jeering in the cold air, followed by raucous laughter. I was spooked. It would be easy to shoot someone and say it was an accident if that sort of thing entertained you, to hold someone under water until they drowned. I kept on, quiet and fast as I could, stopping behind trees to look back, walking on soft mouldering leaves. Once I thought I heard their breathing, but two are noisier than one and I was able to steer away. In fading light a shoreline came into view, and two cabins perched on a point alongside a couple of boats. Further out was one of the squat old lighthouses, dark but for a red light on its pointed roof. I heaved a boat free, persuaded Hurtle in and dragged it into the water and rowed out, taking care not to splash with the oars, tethering it to the steps, and with some difficulty heaved a reluctant Hurtle out again. She growled, maybe from some tender spot I couldn't see. She had plenty of scars. We climbed the flight of steep metal treads, and beneath us the water moved dark and uneasy, catching and breaking the moonlight. It was dark at the doorway; the wind buffeted, that hollow sound. Hurtle pressed close. I found the handle, turned it, and pushed the door open.

It was quiet inside and the darkness was mottled and approached in waves that darkened and darkened but never absolutely arrived. A rustling came from above. It smelled of wood smoke and burned oil and candlewax, and was not unpleasant, though close.

'Hello?' I called softly, even though no one could be there since there was no boat when we arrived.

Hurtle barked.

'Shh, Hurtle.'

She looked at me and moved her tail. I stroked her cheek. There – as long as I had a living creature beside me I could repel the darkness, the same as when I was a child. My eyes began to adjust and we started up the narrow corkscrew stair cavity I found behind a low door. My hand traced the chill walls – timber slats by the feel. The small doorway at the top was open and a lighter grey bled from it. We climbed through. It was a tiny space almost filled by the vast refractive light at the centre, its unmoving, unlit facets gleaming. Windows all around looked onto seething water, a star-filled sky and the masses of dark pines I had come from, their toothed outlines biting at stars and sky. I shut the small door and latched it, and opened and bent to climb through one of the windows onto the narrow walkway and lifted Hurtle through. The cold wind struck my face, but it smelled good out there. Hurtle looped the lighthouse tower. I looked onto the world obliquely, at the flock of oil derricks further up seeming to stalk our way, one or two warning lights about their edges. A raucous cry sounded across the water. 'We know where y'are now.' And there was a splash, and another, rowing.

'Hurtle,' I whispered. 'Not a sound.' I pulled my gun from my pocket. The water was slippery looking, heaving, as if searching for something to swallow. I waited until I could see them, a denser black moving in that stuttering way of rowboats. 'I see you now,' I called. 'And I will shoot if you come closer.' I detected some hesitation in the rower's stroke.

'You haven't got a gun – or a wolfdog. Bad day for hunting, but it's not over,' the voice taunted. And they began again. 'Like shooting fish in a barrel,' one of them shouted, and the other laughed and said, 'Pigeons in a loft.' They were getting closer.

'I don't want to shoot, but I'm not afraid to,' I shouted. 'I won't warn you again. I prefer not to kill.'

'Ha!' And they came faster.

I lifted my gun and took aim. The conditions were not ideal – I could barely see them. I could see where they were not, though, and I didn't want to hit them. I shot. They bellowed their alarm. 'That should have holed the boat, fellers. The light's not too good. One more to be sure—' I shot again, and heard a sort of thud.

'Fucking crazy bitch. Can't take a joke.' Their boat was drifting now and one of them was fumbling – for his own gun, no doubt. So I shot again – still aiming for the boat. I didn't want any more people on my conscience. I hoped they could swim.

'Is your boat filling? It should be. Head for shore is my advice,' I called. 'You come closer and I'll shoot again. You going to waste time when your boat's going down?' It was wallowing and dragging in the water now, like that seagull Josh shot. All their muttering and cursing, which I could still hear, was only for themselves, and their boat kept drifting, carried heavily by the blackness.

My heart was skipping around. When I put my hand to my chest I could feel it, and wondering if I might faint, I sat for a moment, watching their inexorable slide away, and then lay looking at the stars, at all their untouched patterns. I had not killed them.

Hurtle made a sound in her throat. 'Okay,' I said, and in a couple of minutes we went back into the lighthouse. Downstairs, I scooped out a handful of dog food for her and had a few pieces myself (it's not so bad if you're hungry). I shone the light around. There was some timber in the wood box by a small pot-belly stove, and tucked to one side some paper and candle stubs. I lit the fire. I remember this night so well, it kept me going for so long, the security of it, the knowledge that I had seen off danger and not hurt anyone, and had a little warmth and the company of my strange dog, and I vowed that if I got back I'd try to provide the same for other travellers. Food as well, not only here, but in other places too. I briefly dreamed of lighthouse life; what is a lighthouse but another sort of island? A dog will always be in need of a garden and a walk, though, and I could not imagine life without a dog. I sat cross-legged before the fire and brought my notebook up to date as best I could. I got things wrong and out of order and felt bad already about my early feelings towards Hurtle, which I tried to be honest about in my words. I stroked her head and her ears.

She made another sound, a soft groan. 'Okay,' I said, and when I lay down she flopped against me like I'd thrown down her bed and we curled up close and she promptly went to sleep. It got cold in the night and I wrapped my coat across and around Hurtle and put my hood over my head. She breathed her warm dog breath on me and I can't say it wasn't welcome. The fire burned out and one of us would shiver and we'd squeeze tighter together and come good again. We needed each other, something that Girl and Sweetie and Missy and the others had never taught me.

Hurtle's whining woke me at first light – she'd be needing a pee. It's easy to think of letting a boat drift in the hope it might find another island, but a dog changes things. You can't not take them into consideration. They make you; it's the blessing and curse of them.

I was cautious returning to shore, and I kept watch for a long time, moving through the edges of woods rather than along the roadside. Once I thought a truck that drove by was the huntsmen's, but I couldn't be sure, only saw that the men in it had guns on their laps pointing from the windows. I wasn't what they were looking for – a woman with a dog and no home, but they might kill for sport and agree afterwards to be silent. It can easily happen. People get a little hunting lust up and it has a drive to come out so the host can settle again. No point in taking chances. I stayed still and waited until they'd passed from sight. I had a little food for Hurtle and therefore for me and we walked through that day and stopped only a couple of times. I found an abandoned house that night. There was a woodpile at the kitchen door, but not a match to set it going. I searched until it was too dark to see, then Hurtle and I curled in the bottom of a cupboard upstairs to be out of the drafts and ate the last of the dog food. It was a long uncomfortable night. I made a list in my head of things I wished I had.

Emergency survival pack
- *Matches / lighter*
- *Energy bars*
- *Dehydrated food*
- *Soap*
- *Small towel*
- *Space blanket*
- *Quick-dry change of clothing*
- *Can opener*
- *Miniature gas stove and a tiny travel saucepan, like the one I got from the camping store and left behind*
- *A few coloured pencils*

- *Powdered milk*
- *Small jar instant coffee*
- *Narrow-gauge wire*
- *Strong string*

I didn't know how much further there was to go, but feeling hollow inside, I set myself up outside a library in Manahope, a name I remembered, so I was getting closer to home. The library was a fine old red-brick building, puffed up with white pillars and fancy lettering. Hurtle curled up in a cardboard box I'd picked up from a store. It kept the wind at bay; her fur lifted and occasionally an eyelid and occasionally her ear and occasionally her reproachful gaze. She was not a dog to inspire giving but she was my dog and she needed food so I did this for her. Before us I placed my woollen scarf formed into a nest for money. It lit up on the sidewalk like a fallen sunflower.

I began calling, at first quietly, and then louder, taking care not to use my island accent, and really not caring after a while what people thought and how they judged me or my homely dog. 'Hungry dog here. Still got a way to go.'

Two police officers wearing dark glasses and thick jackets approached with more caution than I thought necessary for a woman down on her luck and her sleeping dog. Their hands rested on their holsters. 'That a wolfdog, ma'am?'

I thought of saying something smart, like, 'Does it look like a wolfdog to you?' or, 'Do you suppose a wolfdog would fit in a box that size?' Pure recklessness. 'No, sir, it is not. No idea what she is. Someone dumped her on me, can you believe?'

'Well,' one said. 'We're looking for someone who's got one.'

'There's a few of them around.'

He showed more interest. 'You seen some?'

'Not around here, no, sir. I have seen them in the past, I mean.' I spoke in a dull way and didn't look in their faces in case they'd remember me, or glance at my scarf in case they took note of its colour, or speak to Hurtle in case she stood and growled or snapped and became memorable.

'We don't like this sort of thing in this town.'

'Excuse me?'

'Begging, ma'am. We do not appreciate it.'

'Oh, okay. It's for my dog. You won't see me again. We're moving on.'

'Which way's that?'

'North, heading north.'

'See that you do.'

I picked up the few dollars we'd gathered and we kept on south. At a convenience store at the edge of town I bought some bread and a piece of only slightly mouldy cheese from the discount shelves, some matches and a bag of dog food – a different flavour.

I wish I had pictures of the car graveyard that Hurtle and I slept in that night and of the four or five teenage girls we found living there. Runaways, not runners, they told me. They were hard, fierce, lean things, and came and sat with us in our car, moving like cats using all their limbs to crawl over the seats. Their eyes darted around us so fast. I gave them the rest of my cheese, which they ate wolfishly. 'My God, cheese,' one said. 'I know, right?' another said. It went down in great chunks that I could see the shape of in their throats as they swallowed and swallowed, stretching their necks to help it down.

'Got anything else?' a redheaded one asked from behind. She played a long bootlace through her hands as if it were rosary beads, wrapping it around and pulling it tight.

'Here you go.' I gave them the bread too, after tearing a piece off for Hurtle.

Another girl said in a wheedling way, 'I like your jacket.'

'Yeah,' I said. 'It was my dad's, so . . .'

'Mmmm,' the girl said, feeling the fur lining peeking from a sleeve. 'Looks warm.'

'It is.' I patted at my side. 'Good deep pockets too so I can fit my gun in, you know.'

She pulled her fingers away and sat back. They became formal after that: 'Excuse me', 'Thank you so much, ma'am', 'You've been so kind', 'Your dog's such a cutie', that sort of thing, fake, but polite, carefully reared as far as words go – as if they'd come over for a tea party bringing a bunch of flowers. They scampered off at sundown like wolf cubs, like jungle cats, like hyenas, one with the bag of dog food under her arm. I envied them in a way. We weren't far from a town, so perhaps they swarmed through it in the night getting the things they needed. There are all sorts of ways to live and they seemed to have each other's backs, but they were wild things, fragile in one way even if they were tough in another. I wondered about their families and where things went wrong. A thought raced: *A girl needs her mother.* Was that true?

They reminded me of Claudie, who would have been about their age when I returned to Wolfe. She'd had that lithe eagerness, the fierceness, the desire to break away and be part of a gang. She had Hart those years; she had her father. But without me there, what would she break from? I'd been so sure she didn't need me – I'd persuaded myself of that.

I took the indicator arm from the car interior, also the rearview mirror, which I used right there because of its weight. I had to so I could keep going. I made a figure from a roadside stump and affixed the mirror to it, facing south, and wired it there securely. I laid some long branches in tracks from its base, and bound them with grasses. It seemed unfinished. It needed some metal – brass that would weather to verdigris in time – riveted to its body. I made a note of that and wrote a little beneath.

Now the deep cold of evening has set in along with some light drizzle. It's not cosy in the car, but it is at least dry. Hurtle and I have moved to the passenger seat, windows up, facing forward, like we're waiting for a driver. There is an old car smell – of grease and dust and distant journeys, and maybe a little coffee, and a wild smell outside that's trying to break in. The drizzle has cleared and the moon has started to slide across the window. It's almost too dark to write now. Soon I will be imagining homecomings, as I do every night, trying to lull myself to sleep. Sometimes Doree is there and sometimes Hart. It is always warm and clean and sweet-smelling and I am clean and they bring me food. Hurtle is her best self. It is better that than thinking of prison. People have died and I made that happen. There is the law and there is justice and I consider the second to be more important than the first. Still, I can't stop remembering when my eyes close. It comes in storm surges. I am glad of Hurtle in those moments and glad of the future brought close. It pulls me along.

It hardly seemed worth standing in the morning, but cold was worse than hunger; we found a slice of sun and stood in it.

I thought I might steal at the next town and wouldn't judge myself for it. Hurtle was depending on me, after all. I felt around in every pocket and found the Silverado key, a box of matches and three pieces of dog food wrapped in a frayed tissue. They were in my hand, chunky and rough, and they looked good. Hurtle stared unwaveringly, drooling. I would have shared them between us. I thought of it. Then I lowered my hand and unfurled my fingers. 'There you go,' I said. They were gone, and Hurtle was quivering in expectation of more. 'That's it.' She shuffled her haunches along the ground, being a good girl. I knelt and opened my pockets so she could see I wasn't holding out on her, and we started walking, not fast, just keeping on. She stayed with me. She might have been looking after me.

Nothing stopped, nothing even slowed, and at dusk Hurtle and I walked off the road into the dark woods. Sleep seemed like the only peace there was. I could lie behind a bank of grass and see those stalks moving above, and even if they were hit by the draught of a passing truck, all laden up with local militias with semi-automatics and assault rifles, if I could not see them, I would fall into a sleep so deep it was another world as far away and safe and beloved as Wolfe Island.

Sometimes I dream that I am still on Wolfe. The closer it is the more *now* it seems. Someone once told me that dead people are everywhere, they follow us along the roads we travel. (Eddie. It was Eddie.) They are here, like Wolfe Island, the past too. Those times are strange and bright. Sound rises out of memory: a few words, a song, a shout – otherworldly, you know? Did we live in that place? It will be a story that people tell. People might look to their grandparents and ask was there a place called Wolfe Island where they really once lived.

Perhaps they'll notice the shadowy contours on sea charts and say, 'Imagine – all of it underwater now.' I might too, tracing the route from dock to my house, up the marsh road and beyond to Stillwater and even to the old pine that Tobe felled at Pine Point, angry or sad or both. There are sunken worlds all around that have no certain meaning to me – shallow spots where sabre tooth tigers might once have roamed. Once upon a time watermen dragged up great bones grown all over with shellfish in their oyster tongs. Sometimes it seemed like these islands were just waiting to become sea again. But everything continues in one form or another – ourselves included, even after death, and in that way and others what Eddie said was true.

It was the day they came to see me on Wolfe that Tobe felled the pine – when Claudie asked me to go back to the main with them and Tobe looked back and Hart didn't when they left. Before that, Hart had been fixing a shutter, which was nice of him, and Claudie had been sunbathing on the dock. Tobe found me in the makings room.

'Can't I stay?' he asked, hanging about the door. 'Can't you talk to Dad?' He'd got to that lanky stage, shooting up and skinny as anything, his thick brown hair growing out and falling on his face, a little fuzz starting on his upper lip. Things were happening while I wasn't around. A hug wasn't going to fix things now.

'I don't think so, honey,' I said. 'You know what he thinks.'

'Yeah, but what do you think? *You* can stay. I could stay with you.'

'I'm working. You need an education.'

'I don't need that shit, not for what I want.'

'Tobe.'

'What are you going to do – fucking ground me?' His eyes were bright. He must have been desperate to lash out like that. But he was right. I'd given up any claim to chastising him.

I looked at him as steady as I could. I couldn't bear to tell him that what he wanted – the old life – was dead and gone on Wolfe. My face probably told him. He stormed up the marsh road, punching his leg and whipping the reeds either side with a long stick until their heads flew up. I saw him from my makings room. And then I looked away. I didn't hear anything or notice anything until the next morning when I went mudlarking, and felt a hollowness on the skyline. Wolfe's Pine was gone. That sent me out on my bike. All the way out I was hoping I was wrong, that it had merely fallen. But it was true: Tobe had cut it down. He'd left the chainsaw right next to the stump so there could be no mistake. At least half the tree was in the sea, with the waves breaking in line after line through the branches. He was lucky he hadn't been injured or killed right there. I was thankful for that, believe me. But I felt as if I'd been struck. It was like a mortal blow to the island. I don't know what he meant by it exactly. He knew hurting the island hurt me, and he knew what my mother had always said about Wolfe's Pine. I dug up a few pine seedlings I knew of from elsewhere and planted them at Pine Point and watered them, but they all died. It seemed like they needed the shelter of the big tree to survive.

I never mentioned the tree to him, and he didn't speak of it to me, even when he came back to stay. He knew where to strike at me. He knew me well. It was a bad memory.

Chapter 25

WE CAME UPON a car wash on the outskirts of the next town. A man and a woman were sitting on a bench outside waiting for their cars and I joined them because of the sun. We were like birds on a wire, perusing the day and the neighbourhood. The woman got out a packet of beef jerky, teriyaki flavoured, and held it out and nodded at us, Go on, and we did go on.

'Your dog like a piece?'

'I think she would.'

She gave Hurtle a piece. Hurtle edged closer, like she was reconsidering her options, and stared fixedly at the bag's progress up and down. I gave her a sliver more. The man fluffed out the zip edges of his jacket, the way a hen does its wings and feathers when settling into a good patch of fine and sunny dust, half closing his eyes. It was quite a rapturous moment for us all. He said it was good jerky and we agreed. I could have eaten the entire packet in a few minutes but I took care not to look desperate. After a bit, the woman shifted towards the man. Heat has a way of releasing scent and stench both. I took my leave, using my politest voice, and they wished me a good day.

I used to be comfortable sitting near folk like that. Girl had commanded respect and I hadn't liked to let her down. I missed those things, but Hurtle and I were survivors, we suited each other, and we'd look better with a feed and a wash. It was circumstances that made us this way. I bent and smoothed Hurtle's soft cheek and straightened her ear so she looked her best. 'Good girl,' I said. She picked up her feet, almost jaunty, and gave me a look like we were partners in something. It lifted my spirits.

We got a ride with a trucker right there at the car wash exit, the first I'd ever caught with Hurtle. She leaped up without hesitation, making me wonder whether somewhere in her murky past was a truck and a warm cabin and easy days. She lay against my lap, jiggling with the truck's movement. We got so warm I undid my jacket and dozed, head lolling against the window.

I woke with a start on the fringes of a town, about to shoot or be shot. I might have cried out. Hurtle barked. The trucker was looking at me wild-eyed. 'You okay?' he asked. I rubbed my eyes and nodded yes. He didn't ask about my dreams, just held the backs of his fingers to his nose and leaned away.

'What day is it?' I asked.

'Thursday.'

'I mean the date,' I said. When he told me the answer, I knew already. I said, 'That would be right.'

'Why's that?'

'Someone I know is dying today. It's the day of his execution.'

He looked at me and looked at me, rubbing the side of his finger over his lower lip. 'Anyway,' he said, 'I'm heading further east. I'll drop you here if that's okay.' It was a bus shelter he pulled into, not a big one. I thanked him for the ride. He said, '"Make sure you take care of strangers. Might be your turn one day." That's what my mother always said.'

I told him I supposed he was right.

*

Hurtle and I sat pondering things. She might have been thinking of beef jerky or why we left the truck. I hauled her onto the bench and she settled there. While waiting for a bus, which the timetable said was passing through Blackwater, and for the further kindness of strangers, I saw that I was in Thornhill, a town I had driven through more than once on the way to the prison. The depot wall to my side advised anyone interested of the prison shuttle service timetable. It was peeling up at one corner and had a pen mark next to 9.40 am, and 1.30 pm underscored. My gaze kept returning to it, though I tried to distract myself with thoughts of home, with picking at stickers peeling loose on the wall, with the sky, which was a high water-wash blue. I couldn't remember the time of the prisoner's execution, and that troubled me.

I had been back to see him a couple more times after he'd confessed, though I'd sworn I wouldn't. I had failed Tobe was my thinking, and this man was the consequence, yet I felt tied to him in some way. We did not speak about Tobe again, that young murderer and me. It was as if he was trying to work himself back into favour, like I might forget for a while who he'd killed, and what that person had been to me, or that I might even feel a bit of mother love for him, lacking as I was a son of my own these days. A bit of me could edge around the hardness that was inside of me then and see the lonely thing he was on the other side.

The last time I saw him he asked if I'd go along and be witness to his execution or, as he put it, 'to keep me company while I pass over'. Seems like people cannot have enough of killing, like an execution is a 'by invitation only' RSVP function. By then I had made up my mind on the subject of killing. If that had been Chas Dartmouth's aim, it had finally come to be. Why he asked, I wouldn't know. I would have killed that boy to save Tobe, but that was done now. Nothing could change it or the way I felt. Perhaps it was a gift he thought he could give me after this time: 'You can come see the price I have paid. We're square now.' Something like that. Maybe I was the closest thing to family he had left in the world. If that was so, how could I refuse him? Chas rang to ask me as well. The prisoner had asked him to, he said.

'I can't,' I told him. 'I can't watch someone being killed. Not for anyone.'

'Why?'

'It's a sin. It's another sin to keep a person in a place like that without hope. I'm not watching something they tell me is justice.'

Once, I would have thought that death would mean freedom for the prisoner who killed Tobe. What kind of life did he have? But I read once that it is not easy to raise the veins on a person facing death by lethal injection. As the needle approaches, their veins recede far down into the flesh, like a whale diving deep, a bird plunged into a thicket, or a person behind a door or a haystack, beneath floorboards, in tunnels, in roofs. The body will try to save itself even if the mind says, Please let go. Release me now.

If that is so, it might also be that when the water finally, entirely submerged Wolfe, instead of watching the water rise around my feet and engulf my home and cover my eyes and lift me from my feet until I was a wraith in the water, I might fight to rise, erupting into the sweet thin air and drawing breath and choosing life. We do the same for others – help them rise,

I mean – if we care for them, and sometimes, less often, even if we don't. Tobe was beyond our reach, truly gone in every way but memory and in the things that he left behind, in his neat shanty and its few special things, gone now I didn't doubt.

I wished I could be with the prisoner in the moment, not to see him killed, but because he was lonely and it was his wish, and because I hadn't been with Tobe when he died, or often before. Nothing could change that. It is hard to believe in mortality. I find it hard despite the dead people I've seen. The ones I'd seen in the year just passed were mostly surprised, if they had the time to show anything. It didn't make sense. Tobe didn't make sense. But doing something right is not the worst way to die. He was a good person. I couldn't separate that boy prisoner from what he'd done. Still, not a person or any creature deserves to die alone, unless they wish it so. We are all as broken as can be and most of us (people, I mean; I cannot speak for other living things) would wish some moments unlived. I declined the invitation; that is, I would not go, and now I was sorry for it.

I was glad I had Hurtle leaning warm against me. That boy could have done with a dog at his side in his final moments. I sat there for a while, and put together a small making, a winged figure with three sets of eyes: one set like Tobe's, the startling blue of his father's; one like Luis's of shining black; and one like the prisoner's, green-gold and wild. It was gazing upwards, taking flight. 'Set them free now, set them free,' I said, and held it to the light.

Part III
Home

Chapter 26

I STOOD ON the bus step when it arrived. I said, 'I've got no money right now but I can pay you back.' The driver looked at Hurtle. Hurtle glared.

I said, 'She's a good dog.'

'Doesn't look it. What kind is she?'

'Dog.'

He nodded in appreciation. 'She bite?'

I considered this. 'Sometimes. Not always for a good reason.'

'You're really selling her, ma'am.'

'I didn't raise her. I'm telling you the truth. We both need a ride.'

He listened seriously. I liked him for that. 'Seat up the front's good – a reward for your honesty. My grandmother came from down your way, by your accent.'

'Oh yeah? Where's that?'

'Sutters.'

'Right. Long gone.'

'She talked about it a lot.'

'People do who've lived out there. I thank you.'

He tipped his cap with simple elegance, an old-fashioned gesture. Hurtle fell asleep after a while and I sat in a daze and when I came to we were in Blackwater. That driver took us the whole way.

'Ma'am,' he said when I stood. 'No charge.'

'Thank you, sir,' I said.

'You're welcome.'

I thought I might cry.

Sometimes on Wolfe I lay on the docks looking at the stars and sometimes I felt the world turning. I lost myself in it. I didn't matter, nothing did, except that it should go on. I never felt that on Wolfe after everyone came. Once or twice I did on my travels – in the lighthouse, and on the bus. That bus driver taking me along so softly and plainly, the bus flowing through the salted fields and raddled woods and marshes, past broken lives and houses and travellers, which flickered by in endless stream, the sunlight falling and falling on me, and I part of that brokenness – well, it was peaceful. I didn't want to leave.

A light snow was falling and everything smelled fresh when I arrived in Blackwater. The ruts of soil were frozen hard beneath my feet and the snowy grasses rustled. I could have fallen down there and hugged it and never got up, but I kept walking away from the bus stop, taking a moment to get my bearings, the light being milky with snow which blurred street signs and colours. All the prettiness of that town had been drowned and picked clean; all its bones washed to the shore and become apparent and more like Wolfe. My markers were gone. There was just the old brewery, fancied up into apartments upstairs and shops below. I was all right then, back somewhere familiar if it was not exactly home. The snow's big wet flakes melted on my cheeks and caught on my eyelashes and I wiped them clean and pulled my hair back and tucked it away. It was all rough and tangled and snagged to my hands. What a sight I must be.

I headed for Doree's. In one of my imagined homecomings it was night and I curled with Hurtle on her doormat. It was the middle of the afternoon when I stood between her flags and rang the bell by her bright red door.

Doree's high call came from inside – 'Coming.' The door opened, and the screen door, and there was a pause. 'Oh my God. Kitty. It's you. Thank God it's you. What's kept you this long? What has happened to you?' She put her arms around me and drew me in, very gently, as if she thought I might crumble or fall. I must have looked worse than I felt. 'Honey, no offence, you could use a bath.'

'My dog.'

Doree looked past me to Hurtle, who appeared resigned to whatever would happen next – she seemed to expect something bad as inevitable, more or less. She didn't even bother standing or stepping forward. She'd begun to separate from me already, sparing herself my turning against her. A dog can tell you their whole life without a word if you pay attention. They are eloquent in their way. 'That's yours?' Doree said.

'Hurtle. Here, Hurtle, come on, sweetheart,' I called. She stepped forward then to my side and I put my hand on the side of her head and held it to my knee and crouched and put my arms around her. She pressed against me and I felt the soft quiver of despair running through her. 'I hope she can come in because if she can't neither can I.'

'Always room at the inn,' Doree said and stepped aside so we could enter the light and warmth and stillness and calm of her house. 'What happened to Girl? I hardly recognise you without her. It's like you lost a leg. Oh, pet.'

'Dead. A man shot her.'

'What did you do?'

'I shot him.'

'Stop talking now. Never tell me such a thing. I won't hear another word until you know what you're saying.'

'I saved a pup, though.'

'Where is it?'

'I gave her to someone who needed her more than me.'

'Girl's last pup. Oh, that's hard. You just went at life straight, didn't you? Looks like you crashed.'

'The path went wrong. I couldn't stop it, Doree. I tried.'

'Never mind that now. Come on, I'll run you a bath.' She took me upstairs, slowly, and ran me a bath. I sat on a wooden stool watching the hot water steaming in. What a miracle that was. She helped me out of my clothes and I didn't care. 'You need to eat more,' she said. She went away and came back with a cup of hot chocolate, which I drank in the bath, and a pile of buttered toast. Hurtle sat on the bath mat and we shared the toast.

'I ran out of everything, even dog food. I lost my wallet.'

'Should have rung.'

'No phone. I didn't know if I was wanted.'

'Only by Hart. He put out a missing persons thing on you.'

'Did he? Why ever for?'

She gave me one of her sideways eyebrow-raised looks and pursed her lips and went out and came back with a pile of clothes. I said maybe she could let him know I was okay. I'd go and see him when I was ready. I couldn't think about that. I scrubbed myself until I was pink and scratched-looking, and got out and ran some fresh warm water and heaved Hurtle in. She scrabbled and snapped and I told her it would be okay,

I would never hurt her, and my voice seemed to calm her even if the water did not. I towelled her dry as best I could and she began to look more respectable despite her air of betrayal.

Doree made waffles served with whipped butter and maple syrup using her famous Wolfe Island waffle recipe. (She had a trick of substituting some flour for corn starch – it helped to keep the waffle crisp, she said.) Hurtle and I ate half a one each. I couldn't speak. I was drifting emptiness. I fell asleep at the kitchen table. Doree made up a bed for me in my old room from the week when Treasure was born. She had the sense not to ask too much.

In the morning I said, 'We should, I don't know, talk about – arrangements . . . I can't . . . My house, Wolfe . . . I don't know if it's there still.'

'Honey –' she put her hand on my arm '– there is no need. You take your time.' She took me out and showed me her pride and joy, her new oyster farm skiff, hauling it out of the depths off her dock. 'Everyone's got one,' she said. 'Best thing anyone's tried.'

'I knew a guy at Stillwater did the exact same thing.'

'Nate Strudwick,' she said. 'Writer.'

'That's it. That's him.'

'He could buy a few oysters these days. No need for a boat.'

'The book made it?'

'Sold an app. Sold a couple, I think. Monitoring water quality for the home oyster farmer. And mussels. There's some gizmo goes with it to treat the water. He bought an island, I believe. Hell, maybe he still grows his own oysters.'

'He bought his own island?'

'They are pretty cheap around here.'

'He did grow a sweet oyster,' I said.

She gave a little sniff. 'I never cared for them. Except as pets.'

'And the books?'

'That's the killer. Still hasn't been published and it's the only thing he really cares about. He says if he was still on Wolfe he would have done it by now. Apparently there are too many distractions on the mainland. A friend told me that.'

'Maybe he's right.'

'You should come out next week. We're sowing oysters; we collect old oyster shells from islands and people's yards and throw them back in the water.'

'What a fairytale world you live in.'

'I get a kick out of it. We're thinking of checking out Wolfe.'

'It was covered in shell.'

'You wouldn't mind if we . . .' She left a delicate pause there.

'What would I do with them? They're not mine.'

'I meant to say – I've been past. Your house is the last one standing. I didn't land, but you could still walk it if you wanted.'

'Maybe,' I said.

'Did you hear about Josh? I suppose you didn't; I don't know how you would have.' Doree looked at me in her measuring way. I was eating breakfast in the kitchen. 'Bacon? Hash brown? Some more syrup?'

I shook my head. 'Josh?'

'Cat's boyfriend.'

'Right.' Just hearing his name brought that day back, him sliding across the water in his sinking boat, his bleeding arm. 'What about him?' I couldn't look at her, and thought about the sound of my voice, whether it had betrayed me in some way, and when I glanced at her and saw her casual gaze in another direction I knew that it had.

'He came up here one day, soaking wet and freezing.'

'Here? Why here?'

'He'd had a boating accident. He had a cut on his arm. That's what he said it was. It wasn't.'

'I don't understand. When was that?'

'Just before the big storm. A couple of months ago now – remember that? Were you all still out on Wolfe then? It would have been something if you were.'

'Yeah, it was some storm. Water running across the whole island just about. He and Cat broke up. He was upset about it. We left the next day. Town had been evacuated when Cat and I came through. But how did he know to come to you?'

'Kitty girl.'

'Yes?'

'I know who was on Wolfe.'

'Cat – and Josh. I should have told you that. There was some trouble he'd got himself in.'

'And some other people.'

'Who do you mean?'

'Alexander and Louise.'

'Alexander and Louise. Those names I don't know.'

'I suppose not. It wasn't their real names. And the names you called them I never knew. They weren't their names either. Not even Cat and Josh knew their names.'

'He told you about them when he came here?'

'A long time before that. Last winter. Come on, Kitty. You can work this out. You know about me, if you think about it.'

'Wait.' I took a moment, my thoughts lurching, trying to keep me above water. 'They came here because they knew you?'

'I knew Cat was Claudie's girl, would have known if she hadn't said a word, her being the dead spit of you. I suppose she could have been a by-blow of Tobe's. Not his style, though, to abandon a girlfriend. It was a teacher at Josh and Cat's school who had the connection to me; he needed to lie low for a bit, Cat too. I suggested Wolfe to keep them safe for a while.'

'Why didn't you say?'

'You know the rules. You knew them then or you would have said something. If you don't know, you can't betray.'

'Who started that?'

'Someone who'd seen things, a long time ago.'

'Right,' I said. 'Anyway, Josh was okay, you're saying?'

'He was. Well, he was alive anyway. But upset. Angry. Yelling about Cat and someone else. I can't remember the name he used. It was Alexander I guess.'

'Luis.'

'That's it. He was going to tell his dad. He was a mess. You know who his dad is?'

'Not exactly.' I shook my head.

'Homeland Security adviser, immigration official, I forget. I'm talking high up.'

'Oh God.'

'Tell me, Kitty, did you have trouble?'

'Did we have trouble . . . I can't even . . .'

'Tell me later. But did they make it? Tell me they made it.'

'Luis.'

'No. Oh, he was a good kid. They caught him?'

'They killed him. I have to go out now. I need to be on the water. Come on, Hurtle.'

We went outside. The screen door banged behind us and we were down the stairs and gone.

The boat was waiting in the harbour, not so many months since we'd left it there. There was not a mark on it, and it felt so much like part of me that it made no sense, as if the last months had been nothing. It should be a haggard old thing, scored and knife-wounded, thinned out in places so it hardly kept afloat. I took it out, feeling the grain of those old waves beneath me, the roads they made if you understood them. I felt the shift where Sutters used to be. I'd know it in my sleep. In the distance there was a hummock, a stark tree trunk, a foundering house, a chimney topped by an eagle swivelling its head in that abrupt way: You are nothing to me. I circled and circled it in large even swoops, over the waves, noting the fierce black lines of jetty beneath me and the Watermen staring the length of the staggering docks. The eagle took off and circled, flying helix to me, not sparing a glance. I turned back before I reached Wolfe.

You might not believe all this, but it is true just the same. The world is inexplicable in its miracles and horrors. Writing the last of my journey into the notebook reminds me of that. I couldn't write at Doree's. Sometimes I sit in my boat, the water shifting ever so softly. It feels like it's holding me. The words come out not too haltingly. Perhaps they're lulled, as I am, by the movement. I read some sections of the notebook and it comes back to me. Other parts I skip over quickly.

The grip of life and death is everywhere, and despite everything I've been through and everything I'd caused my heart has kept beating. Hart – I haven't said much about him, though I've thought of him often. He'd been in touch more than once, Doree told me on the third morning.

'Oh?' I said, casually. 'How was he?'

'He was worried. He was asking about you.'

'Was he mad about the Silverado?'

'He didn't mention it.'

'I took it. I left a note. He knows it was me. He probably wants it back.'

'I don't think he'd mind. It's you he cares about.'

'Oh. Tell him I said hey, next time he calls. I have to go now.'

'You should talk him to him, Kitty. Set his mind at rest.'

'I'm going for a walk,' I said.

'Where you headed?' And when I gave a look she threw up her hands in surrender and said, 'I'll be at the shop if you need me.'

I whistled up Hurtle and put her on a lead (I had never needed such a thing before; she was a different sort of dog) and we walked around to Hart's. I stopped on the street. I imagined going around the side and finding him lying on a chair in watery sun. I'd go over and kiss him and put my hand on his chest and feel the beat of his heart. You wouldn't believe his eyes. He could have had a decent political career on his eyes alone; he was a good-looking man. I'm sure his mother thought so. Those years on Wolfe took it out of him.

I couldn't make up my mind to it. Hurtle began straining towards a leaf. I began to lose my nerve. The front door opened.

'Kitty.' It was Hart.

'Oh,' I said. 'Hart.'

He goggled at Hurtle.

'Hurtle,' I said.

'There must be a story there,' he said.

'There is.'

'Would you like to come in, Kitty?'

'I think I would. I should tell you now that the Silverado's gone.'

'I heard.'

'Doree told you.'

'Police. They found it burned out, got the chassis number.'

'I didn't think of that. It wasn't me.'

'Doesn't matter. If it was, I thought you'd have your reasons; if it wasn't, I was worried. You've been a missing person. Did you know that? People have been looking for you.'

'Not all of them for good reasons.'

'No? You'll have to tell me.'

'We'll see.'

'I thought you'd have Girl. I told them you would.' He took a couple of careful steps closer.

'Oh God. A woman with a wolfdog. Police asked me a couple of weeks ago. I don't exactly remember. I showed them Hurtle. That was the end of that. I thought they might be looking for me for . . . some other reason.'

'Like what?'

'Oh, just some things. People. Never mind now.'

'You mean it would be better if I didn't mind.'

'I do.'

'I see.' His face was as alive with thoughts as ever, roiling their way across him like weather systems, arriving, being considered and discarded in rapid sequence. 'You've been in danger then.'

'Some – but less than others, as it turned out.' I just took him in for a moment. 'It's good to see you, good to be home.'

He let out a great breath and his expression stilled. 'May I – I hope you don't mind – I will have to hold you in my arms for a moment to be sure it's really you. Can I do that?'

'You may.' I moved towards him and he towards me and we came together and it would be a great lie if I told you that it was anything other than a pleasure and relief. I really felt I had come home and forgot in that moment the many things that word can mean and was purely content.

'But you're not.'

'Home? Not really. I'll have to find a place.'

'Well, come on then. Never mind about the truck.'

'You don't seem very pleased to see me.'

'Being careful. You startle so easy, Kit.'

I sat quietly on the porch that night, my old jacket pulled around me and Hurtle by my side. I liked the cold air on my face. I planned on taking the boat out to Wolfe Island, on my own but for Hurtle, because life changes. And I thought of being out there on a warm spring day and puttering its roads again in an old wooden skiff, and looking down and seeing their ghostly presence and the fish nosing their verges and crabs (if there were any) sidling about the stone markers, glaring as the vast shadowy bottom of the boat slid across the sky above them, filling it, gliding away.

I imagined the land – rank from drowned grasses, rotting grasses, sodden timber, and waters turned brackish and brown as tea, and rain falling on lone trees, and water and soil running loose. Fish swimming up roads, crabs finding new homes beneath drowned stairs and fallen shacks and one day walking in through doors opened by sea. The old ladder-back chairs floating to the ceiling. Fish, maybe sharks, nosing through the front door, washed open, into the kitchen and looking out of the windows, surprised.

The truth is not that I was lonely or sad out there, whatever people might choose to believe. I was as contented as I'd ever been. The thin snow might beat my window, the fire might need wood, the wind might moan, but I had Girl at my foot and my makings table busy with life and the lamp above swaying just a little (the house alive to the land it rested on), the glow of it feeling its way into the darkness, the tussle between them apparent only to a noticing eye. Sharp feeling was gone; it might never have been. It was the keenest gift of that time.

I would look in at my makings room, if it still existed, and see what I could salvage from the house. That might take time. I couldn't go back for good. I knew that already. It wasn't my Wolfe anymore. There's a photograph of Girl I always liked. She's picking her way up a shadowy gut at wolf light – that between time – dark in the half darkness, lifting her feet in that high prancy way, looking up, her yet-darker shadowy twin stretched on the ground beside her. I'd look for that making of the boy in the skiff, the way he paddles along, flicking those oars at the end. It's jaunty, you know? I thought Hart might appreciate it. I'd like him to have it.

I planned to see Hart again, though I didn't know what would happen. I liked him. I loved him, actually. I always did. I worked that much out on my travels. (This is not really about him, though.) I might look for a place of my own or I might not. I had some ideas for makings. There were a few things lying around town no one seemed to care about and they were on my mind. And I had my notebook filled with ideas and sketches.

Chapter 27

Autumn (some years later)

IT'S A LONG time ago, but it doesn't seem to matter. Memories are as faithful as dogs in their way, though not always tame.

Alejandra came visiting as I always said she should. 'You would *not* believe the fucking paperwork,' she said the month before she came, reminding me of Cat. She made me laugh; she made Cat feel close.

I was at the hall table putting a pomegranate stem in an old milk bottle when I caught sight of her. She was at the edge of the porch, gathering herself, looking all about at the sea and my dock and my yard. I had painted the porch floor green in some endless summer, that same light dark green with a hint of milkiness of Shipleys' porch, and it might have been reminding her the way it does me. I always liked it. I don't know what you'd call the colour; I've never seen it in nature; they mixed it for me at the hardware. She lifted her face into the sun and I imagined that she had shut her eyes. I didn't know that for sure, though I did know the light was too bright to look at directly from there at this time of day and had raised my head the same way to feel the warmth of it. True autumn had come, with cattails drying brown and rasping and rustling, louder in death than life, and the other grasses (three-square, cordgrass, needlerush, switchgrass, cattails) turning grey-brown, golden-grey, silver-yellow, all the in-between colours of softness, their differences clearer at this time of year. Sparrows fossicked for seeds about the dying goldenrod. A blue heron stood a little distance off, ignoring us in its haughty way. That was a rare sight on the main, and I wouldn't be telling anyone.

Alejandra turned to the house, set her shoulders square and, seeing me, stopped and waved her tentative half-wave from the waist – the very one that broke my heart when she was waiting in the bus queue in the town we called Freedom, a minute before her brother died. 'Kitty?' she called lightly, and I went to the door to greet her.

At first she was a stranger; she was so tall she could look directly into my eyes. A minute later it was hard to remember what she had been. She was exactly what she was going to become, only I didn't know what that was until I saw her. Her liquorice hair was still long and loose, and she had the same sadness. It was part of her. 'Grief is like childbirth,' my mother said once, after Baby died. 'You've got to get through it yourself. No one can take it away, or live it for you. I'm not saying it's not hard. I'm here, though.' I have learned that she is right, that feelings will have their way, eventually, and the world will have its way, eventually. People mostly pretend that's not so.

'All the way out here, Kitty. What are you thinking? Did you not learn a thing?' She touched my arm as I would an unfamiliar dog, from affection and so as not to alarm, as if I was the one who'd suffered a great loss the last time we were together, not she. She was a woman grown, big enough to look out for me.

'What do you mean out here?'

Where I live now is a sliver of higher ground with a small wooded lot and an old farmhouse set in acres of marshland at the edge of the sea. It's not so far out of town: as close as I can stand it and far enough away that I can hear only the wind through my woods or the sound of a boat sauntering past in the distance. I can drive if I want to, or make the journey by water, puttering along the coast and pulling up at Doree's dock. She waves from her kitchen window if she happens to be there. We discuss packages coming through and supplies, a sort of business we have developed.

Alejandra and I were laughing. Behind it, I was remembering the very first day. That's how close to the surface it was, nosing along and bursting up for air. Life, what a thing it is. It was the pleasure of seeing Alejandra, and of being with someone who knew. 'Oh, I think it's a while before it'll be an island,' I told her. 'The water's not touching the road yet.'

'You be careful,' Alejandra said. 'You could get cut off. Your drive's no better than the marsh road. Does it stay open? Tell me now.' She looked stern and peered into my face with searching eyes.

'Mostly.'

'I knew it. It's not safe.' She looked so concerned I felt queasy about my age, which is not so advanced in my view. Also, I was as fit as a fiddle. I was about to say something on the subject when she looked around. 'No dog?'

'Not since Hurtle, a few months ago.'

'Hurtle, that's right.' Her face twisted. 'Oh, I'm sorry, Kitty.'

I put my hand to her cheek. 'It's okay, honey. We went through some things together. I miss her, which considering the way I felt about her when we met . . .'

'I heard from Cat. Claudie told her.'

346

'Claudie was here when she went. And Hart, Cat's grandfather. You probably know that. It's like I lost my shadow. That's the truth. We gave her a send-off. I'll get another one sometime. Or one will arrive. I'll wait and see.'

It was springtime. We'd got Hurtle through the winter, which was not severe – winters seldom were anymore – but cold enough for an old dog. She had stumped around as cantankerous as ever, keeping me company, groaning from time to time, eating the small treats (pâté on toast, poached chicken, pinches of grated cheese) I tempted her with so she'd live another day. She flopped to the ground, sides heaving, eyes filming up but tracking me with them just the same, and a sob and whistle sounded in her chest and she ran her paws if I moved from her sight, and when she got worse there was nothing for it but to lie down too and curl around her the way we had in the dark forests and the lighthouse and in the grassy verges, just the two of us safe for this time, and she'd be peaceful again. Hart came over and creakily curled around me, his arm a pillow, his body some warmth, and held me when she finally slept.

'I don't think I can do it,' I said.

'You can,' he said. 'You can. Look at her.'

'Wait for Claudie,' I said.

'Does she like her?'

'Probably not.'

'Probably right,' he said.

'Don't make me laugh. Don't wake her.' I stroked her velvet cheek.

'I won't,' he said.

347

'Will you stay the night?'
'Of course. You know I will.'

The first makings afterwards were memories of the things I made on the journey south. Rivets and wire did well for some; the first versions of others troubled me. The passingness of some things is unbearable and therefore powerful, and the first makings of them in their hardness were lies and ghosts. I learned new ways with grasses and fibres, weaving and braiding and knotting. The connections they made seemed true, since toughness and loss were built into them. Mary Dove thought well of them. I would have been pleased once. Now I thought: Can I sleep or not sleep knowing that I put them in this world? I think that Eddie, the young man in the cave, had learned this. There are things he said that I'm still learning to understand.

My new makings reminded Mary Dove of the Watermen. She made me go and save them, and came along to be sure we did the job right. Hart came too. He said he'd been hearing about them for years and wanted to see what the fuss was about. He was quiet at the sight. He took some pictures of them and of me standing with them. 'I'm sorry,' he said to me. I believed him. We took a crew of men, including two of the people who'd helped install them. There was some swearing about the care they'd taken years ago, but we paid them well for their trouble.

Mary Dove sold the Watermen to a museum. I said they didn't owe me anything; they had served me well. Once we left Wolfe Island we were on our own; it was not their failing, what happened. My mother would have agreed and my father would have smiled, because what would be the point of arguing the matter?

She called the show *Vagabond Winter*, which I had misgivings about, but Mary Dove had her way. An interviewer asked where I got my ideas from, and what my images were metaphors for. What were the meanings behind my iconography – 'or visual lexicon, if you will?' – and what was their source. I said that ideas came to me like wolves down shadowy creek beds in failing light. I could let them kill me or wait for them to approach – get to know them, you know? There was nothing between but lies. And the interviewer said that was interesting.

I have included the names of some of the pieces to give you the flavour. You will see from the titles that the show was in some ways autobiographical, though not strictly representational.

Some pieces from Vagabond Winter
- *Ghost tree*
- *The runners*
- *Silverado*
- *Shootout*
- *Girl*
- *The burial*
- *Burning house*
- *Cub and basket*
- *Cub and child*
- *Holed boat*
- *Drowning boat*
- *Boy and girl*
- *Wife and husband*
- *Speed*
- *Silverado pyre*

- *The island is sinking*
- *The mountains*
- *Man on roadside*
- *The Samaritan*
- *Campfire talk*
- *Dead chicken*
- *Wolf girls*
- *Teriyaki jerky bench*
- *A lighthouse is an island*
- *Hunters*
- *The boys are flying*

This was how we had worked things out. Hart kept his house. I bought a place of my own – close to rising water on the edge of fraying land, like Wolfe. It felt a little like home, the way it sat lightly, as if it had just touched to earth and might take flight again. It was a stranger to me in other ways. Its marks and scars were silent. I would never hear them or know their causes.

The house on Wolfe had been a living thing. I felt the lives of hundreds of years moving about in it in the smooth banisters, the scrubbed elm wood kitchen table, the declivity of doorway floors from the passage of steps, the pantry door and walls where children's heights had always been marked. My makings room had been different things to us all: my mother's gardening shed, my grandmother's sewing room and my great-grandmother's withdrawing room. My study was little changed from when it was my father's reading room.

Long ago, when Mary Dove first came to Wolfe Island and walked through my house to the makings room, she murmured 'antebellum' over the hall table and 'eighteenth century,

I suppose' at sight of the bread bin. The kitchen table stopped her dead. 'How long did you say your family had been here?'

'Sixteen eighty.'

She put her hand on it. 'That's about right.'

'It's a nice old thing,' I said, and she laughed.

I salvaged some things – furniture and a few items from the makings room – and now the watermarks of the floods they survived are part of their voices. There was never much sign of Tobe to speak of in the house. He was a person of the outdoors. His favourite place had always been his oyster shanty. Hart and I took his ashes there one day and emptied them about its ruins. They sat on the water's surface and then sifted down or floated away. I did not feel much of anything then, except rightness. Hart cried.

Hart stayed with me for days on end on what he called 'Kitty's island'. ('Only a matter of time until it's true,' he said.) But there were times I preferred to be on my own, if my work had taken hold. I might be up in the middle of the night moving things around and humming, maybe playing a little music; I could spread my things about, while he liked things just so. He'd grown used to his own ways as I had mine, and things got testy before we found the right way to deal with it. I loved him and told him so often and freely. It was a relief.

'I'm sorry,' he told me in the beginning, after the long walk home.

'I know you are. It's done now.'

He looked at me as if there might be more to say. There wasn't, though. If he wanted my forgiveness he did not have it. If he wanted me to forget, that would not happen. All *that* was like a fast-flowing gut that must be jumped over or built over or crossed somehow. It would not close up. It's not the nature of some wounds to close. They can stop weeping, though, the edges can dry, and you can find ways around them, even sometimes by pretending, by looking ahead, by keeping your balance, but they are there just the same. Tightropes and a steady gaze can get you through a lot I've found. The steady gaze I maintained on Wolfe those years held me together. Hart would like something more, I suppose, but what I am is the best I can do with what I am. Whether or not that was enough for him was not up to me. I told him so, and it made him angry and he stayed away for eleven and a half days, a time during which I considered the idea and limits of personal resolve, and when he came over again he looked like he had learned something about tightropes and a steady gaze too. (No doubt he had things he couldn't forgive either.)

We've got kinder to each other. Even if our failures hadn't led to Tobe's death, I couldn't bear that we had added to the sum total of his sadness. There was no being free of that. Hart might be the only one who would understand, but neither of us could outright utter the words. The only way we might have acknowledged it to each other was in small kindnesses, each understanding the pain the other was in. If Hart, with gentleness, said he admired a making, it was as if he was saying to his son, 'You did well there, Tobe. I'm proud of you.' And if I brought Hart cookies and a coffee, in some ways I was doing it for Tobe, to show that I did know how to care.

I wanted Claudie there when Hurtle died.

'Why?' Hart said.

'I don't know. Who ever knows exactly what they're doing? To see what it means.'

'What, though?'

'That's the bit I don't know.'

There is something about a dog. They love freely; they do not judge or blame; they forgive. That's a blessing every day of their lives and you pay for it when they die. It is a pure grief, and it carries all your other griefs along with it and sets them free, sweeping them up and carrying them along as fast and awful as any body of running water. Your lost parents, all the lost dogs of your life, your lost island, your lost granddaughter and her dead lover, the lost girl you took under your shabby and broken wings, your lost daughter, your lost boy. Hope that there is someone to hold on to. Hurtle wasn't dying of anything but old age. She wasn't in pain. She was waiting; we all were. Her breathing whistled and her eyes tracked me and if I moved away she tried to follow me. So I curled around her, as I said. She seemed cold. I found my old aviator coat with its great fur collar and its furred insides and put it on and all the old smells of our travels were there. I pulled her in close and wrapped the coat around her, right around. She was breathing into my neck and I stroked her ear and her head and she gave a sort of whistling groaning sound and we lay like that for a bit and after a while she was gone. I hope I die like that, with someone watching over me and holding me, smoothing my hair, travelling out with me on that thin spit.

Claudie hardly knew Hurtle but she cried just the same. She had plenty of her own things to be going on with, plenty to cry about, including Cat, seldom seen except on the news or on the internet, haranguing the world or cajoling. She's something. And there's Treasure, who Claudie has not seen outside of a photograph since she was a few days old. That's a hard thing. She's hoping for a visit one of these years and it might yet happen. It will, I'm sure. 'Look at us,' I said to her and reached up to smooth a piece of hair from her cheek.

And she opened her eyes, sudden and startled, as if the idea had never before occurred to her. 'That's so,' she said. The thought seemed to lift her.

Her tears kept falling the whole afternoon that Hurtle died until her face was smeared with them, like land that can't absorb another drop and must release it. Every once in a while she'd say, bewildered, 'I can't stop.'

After a drink in front of the fire, Hart and I went up to bed. Not long after there was a knock at the bedroom door.

'Claudie?' I said.

'Can I come in?' Her voice quavered.

Hart turned his head in the shadowy light, just a little moonlight blooming at the curtains' edges, and called out, 'Of course, sweetheart.'

She edged in sobbing and shuffling, broken. Not since the day she started school had I seen her in such a state. (I'd found her on the stairs sobbing her heart out and asked her what was wrong. She'd looked up through her bedraggled hair. 'It's you, you, you!' she screamed. 'This stupid island.')

'Oh, honey,' I said when she reached the foot of the bed, the great soft golden thing that she was.

'Can I sleep in here?'

It seems like we all carry our child selves around with us and sometimes they come out for a visit; they're in some kind of trouble as often as not. Habit woke in us and Hart pulled towards his side and I pulled towards mine and a space formed there between us. I patted it and she crawled up on hands and knees in her polka dot pyjamas like she was six. I reached for the old apple quilt at the end of the bed – one

I'd rescued from Wolfe when I first came back – and heaved it up and across her. Presently her shuddering subsided. 'It's just sad,' she said. 'You know?'

'I do,' I said.

'I don't know what. Everything . . . everything. So fucking sad.'

'It'll get better, sweetheart,' Hart said.

I did not say my true thoughts: that she might do no more than get used to it, the knowledge of it, that she might work out ways to hold its roar off at a distance, like a mad dog on the other side of a screen door. Something like that. We're all of us close to its hot breath; we feel it sometimes if we don't always know it. Don't look too hard now, you don't want to provoke. Some people pretend it's nothing but imagination. They frighten me, those people.

Hart patted her hand and she held his and I hooked my arm through hers and held it in tight by my side. She turned her head and stared hard at me, or so I assumed since her head was at an unnatural angle and remained there; I could just discern the movement of her eyelashes, like butterfly wings in sun. 'You stay here,' she said, grinding the words as if they were stones and that would release their meaning.

'Okay,' I said.

She and her boy Hartford, born the year after Cat headed north, visit quite often, and after the first few days tut-tutting at the dangers of living alone and why I won't be sensible and go and live with Hart in town, and my untidy workroom and the lack of vitamins in my bathroom cabinet, Claudie pulls on old boots and stamps around like an island girl. She and Hartford drag bikes from the barn and pedal the busted roads and she gets freckles and lets her hair go wild and dry as late summer grass, and draws pictures, beautiful pictures actually, sometimes of ugly things: bones, dead birds, dying trees, rotting fruit, trapped creatures. She lies on the end of the dock and stares into the water at the sea grasses and I wonder what she thinks staring through that queer membrane into another universe. I forget myself in wondering – the wondering of the outsider now, not of someone waiting to become part of it and looking forward to it in some part of myself, though I don't remember it being hard and terrible when I thought and felt that way. It was a peaceful prospect then.

Hart has the wire skiff and the boy traveller making from long ago. 'My boat boy' he calls it. It means a lot to him. He has it where he can see it. I've seen him resting his hand on it. It is best to take the long view in life. I have often failed. It sometimes felt like I suffered more for my failings with the living than over the people who lost their lives at my hands. (*Say it, Kitty*: who I killed.) I built a new making: a skiff of wood and another boy. I was slow and careful, trying to remember the things I had seen in boatyards. It looked sturdy to my eyes. I took care over the boy too, and when I had finished him I saw that he resembled Claudie's boy Hartford. I will give it to him one day, I suppose. He seems to like it.

Claudie and Hartford come on some of my expeditions through the backwoods and byways on the roads heading north, mostly near the coast where people got dropped at water's edge. Folk travel in different ways now, the old ways and borders being so dangerous. Water has been useful, time out of mind. You leave no track and no scent; it is quiet; you are there and you are gone; darkness is a protection, not only a shroud. Hug the shores and you can miss the big boats. The little ones can dart in and drop off; big boats will tear out their bottoms if they try. Who knew all those failed jetties would yield such benefits. That all blew up a while back, when they started caging children, the separations and worse. People learned from those things, though they didn't always learn the thing intended. They heard Stop, and thought: Try another way. We will all choose a chance at life and future over death and despair, especially when children are involved; that was never going to change.

A few old watermen of my acquaintance have newfound careers ferrying people passing through. It's simple economics. People will pay what it takes. I put a bit in to keep things running smooth and Nate Strudwick the writer helps keep the boats in good order. (It appeals to his 'countercultural nature', he says.) It would have been a good line of work for Tobe. It saved Owen Jims's mind and their marriage, his wife once told me. It's strange how a skill can be valued for centuries and then be worth nothing. I'm glad for it to have a use again. It's a little bit of Wolfe to me. Some people feel the water different, like a muscle under skin, the way it flexes and rolls, the way it's knotted in places if something isn't right beneath. That can save people.

I visit the houses I stayed at with Cat and Alejandra and Luis and Treasure, and on my own. There are other places I come across that seem convenient and likely stopping points (cheese houses, iron sheds becalmed in fields, barns, abandoned farmhouses), marking them on a map so I don't forget, and stock or restock the cupboards. I use the lists from my notebook of things I wish I'd brought on my journey south as a guide. Looking back, I can see now how each new list

I wrote prepared me for the event just passed. I only needed bandages the once, for the runner, and I made do without. Food, warmth, and shelter are the essentials. I plant fruit and nut trees all over the place – near doors, mostly, so people can't miss them. I think of the apples Alejandra collected not long before Girl died, and of the nut trees I once found in the woods with Hurtle, and how a walnut or a beechnut or a hickory nut is the best thing you've ever tasted if you're in need. They are life itself. I throw the seeds of lettuce and peas and beans and pumpkins, in hope, and sweet peas, petunias, sunflowers, zinnias, cornflowers and chicory too, for the bees and butterflies, should any be around. I see the signs of plants sometimes having grown (orange pumpkins in a sea of blackened vines, lettuce gone to seed, pea pods spilling their dried inner selves), and that people have passed through. Claudie thinks I've lost my mind and tells me so.

'You don't know what it can be like,' I told her on one trip, and handed her the spade to dig the next hole. The spade hissed into the soil and a sweet smell rose. I pulled the sapling – an apple – from its pot, and loosened the roots and put it in, scraping the dug earth back in around it, taking care with a worm worried for its life. We trod the soil snugly around the roots and I poured over some water. There. It was nothing but a collection of twigs, but it felt good to have it connected to the earth and to feel that it might help someone out if it survived.

We collected bundles of kindling and put them on back porches and inside doors. Next time I passed through it was gone often enough, or a new pile had taken its place. Sometimes people were in a hurry. I made a note in my little book, which was filled with tiny maps I'd drawn.

'Will you tell me what happened one day?' Claudie said.

'I might. Some of it.' I stacked a few pumpkins up on the porch of the house we were at and they glowed like fire-filled eyes. (I remembered the day that drone appeared and started the end of Wolfe, the first frost of the winter.) The porch roof drooped like an old-time movie star's smouldering gaze. It was a fearsome sight at first glance. 'I'll see. I'm too old for jail.'

Claudie laughed, and when I didn't join in or even smile she said, 'No, really, Mother, what did happen?'

'Explanations don't always reassure, sweetheart,' I said. Still I keep writing in my notebook, whichever one I'm up to. She can read it all one day if she wants and I hope if she does that before judging me she will take into consideration what I did to save the lives of people she holds dear. (*Please remember this, Claudie.*)

Every time, I missed her when she went. Every time. And I thought of the time I might have spent with her and didn't and wondered at it all. Mostly I was grateful.

But this was now, and Alejandra came inside. 'Oh, pomegranates.' She touched the fruit and it swayed.

'Planted a tree the week I moved in. Cat and Claudie – how about that? I'm glad they're speaking; that's a good thing. *I* think it is.'

'Oh, me too,' she said.

Then she saw something on the coat stand – the satchel I found on the edge of Deadness. I had fetched it from my house with my other things. 'Luis's bag!' she exclaimed.

'Really? I didn't know. I found it on Wolfe. He saw it and never said.'

'That's strange.'

'And the initials – H and G – of course. What did that man call him?' I was thinking of the man who shot him, but couldn't say the words, not to Alejandra.

'Oh. I don't remember.' She became carefully blank, so I knew she understood what I was saying. 'It was just a bag he had.'

We followed Cat on the news and elsewhere and heard from her once in a while. She was a notable troublemaker or beacon of hope, depending on your point of view, and would likely be arrested if she tried to come back. 'And Treasure, how's she? And Teddy?' Teddy was Cat's second child, a boy the same age as Hartford.

'They're good.'

'That's what Cat says.'

'She loves them and she has things she has to do.'

'Sometimes you can't stop. If you can, it'll break you.'

'Hard on the people around her.'

'They could choose different.'

'The children couldn't.'

Suddenly I was remembering a conversation I had with Cat in Freedom, not long before we went our separate ways.

'Do you ever think about Josh?' Cat had asked.

'Not much,' I said, which was a lie. 'Do you?'

'Only, was it my fault?'

'That's what I wonder. But you didn't make him threaten his daughter, and neither did I. He chose that himself.'

'But what was I thinking? That's what I think about. I feel like I don't know myself. What if I did something that stupid again?'

'We all have to live with that, our own stupidity.'

'I thought he cared about people. I don't think he did. Maybe he did a bit. He was kicking against his parents, after some adventure. I know I was too. But there wasn't more to it for him. I don't think there *is* more to him.'

'There might have been. He cared about Luis. He wanted to impress you.'

She made a disparaging noise.

'And Luis?'

'Honestly, I don't know much of what he thinks. You can tell what he is from what he does. He has things he must do. He's determined, you know? He will make a family and a life. He lets me be what I am. And if he doesn't, that's the end for us.'

I told Hart about this conversation a long time later and he said, 'That's our granddaughter?'

'She's wonderful. She survived that. She kept them together. She loves them all. She's got things to do. She's something.'

'I will never know what happened, will I?'

'You might not want to.'

Alejandra gave me a look, thinking about Cat, as I was, moving a few pieces around in her mind by the looks, and deciding to let it go. 'Is the island still there?'

'A little piece of it at least a couple of months ago. I give it another year, maybe two, depending on the weather.'

'I'd like to go see. Would you take me? Could we do that?'

'Sure,' I said. 'Good idea before winter sets in. You'll get a surprise. *I* might get a surprise.'

'Do you have your collections still?'

'I do. And new ones.' We wander to my makings room and she looks around with a more knowing eye, picking up pieces and looking closely. 'Some of these things, they're pretty rare, you know.' She is on her way to becoming a scientist, a biologist, and I know she's right.

'I know. I don't really care about that.'

'Unless you need the money.'

'My makings take care of that.'

'What about your Watermen?'

'Sold them when I got back and bought this farmhouse. They did their job. I miss them, though.'

'I hope they're outside, with plenty of space around. I wouldn't want to live with them. The first time I saw them . . .' She made a face of childhood horror.

'They weren't designed to be friendly.'

'You know, when we came in the boat, the whole way in Josh is saying, "Shit, holy shit. Would you look at those fucking things? Are you sure this is safe?" and Cat's saying, "How would I know? Have you got a better idea? A nice hotel in town?" It was pretty funny looking back. I hated him.'

'Yes. Anyhow, he's dead, did you know?'

'He is?' It was the strangest thing, watching her in that moment, as if something collapsed inside her, as sudden as if it had been punctured. 'Oh God.' She shut her eyes. Her skin turned pale, the way it was when we first met on Wolfe. I thought she might faint.

'Alejandra.' I held her arm and her hand and rubbed it with a thumb.

She opened her eyes and shook her head a little. 'It's just a relief, you know?'

'Not really.'

362

'I thought, I don't even know I thought, he might appear again. I hated him. I really hated him. What happened?'

'Killed in the war. He was a good soldier, they said.'

'It's not enough.'

'It was something for his parents to hold on to.' Way back, I heard from Claudie that Josh had gone into the military. His parents had got a good lawyer, pulled some strings, and got him off any charges. I suppose that's what justice looks like for a person who looked like him. Not a lawyer in the world could save Luis and Alejandra's mother.

'I don't care about them.'

'You might think differently if you ever become a parent.'

She looked clear at me. 'No. No one's going to do to me . . . My girlfriend wants one.' She nodded very slightly a few times, piecing out her thoughts, would she give them voice or not. 'It doesn't matter what country you're in if you need something and no one cares. There's no help comes for nothing. Not much anyway. I learned from you, Kitty, and from my mother. I saw what happened – that day we found Mama. That guard taking her into the trees, remember? I'd seen that before. I never told you. I know what I saw that day. I knew it then. Mama always said they wanted to ask her some questions. But I know. I saw things and I think she knew that. But she had to pretend for me and I had to pretend for her; otherwise we would know too much – both of us. It would be so easy to see it in each other's eyes, less than one second. Once, it nearly happened. I could see it when she realised I knew something and it made her afraid. So I asked her what was for dinner. It was a little trick of mine, you see? This was all she wanted, for me not to know, for me to feel okay, because then she had been a good mother; no matter what things had

happened to her, she had done her job. There was a man.'
She stopped and circled the makings room touching things,
some cut-out sections of flattened tin, an oyster can, a creature
dangling from the ceiling, and circled back. 'There were things
that happened. I don't want to talk about that. "Don't tell your
mother, little girl. Wouldn't want anything to happen to her."
That's what he told me. If I did, my mother would know she
had failed and I wanted her to feel good about something, that
she had taken good care of me. This was my life. Treasure's
normal is a mother who loves her; for sure she loves her. No,
I don't know what normal means for a lucky kid, that shitty
word. I never lived it so how would I pretend it right? Any
man takes you by the arm and marches you into bushes or the
long grass or a shack or an office is not stopping until they do
what they're going to do. I carry a gun. I learned that from
you, Kitty. I'm not afraid of using it. I'm afraid of something
going wrong with the gun, of someone tricking it from me, of
losing it. I will use it if I have to. Believe that.'

'I believe you.'

'I can't stop talking, Kitty. Why is that?'

'You've got things to say.'

'I do. You shouldn't have left us. That is the other thing
I have to say. That is the main thing, I think. You shouldn't
have. That was wrong.'

'They wouldn't take me. You know that.'

She narrowed her eyes like she was looking at me through
a telescope and trying to make me bigger, trying to see clearer,
seeing if the focus would change. 'I saw in your face. I can read
faces very well – and fast. I know that a little piece of you was
relieved. I saw that little piece in your eyes.'

'Alejandra.'

'And you said, "Take Niña," to make yourself feel better, like you were the good one. It was nice of you to give me Niña. She is a wonderful dog. I miss her like crazy, like right now I miss her, you know? She is very good with the children.' She looked about like she was expecting her to come up a creek bed, the way Girl used to, shadowy in the blackness, wild but connected to me anyway. There was nothing there. 'I feel like I have no clothes on without her. Anything could happen to me. I couldn't bring her. I thought someone might take her. I thought you might want her back and I'd be too weak to stop you.'

'I would never do that. Never. Never. Never take another person's dog no matter what. She would never leave you. A wolfdog doesn't do that. It's not in them. My last dog someone gave me, in a manner of speaking. I would never have taken her. She was broken, that dog. But broken things can still be something. She was something in her way, to herself, not just something to me. She decided to stay with me when she could have run off.'

'Okay, okay. I'm sorry. I shouldn't have said that. But about the other thing, I am right about that.'

'I don't remember exactly. Only I couldn't go; I would have gone if I could. Maybe the other thing you said, maybe that's true. But I would have come even if I didn't want to. I wouldn't have left you. Were you safe? Or is it like with your mother, you've been telling me things?'

'No. We were safe, but it was . . . it was hard anyway. And my mother and Luis.' She blinked rapidly here and crossed her arms and held her elbows.

I didn't say anything for a minute at least. What would I say, what would I ask? Is there any news? Has she been found? Your baby sister? If she had not told me, she'd heard no news, they were both lost to her. I did think hard about her sister. Finally, I said, 'I heard that Alejandra wasn't your name.'

'Doree?' When I nodded, she said, 'That's right, it wasn't. But it is my name now. I don't want the old one. I'm sorry I can't tell you. Safer. Out there on Wolfe Island I thought we were safe, for a while I felt that. That was the first I knew what safe felt like. I thought it was like, do you have enough food and water, have you got some place to go, a home, you know? Do the people there care about you . . . love you, I mean? All that.'

'Yeah. I used to feel like that,' I said.

'And now?'

'Not exactly. I can live like this. The old feeling is gone. This is the best I can do. That's all. But Hart is around. I'm lucky really.'

'Yes. I am lucky too.'

I looked at Alejandra's eyes then, the little turn at the outer corner, that thing she shared with her mother. There was one more secret.

Some months after my vagabond journey I had made up my mind to go see Josh's father, Lionel Starkweather. I had learned his name and what he said he was, which was a lie. I had only to ask Claudie to get Lionel Starkweather's address. I wanted to write him a letter, I said. Claudie didn't know I'd shot his son, of course, or about the other things, or she might have answered differently. I wanted to look him in the eye and tell him the truth.

I thought a lot about what I'd say on the drive to his town: how he'd caused the death of one of the best people I ever knew, and destroyed a family, how things have a way of catching up, as Luis said. It was almost two hundred miles, so I had plenty of time for ruminations. I had my gun with me and I hadn't ruled out using it if he raised something against me.

Calverton was a beautiful town, grander than Blackwater. Even the poorer parts were tidy, the yards neat and mown. It was strange to think of Cat spending her growing years here, going to school with Josh, meeting Luis, her life changing direction because of her parents' aspirations.

Lionel Starkweather's house was a lovely thing, a three-storey clapboard with a circular drive, and twin copper beeches out front. I expected a maid or perhaps his wife to answer the door, but it was Lionel Starkweather himself. He was much like his photographs: tall and not quite running to fat – handsome, I suppose, in his navy cashmere sweater.

He stood in the doorway, remote and puzzled. 'Can I help?'

The million ways I could have answered that question . . . 'I'm Kitty Hawke,' I said. 'Claudia Hawke's mother, Catalina Hawke's grandmother, your granddaughter Treasure Hawke's great-grandmother.'

'Excuse me?' He looked to the side then and I heard a small peeping voice: 'Papa, Papa,' and a wee girl with black hair ran from somewhere and wrapped her arms about his legs. He scooped her into his arms. 'Selina,' he said, and now she put one arm comfortably around his neck and faced me like a queen. I would know those eyes anywhere. I was thinking very fast.

'How old is she? Two and a half? I know her sister. I knew her brother, who, by the way, I know you had—'

He looked to the side again.

'Stay there.' I patted my pocket so he knew what I carried with me.

'You don't know.'

'I certainly do.' That old dangerous calm had descended on me.

He leaned forward and in a hissing voice said, 'I said you don't know. She's mine too. *My* daughter, do you understand?'

I felt winded and took a breath in, when I could, and out, and spoke: 'So you raped her mother, let her go to jail and took her daughter. No wonder Josh is a screw-up. That poor kid. Can't believe I said that.'

His face twisted. 'Call it what you want. You don't know. I kept her safe until other people got involved. She gave me the baby so she had a chance. Understand that. *Her* choice. We've adopted her. She's ours now.'

'What a hero. God, it would be embarrassing if people knew.'

'I know the other one's alive.'

'Her sister, you mean? You never even knew her name, did you?'

He looked pained at that. 'What do you want?'

'I wanted to look you in the face and call you out, tell you about the boy – your daughter's brother, think about that why don't you? – you tried to trap and then had murdered.'

He lifted his hand to Selina's head and pressed it against his shoulder, covering her ear.

'Not nice to hear that word, is it? He was really something, but you would never understand it. I suppose you'd say you were doing your job.' He glared and curled his fist, the way I'd seen Josh do more than once. What a sorry thing he, Lionel Starkweather was. 'You're hardly a person.'

He was recovering by then and he brushed it off. 'You wouldn't understand. You leave us alone and I'll leave your family alone. Got that?'

'You get this, Lionel Starkweather: I wouldn't trust you for anything. I knew that before I got here. I've got all this recorded, and the minute I leave here I'm making copies – I'll send one now – and I'm putting one in a bank, one with my lawyers. If any of my family gets as much as a scratch, you know what I'll do, and I'll make sure your daughter here knows someday about what sort of man you are.'

Chapter 28

WE WENT OUT the next day, it being as fine and still as any other I have experienced, if not as warm. The algal blooms had died and the water had turned old-fashioned blue: taut, brimful, sequined. The main shore smudged then faded to nothing. Alejandra was quiet and held herself in a small tight ball, occasionally scratching at the peeling red paint of the boat's edge with a thumbnail and picking it out of her nail when a shard caught and looking around and back down at her fingernail.

'You okay?' I asked.

'I've only made this journey once before.'

'I should have thought.'

'It was my idea. *I* should have thought.'

'Nothing's going to happen. Hardly a thing to see. Maybe nothing by now. We had a storm a couple of weeks back.' But I knew she wasn't seeing what was happening now. She wasn't in this time or even in this place. She was roaming inside, a place that is vast beyond reckoning.

Alejandra said, 'I think about it. Why is that?'

An osprey hovered, watching the water with its fierce gaze, turning its head, tilting, feeling the air with its subtle wings.

I said, 'I always wondered. I carried a gun; you knew I used it. How do you trust a killer?' I wasn't asking a question, or not one of Alejandra, but she answered anyway.

'Some killers you trust; some you don't. That's all. I knew killers before you. My father and mother were wanted. That's all I can say about them. I heard of other killers, plenty of them.' She didn't say it to shock. She didn't even look at me. 'Not story-heard. Actual people. So-and-so's brother: that sort of thing. It's not what you do, it's why. That's always true.'

'You look at it one way that man was protecting his friend's place.'

She made a sound of disgust. 'He was nothing, a liar, lying to himself about that. He was scaring a woman and a bunch of kids without a home to puff himself up. Probably made his day, up to then.'

'I don't know why I did it. I shouldn't have. I'd do it again. I know I would. I can't remember it right. It might be I'm the liar. I wrote it down but I don't know if it was true, what I wrote.'

'It doesn't mean it's a lie if it happened different. The way you feel is true. I think it is. What did you write?'

'I don't know. I'll show you sometime.'

'I don't remember it either. Just Girl. Blood. Afterwards. I thought as long as you were there we'd be okay. I knew what you were. I didn't know before that man came to the island what you would do for us. I wish I'd known earlier. It might have made a difference. I wished you'd killed Josh.' Her voice brightened. 'I remember the makings room. A lot.'

'Yeah.'

'I loved that room.'

'Me too.'

She shook her head irritably. 'I don't mean like I love

371

chocolate, or pesto. Or – or dogs. I mean that place . . . it made me, you know? It put me together, it held me together. If I feel bad I go to that room. Even now – still. A shrink told me this once: "Shut the door," she said. "Leave the world outside. It doesn't belong in there. It's for you – and if you want to invite anyone in that's up to you. You've got the handle."' She paused and looked at me kindly. 'She was speaking metaphorically. Obviously it was your room. I know that.'

'It's okay. I never minded sharing,' and at her small smile and twitched brow I added, 'after the first little while, I mean.'

'It's kind of a knack. I do what she said: open the door, go inside and sit at the bench. Girl's there at my feet and her fur is soft. It's warm. I push my toes in. There's her heartbeat, her stomach is rumbling, you're humming your tune.' Her voice was a soft pulse.

'What tune would that be?'

'I don't know. I never heard it anywhere else.'

'I didn't know I did that.'

'Like this,' and she hummed along for a bit.

'Oh, Song of Wolfe.' I sang a line or two and Alejandra hummed an accompaniment.

'I feel it now. I'm feeling it.' She was so surprised that it sounded in her voice and her eyes were wide, wide open. 'Sing some more, Kitty.'

I sang it through to the end.

'I didn't know the words. Or I forgot them – you'll have to teach me.' She hummed a little.

We were quiet again and everything was so clear and calm that looking up I half expected to see reflected an old skiff and two women gliding along the cornflower sky, looking overboard deeper into the heavens.

A speck of an island, low and flat, came into view with nothing on it but a yellow-sand beach and sparse grasses and a tall red-brick chimney very bright in the sun, its long black shadow flung aside like a fallen tree. 'Shakers Island,' I said. Another time I might stop in and poke around for things I could use, that might have been washed up since I was last there, which would be quite a few years before.

Alejandra turned her head towards it and away like it was nothing more than a wrapper blowing along a street. She said, 'Sometimes at night I wake up after a bad dream. I go in there again. I open the collections drawers. I look at all the things, the shells, the bottles, do my drawings, keep my lists. The smell of tomatoes coming in. Girl is at the door and we're safe, you and me. You know?'

'I do.'

'Nothing can touch me. No one.'

'Well who would, honey, out there?'

She didn't answer.

We came towards Wolfe, which I could tell from the water and the distance we had travelled, and then by the sight of my house still standing, flat and bright and shabby against the sky and the water, a distance off still. I shifted course towards it and slowed, looking over the side and ahead for jetties and drowned buildings. The water was bright as tin and made my eyes sting. Alejandra was on the verge of saying something and paused more than once and took breath again and frowned. 'That's . . . is that . . .?'

'Wolfe. My house. The last one standing. My father always said it would be. It drove Mrs Beaufort crazy. I wish he were here to see it. He loved to be right.'

'My God.' Her eyes moved along, though there wasn't much

to halt her gaze: a few hummocks, a sweep of golden grey marshland run through with water and dead tree trunks poking up. Presently, we saw buildings slumped to water or grass, as if they'd paused, exhausted, and lacked the will to rise again. I lined myself up with some posts and piles and came in over what I judged was the dock landing – its slats failing and falling away, swaying deeper into the dark like living things.

Off to one side was a pile of tarnished timbers. 'Your old home,' I said. 'Shipleys. See the little bit of green – the porch floor?'

Alejandra stared at it without expression. 'I don't—'

'Recognise it?'

She shook her head, no, but kept looking like she hoped something would remind her.

I turned the engine off and pulled the motor clear. It was quiet but for the muffled sound and feel of water slopping through wood, timbers bumping hollowly underwater, at the movement of our boat maybe, the smallest movements taking effect in the body of water, a feeling as much as a sound. That was all and it was eerie, as if something other than us was alive there or had only recently departed. I took hold of the oars and we kept on slowly – the sound the oars made and the drip and scoop of water an intrusion – until we came to a tall post and a pile of timbers and sheet metal with CRAB H in large capitals the colour of dried blood staring at the sky, and half fallen into water its pair: OUSE.

'The street should start about here,' I said. Sure enough, the white pebbles of pathways silted greenish led from the dark line of submerged asphalt on both sides and close beneath us. I poked an oar down until it hit bottom, no more than the depth of the paddle. A salty mossy pungency lifted. Alejandra stared, her eyes very black, gripping the boat's side like the whole world was dissolving and only this vessel would save her.

'Kitty.' Her voice was a choked thing.

'What, honey? It's okay. Just things have got drowned is all. Not you, though. You're okay. I'm here. I'll look after you. Like I did before. Oh, don't sweetheart, don't.'

She began to pant in soft distress and she shut her eyes. The boat scraped the bottom and shuddered and would go no further.

'We'll have to walk now. Can you walk?' I said. 'Can you get out? You'll feel better when we get to the house, inside, or we can go back if you want?' She didn't speak and her eyes remained tight closed. I took off my boots and rolled my jeans as high as they would go and stepped out of the boat knee deep into that cold Wolfe water. The smell of it rose sharp and salt and the faint movement of water was like icy breaths on my legs. The boat came free. I pulled it a few more feet along and took hold of Alejandra's hand and held it tight between mine, the side of the boat between us, like a pregnant belly. She was shaking, but I smoothed her hand and made a few sounds and words and she opened her eyes and let me help her with her shoes and jeans and I took her hand to help her out.

She flinched at the water, the gritty feeling of the road, its silty surface like sodden fur – it was as if her balance had gone – and for a moment she wouldn't let go. 'Sorry, Kitty. I'm so sorry.'

'It's okay.'

'I didn't know.'

'Not to worry. We're here now. We're on our own – no one else here.'

She released my hand and waited while I tied the boat to

a rusted light pole. We sloshed towards the house, moving carefully, feeling along with our feet and coming upon rocks, more drowned wood, branches and so forth. A mouldering smell of wet wood and plaster grew stronger as we came to the house. The porch railings sagged and the stairs hung loose as a busted jaw. We pulled ourselves up gingerly. The raw edges of the rotted timbers crumbled a little in our hands but took our weight. The porch was strewn with storm wrack – seaweed and plastic bottles and bags and a dead bird or two spilling more plastic – piled up against one of the old petunia pots.

I shoved the door. Evidently people had visited since I collected my boat boy and the Watermen and other things. Books – their pages speckled and buckled with damp – and the remaining furniture and so on had been thrown about. Wallpaper hung off the walls in sheets and the ceiling hung in swags. It was a shock, but not one it seemed worth remarking on. It had happened to every other house on the island, invisibly it seemed, and mine was no different; left to itself nature is impartial, and without witness people are impartial. I picked up three books and stacked them to one side, but they were so buckled not even those few would lie flat. And they smelled mouldy, which is unpleasant in a book. There was a bigger shock than this chaos. The house stopped past the stairs, as if a meat cleaver had cut clean through. The back wall had gone. Beyond were the island, the marshes, everything trying to rush inside it seemed. It was a beautiful view, I will say that, the framework of the house shaping an enormous picture, more focused for its framing, but it took some of my breath and all of my attention. A corner of my mind wondered about setting it to rights and restoring the missing wall. Alejandra shook the stair post and rail and, when it held, started up the stairs. I followed.

At the top was the landing and the two front rooms facing east and south, the vast sky where the two back rooms and half the garret had fallen away, and the little window facing north-east where I used to look over the dock and Cat's house. The window was cloudy, the salt dust settled in the waves of the old slumped glass. I wouldn't have minded saving it, but I didn't have the tools. You can't save everything, try as you might, except in memory if you're lucky.

We moved from window to window. Looking north: the boat had settled like a tethered horse swaying gently at the nose, the rubble of fallen buildings surrounded by water, the great sweep of saltmarsh, an eagle on a dead tree, an egret as still and white as candle drippings, gannets – all stark with a queer dimension from this elevation. South and west were the sparse drifts of drowned meadows and encroaching sea, the old exca-vator rearing from the water, Stillwater flattened as if by giant wave, and the broken thread of the marsh walk still trying to stitch the island together.

Alejandra came to my side. She heaved the window up and a sweet light breeze hit us, shivering our hair. It was like looking out at the end of civilisation and being there, standing within its last remnant and knowing the strange wonder of it and knowing it was not my world any longer.

'Remember that story you told us about the lady who died? Your . . . not your mother . . .'

'My grandmother,' I said.

'Right. And there was a hut.'

'A storeroom.'

'Yeah. A storeroom.' She said it slowly, carving the word into herself; she would not forget this time; she would remember these details and maybe add to them a little of herself. She

377

nodded, as if more was coming back. 'And she died before she could be saved and was put in the storeroom.' She paused and looked at me with questioning eyes, caught up in the story and seeing it – the thought, the living power of it. 'And your mother prayed for a miracle and thought it would happen.'

'Yeah.'

Alejandra drew in a deep breath and let it go, and stood squarer. 'But it didn't happen.'

'No. It was too late, but she held that hope close her whole life and it meant a lot to her.'

'I prayed for a miracle, and one came. I prayed on my hairclip. You remember that clip, the one I gave my mother the last time I saw her? Remember, Kitty? And it came true.'

'You prayed for a miracle? What miracle was that, sweetheart?' She didn't answer, just stood there looking at the tilted world. I thought she might be ignoring me or hadn't heard or had lost heart, or didn't think the question important. It seemed like her mind was running some other track.

'This is where I saw things from, up here,' Alejandra said.

'What?'

'Oh, a couple of things. That time the man's boat went on the rocks. You remember that time?'

'You saw?'

'Oh sure. I saw him from our place, from Shipleys. I knew him. Him and the one at the church. And one more. They were not . . . nice men. Luis killed the one at the church.'

'He what?'

'The first one. That was just before we came here. I don't remember. One or two days. Not *in* the church. Luis found out about the man, what he was doing.'

'What was that?'

'Messing around with people passing through, waiting for the legals, waiting to be free. Only the women. He called it rent. "Just a little rent due," he used to say. If they didn't pay, we didn't see them again. There was another man who came not so often. He had the prettiest ones. My mother. He collected the rent in an office. I don't like that word. "Study" is okay. I liked how you had a makings room. I like that a lot.'

'Sweetheart. Alejandra.' The man who had the pretty ones – Lionel Starkweather, I supposed. I kept that to myself.

She looked at me sideways and gave a sideways smile and shook her head a little. 'It's okay. It's all done now.'

'How did Luis do it?'

'I don't know. He put his hand in.' She moved her hand forward, feeling and seeing it at the same time. 'And then he –' she twisted her wrist '– did like that.'

'Oh,' I said. 'I think a knife.'

'I suppose.'

'The knife in the satchel.'

Alejandra looked at me. 'He said he threw it in the water because his name was in it.'

'It was in a way. And after the man?'

'Cat and Josh came, and I don't remember after that.'

'I killed the man on the rocks, that was me. Luis just followed me.'

She shrugged. 'I wouldn't mind if he did. He was another bad one.'

'What did he do?'

'I used to see him sometimes. I would have shot him if I had a gun when he came to the door. He saw me on the stairs. He knew about Luis. I didn't mean him to see me. I was just there.'

I made some sound of distress.

She didn't look at me. She put out her hand to hold me off, to stop me. 'Don't get angry. Please don't get upset. It's better that way for me. So don't. For me.'

'Okay. I'm glad we got him then. I'm glad of that.'

'You get a good view from here. You'd see anything. Josh used to lie out on the walkway – near the end – lie flat, only I could see his hair, and he'd take aim with his rifle. He didn't shoot but he pretended he did.' She held the rifle of memory to her shoulder – somewhat tender and awkward – and squinted into its finder, and made the sound of a bullet being fired, a child's approximation – *pyouh*, something like that, breathy and nasal – jerking the rifle and raising the muzzle, assessing the result. 'Sometimes it was a bird.'

I said, 'I saw him shoot a gull once, in Stillwater. He was a fair shot. I don't know where he got those bullets. I was worried he'd find more. I hid all the ones I knew of after that, and any guns. And he went looking, I know he did.'

'I know he did too. I was in this house when he did it.'

'You were?'

'I hid in a cupboard. He aimed at you a couple of times when you were out walking. I thought it might be real.'

'But it wasn't.'

'No –' gravely '– but I wasn't sure. And even if it wasn't, it could be another time. That's when I prayed. I prayed we would be saved from him and he wouldn't be saved at all. I got my miracle. That was you, Kitty.'

'Oh, Alejandra, no it wasn't. I came along for the ride. What was I thinking? That I could be useful? I was so stupid.'

'You did save Treasure, and you saved us. That's the truth.'

'Look at it another way and I got you into trouble. But here we both are.'

'Will I go to hell for that?'

'Who would send you to hell? Who would want heaven without you, sweetheart? If there is such a place.'

'I prayed anyway. Maybe what happened to Luis was the punishment.'

'No, no such thing. I prayed for things too, all the time, still do, for all of you, that it would work out, that I would see you again.'

'You know what he, Josh—' She didn't want to say his name, but some people have that kind of courage. 'Do you know what he said to me?'

'No.'

'He said, "I know you've been watching." I asked him how and he said because of the way I was around him, keeping a side eye out – that's what he called it – staying away from him. He wasn't stupid. Like with Cat and Luis, he knew something was going on before *they* did.'

'I think he did shoot sometimes. Not at me – at least not that I know of. A couple of times I thought I heard shots and thought it was hunters I hadn't seen coming and I went looking. They used to come by in summer. It might have been him.'

'That sounds about right. You know what he said?' She kept looking out over the watery land, watching the past, I supposed, and not waiting for my reply. 'He said, "Say anything to Cat and I'll have you deported. I know things – remember that. Agents will get Luis; you'll never see your mother again. Kitty will go to jail for . . ." He didn't even know what for. He said, "For helping aliens." I told him the word he wanted was "harbouring" not "helping" and he hit me.' She put her hand to her shoulder. 'Then he said no, he wouldn't, and I thought he was saying he was sorry, but he wasn't.'

381

'What did he say?'

'He said, "You could hide anything you like out here." I told him Cat would never love him no matter what, but he didn't believe me. I promised him because I believed what he said. And I never broke my promise until now…superstition. But I think it would be okay now. Do you think so? Or do you believe in ghosts, that he could come back?'

'I think he's really gone.'

She turned to me. 'Do you think he would have done what he said?'

'I don't know. What he did was bad.'

'He really is dead?'

'He really is.'

'Well.' She nodded her head sharply, once, like a punctuation mark or an axe. He was gone. She had decided to believe it.

'It didn't suit him out here, but what he did must have been in him. Some dogs need leads. Same with some people. They don't realise it, though. That's the trouble.' I looked down at the marsh and then away over the water and I couldn't see anything, not a speck of any other land at all. 'An island is a kind of leash for some. Not for him.'

She started to cry and kept on, the tears flowing down her face and neck into her clothing. She pushed some aside with the back of her arm and her fingers and pressed a hand at the base of her throat to stop them in their tracks. I put an arm around her and we stayed until she was done. 'I'm sorry for it all,' I said.

'I am alive, Kitty. I am *alive*.' She almost sounded triumphant. 'Every day I breathe I remember what you all did for me. You saved me, Luis most of all. I will not fail you. I will not waste this life.'

I thought about that last secret, about her lost sister, but there had been enough already for her to deal with. Let it stay buried for now, I thought, keep her safe. When they read this notebook I hope they understand why I stayed silent. There never is an end, only way points between past and future, and the future is always coming for us like a flood, like a train. These days I don't picture Wolfe Island in holiday time, with the motorboats bustling around and white sails on the water and people laughing and talking on the docks, catches coming in. I remember the time in cold first light when we left, Cat and Luis and Alejandra and Treasure and Girl and me, the way the dark and driven water rushed over the island and across the steps of my porch like a river and how it seemed determined to wash that world away. I knew I was done with Wolfe even if some of it still remained. I wonder where good lies. The ties of affection are a sort of good, I suppose, though we make the world bend to them to its detriment. I do that. What kind of monster does not? The shape of it's going or gone, but the world will have its way. 'The lion will not lie down with the lamb,' I used to say to Doree. I believe that.

It was mid-afternoon when Alejandra and I left, the sun was plummeting from the sky, burning up brighter, brighter, the closer it got to the edge of the world, and I knew it was the last of Wolfe Island and didn't want to look back. I didn't mind the thought; it was welcome, if anything. The marshes would last longer than I would and be home to things even when there was no place there for me.

I like the thought of it persisting and of that having nothing to do with me. I am not done, not quite. I might yet go out on the water, flood the engine, drop the oars, and wait for where it will take me. There's a wildness in it I miss. But there are things to be done and things to hope for even while I'm waiting for the long night ahead.

We saw three geese circling in and heard the one below calling to them. Alejandra called out, 'Kitty, see the geese,' or I might have missed them, but we were quiet for the most part, me wondering whether a lone goose would keep calling or call once and remember and fall silent, and would there be nothing but silence when the sound it made had meant something: to itself, to the creature being called, to everything around? When we drew into the dock, feeling the heaviness of the boat in still water and the drag of the water through its sides, a quick breeze sprang up sending the rushes hushing on either side, and the sun finally drowned. The house's eyes were winking. Kind Hart had lit the lamps to call us home, and we walked in wolf light from the dock. I felt some misgiving then, but we had only to get to the door to reach shelter on the other side.

Endnote

PEOPLE SOMETIMES ASK me about the sorts of things I used to find. Each one had its own story and its own world. When I hold one of those things or touch them I imagine the things they might have been surrounded by: ferocity, ladies in crinolines, high seas, illness, the firmament of history. It helps to take the long view.

Interesting finds from the final years on Wolfe Island
- *Megalodon tooth, cretaceous, south end of Wolfe Island, very rare, collection of Alejandra. Impossibly lucky find.*
- *Quartzite shard, broken arrowhead (?), not native to this region, western reach.*
- *Sewing machine, 1880 or thereabouts, washed up by storm.*
- *Long-arm oyster tongs – too many to count.*
- *Bottles, various: vanilla bottle, 1890 or thereabouts, opalesced by time, Darkness Bay, common; Coca-Cola bottle, 1965, marshland, Smiths End; poison bottle – unusual cerulean blue, mid-1800s.*
- *Fallen angel wing – a shell, edge of embankment, Stillwater, post-subsidence. Undamaged and rare.*
- *Dentist's spittoon, possibly 1990s. (I date this from*

recollections of dentists' visits, the worry over teeth, the children lying back like sacrificial lambs, mouths agape, and their bloody spit splattering those small white basins. They might have spat into that very one.)

- *Four children – family for a time.*
- *Marsh periwinkle – once common, waterline, Marsh Road, collected by Alejandra one July of the twenty-first century, the year Catalina came.*

Acknowledgements

THANKS TO MY lovely family: David, Jack and Tash, Will, Catherine, James, Josie, Aileen, Nancy and Patricia, and, because dogs are family too, Gussie and Nell.

Thanks to dear friends: Kate Richards, Jenny Green, Trish Bolton, Dana Miltins and Clare Strahan.

Thanks to the wonderful people at Pan Macmillan: Mathilda Imlah, Danielle Walker, Cate Paterson, Tracey Cheetham, Katie Crawford, Clare Keighery, and to Ali Lavau for her sensitive editing.

Thanks to my lovely agent Fiona Inglis, and to Geordie Williamson for timely reading suggestions and for believing in the project from the beginning.

Thanks to my amazing supervisors Paddy O'Reilly and Alexis Harley at LaTrobe University, and to Sian Prior and Kelly Gardiner for their help. I am grateful for the RTP and David Myers scholarships that supported the writing.

Thanks to Sandra Leigh Price, Nina Killham and John Bartlett for their support.

The Wolfe Island of this novel is fictitious, and is located in the Chesapeake Bay on the east coast of the United States. Thanks to the people of this beautiful region, especially Smith

Island and Tilghman Island, and Mary and Jim Oliver for their warmth and generosity of spirit.

I am grateful to the Australia Council for a grant to support this project, and to the City of Melbourne's Arts House the Meat Market where I wrote this book.

A Note About Wolfdogs

WOLFDOGS ARE BEAUTIFUL but unstable and wild animals, completely unsuitable as pets. They are more stubborn, territorial, predatory and aggressive than domestic dogs, and can damage homes and injure or kill smaller animals, including children. Wolves belong in the wild, while dogs are domesticated companion animals. Nine out of ten wolfdogs are lost to neglect, abuse, euthanasia, escape and misunderstanding. They are outlawed in many parts of the US, and are prohibited in Australia. This book is not an endorsement of breeding or keeping wolfdogs. The wolfdogs of Wolfe Island would contain only a relatively small proportion of wolf blood after centuries of hybridization with domestic dogs.

For more information, visit Mission Wolf: https://mission-wolf.org/wolf-dog-introduction/ or the United States ASPCA: https://www.aspca.org/about-us/aspca-policy-and-position-statements/position-statements-hybrids-pets.